Which Way to Go Now

By Curtis J Hines

Table of Contents

Acknowledgements

I want to start off by thanking everyone that read my first book, "Which Way to Go"! With that being said, if you haven't already, please grab a copy of that one before you read this book! You'll thank me later. To my wife Lashanda, you are appreciated for your unconditional love and support. Thank you to you and our kids for encouraging me to continue to chase my dreams as a writer. To all my friends that holds me accountable and never let me forget that they're always waiting and ready to read my next story! You all keep me focused and motivated!

One thing about this writing journey I've learned and cherish is the ability to create freely and fearlessly. I encourage others to go after that idea or goal you have wholeheartedly and watch what happens! Don't be afraid of the unknown. It's a beautiful thing when you overcome the doubts! Go for it!

I dedicate this book in memory of a good friend and coworker Patricia Chaffen. You are missed and loved. Thank you for unforgettable good times and laughs!

Introduction

After making the dire decision to attend Northwestern University fearing the worse for his wellbeing had he stayed home, Cedric Mason is reminded that all actions come with consequences. Running from the neighborhood menace, Melvin, who has a questionable desire to see Cedric make it to the big leagues as a top baseball recruit to losing David, his best friend that was like a brother to him over selfish lies told by a girl, Charlene, he once saw a bright future with, gave him more than enough reasons to want out of Jackson, Mississippi. Having the much needed love and support of Mrs. Anthony, David's mom, who took Cedric in as her own, still wasn't enough as he immaturely struggles with fighting the temptations of his flesh, while coping with the new freedom he has in an unfamiliar place as freshman in college, way up north in Chicago, he continues to put himself in serious situations that requires some life changing behaviors. With no one to shift the weight on as his load starts to get heavier, he is left with the feeling of failure and defeat. To make things even more hectic for the young guy, it only took two phone calls to ignite a flame of chaos for him to go from "I think I can handle this" to full out panic and uncertainty thinking, "What the hell am I'm going to do?" Every step forward he tries to take, will only have him going in circles if he doesn't change his perspectives on life. He's stuck again trying to figure out which way to go now!

Chapter 1

What to Believe

"Do you, Cedric Mason, take Rachel as your lawful wife, to have and to hold from this day forward, for better, for worse, for richer, for poorer, in sickness and in health, until death do you part?" Pastor Clayton asked. I looked in Rachel's eyes as she stared back into mines. I felt at ease, calm by the glow she was wearing looking beautiful as ever. "I do!" I waited no longer to say as a tear appeared in my eyes. I tried my best to hold mines back as tears started rolling down Rachel's lovely face. I took the tissue Rico handed me then wiped her face making sure I didn't smear her beautiful make-up too bad. She smiled at me holding her head still enough for me to dab her face a few times. Pastor Clayton then said, "Therefore, it is my pleasure, that I now pronounce you two as husband and wife. You may kiss your bride." I glanced over at Mrs. Anthony as tears were flowing down her face while she was trying to keep Cedric Jr. under control. She smiled as she nodded her head giving me the look of a job well done. "Way to go Cedric!" Rico yelled as others stood up clapping and cheering as well.

Yes, I know this comes to a surprise to most of you who have been with me on this wild ride of my life! This journey has had many ups and downs from losing my best friend because of a lie to making the right decision to take my talents in baseball off to college in Chicago. Just when I thought I had made the right choice, leaving all the craziness behind, somehow it followed me in the worse way! I have regrets, but some lessons are better learned from some of our bad mistakes. Confused and ashamed of it all, I felt I was way too young to have to deal with the thought of being a father not to just one child but two, by two different girls mid-way through my freshman year of college! I can explain all of it. Forced to make adult decisions and choosing which way to go again wasn't the easiest road to choose but I'm glad I did. So much happened to get me to this point in life so let me share with you the adventure that lead me to that alter with Rachel. Let's go back to those calls...

Sitting on the sofa with Lauren after the back to back phone calls had me shook up! How was that even possible that they both were pregnant at the same damn time? Of course, a rhetorical question I asked myself as I sat there feeling numb inside. My stomach felt hollow as if I hadn't eaten in days. I didn't see any of that coming, not at that point in my life. I knew having sex with Charlene and Rachel was wrong as far as what Mrs. Anthony had warned me about many times. I could also hear my pops voice, yelling at me from his grave, "See Cedric, I told you! If you play with fire, you're sure to get burned!" Lauren didn't know what to say or do as she sat there in silence. I planted my face in the palms of my hands trying to keep my head from exploding! The moisture from my sweaty hands gave me a light rinse across my face. Lauren moved over closer to me as she rubbed the back of my head. I was sure she going to be grossed out from the wetness of my hair as it too was damped from my stressful thoughts. She wasn't fazed as she continued to slowly massage the back portion of my head. "This can't be happening... This can't be happening..." I whispered to myself. My head started pounding as my chest tighten as if I was about to collapse. I started to lean on the arm of the sofa because my head felt like it weighed a thousand pounds! Lauren ran over to the kitchen area. She brought back a glass of water for me. My hands were shaking as I tried to drink the water without spilling it. Lauren went on to help guide my hands with hers as I took sips of the cold, refreshing water before setting the glass on the coffee table. "Whatever it is Cedric, I'm here for you. I'm sorry it has you so upset like this." Lauren whispered to me as she started back rubbing the back of my head. I rubbed my face a few times. I took some deep breathes as I tried to calm my emotions and relax. "Thanks for saying that." I replied. I knew she wanted to know what was going on because she's never seen me so worked up about anything. I had been sure of myself. I wasn't too closed in with Lauren. We had been very opened about any and everything with each other since day one. We had shared many deep pains and frustrations of our past. From our day to day college life to our lives back in our hometowns. If there was a thing or two, she hid from me, I wouldn't have been too offended about it because I was sitting there next to her knowing she was oblivious about me having sex with anyone from my past or present. Since she had made it clear she wasn't a virgin as she had mentioned it a few times about how her first and only time was a complete disaster. She would go into full details about it, but I would always find a way to change the subject as I wasn't too proud of the two times I did it. I knew I should have said something about it, but she never asked me directly if I had done anything with anyone. "Want me to make you something to eat? I'm hungry." Lauren asked as she stood up looking down at me. I knew it was a matter of minutes if not seconds that she would blurt it out and ask me for the details of my worries. I stood up quickly as I replied, "Yeah, I should eat something before I pass out." She smiled at me and nodded her head as she walked over to the kitchen again. I followed her dragging my feet then sat at the kitchen table while she gathered things from the cabinet and out the fridge to cook. Cemented there in my chair as my thoughts went from scared out my mind, to the thoughts of all of it not being true. I was wishing for them to had been playing a sick trick on me together yet again. I figured since I was gone, maybe Charlene swindled her way back to being friends with Rachel and somehow convinced her to do me that way. The more I thought about it, that was the scenario I was basically begging for. I could live with that outcome the most. I must have been extremely out of it and deep in my uncertainties because Lauren scared the hell out of me when she screamed my name! "Cedric!" She yelled at me and I was startled! She caught me off guard sitting there. I looked at her as if she was pointing a knife at me with fear in my eyes! I knew she was frustrated with something if she called out to me like that. "What, what's going on?" I asked as she was standing in front of me, staring at me. She was trying to keep her cool due to the fact something was bothering me. She shook her head a little and said, "I've only called your name like thirty times." I couldn't believe it, but I knew she wasn't making it up. "I'm so sorry, my mind is doing too much for me to handle right now." I replied. It was just my luck to say that which ended up giving her the opportunity to ask what she had been dying to ask that whole time. Without a second to pass, Lauren went for it. "So, what is it that has you so discombobulated? I hope it isn't anything about Mrs. Anthony or something tragic?" She asked. She was thinking the worse possible things I guess from the way I was acting. I didn't hold it in any longer as I replied with, "No, nothing that bad but just as crazy to deal with mentally." She didn't interrupt as she walked back over to the stove. She continued cooking up what looked like an omelet. I went on to say, "Here's the thing, I'm not a virgin if it crossed your mind. I didn't say anything because... Well, they aren't my proudest moments." Lauren paused from cooking and turned her head towards me and said, "Moments huh? Plural? You've done it more than once!" I wasn't for sure if she was excited or mad? It seemed as if she was more interested in the details of me having sex than the reason why I was frustrated. It felt weird for a second because I haven't spoken to anyone about it at all until then. I continued, "Yeah I've had sex… twice… That's the main reason shit just got real!" She immediately turned the stove top off, slid the skillet to another spot because she almost burnt the food! She was so stunned as she started to connect all the dots from what I was saying! She then turned completely around to me with a shocked look on her face then said, "Wait! You got someone pregnant didn't you!? Oh, my god Cedric! Is that what's going on?" My eyes lit up like a lighter in a crack house! My eyes were just as wide as hers as I couldn't believe she hit it right on the head! She could see it on my face that she was dead-on. I didn't have to answer her at all. She walked back over to me. She kneeled in front of me as tears started to pour from my face. I felt hopeless and weak. She whispered, "It's going to be okay Cedric. I know it is. Please don't be discouraged. You've come too far to have doubts or feel sadden by this. I know it's scary, but I believe you can handle it. I believe in you Cedric." I sat there for about five minutes while what she said sunk in. Her words did give me sanity as I wiped my eyes. "You're right. There's always something trying to steal your joy. Something Mrs. Anthony would tell me when things happened suddenly that was out of my control. I know things will be okay, I'm just not sure where to begin in this situation. I'm so lost right now. I know it's all my fault. I have to deal with it." I finally replied. Lauren took her hand and rubbed my cheeks to clear up the last of the tears that rolled down my face. "Cheer up my guy, you'll come out of this, I just know you will. If you don't mind, let's eat! Let's try to take your mind off all of that." We both smiled at one another then she went back over to the stove to finish making us omelets and French toast. I wasn't a huge fan of omelets, but Lauren made them as if she invented them! I couldn't resist. I gobbled mines down within minutes with syrup dripping from the French toast! It was so good that my attention was more focused on Lauren's plate in hopes she wasn't going to finish hers. She must have felt my eyes locked in on her plate while she was taking her time with every bite that she slid the rest of her omelet over to me. "I'm sure you were waiting for me to do that, Mr. Greedy!" Lauren said as she looked at me shaking her head. I nodded my head as I accepted the generosity not wasting a second stuffing the leftovers in my mouth. After we were done, I washed the few dishes that we used. It was a Saturday I believe and there were no classes or practices for neither of us. Lauren wanted to go shopping for sunglasses and a new swimsuit since Spring Break was approaching. I was in need of getting out to clear my head. It was the best thing to do so I agreed to join her. Not only did I need a break mentally but physically as well from all the training. My baseball season was in full effect. I thought I wasn't going to start but I was so focused on my game that all my skills had improved extremely well! I wasn't complaining one bit about playing my first year because I put in the work to earn the spot. I know it was from staying in Chicago during all the holiday breaks. It was tough as hell, but Mrs. Anthony suggested it. She wanted me to study more and train harder. She said it was best I stayed than to come back home in fear that something happened to keep me from going back. Lauren's dad drove her a car up to Chicago as a late graduation present a couple of weeks after we started classes. She wasn't a bad driver, but I had to make sure my seat belt was on extra tight whenever I rode with her anywhere! She had to go freshen up and grab the keys, so I took a quick shower too before I met her downstairs at her car.

We went on to the mall. Of course, Lauren wanted to go into every single store! Had my feet burning because I only had on my flip flops. Bad choice of footwear when you're unexpectedly walking around for what seemed like miles. She finally found what she was looking for and for me being a trooper, she bought me a pair of sunglasses too. I didn't have a clue that sunglasses were that expensive or there were so many different options. We had worked off the breakfast she cooked and decided to grab some food from the food court in the mall. Lauren didn't ask me what I wanted, she just told me to follow her as we approached the center of the food choices circle. I wasn't sure what she was up to because she was a bit anxious. I just did as I was told. We walked past some good places I wanted to try but I didn't say anything as I kept walking slightly behind her. She led us to a place that was sitting alone in the far-left corner of the food court. There were three guys with white robes and hats on preparing food. I wasn't sure what exactly it was from where we were standing. All I could see was white rice being rolled up stuffed with other foods. Lauren turned to me with a big smile on her face then said, "I've been dying to try this place yet alone anywhere that had good sushi! I haven't had any since moving up here for school. You just don't know how much I love sushi!" I was speechless for a second as I struggled to comprehend what sushi was. Me being a lover of seafood as I started to see all the shrimp, crab meat, and other cuisines from the sea, I was ashamed! Not beating myself up too bad as I thought, I hadn't been anywhere in my life that was known for their sushi. Lauren wasted no time asking me if I had it before. I didn't want to seem far out of the loop, so I said, "Well yeah I haven't had it myself, but I know other people that like it. I just haven't had the chance to get around to it." She was overly excited about my statement as her eyes lit up! She replied, "Perfect! I think you'll like it! Please! Please! You have to try it!" I would have just been fine with pizza or a double cheeseburger, but I knew I couldn't get out of it. She was way too hyped about it. I didn't want to kill her excitement on introducing me to it. I agreed to try some. Since she was paying it wasn't a hard decision. She didn't give me any choices or asked if I wanted to try one over the other. She ordered, then the guy started loading our tray with all kinds of various rice rolls. While she paid, I went ahead taking the tray because I didn't want Lauren to strain an arm muscle with the ten pounds of food that she ordered! Well it looked and felt like it was. I found us a table then waited for Lauren's directions and summary of the sushi before I touched anything. The presentation was nice, but I was more concerned about the taste. Lauren brought over some soy sauce which she described as a tasty condiment. She poured some in a small container for us to share as she explained the different sushi by names and ingredients. She even showed me how to use the chop sticks as she grabbed a few of the rolls then sat them on the extra plate she had for me. I tried until I got it as Lauren laughed at me while I fumbled with the chop sticks. I finally had control then picked up one of the rolls she said that had fried shrimp in it. As I was about to stuff my face with the roll the strangest thing happened. I wasn't a hundred percent sure, but a lady walked by the food court that looked exactly like my old principal from my high school, Ms. Harris! I immediately started to feel the goosebumps crawl all over my body! I wore a look on my face as if I was a frighten small child that thought they saw the boogie man! Lauren was so busy making love to the sushi that she wasn't paying me any attention. I dropped the sushi roll back on to my plate and that's when Lauren looked up at me confused. She looked over her shoulder trying to find the thing or person that had me speechless as I followed the lady's every move as she disappeared in the crowd of people walking by. "Cedric, what's wrong? You good?" Lauren said as she waived her hand in front of my face trying to get me to snap out of the daze, I was in. I shook my head in disbelief as I replied, "Yeah I'm good. Sorry." I couldn't say anything about who I thought I saw because I knew it would have led to other questions. I fixed my chop sticks in my hand again then grabbed the roll to eat it before Lauren threw more questions at me. As I was still in shock while eating the sushi, the taste of it was surprisingly delicious! I hurried chewing that one to grab another one! I tried more of them that looked different, yet they all were just as good as the one before it. Lauren was just staring at me as if she was waiting for me to say something. I finished eating the third roll then said, "What's up? I'm good." She looked at me as if she wanted more explanation than just that. I knew I needed to say something else as she had placed her chop sticks down. "I don't know why I thought I saw David. That was weird. I think my mind is playing tricks on me." I finally said. It was the best I had at that moment. I thought it was a very believable thing I could come up with. I knew she wouldn't question that. I couldn't tell her that I thought I saw the woman that tried to rape me in a school office. David was the only person that knew about Ms. Harris and me. I planned on taking that secret to the grave with me as he did. I was ashamed of it more now than I was back then when it happened because I thought it was something cool. Well at least David thought it was, so I didn't feel as bad about it after it happened. Thinking about it, fearing someone else finding out felt embarrassing. Lauren's facial expression changed from being disturbed and worried to sad and concerned. I was wrong, but it kept my secret safe. She said, "I'm sorry Cedric, I know it still bothers you I'm sure." I didn't want to keep that topic on our minds, so I replied, "Yeah I do think about David and often find myself trying to picture him here with me. Sorry I spaced out on you. I'm good now." We both sat there for a moment. "Well he is here with you in spirit. Long live David." Lauren replied. That really did make me feel a way as if I would never actually be alone. I needed to hear that. She was right about David being with me in spirit. I smiled and said, "You're right. Long live David! I will never forget that. Oh, and I know he would have loved these sushi rolls too!" We both laughed as we finished off the rest of the food. They were all great. That day they were added to my favorite food list. We walked the food off with a little window shopping through the rest of the mall. After about thirty minutes of that we left. We headed back to our apartment.

We didn't talk much on our way back because I was still thinking about Ms. Harris. I couldn't shake how much whoever that lady was I saw looked exactly like her. I didn't recall her having a twin sister. Whoever that was, was as close as you can get! I just stared at the clouds, basically reliving the sketchy interaction I had with Ms. Harris in her office that day. I thought about it many times if things would have gone all the way with her and how would I have handled it as far as living with that fact. Lauren kept glancing over at me, which I was sure she saw that same discomfort look I had on my face from the food court. I quickly asked, "So, what's on the agenda the rest of the day?" I couldn't have her thinking too long or searching for the truth behind my worried face. She took a second or two to think about it as if she wanted to ask me something but held off. Just as we were pulling into our apartment's lot she answered, "Hmmm? Good question. I think I want to try out my new swimsuit and sunglasses! Since the sun is out. This weather is too nice to be cooped up in an apartment. Let's go sit out at the pool! I could use a good swim too." I didn't mind that idea at all. There was never a time I would pass up seeing Lauren in a swimsuit, a nice skirt or that dance uniform they wore during games or cheer competitions. We were indeed good friends. There weren't any doubts she knew I admired her figure. "Sounds good to me. I can deal with that. Yeah I need to relax and enjoy some chill time by the pool." I replied. Being that most of the other girls that were on the same squad as her, volleyball and soccer teams lived in the same apartment complex, gave me even more eye candy to see! "Okay, well let's get our swim wardrobe on and get down there to get a couple of pool chairs before they're all gone. I'll get sunscreen and a few sodas." Lauren said smiling at me as she parked the car in front of our building. "Okay I'll grab some chips and cookies to snack on. I'll slide my speedos on too if you're cool with that?" I said as I tried to hold back my laughter. "Yeah right, I'd like to see you in those if you're brave enough to wear them! I'm sure you'll be flexing hard to get all the other girls to stare at your little bitty package if you wore something like that." She replied as I burst out laughing while we were getting out the car. She added, "I thought so." I replied, "I'm good, just joking about that part. I'll never need a pair of speedos for that. Plus, I don't think I'll be able to fit all this in speedos anyway." We both laughed as we walked up the stairs to our units. "Yeah right. I hear you. Hurry up grand pa before everyone else comes out." Lauren said. "Okay, I won't be long at all." I replied. She gave me a look that had curiosity written all over it as she paused for a second then she hurried inside of her place. I could tell she didn't want me to say or add anything else. I laughed to myself as I went on into my apartment. All of that kept my mind busy enough to forget about Ms. Harris and everything else that was stressing me out.

Fifteen minutes later, we both met down by the pool. Lauren looked like a hot slice of apple pie as she walked in the gate to the pool! I always told her she was perfect and flawless because I couldn't find a damn thing wrong with her. She had smooth skin, fit and was out of my league sexy. She didn't look too muscular like some of the other cheer girls on her squad. She was short. Not too little. When she would put on heels, she was like the right height for me! We hung out there for hours. There were a bunch of other people coming and going during that time. Mostly pretty girls from school. There was music playing low from a speaker someone had, with snacks and plenty of sodas going around. Daniel even popped up to hang out as well. I had an extra pair swim trunk he borrowed so he could jump in the pool to cool off. The sun was beaming down hard that day. Daniel always kept me honest by preventing me from staring at Lauren or even talking about her past the limit of friendship. He knew I had this secret thing I wouldn't confess to anyone else about how I really wanted to date Lauren. I never said it but of course it had crossed my mind. I just stuck with the fact that she was a very innocent girl I had as a friend. Daniel and I sat next to one another watching all the traffic while talking about which of the girls were pretty on a scale from one to ten. Lauren threw her comments in here and there whenever she was listening in on our conversation. She laughed most of the time on how Daniel would describe the things he would do to certain girls that were patrolling pool side. I had to keep my comments innocent when Lauren was listening, so she wouldn't know how I really felt the same as Daniel did about the ideas of being with some of those girls. I had to make sure I didn't mess up my chances, if any, of being more than friends with Lauren in the future.

Chapter 2

You Get What You Ask For

After another hour of hanging and seeing many faces with flawless bodies we decided to go back up to my place. Daniel wanted to order something to eat and watch a movie or two. He agreed to pay for the food after Lauren promised to get a couple of her cheer team girls to come over to join us. Daniel was always willing to pay for whatever if there were any chance of being around girls. We all wanted hot wings and pizza, so Daniel ordered from a place we loved. After making some calls, Lauren stepped next door to her place to shower and change clothes. I went on to wash up as well before the other girls headed over. Daniel changed back into his regular clothes since he didn't get in the pool like Lauren and I did. After I was out the shower, I picked up a few things around the place making sure it was presentable for the guests. Daniel helped by taking the trash out and sweeping up in the kitchen area. An hour went by fast and the night settled in. Just as we were finishing up, there was a soft knock on the door. I was wondering what was taking Lauren so long to come back but when I opened the door, it was her accompanied by two gorgeous girls! We didn't see them at the pool. Both girls were about the same height as Lauren, one with sandy brown skin with long black hair, the other had pale skin with long blonde hair. They were both just as fit as Lauren was and had jaw dropping jean shorts on that revealed every curve they had. Lauren had on a fitted short skirt that had me zooming in as they all walked past me. Lauren was leading them through the door. The two girls' eyes perked up when they saw me and they both said, "Yeah he is really cute! Thanks for having us over!" Lauren looked back as if she was shamed but smiled with guilt from the girls' comment. As I was shutting the door I looked over towards Daniel and he was wearing a huge smile from ear to ear. I couldn't help but grin too as I closed the door. I walked over to Daniel then gave him a fist bump with excitement! Lauren and the girls all sat on the couch as Daniel and I quickly grabbed two chairs from the kitchen. One of the girls had a small bag with her that she sat on the coffee table. I looked over at Daniel after we both eyes balled the bag, we were sure we knew what was in it. From the way the girls continued to giggle softly, indicated it was some liquid courage. Something my dad called alcohol. As the girls whispered to one another, laughing in sync, there wasn't any doubt they were feeling bold. I had to say something to keep them from thinking Daniel and I weren't just two staring owls. "I can't believe that there are other pretty girls that don't mind hanging out with some lame dudes." I said smiling at the girls. Before they could answer, a loud knock came from the door! One of the girls quickly grabbed the bag off the table then stuffed it behind her back as they all sat closer to each other with their backs all pressed to the couch. Daniel jumped up and said, "Who's that knocking like they're the police?" Lauren looked over at me as I started to laugh at them all. She was shaking her head in confusion. They all gave me that same look. I slowly got up to get the door and said, "It's about time they got here!" Daniel and Lauren asked almost at once together, "Who!" As I was opening the door, I said, "The food is here, relax!" They all looked relieved after seeing it was the delivery guy with the food we had ordered earlier. Daniel immediately walked over to pay the guy as I took the food to the kitchen area. When Daniel closed the door, they all burst out in laughter! "Man, I just knew that was some trouble, knocking on the door like that!", One of the girls said. Lauren replied, "Yeah I forgot we were expecting food." I grabbed some paper plates and napkins from a cabinet then sat them on the kitchen table. Daniel walked over shaking his head and said, "Yeah I forgot too, that fast! But I see Mr. Cool over here wasn't worried at all or you're just hungry enough to had remembered that?" I laughed and said, "No lie, I'm hungry as hell! I was about to call and see what the holdup was on our order!" Daniel laughed as Lauren did too then she walked over just in time, hearing my hungry confession. The other two girls came over bringing their brown paper bag with them. "Ladies first..." I said as my stomach growled. Lauren was the only one close enough to hear it. She slightly bumped me with her elbow and whispered, "We may need to let you go first? Your stomach is screaming, "Feed me Cedric!"" We both laughed, then I replied, "I'm good, I wasn't raised that way, so you ladies go ahead. Don't be shy, it's just food." The girls all filled their plates up with slices of the steaming deep-dish pepperoni pizza and some of the dripping saucy glazed hot wings. Once they had their plates loaded, they went back into the living room area leaving their little bag on the kitchen table. "Do I really have to ask are you ladies going to share what's in the bag? I mean, there are house rules!" Daniel said with a big curious smile on his face as he winked his eye at me. I wasn't sure if he was serious or just messing with the girls, but I knew I wasn't going to partake in whatever it was in that bag. Lauren held her head down as a sign that she wasn't going to say anything in response to Daniel's statement. The two girls giggled as they looked at one another then nodding, agreeing they should offer him some. "Wait, before I accept anything from you beautiful ladies, what are your names!" Daniel said as he gave a side eye look at Lauren. He slightly turned his head towards her to let Lauren know it was rude for not properly introducing the girls. "Yeah what are your names?" I added then gave Lauren the same look Daniel was giving her. "Oh, I'm so sorry fellas! My bad, how rude of me? I didn't introduce you all at all." Lauren shook her head with a grin on her face. One of them stood up and walked over to the bag then said, "Well my name is Ashley and she's Sasha. But I'm the fun one! So, grab a cup if you really want to know." Daniel didn't waste any time getting a cup from the dishwasher! He sat it on the table near the bag. "Wait, let me get my guy here a cup too." Daniel said as he went to get a cup for me. "I'm good, I'm sure you'll let me know what it is!" I said as Lauren stared at me trying to see what I was going to do. After hearing my reply Lauren got her plate then went to the living room. "No wonder Lauren likes you so much, you're just as square as she is." Ashley said smiling as she filled Daniel's cup. "Oh, is that right?" I asked. "It's okay, everyone can't handle it. Let's see if your boy can." Ashley whispered back to me. "And what exactly is that?" I asked. "We call it Hunch Punch!" Sasha and Ashley both yelled so that everyone in the place could hear them! You would have thought they were shooting a commercial for it the way they said with joy and laughter. Daniel smiled as he grabbed his cup then said, "Sounds good to me! I know about 'Hunch Punch' and from what I heard, it's quite a bit of alcohol used to make it." I didn't want to ask where they got the alcohol from. From the looks of it, we were all just freshmen. Neither one of them were 21. I just shook my head as I fixed me a plate, so I could finally eat. I wanted to say something to Daniel about not doing it, but I didn't want to seem like I was cutting into his fun. He had a habit of telling me I was being too up tight when I would try to keep him from doing certain things. There were a few times where I had some words for him about his nonchalant behavior towards serious situations that could have turned ugly. Had to tell him several times that he needed to chill out a little instead of being so eager to do whatever whenever. I always felt that was his way of trying to fit in with whoever to get them to like him. All I could do was watch as Daniel turned the cup up, drinking it until it was gone. "Wow! That was better than I thought!" Daniel said slamming the cup down on the table. Everyone looked around at each other nervously. "Please be careful drinking a lot of that stuff! It will sneak up on you. It will have you doing stuff you know you shouldn't be doing." Lauren said to Daniel with a concerned look on her face. "Yeah be careful my guy. I'm not sure if downing it that fast was the best idea." I added. Ashley and Sasha just giggled as they continued eating while passing a cup of the Hunch Punch back and forth to one another. I sat by Lauren in a chair and Daniel slid in between the two girls on the couch. We all ate and joked about school, the cheer team stuff and how good Daniel and I was in baseball. We watched a standup comedy special that was on TV which helped with the mood. It also made it easier for the girls to giggle as much as they wanted to since they couldn't stop laughing at everything Daniel was whispering to them. I was okay sitting next to Lauren laughing together about the funny stuff the guy was saying on the TV. I could get in a few words in between the jokes as I tried to investigate the things that were said about me from her mouth. The parts about her liking me more than I knew. "Enjoying yourself?" I whispered to Lauren. "You know I am. This was a good idea. Are you?" She replied smiling. "I do agree. Thanks for inviting some distractions for Daniel." I said jokingly. "Yeah yeah... I know you really wish it was you over there sitting on the couch with them." She said as she got up then walked into the kitchen. She dropped her pizza crust and wings bones in the trash can. I sat there for a second then followed as she poured herself some soda from the fridge. I dumped my trash as well then slid in up close to her. She had her back to me as I said, "Being close to you and having you around is what I prefer." She turned around towards me. She looked me in the eyes then asked, "Is that right?" I stepped a little closer. As I was about to speak, Ashley shouted, "Aww You guys look so cute!" Of course, that made it weird with everyone suddenly staring at us. I asked, "You think huh?" Lauren immediately grabbed her cup. She hurried back to her seat. I could tell she was embarrassed again, so I went to the restroom to refresh myself. Felt like I had some chicken stuck in my teeth. I relieved myself from all the soda I had. I had to brush my teeth making sure I wasn't crazy. While brushing, those random thoughts kept coming back to me. The idea that Ms. Harris had moved to Chicago and she was just casually passing through the mall. I quickly finished up when I heard the front door suddenly slam shut! I didn't want Lauren to leave without saying bye or at least made sure she was okay. I walked out the restroom bumping my elbow on the door frame trying to move fast! I rushed into living room to only see Lauren sitting on the couch alone. I was puzzled looking around the place for Daniel and the girls. As I was about to ask what happened to everyone else, Lauren said, "Not sure if Daniel leaving with those two was the greatest idea, but you can't stop anyone once they're filled with Hunch Punch." I marched over to the window looking through the blinds trying to see if I could catch them in my sights, but they were long gone that fast! "No need to look for them or try to stop them, they'll regret whatever it is they're about to do." Lauren said as if that was the norm for the girls. "That's fine and all if they're that way but I don't want Daniel to get in any trouble! Our coach has given us enough strict warnings to not get caught up in anything that involves alcohol and girls. He said the outcome could cost us everything including getting kicked off the team!" I said concerned about my friend and teammate. "Well honestly I haven't heard of anything that wild happening with those two that would cause that much trouble for him. I wouldn't worry too much about it." Lauren said to keep me calm about my worries for Daniel. "I'm kind of glad they're all gone now. They were getting annoying as hell with all the extra snickering." Lauren said. I went to the door then opened it. I stepped out looking to make sure they were indeed gone. I came back in after a minute or two. I shut the door then locked it hoping she was right. "I mean you did invite them over out of all the girls you knew or hung out with." I replied. "Yeah you're right. They are fun chicks to kick it with up until they start drinking. They go from super cool to super irritating. That's why I don't give in to their encouragement to drink that stuff! I don't want anything that's going to make me act anything differently than my normal self." Lauren replied. "Well, that makes sense to me. It's like the way I feel about Daniel. He's funny, plus one of the coolest people I've met, until he's trying to be too damn cool!" I added. We both paused in thoughts about them and laughed a bit. We went on to talk about some of the craziest things we've seen so far happening around the campus and at some of the parties she's been to. I wasn't the best studier, so I couldn't attend many parties due to wanting to stay ahead of my class work. Especially if I wanted to continue playing baseball. I couldn't afford the luxury of parting all night and that's one of the many reasons why I enjoyed hanging out with Lauren more. She didn't prefer to be out too late around the party animals. She said she only attended a few parties because her cheer team was hosting them to recruit new cheer girls. I was trying hard to stay up, but I started to nod off during one of Lauren's stories until she punched me in the arm! "Open your eyes sleepy head! Don't be rude, I'm telling a funny story." She said smiling. "I'm trying, I'm trying. Your story is actually what's causing me to doze off because it's taking your ass forever to get to the funny part." I replied, laughing as I was saying it. Then she punched me again! "Oh! You're just going to be an ass about it huh?" She said as she jumped on me causing me to lay on my back on the couch. She straddled me trying to pin both my arms down. I didn't wrestle with her at all and she noticed it right away. "Don't let me... Fight back!" She said as she held my arms down. "Why would I? You know how long I've been waiting to have you on top of me…" I replied. I didn't think twice about expressing that in that moment at all. I couldn't hold it in. I didn't have any other come back for her than that. I was trying to test her to determine if the rumors were true. That imaginary line wasn't there anymore. I didn't want to cross it since I've been restraining myself since we were so cool as friends. I shot my shot! "I don't believe you." She replied as she rolled off me back on to the couch. "Wait, is that a serious question?" I asked as I sat up. "Maybe I should just leave and not make things awkward between us." Lauren said as she stood up. I grabbed her arm pleading with her as I whispered, "No, please don't go. I wasn't expecting that or wasn't thinking you were for real?" She turned around facing me then said, "I don't want things to be strange, but I've really liked you from the first day we met. You are not like any guy I've ever dated which is a great thing. I really enjoy being around you more than you know. You're so different and it's cute that you don't have a clue. You don't know how special you are." My heart may have skipped a beat hearing her say that. I felt as if I was daydreaming or something. I had to pick my whole bottom of my mouth off the floor. I had to take a moment before I replied to let what I heard marinate. "I figured it was just safe to stay in the friendzone. I did not want things uncomfortable for you. What I said earlier were facts. I liked you a lot since day one too! I have had so much on my mind from the way things played out for me back at home before coming to school here. Well… You know now from the phone calls I've received since I've been here. I knew for sure you wouldn't be interested in dealing with a guy with so much craziness going on." I finally replied. She shook her head as if she couldn't believe what I was saying. "What is it?" I asked as I was trying to understand the purpose of her shaking her head. "Cedric, who am I to judge you for your past or any mistakes you have made? I admired your concern and passion to handle it all. That drew me closer to you. Most people would have freaked out or shut down but not you!" She replied. I knew she was being honest to have said all that which had me feeling myself. I didn't think she looked at me that way. Not with that much dept. I was too busy trying to act like the playboy I use to be, instead of embracing the man I was becoming. Lauren was seeing it herself since I arrived there. She was witnessing change within me as well as my ability to step up to the plate of responsibilities. My palms were sweaty, but I had to show her I appreciated her attention to the details of my growth. I replied with action. A soft kiss I placed on her lips. I pulled her in closer to me then said, "Thank you for seeing something in me that I don't fully recognize myself. It means a lot to me hearing it from you." She then jumped on me again, straddling me then whispered, "Don't ever doubt my words, it took all my nerves to confess that to you. Please don't become a jerk towards me..." I placed her head on my chest. "I don't know how to be a jerk. I think we both just lifted some weight off our shoulders. I'm glad we both opened up more tonight. Not sure where this will go but I'm willing to found out." I whispered back to her. It seemed like I could feel her smiling as she was laying on top of me with one side of her face pressed against my chest still as she said, "Yes I agree, I'm willing to see too." We both sat there quietly as the sounds of the late-night party people carried on outside. I didn't want to move a muscle although they were stiff and numb from Lauren still laying on me after about a half an hour. I believe we both enjoyed being that close to one another as if we were Siamese twins until we were both sound to sleep.

I nearly jumped out of my skin as I almost pushed Lauren on to the floor when we were surprisingly awakened by loud bangs on the door! Lauren and I slowly got up looking at one another dazed as hell about who would be knocking with that much force other than the police! I knew it was late morning because of the rays of sun light shining through the blinds of the window. The knocks started to get louder as I hesitated to open the door yet alone ask who it was behind the door! Lauren signal me to go ahead and say something or at least answer the door. My hands were shaking as I reached towards the door handle. Lauren whispered, "It's okay I'm sure, just open it." I replied, "Easy for you to say but I'm going to." I finally twisted the doorknob, opening the door as I braced myself for the mystery. Daniel came running through it like a wanted man! Just when I thought for sure it was the school or local police beating down the door! He came in looking like he had seen a ghost and he had rushed over to warn us about it! He was pouring down sweating with the same clothes he had on the night before. "What's going on, you good?" I asked as I closed the door quickly. He was gasping for air as if he had run there from the next town over! "Daniel, are you okay?" Lauren asked as Daniel gathered himself to speak. He walked in circles as if he were trying to figure out something in his head. "Daniel, you better start talking now and stop acting like a fugitive!" Lauren shouted at him! She was nervous and worried. I was just as concerned myself but was trying hard to be patient. I knew Daniel could be dramatic when he did something he wasn't supposed to do. I stood there quietly as we waited for his response. "I didn't know what to do or say so I ran here!" Daniel finally said but almost as a whisper as if he wasn't sure about what he wanted to say. "What's going on man? What have you done now?" I asked breaking my silence. I stepped in front of him during his small circle dance he was doing. "I'm not crazy... and yes I was really buzzed! But... I don't know how that could have happened?" Daniel said as he shook his head in disbelief. Lauren walked over closer to us as we were standing face to face, Daniel and me. She looked as if she was fixated on Daniel's next words. I asked, "What happened? Did something happen with you and the girls?" I figured it had to have something to do with them when he said he was buzzed. As Daniel was about to respond, he was interrupted by loud thumping on the door! The knocks were just as loud as Daniel's knocks! Lauren and I immediately looked at Daniel as we both launched a series of questions at him! We both knew those knocks had to have been for him. "What the hell man? Who's that Daniel?" Lauren and I asked right after each other. Daniel started walking backwards slowly away from the door as he said, "I promise you two, I do not remember what happened last night, but I do know I didn't force anything on anyone!" Lauren then walked over to the door as if she knew who was outside knocking. "Wait, what happened?" I asked him. Lauren was standing by the door, waiting to hear his answer before she opened the door. "Okay, okay… We went back to their dorm room, right… After walking around campus talking, laughing and daring each other to do stupid stuff." I cut in and asked as he was talking, "Stupid stuff like what?" Daniel walked over to the couch and sat down at the edge of it, with both his knees shaking as he went on saying, "Once we made it to the building where their dorm rooms were, of course they snuck me in. Okay… We were in the room, whispering as we were still daring one another to do silly stuff." The knocks at the door were getting louder and louder by the second! I could tell Daniel was scared out his mind but was struggling trying to piece everything together that happened. "I'm sorry guys but seriously, we have to open this door before they break it down." Lauren whispered as she was waiting for Daniel to hurry up with his story. "I know I know! Daniel please tell us why someone is here beating my door down!" I added as I stepped over closer towards him. He suddenly stood up then walked quickly over to the door! As I was about to ask him what the hell he was about to do, he opened the door! Lauren stepped back out of the way as two men stepped in, rushing towards Daniel! Lauren and I were speechless! One of the guys was the head of the room and board for the school, escorted by one of the guys from campus security. The campus security guy was the first in and immediately grabbed Daniel by his arm! He said, "You shouldn't have run son! Now you have to come with us!" Daniel didn't put up a fight. The look of guilt and confusion was all over his face as he walked out the door with the two men. "Wait, please tell us what's going on here!" Lauren said to the two guys escorting Daniel out of my apartment. They didn't say anything to her. Lauren and I followed them out the door. I had to say something. I was beyond worried at that point knowing that Daniel had done something he couldn't talk his way out of! "She asked you guys a question! One of you can tell us something! Please..." I said. The campus security guy looked back right before they got to the stairs then said, "Your friend may have had too much fun last night. We need to ask him some questions to get to the bottom of it." They took him down the stairs to a campus security car. As they were putting Daniel in the back seat, he looked up at us and yelled to Lauren, "Lauren please tell your friends to tell the truth about what happened last night!" I looked over to Lauren confused and thinking of the worse possible things he could have meant by saying that. "Please tell me those girls wouldn't do anything crazy like lie about something serious enough that the campus security had to get involved in." I said to Lauren before we walked back into my apartment. The car pulled off in a hurry. "I honestly don't know what they would do. Especially if they were trying to avoid getting themselves in some trouble." Lauren replied.

Lauren wanted to change before we headed over to the dorms to see if we could catch up with her friends to get a better understanding of the foolishness. I agreed I needed to put on something else too. Lauren went next door to her place while I got myself together. My phone rang as I was getting out of the shower. I hurried to my room where it was plugged up at to answer it. I didn't look to see who it was, I just picked it up then said hello. There were a few seconds of silence before I heard Ms. Anthony's voice. "Cedric, I'm glad you answered. I wanted to ask you a few questions about your old principal, Ms. Harris." She said it with a concerned tone as if she discovered some terrible information. My heart and stomach dropped on the floor by my feet as I was in complete silence waiting to hear the first question! My heart was racing, and my entire face became sweaty! I had to take a seat on my bed. "Cedric, are you okay? Did you hear my question? Mrs. Anthony said. I guess I checked out mentally and was thinking of what not to say not hearing a word she said! "I'm sorry, I just got out the shower and was trying to put my clothes on. I missed the question." I quickly replied. "Well there's a lot of talk going around here and even on the local news that she hasn't been seen around here since school was nearly out. It's very disturbing news to hear some of the things she's done. I've heard she was in some trouble for some sexual misconduct while working here at the high school. Do you know anything about this?" She said gradually. I had to be careful with my words and the way I responded. She hadn't heard too much or anything close to linking me to any of it. "Wow! That's crazy. Are you serious?? I can't believe that!" I said as if it was the most shocking news I've ever heard. She replied, "Yes it's a serious matter. Some of the policemen have been to some of the current and former students' homes asking detailed questions! You know Herman's mom, Ms. Baker? Well, she called me this morning asking me about you and if you knew anything. She is taking this hard because she just found out that her son was touched in places, he shouldn't have been touched by Ms. Harris last year! Ms. Baker was clueless and is terribly upset about it all! I know you and Herman played baseball together, so I told her I would call you. Is there anything you need to tell me Cedric?" I was speechless at that moment. It was nothing to brag about, but I really thought she only did me that way! I was keeping it to myself since Ms. Harris had left town and I figured I'll never see her again. I couldn't believe she had been doing it to other young men like myself for years! I had already told Mrs. Anthony I didn't know much. I couldn't change my story. "No ma'am... I didn't know about any of that! I can't believe I was around him and he never said one word to me or any of the other players. I mean we hung out a little outside of school but never talked about much about anything else other than baseball. I'm sorry that happened to him! I hate it happened!" I replied as convincing and concerned as I could. I swallowed my whole tongue after saying that knowing it was a big lie! I hate I had to lie to her, but I didn't know what else to do. Suddenly a knock on my door which felt like it had made the entire apartment shake due to me being insanely tense, holding the phone nearly dropping it! The only benefit I was getting from the knocks on the door was having a legit reason to end the nerve wrecking call with Mrs. Anthony. I didn't think I was going to keep my story together any longer. "I'm sorry Mrs. Anthony but someone's at my door. Can I call you back later?" I said. I heard Mrs. Anthony exhale a deep breath as if she had more to say. She was somewhat relieved at my answers to her questions. "That's fine. I'm glad nothing happened to you, but I'm saddened by the news of the other young men. This is something that should never happen to a young person ever, yet alone at a school! Please be careful Cedric. I hope you understand that if anything remotely close happens to you like that, you will not hesitate to say something to me or anyone, okay." She replied calmly. I agreed with her and assured her I would speak up immediately before I hung up the phone. It felt like a thunderstorm cloud formed over my head as I walked to the door to answer it. I knew I was wrong, but it was better that way in my eyes.

I answered the door and to my surprise, it was Lauren and one of the girls from last night! The one with the blonde

hair, Sasha. So many things were running through my head as I
wanted to scream at her with a bunch of questions. I couldn't
do it without mixing my emotions with what was going on
there, with what happened back at home in Jackson! Lauren
walked in first followed by Sasha with her head down as if she
didn't want to see my face. I shut the door then followed them
into the living room. Lauren sat down while Sasha stood by the
couch with her head still down. I looked over at Lauren as I was
confused and curious on what was going on. Lauren shook her
head as if she was frustrated then said to Sasha, "Girl, please
don't be rude! You know why we're here! You're not going to
say anything? Please tell him what happened before I do!" I sat
down next to Lauren as my attention was locked in on Sasha.
She finally looked up at me after Lauren's pressing words to her.
"Please tell me what happened last night." I added. Sasha had
this look of guilt on her face as she started to reveal to me the
truth about their night. "Well we went back to our dorm room
which we had to sneak Daniel in. I didn't want to personally,
because we had already had another situation where we were
in trouble for, similar to that. I couldn't afford to do anything
else crazy. Ashley didn't care. We were all really drunk as we
were making all kinds of noise that late at night. Daniel was in
and out, blacking out while we were all laying in my bed playing
"Truth or Dare". We both knew he was falling asleep or I guess
passing out, but Ashley kept hitting him, making him stay up
with us. After a few unsuccessful rounds of that, Daniel
eventually fell asleep. I wasn't going to move him or tell him to
leave so I left him there as I was crashing myself. Ashley was
wide awake as if she had a triple shot of espresso, she didn't
share with us. She whispered to me that she wanted to do
something crazy, so she went and got some of her make-up to
put on Daniel's face while he was passed out. I promise I didn't
have any energy to neither talk her out of it or physically try to
stop her. I was completely done and couldn't keep my eyes

open. I laid down on her bed which was directly across from mines. Within seconds I was out! All I remember, was tossing and turning a bit. I may have seen Ashley kissing Daniel at one point then maybe seeing her on top of him. I just rolled over thinking I was probably dreaming or something. Then suddenly I heard loud screaming with the lights being turned on by the Resident Head of our dorm rooms and campus police! I could tell something wasn't right because Daniel's pants were pulled down! Daniel jump up scared, as if he was having a nightmare. He immediately plowed his way through the door nearly knocking the campus police down! Ashley was the one screaming like Daniel was a monster trying to get her as she too jumped up! She then huddled up behind the two men as they were picking themselves up from being pushed by Daniel. I was so confused as the Campus Police then ran after Daniel! Ashley started yelling, "I don't know how he got in here! Help us please!" I looked at Ashley and gave her my "WTF" face! I didn't know what to say or do!" She said as I had to cut in at that point, feeling disgusted and furious! "Are you fucking serious! You mean to tell me you were somewhat aware of what was going on yet couldn't do anything to prevent it! On top of that, you didn't step in and immediately explain to them, you two invited him over, basically snuck him in!" I shouted at her! Lauren placed her hand on my thigh, in what was an attempt to calm me down, but I was boiling with anger! I never raised my voice at a female that way. I just couldn't believe they would do a guy like that! I mean, I know I had my experience with one heartless girl. To think that two would pull something like that was beyond me! Sasha started to cry as she said, "I promise you Cedric I didn't mean for anything like this to happen. It all went downhill so fast and before I had a second thought, Daniel was running out the room!" I got up and went to the kitchen area to get Sasha a napkin to wipe her face. If her story was true, I couldn't blame her for any of it. On one hand I was thinking

Daniel deserved it because he got himself in it but on the other hand, that wasn't cool at all for Ashley to do him that way! I gave Sasha a few napkins as we all sat there with our thoughts crossing all over the place. About ten minutes went by as our silence wrecked my nerves thinking we should find Ashley and make her tell the truth! "Where is Ashley now?" I asked Sasha. "I don't know. After Daniel ran out, she rushed into the restroom locking herself in there for a few minutes. The Resident Head convinced her to come out and go with him to give a statement on what exactly happened. I was confused because she didn't ask me to come too. That's why I came on over to Lauren's place." She said. I jumped up then grab my keys and shoes! "Come on! We have to go to make sure they hear your side too! That's the only way Daniel can get out of this!" I yelled! Both agreed and got up.

We all walked over to the campus police office as fast as we could. When we approached the building, there were a few students standing outside. We weren't sure why they were out there for as they were all standing in small groups talking to one another. Most of them were female students in their pjs and flip flops. We were at the doors of the office when we saw Ashely sitting, talking to some girls that were planted around her. One girl was standing next to her shaking her head as she was rubbing Ashley's shoulder like she was comforting her. I was putting all the signs together at that point and knew exactly what was going on. We walked in and Ashley's eyes lit up like a lightning bolt when she saw us! She immediately jumped out of her seat! She ran into another door. We were following her when out came one of the campus police officers! Ashley was trailing him closely as he was standing in between her and us! "What are you all doing here? Are you all trying to attack this young lady?" He asked. I know how I really wanted to respond but Lauren spoke up before I did. "We are here to tell the truth! Nothing but the truth! Daniel is innocent! Ashley's roommate

Sasha is right here. She can and will prove that, with her side of the story!" Lauren yelled! I believed Lauren was damn near more upset than me from her reply. I was glad she said something because I wasn't going to get anywhere if I had said what I was thinking. "There's only one side and that's my side! I was attacked, and you were sleep Sasha!" Ashley yelled back at her! I was so angry at Ashley for her statement that I yelled out at her, "Wow, you slutty trailer trash, you know he didn't attack your dusty ass..." I believe the entire building heard me say that! It was completely silent. You could hear my heart beating through my shirt. Ashely instantly started to cry, while everyone stared at me as if I had stabbed or punched an innocent girl. The campus police guy stepped in then said, "You need to leave now young man! You will not talk to her that way! If there's more to the story, we will get it. As of right now, your friend will be right here until we have cleared him!" I didn't want to cause any more trouble, so I walked out the office. Lauren and Sasha said they were going to stay to make sure the officer heard Sasha's statement. I told them I was going to go back to my apartment if they needed me. I didn't want to hang around outside because of all the commotion and people thinking I was a crazy person after yelling and saying what I said to Ashley. As I was walking back to my place, my phone rang. There was no number showing like normal, it said it was from an unknown caller. I was hesitant to answer it, but I did any way. There was hardly anyone who had this number. I held the phone to my ears, saying hello for about a minute but no one said anything. It was just silence, then I hung up. I finally made it back to my place. I was starving so I put some of the leftovers from the night before in the microwave. I kicked my shoes off then turned the TV on. My phone rang again as soon as the microwave buzzer sounded! I quickly answered the phone as I walked back into the kitchen to get my food. No answer on the other end again, just background noise. I hung up again then proceeded to feed my face. After I ate, I just laid on the couch watching an old movie that was on I hadn't seen in years. Eventually I fell asleep and was out for a good time.

From the loud knocks on the door that woke me and then glancing at my phone, someone was really trying to get to me. I slept for over three hours according to the clock on my cell phone. It was well past noon when the movie started that I was watching, and the clock read four thirty! I had five missed calls and had to rush to the door before it was smashed in! I heard Lauren's voice through the door saying, "Cedric open the door it's me! I know you're in there!" I quickly opened the door. "Hey, what's up? Come in." I said as Lauren walked in. She looked me up and down then looked around the place. "What the hell is going with you? What have you been doing? I have been knocking on your door for like 20 minutes! Is someone else in here with you?" She said aggressively. I was stunned to hear that from her. I wasn't expecting that. I couldn't believe she had been knocking that long because I'm a light sleeper. For some reason I slept harder than I've ever slept before! "Yeah I'm just as shocked as you. Why would someone else be here? I don't know why I was in such a deep sleep like that. I'm sorry... I think my body, well mostly my brain was telling me I needed to rest?" I replied. She got her some juice from the fridge then drank it within seconds before I could fix my mouth to ask her to pour me a cup! "Damn you was thirsty huh? Nothing to drink at your place?" I asked jokingly as I washed the cup, she had out to pour me some. "You know I have plenty to drink at my place. With so much going on earlier after I came back to my place to freshen up, I was stepping out to see if you wanted to get food, but I locked myself out of my apartment! You didn't answer the first time I knocked so I had to walk over to the office building. The maintenance people said it was going to be a few hours before they could get me back in, which left me outside your door knocking and banging on it. I knew you were in here because I heard your phone ringing. That's when I was starting to get worried!" Lauren said as she laid down on the couch with her head on one end and legs propped up on the arm of the other end. "It took 20 minutes for you to get worried about me?" I asked with a grin on my face. "I mean you had the door locked and all. I thought you were in here jerking off or something... I also know it don't take that long to do that so..." She said then started laughing. "It depends." I whispered as I started to laugh with her. I looked through my phone, seeing there were no familiar numbers showing up. Just five missed calls from "Unknown Caller". "Yeah, I hate that happened to you. I should have just kept the door unlocked. It's not like anyone else is going to run up in here but you or Daniel." I added then finished my cup of juice. "Speaking of Daniel, what happened when I left?" I asked. "I don't know, I wasn't able to speak to him much because they kept us in separate rooms, coming back and forth asking Ashley a bunch of questions. I know you wanted to be there for him, but it was probably for the best you came on back to chill out." Lauren answered. "Man, I want to go back up there. It's been hours! They have to had let him go by now!" I said as I was looking through the blinds out the window. "You may be right but I'm sure Daniel will come by or call. I don't think it's a good idea to go back up there. Ashley gave them the truth with good details about last night! She was worried and very apologetic about it all." Lauren said. "Well she should be! I am glad she came to her senses about it unlike your lying, pathetic friend Sasha!" I said then walked to my room without waiting for a reply from Lauren. That was rude of me. I instantly got angry when I thought about how evil Sasha had been. I was letting it get the best of me, so I wanted to lay back down. I laid across my bed on my back staring at the ceiling. Lauren came in after about three minutes of me giving her the silent treatment. "I get it Cedric, trust me I do! I could have slapped her whole damn head off! Daniel is a

good guy and shouldn't have been screwed over like that."
Lauren said as she walked in my room. I didn't say a word. I laid
there thinking about what Daniel was doing and who had called
my phone that many times. Lauren laid down beside me on her
back as well. We laid there together, quiet in our own separate
thoughts. I was trying my best to avoid turning my head her way
because she had laid as close as she could next to me. Finally,
she asked, "what are you thinking about right now?" That was a
question I wasn't prepared to answer, given the fact I was
thinking of kissing her. Her lying next to me with so much going
on, I needed a release! "I honestly have at least a million and
one things on my mind, plenty to choose from." I replied as I
exhaled with exhaustion. She turned over next to me with her
face facing the side of my face. Just inches away. So close I
could have just turned with the slightest effort and our lips
would have touched. I did not want to make things weird, so I
stayed in place. "I'm worried about you. I want you to know I'm
here for you through it all. Anything I can do to help, I will." She
whispered softly in my ear that made the hair on my arms raise.
The way she said it, led me to believe she too may have needed
a release. I replied jokingly saying, "Well, there is this one
thing… maybe, you could do… if you really want to help." I then
turned towards her with my face barely inches away from hers.
She smiled then replied, "I wonder what that could be?" The
courage train was rolling, and I wasn't getting off it until we
reached my destination! I did not want to waste another
second, so I went in for a kiss! I gave her two soft pecks. On the
second one she pressed her lips harder on mines to confirm she
was feeling the same way! "Something like that." I whispered to
her. She smiled innocently as she replied, "Yeah I could help
with that. Only for you." I felt some kind of way as my heart
started to beat faster as I was thinking about my first two
mistakes in that field. I was trying to come up with a smooth
way to get a condom from the nightstand drawer beside my

bed. Before I could even make my attempt, Lauren said, "Given your past Mr. Jack Rabbit and not trying to ruin the moment, please tell me you have protection?" I laughed out loud because that caught me off guard yet gave me the perfect chance to roll over to grab the condom. I turned back over with the condom in my hand then said, "I know better now. You have nothing to worry about." She smiled as she was shaking her head, agreeing that I should know better. I couldn't disappoint her and make her second time worse than her first. I understood enough to know it was better for me to just relax and take my time. I wanted to do all the work to ensure she was comfortable, and she could trust me. Thinking about how it was going to affect our friendship wasn't my biggest concern but soon it would bite me in the ass! I went right to kissing her on her lips once more then made my way down to her neck as I let my tongue slide along her skin gently. I slowly rolled her on to her back as I continued kissing her neck moving myself slightly on top of her. I took off my shirt first to give her a moment to remove any second thoughts about going on with it. She wasn't backing out at all as she joined me by taking her shirt off too! I tossed mines down to assist her with hers. I slid my hands up her arms as we both guided her shirt over her head together. I kissed her on her lips more as she unfastened her bra. She laid it on the floor as she stretched her arms in the air shaking with every touch my lips gave her soft skin. I licked and kissed her breast as she was unbuttoning the shorts she had on. I pulled her shorts off then she whispered, "Can you put on some protection now before we go too far without it." She laid up by the pillows as she then pulled off her panties. She slowly got under the sheets. I was as ready as I could be as it didn't take me long to get my shorts off to put on the condom. I crawled on the bed then underneath the covers with her. She instantly pulled me on top of her! I admit I was nervous, but it felt right for a lot of reasons yet wrong for just as many. I didn't want to ruin anything with my doubts of preforming well because Lauren was giving me a look as if she wanted me more in that moment than anything! I would have been a fool to change the way things were flowing. I couldn't wait any longer as I slowly pushed myself inside of her. We went at for about ten minutes! Maybe it was five minutes? However long it was, it was amazing! With ever thrust I gave, it felt wetter and tighter! She pulled me in closer as we kissed for what felt like forever! I was about to bust my load and it was like Lauren knew the exact moment. I knew I was about to and right when I was pulling out, making sure I didn't make any mistakes even though I had a condom on. Lauren locked her legs around me then pulled me as close as she could as I came inside of her! It felt so damn good! All I could do was lay there as the sweat dripped off my forehead on to hers. She looked up at me with an evil grin yet a very satisfied look on her face. I didn't say a word until my arms started shaking as I was still holding myself up to keep from crashing down, suffocating her. "Damn...That felt so good." I whispered as I finally rolled over slowly next to her. "I have no complaints at all. Sorry for that last second super leg hug I did on you." Lauren said as she giggled. "You knew what you were doing." I replied as I smiled while shaking my head. I then got up to use the restroom. "Excuse me for a second, I need to go to the bathroom." I whispered as I rolled on out the bed. "Come back and lay here with me when you're done please." She said as she pulled the sheets back over her. "I don't have any other place to be... I can do that." I replied. I closed the door behind me as I rushed into the bathroom! I was slightly freaking out as I hurried to look and examined the condom. I wanted to make sure everything was still intact and not a drop got out! I took a risky chance doing it in the first place but wanted to be a thousand percent positive that there were zero chances of Lauren saying she was pregnant out the blue months on down the road. After, triple checking everything and myself, I slipped the condom off then flushed it down the toilet. I didn't want to leave it in the trash can at all! Only because I'll never forget the night, I was watching one of those weird investigation shows a few months before on how an insane chick that was stalking this guy, broke into his home. He left a used condom in his trash can, and the crazy chick stole the condom! Months later she shockingly had the guy's child! That was something I couldn't imagine anyone doing to me, but I swore that if I ever used condoms, I would flush every single one of them. I even flushed the toilet several times to ensure that it was gone. I washed my hands, splashed some water on my face then flushed the toilet once more before leaving out. I walked back in my room quietly. I heard Lauren snoring. I laughed to myself thinking I had really put in some work to have her sleeping after what we did. I didn't want to wake her, so I went to the kitchen to get something to drink and turn off my television since it was still on. I got myself the biggest cup I could find to fill it up with cold water. I went to turn the tv off and heard knocking on a door close by. I walked to my window. I peeped out and noticed one of the Maintenance guys standing in front of Lauren's apartment door. I ran over to my door then stuck my head. I told him she was over at my place sleep. It was hard convincing him to let me go in to get the keys to her place. He wasn't okay with that which I understood because I didn't want to get her up. I didn't have a choice, so I told the guy to hang on while I got her. I stood next to the bed as I leaned over it, giving her a kiss on her forehead. She started to smile as she opened her eyes. "Why aren't you lying next to me?" She asked. I wanted to be cool about it, so I did say, "I was, I just heard knocking outside and got up." She looked at me as if she knew I wasn't telling the truth but didn't want to bust my bubble. "Yeah yeah, so who was it?" She asked. "Oh yeah the guy is outside waiting in front of your door to let you in." I replied. She jumped up then put her clothes on as she said, "Why you just didn't say that at first?" I laughed as I replied, "I didn't want to come back in here yelling, scaring you out of your sleep. Plus, you looked like you were comfortable. I think I saw a little drool too." She smiled as she slipped on the rest of her clothes and flip flops then said, "I guess that was kind of you because I probably would have gotten up swinging! I don't do sudden noises like that especially if I'm in a deep sleep. Thank you for being considerate." I walked behind her as she headed to the door. She turned back to me before going out the door and said, "By the way, I don't drool!" I laughed and said, "Tell yourself whatever you need to. I know what I saw." She walked over to her apartment. The guy finally let her in. I had my head sticking out my door again, making sure she got into her place. She didn't say anything as she walked into her place then shutting her door behind herself. I closed my door then went back into my room. I could still smell her in the air in my room. It was a pleasant scent that I had to admit that I was looking forward to inhale more of. I picked up my phone and placed it on the charger not caring that there were another three missed calls showing. The way I felt I wasn't stressing at all about anything. I laid down on my bed with my hands crossed behind my head with the biggest of grins on my face. I kept saying to myself how I couldn't believe Lauren and I went all the way! I was thinking about Daniel, wishing he was there so I could spill all the details to him. I knew he would be laughing and saying how he told me Lauren had a thing for me and all. The sun was setting as the sun light was disappearing from the blinds that were hanging in my bedroom window. My eyes started to get heavier as I tried keeping them open as I slowly drifted away to sleep. Within minutes I was sleeping like a baby.

Chapter 3
Attention to Details

Ring! Ring! My phone went on and on until I finally got up and answered it. I was falling out of the bed then rolled over to grab it from the floor after I knocked it off the nightstand. It was very dark in my room and the light from the phone displaying the incoming call was my only guide out the bed. I reached the phone and answered it but like the other times, no answer. I held the phone for a few minutes closed to my ear, trying to hear the slightest clue that was going to tell me something about this crazy person that was getting a kick out of interrupting my life randomly with nothing to say. Of course, I was frustrated by then, but I was also super curious about who it could be. Charlene was the only cruel and heartless person that would have the patience and determination to stomp on my nerves like that. I didn't believe a word she said yet I couldn't deny my guilt in her last statement to me. She was on the top of the list for sure! I was certain Samantha wasn't calling like that because I knew she was busy living her best life. She was not losing any sleep at all about little ole me. I missed her, but I was not going to lose any sleep either at that point waiting for a call from her. Rachel wouldn't answer my calls, so I gave up calling her, although I was still trying to figure out that situation after the news she gave me. I believed it wasn't her. I gave up on guessing as I seen the light coming back through the blinds. I really did sleep like a baby! Puzzled about how I just slept the whole night away. I blamed Lauren. I finally stood up to go to use the restroom. I turned on the shower while I was in there since I didn't get a chance to wash myself up before crashing out. I was wondering why Lauren never came back over as I was standing in the shower. I wanted to go check on her. I hurried with my shower then got out. I threw on some gym shorts and one of my baseball tee shirts. I slipped on my flip flops then headed to the kitchen. I had to put something on my stomach because I felt like I wasn't going to make it anywhere if I didn't eat first. I sat down at the kitchen table eating a bowl of cereal. While reading the back of the cereal box, glancing towards the window as the sun had made its way up. It shined bright through the blinds. Suddenly my phone went off again! I didn't move a muscle. I wanted to throw the whole phone away! I couldn't since Mrs. Anthony was so kind to buy it and kept the bill paid for me. I was stuck with it! I finished my cereal when I realized I could just turn the ringer off. I went back into my room to get the phone. It rang again as I was turning the ringer all the way down to vibrate. The one and only reason I answered it was because I had it in my hand. This was my last attempt for the rest of that day answering my phone. "Hello!" I said as I walked in the living room then sitting down on the couch. The silence wasn't long that time. I could hear clear sounds of cars and people in the background. My ears were latched on to the phone listening to everything until I could hear soft sniffing. "What am I supposed to do Cedric?" Rachel voice whispered from the other end of the phone. I was surprised as hell to hear her voice of all the people I thought of! My phone nearly fell out of my hands as my jaw dropped! "Rachel! Hi! Wha... Wha... What's going on?" I replied fumbling my words. I could hear footsteps as if she was walking with heels on down a sidewalk. About two minutes of nothing as I held the phone giving her time to say whatever she needed to say. "I'm an emotional wreck right now Cedric! I don't know what to do! I know neither one of us planned this! I don't have anyone else to talk to! Nor do I feel comfortable with anyone to talk to about all of this! Sorry about hanging up on you and calling your phone about a hundred times. I realize I'm scared out my mind and alone!" She finally said with passion in every word. I could hear it in her voice that she was breaking apart stressing over being pregnant! We both were but I was trying my hardest to not think about it. "I understand, I do… I do, I really do. Things have been a little crazy on my end here and I honestly didn't know what to do after you stopped answering my calls. My head has been twisted and turned upside down with so many questions. The reality of you being pregnant with my child has had me thinking about my life as well as the next steps for me. I'm sorry you feel alone, and I want to do whatever I need to do to make this right." I said as calm and caring as I could. I didn't want to be an asshole by telling her to get an abortion so neither one of us had to worry about it anymore. I thought about the whole abortion thing because of a similar predicament one of my old teammates from high school was in. He too had gotten someone pregnant. I hate it for the girl because it was so sad that the guy's mom even told the girl he wasn't going to be a father to no one's child that early! The girl was so crushed that she transferred to another school. I didn't want to be like that guy. They both got themselves in it, just like Rachel and I did. Out of respect for her, I had to figure out a better solution. Although, it was a hard pill to swallow, I had to make her feel safe and comfortable with opening up to me. "I'm glad you called. I was worried about you. Trust me, you are not alone. Everything is going to be okay Rachel." I said, which was my attempt to sooth her mind. "I know this is hard for both of…." My front door opened suddenly, cutting me off mid-sentence as I was talking to Rachel! It was Lauren rushing in like someone was after her! "Cedric! I finally got an update on Daniel! She said when she first looked my way then closed the door behind her. The way I was sitting on the couch with my hand holding the phone to my ear, Lauren didn't notice I was on the phone at first. "He was cleared but you guys' coach was called, and it didn't go so well!" Lauren said as she was walking past me to the kitchen. "Hello... Cedric... What's going on?" Rachel asked as I could hear the concern and curiosity clearly in her voice. I scuffled with the phone a bit as I was switching it into my other hand to hear her in my other ear due to Lauren mumbling something to me from the kitchen area. "Cedric can you hear me?" Rachel said with more bass in her voice. As I was saying "I can...", responding to Rachel, I was staring at Lauren as she finally saw that I was on the phone. I couldn't make out everything she was saying as she covered her mouth with her hands as if she was embarrassed to find me on the phone while she bolted in talking loudly. Lauren then gave me a look of confusion but smile then motioned her lips saying I'm sorry without making a sound. I raised my hand at her signaling that it was okay and to give me one minute. I then walked towards my room to finish my conversation with Rachel. "I'm so sorry about that. I'm listening to you. I can hear you." I whispered through the phone until I made it to my room, then pushed the door up some, yet not entirely closed. "What's going on?" Rachel asked again. I leaned up against the wall and gave out a long sigh as I replied with, "Oh, that was just my neighbor stopping by." I was sure Rachel heard me, but she didn't say a word. I even looked at the phone making sure I didn't hang up on her as I was doing a lot of moving when I was switching the phone from hand to hand. The timer of the call was still counting the seconds, so I knew she was still there on the other end. "Rachel, are you still there? You okay?" I asked anyway. Waiting to hear an answer from Rachel, I heard my front door slam! I immediately ran out my room to see what had happened or if someone else had come over. As I was looking around, Lauren was nowhere in sight nor was there anyone else that had come in. I walked over to the window to look out to see if Lauren had stepped out on the porch. Then Rachel finally said something. "Maybe I shouldn't have called so many times. Maybe I should just figure this all out on my own. I'm sorry again for disturbing you." She said as she sounded completely hopeless. I was feeling somewhat helpless as I was drowning in my wave of thoughts with Lauren leaving like she did as well as Rachel's response. "Rachel please, don't say that, please. It's cool, I promise you." I replied. I was convinced that Lauren must have left something on at her place like the stove or her flatirons that she had a bad habit of leaving plugged up. She nearly burned down the whole unit within the first week of living in her apartment. She had never left my place without saying a word which had me at a complete loss. I knew Rachel was getting impatient with our conversation due to the stress we both were expressing to one another and how I wasn't giving her my undivided attention. I continued to comfort her with my words of compassion and confirming that she should have faith that things were going to get better. As I sat back on the couch still talking to Rachel, again my front door opened again suddenly! Lauren returned. She walked right in but with a slower and calmer pace that time. She didn't say anything, she just walked in then sat right next to me. She had a look on her face I had never seen before. Her face gave me an unpleasant feeling that was warning me to be careful on what I said to whoever I was on the phone with while she was sitting next to me! I was beyond nervous but couldn't comprehend why I should have been feeling that way. Rachel went on telling me about how she's been feeling and what she wanted to do about the baby situation. I listened to her go on for about ten minutes until Lauren gave out a deep sigh as if she was running out of patience to tell me something. I figured I could finish the conversation with Rachel at a more convenient time since Lauren was melting the side of my face with her eyes. I didn't want Rachel to regret anything, so I made sure she knew I wanted to hear more about everything she had stated to me. "I know this is unfamiliar territory for us both. I know this is something we're going to have to do together. Let's talk more later please. I'll call you back soon." I said as serious as I could while avoiding all eye contact with Lauren. There was a moment of silence on Rachel's end followed with her saying, "Thank you Cedric. I do feel better a little. If you mean it, please call me back." I replied, "Trust me, I will. Talk to you later." Rachel said okay then hung up the phone. I sat my phone on the coffee table then leaned back on the couch. Lauren was just sitting there looking concerned but kept quiet. After about two to three minutes of staring at the black screen on the TV, I got up to get something to drink. I sat back down then finally said, "I'm sorry for the silence. Just have so much on my mind." Lauren didn't hesitate to reply with. "But we know that already. I was hoping we were passed all the explaining. I know you have a lot going on Cedric. I wouldn't be here if I didn't care." I tried to smile but my face wouldn't agree with me so I just nodding my head. She suddenly kicked her leg over me and straddled me! She was sitting in my lap facing me. I wasn't expecting that at all! That wasn't even the last thing I thought she would do. I guess she was demanding my attention that way, but my mind was too distorted with the unknown outcome with the whole Rachel thing. I had no energy to fake it. I didn't show any enthusiasm with her gesture. She started kissing me softly on my neck then on my lips as I sat there as numb as a traffic light. She was in her own world as she was putting in amble amount of effort to get me going. She was on a mission for another round of sex as she was rubbing my chest then slid her hands down my shorts. With all the kissing and rubbing, it was still no match for the stress I was under with thinking what kind of dad I would be. How was I really going to make things right by Rachel. Should I go back home and help her with whatever support or comfort she needed. About three or four minutes went by as I was still not participating nor exchanging any physical affection towards Lauren. Finally, Lauren got up with frustration. She said, "Cedric what's the problem? Oh, so you're not in the mood? Thought I could at least try to get your mind off the chaos for the moment again." I stood up fixing my clothes before replying. She walked over to the door, but I reached her before she could open it. I think she was mostly embarrassed than anything about her failed attempt. We have been honest with one another since day one, so I was sure she wasn't angry at me. I finally said, "Lauren you know I appreciate you. I know what you're trying to do but I can't focus on anything right now. My head feels like its spinning and there's nothing anyone can do to help right now." I grabbed her by her hand and placed a kiss on it. I stared into her eyes with sadness, guilt and unexplainable regrets written on my face. There were no other words I could express to her on what was happening in my head. She let go of my hand then opened the door. "I was afraid after we went through with what we did last night that things were going to be weird. I hate I was right. I will let you have your space to think things through Cedric. Sorry you have too much on your plate." She said with disappointment. She didn't wait for an answer, a reply or gave me a moment to find something to say. She walked out shutting the door behind her. I was frozen with more weight on my shoulders that had me stuck like a statue. I wanted to run after Lauren and beg her to stay, or maybe let her have her way with me to make things cool between us. I needed her, but something kept me standing there in my apartment looking at my door as if I could see through it. I was able to find the feeling in my body to make my way to my bedroom. I wanted to lay down as the whole place seemed as if it was starting to spin. I knew if I took a nap, things were going to be the same when I got up. There was nothing else I had effort for. I laid on my back with one hand resting the back of my head on it, with enough thoughts that could fill a professional sport stadium. I closed my eyes as I imagined how things would have been different for me if I had never gone as far as I did with Rachel, Charlene and even Lauren. I kept replaying every second that lead to me having sex with them all as well as the moments after. My memories began to mix, and I found myself sitting with David asking him for advice. I knew by then it was time for me to rest my mind.

Felt like I slept for days but it had only been a few hours when I was awakened by my phone vibrating like crazy. It was Rachel's name that appeared on the screen. I made sure I saved her number, so I knew for certain who number it was whenever she called. I also saved Charlene's number, so I knew what number to ignore. I answered it as I sat up in my bed. "Cedric, I know you said you were going to call me, I know. I just can't stand not having someone to vent to. I was hoping we could talk more now." Rachel said. I was glad she broke my sleep because I didn't want to sleep the entire evening away. I wanted to go over to the dorms to check on Daniel for an update. I scooted towards the head of my bed with my back pressed against the headboard. "Yeah I'm here Rachel. I'm sorry I didn't call back sooner. I'm glad you called." I replied. Rachel didn't waste a second as she went right into her bag of worries. She went on and on about wanting to tell someone as she was started to gain weight. She was having a difficult time trying to hide it. She knew she was going to have to go to the doctor soon because she couldn't keep her food down. She said her parents were starting to ask questions more frequently. She went on for about thirty minutes as I held the phone. I tossed in an occasional, "Sorry to hear that..." comment whenever she took a pause long enough to catch her breath. She summed up everything by saying that she needed me more than anyone else. I had given it more thought as she was talking if it made sense for me to go back home. I mean there was no other real reason I had since things were going okay at school. Especially with baseball, we were doing well and heading to the college world series for sure. I was on everyone's top list of Freshman of the year! I couldn't just leave and let down so many people that were rooting for me. I couldn't imagine myself explaining that decision to Mrs. Anthony. She would have thrown a fit if she saw me walking through the doors of our house with the news of me being a father! I didn't want to leave Daniel nor Lauren. I knew I had to make things normal again with Lauren because she would be a friend for life. The same thought with Daniel. I had to make sure he was good too. I had concluded my revelations with allowing myself to use that time to think things through. I finally said, "Again I can't express enough empathy towards how sorry I am that I got us in this crazy situation. I know you're going through so much Rachel. I would come home right now if I could. But... I need time to think things through. I can't leave like that, so I need to at least finish the rest of the semester. I have too many obligations here that I'm committed to and I can't disappoint Mrs. Anthony. Give me some time to pull things together and complete this year." Of course, there was silence from her end after my speech. I waited as I gave her time to digest my response. I was hoping it wasn't too harsh or misleading. About two minutes passed before she replied. "I get it Cedric. I'm not on the top of your list. I wasn't trying to bring a halt to your life. I just thought I could talk with you to get some of the things that's been eating me up on the inside, out. You are the one and only person I could talk to. Believe me, I wasn't expecting too much. I just needed your ears." Her tone and choice of words gave me the impression that she wasn't too thrilled about my statement. She said it as if I was implying that I didn't have time for her or if I wasn't concern with her due to what I already had on my plate. I had to clear the air. "Come on Rachel, I didn't mean any harm. I just wanted to share my circumstances that I have here with you. I wasn't saying you needed me to drop everything and come save you. Sorry if I offended you in any way with what I said." I replied. Without hesitation she added, "Thank you for reassuring that. It's hard to think about and even harder to hide it for me. I just want you to be available when I need to vent. I hope that's not too much to ask for." Her tone was different that time and more calmed. "I can definitely handle that. You can call whenever you need to. If I don't answer, I'll make sure I call back as soon as I'm able to." I said. She managed to giggle a little as she replied, "Now was that too hard for you to say Mr. Freshmen of the Year. I am happy for you. I'm happy we have an agreement too. I feel much better." I smiled to myself then said, "Thank you. I've been working my ass off on that diamond, so I have faith I'll be the one holding that Freshman trophy at the end of the season! I'm glad our conversation helped you with talking to me too." Suddenly there were loud knocks on my door! I moved slowly as I held the phone to my ear as the knocking increased as if someone needed to see me promptly! "Cedric is everything okay. Are you fixing something? What are you beating on?" Rachel asked as she too could hear the loud thumping at my door. "No, I'm not beating on anything. There's someone at my door. Let me call you back in a few to check it out." I replied. "Okay, I hope it's nothing serious. Be careful." She responded. I told her thanks and we both hung up our phones. I made it to the living room as the knocks started to get worse. I didn't think to look or check out who it was through my peephole. I was just irritated yet confused with who would be putting so much effort in to seeing me. I opened the door finally to see Daniel standing there! "Cedric! I knew you were here! I can't believe they're doing me this way!" He yelled as he walked past me! I quickly looked around outside to see if anyone was chasing him again or if Lauren had heard the vicious strikes Daniel gave my door. There was no one outside. I turned back into my place then closed the door behind me. Daniel looked stressed out, frustrated with his eyes watery as if he had been crying. Before I could say anything, he said, "I'm off the team! Can you believe that shit!" I stared at him with a curious smile on my face not sure if he was telling me a joke because I couldn't believe my ears! "What did you say? You're what?" I asked with confidence knowing I didn't hear him correctly. He was pacing back and forth from the living room to the kitchen. He was mumbling to himself as if he was trying to convince himself none of it was true. He looked as if his whole life had crumbled apart and all the pieces were out of reach. I could tell he was really shaken up. I had to ask again as I cut him off in his path as he was about to enter the living room again. "Daniel what's going on? Coach kicked you off the team. You're joking right?" I asked. He tried to brush pass me until I stepped in front of him again. I had to motion him towards the couch with my hands, so he could sit. I wanted him to be still to get him to settle down his mind. I thought that would help him relax. I pulled a chair from the kitchen table then sat it in an angle slightly in front of him. I sat down staring at him as I was waiting patiently for a response. He held his head in his hands as he was looking down towards the floor. Mild sniffing and heavy breathing started to come from Daniel as he rubbed the top of his head. I was close enough to place my hand on his shoulder. "I'm sorry man. I hate this for you." I said as he continued to sit there in defeat. He started mumbling again to himself until he finally raised his head. I slipped my hand away from his shoulder as he pressed his back on the couch. He had tears in his eyes as he looked at me like an innocent toddler. I wanted to tell him everything was going to be alright. I would have been lying. I also wanted to yell at him! I wanted to say so much about why he didn't listen to me or why he never took anything serious enough to have avoided the entire situation! I was angry just as much as I was sad for him. Overall, I wasn't shocked with the decision of our coach. That was one of the critical things on our code of conduct list being on the baseball team. We were to never go into any girl's dorm room under no conditions. We would have been suspended for at least a game or two if we were caught standing around the doors of their building! I knew it was going to end bad for Daniel although he was well aware of the punishment. "I knew better! I wish I could go back and change that dumb ass decision to go with them girls that night! Damn!" He said to himself out loud. I sat up shaking my head at him as I bit my tongue so I wouldn't yell. "You knew better man." I said. Before I went on to go deeper into the word whipping, a light tap was heard at my door that started to crescendo. Daniel placed his face back into his hands as if he couldn't take any more surprises or stress. I got up then walked over to the door. "You good man?" I asked Daniel before I opened the door as if he had a clue who it could be. "No... not really, but what choices do I have! It's over for me." He replied as he went to the restroom. I opened the door after I gave him a second to disappear down the hall. It was our Coach! I invited him in immediately. "Cedric, I hate I have to do this but I'm making stops at all of my guys places to personally speak to you all about the situation with Daniel. If you haven't heard yet, I'm forced to make him ineligible to play here at Northwestern." All I was thinking about was Daniel coming out of the restroom seeing Coach. I had to make my responses brief. "Yeah Coach I heard the news. I get it and it sucks." Coach shook his head in frustration then said, "I really liked Daniel and he was a huge plus to the team. I just don't get why ever single year, no matter how many times I say it, it's part of our rules as a team, why do these knuckle heads give up an almost promising future on the field for a few moments of fun! I try Cedric, I really try to help." I knew it was killing Coach on the inside. That was one of the reasons Mrs. Anthony wanted me to go there. Coach spoke highly on principals, morals and caring about his players character on and off the field. "Well Coach, I won't let you down nor myself." I replied. He nodded his head in relief that I said that. He walked back over towards the door then added, "I want you and all the other guys to succeed beyond here, in life and I want you all to make decisions that's going to increase the number of doors that will open for you, not close them. Be smart Cedric. See you at practice!" Those words hit me harder than I expected. I instantly re-evaluated certain choices I made already on how I may have closed some doors unknowingly. It perked me up and got my mind working. "Thanks Coach. I needed to hear that. All of that! See you at practice!" I replied then opened the door for him. He gave me another nod as he was walking out. With my thoughts racing as I closed the door. I nearly jumped out of my skin when Daniel asked, "Is he gone?" as he was standing right behind me! It was that quick I had forgotten Daniel went to the restroom. "Man, you scared the hell out of me! Yes... He's gone." I replied as I sat back down in the chair. "Did you hear all that?" I asked Daniel as he sat back down on the couch. It appeared that he had been crying because his eyes were red. I asked before he replied to my first question, "Are you okay?" Daniel looked at me as if he was trying to figure out which question, he wanted to answer first. He wiped his face with his hand then said, "I'm upset at myself. I knew better, and I knew the risks! I'm so stupid! You've been warning me, man! Damn... You know... I appreciate you. I'm sorry I let myself down, I hate I let the team down. I'm definitely sorry I let you down." I wasn't expecting that response from him. I sat there as I thought about how painful it was for him. I was shocked he apologized to me which made me feel worse. I should have done more to stop him! I didn't tell him that but deep down I started to realize that. I finally replied with, "I wish things would have went another way too. You're still my guy and this doesn't change our friendship!" I saw a smile pierce through the dismay Daniel was under. I can say we both learned some tough lessons. I stood up again and signaled Daniel up. I met him with a handshake and half arm hug to give him some comfort. While lock in with my one arm wrapped halfway around his upper back, I said, "I hope this outcome doesn't make you give up! I need you here so don't leave just because you can't play! I know it's going to be tough but it's not final! There's always next season!" Daniel was nodding his head agreeing with me as we disconnected then took a few steps back from one another. "You right my guy. I'm not going anywhere. I'm going to ride this thing out..." He replied with a smile of hope on his face. "Plus, I have to cheer my team through the college series! I know y'all going to make it all the way!" He added then said he had to go get his things from the locker while coach was still on campus. I told him to come back over later. I promised him I would order his favorite sub sandwich. That was the least I could do to cheer him up a bit more. I wanted him to know that I wasn't going to kick him out of our friendship nor was I going to stop hanging with him. He agreed to come back over then he left.

About a week had passed since I last talked to Lauren. I was swamped with baseball practice, games and studying. I knocked on her door here and there but couldn't get a hold of her. Couldn't even catch the sounds of her door closing or opening. The announcement had come in about me being the finalist of the Freshmen of the Year award. I wanted to share the news with her which I was sure she knew! I couldn't believe I didn't run in to her on campus nor around our apartment complex. It was like she was strategically avoiding me. None of my calls were getting through nor any of the voicemails I left were getting called back. I knew things were awkward, but I didn't think they had reached the level of ignoring me. When we didn't have Taco Tuesday, I knew things had gotten serious. Lauren never missed my tacos! I talked to a few other girls that were on her dance team but even they were uneasy with giving me any info about Lauren. As if she had put out a campus wide memo telling everyone not communicate with Cedric Mason? I kept telling myself things were okay. She probably needed some time to herself since we were inseparable. I still wasn't sure if she felt guilt about us fooling around or she was upset I was giving more of my attention to Rachel? I wasn't going to let that make me feel bad. I was just proud of myself for using protection. No way in hell I was going to be able to survive someone else telling me they were pregnant! On the other hand, Rachel and I were talking almost every day up to hours at a time. It was like it was meant to happen like that. Since Lauren was missing in action, Rachel did make it easy for me to not worry so much about whatever Lauren was trying to do or prove. Within that week of talking to Rachel I found out way more than I bargained for! She mentioned running in to Charlene a few times! Each time she would bring up Charlene's name, I would clinch on tighter to the phone anticipating her to mention that Charlene told her about her expecting a little person package too! I didn't believe for a second Charlene hadn't already mentioned it to Rachel. I was just waiting for Rachel to finally reveal she knew all about my other secret I was hiding from her and everyone else. She didn't say anything close to that but told me Charlene had been acting extremely unusual. She said that Charlene had been in and out of the hospital. At first, I wasn't too alarm thinking Charlene must had been going since she was aware, she was with child. Rachel went way left with it, telling me that Charlene was in and out of a mental hospital right outside of our neighborhood! She had been hearing it from quite a few of our old classmates she was still in touch with. Rachel said she thought that they were just rumors at first until she had an unpleasant encounter with Charlene just days after she found out she was pregnant. Finally, the moment of truth, I expected I was mentioned if it involved the two of them having any kind of communication. Rachel said she was walking home from the store when she saw Charlene approaching down the sidewalk. She was going to cross the street to avoid any conflict since they hadn't talked or seen one another much after their big fight. Charlene waved at her as she was getting closer which gave Rachel no choice but to proceed towards her. Once they were in front of one another, Charlene greeted Rachel with a hug. Rachel said she wasn't sure if she wanted to punch her in the mouth or hug her back! She just stood there while Charlene wrapped her arms around her. After the awkward embrace, Charlene stepped back. She looked at Rachel as her eyes shifted up and down as if she were examining Rachel. She stared at her for about two minutes before she snapped! She started whispering nasty things at Rachel! Making statements like, "You're not the only one. I did it better. You're nothing like me. You aren't perfect." Rachel said she immediately tried to brush pass Charlene, but she stood in her way. She tried to walk across the street, yet Charlene followed her! It was cloudy and wet from rain that poured down hours before. Rachel said she didn't want to run in fear of slipping from the drenched sidewalks and street. She said she had reached her boiling point and was about to start swinging her hands at Charlene to force her away. Then suddenly Charlene changed her whole demeanor when they made it to the other side of the street! Charlene suddenly started shouting, "It's been so long since we talked! Where have you been? I miss you Rachel girl! We were the best of friends! Wow... What happened to us?" Rachel said she was shocked and sadden at the same time. She knew for a fact that something wasn't clicking with Charlene. She felt as if Charlene was struggling with something mentally, she couldn't shake off. Rachel said she acted as if she was excited to see Charlene just to see where it was going to go in the that moment. She said Charlene tried to hug her again but midway leaning in to put her arms around her once more, Charlene screamed, "I'll never be friends with a back-stabbing bitch like you! Where's that officers. He knows everything!" Rachel said she had to take a few quick steps back! She said she didn't react at all as Charlene then turned and walked away. She said she had to stand there for minutes as she had to collect her emotions and concern for Charlene. She said she had never seen Charlene like that yet alone say those things about her like that. She thought Charlene was going to get the police or something. I was basically speechless after hearing that news about Charlene. I found myself feeling nervous, scared and of course I was worried about the future between Charlene and I. Especially if she was in fact pregnant with my child! What officer? That was strange but nothing made sense. Nothing was said about me, so I bypassed the option to include the one and only concern I had with Charlene's behavior to Rachel. There was still hope that Rachel hadn't found out, which gave me time to figure out what was going on with Charlene and if she was truthful with me.

Chapter 4

Chasing Understanding

Another three weeks had passed with Lauren and I not speaking nor seeing one another. Late Spring with summer easing in. "Spring Fling" was in full effect with some great baseball weather! The college world series were here! We were able to get in with a decent seed in the brackets! We were competing against the best our first round. We had to travel out of state to Omaha. I promised my team I would give whoever we played hell in Omaha when I stepped on the diamond there! I also knew I wasn't going to be able to talk to Rachel as much. We had become accustomed to talking on the phone every day, once early in the morning before my classes and right before I went to bed. I told her depending on how well my team did, it could be a week or so before we got back to talking as much as we had been. She understood and wished me luck. She asked me to call only if I had the time and not to worry if I couldn't. Her saying that made me want to put in the effort. Since Lauren was on the cheer team, there was a high chance I was going to see her during the sendoff rally the school usually had before the baseball team or any team headed off to a big game or tournament.

The day had come for us to leave for Nebraska. I made one last call to Rachel and Mrs. Anthony to let them know. Mrs. Anthony apologized serval times because she wished she could have been there cheering me on in Nebraska. She promised me she would fly or drive wherever if we made it all the way to the championship round. After I said my goodbyes to them, I was all packed up. I locked my apartment then headed to the school. On campus there were students, the marching band and the cheer team all excited for us to hit the road! It was nice the way it was set up and the support the entire campus gave us! It felt good having other students standing around cheering for us, even with some holding signs with my number and name on it. They went as far as to getting a few of us to sign some hats and shirts for the younger kids that showed up from some of the surrounding middle and high schools. It was special, I know I felt that way with all the love that was being displayed! Walking around inhaling the motivation during the celebrations I managed to stumble across Lauren and Sasha as they were coming out of the women's restroom while I was approaching the men's restroom. Sasha saw me first then she immediately tapped Lauren on the shoulder to alert her of my presence! It was as if she had seen the boogie monster or something scarier. Lauren glanced up at me then she turned and ran back into the lady's room! I couldn't get out a word or even react to seeing her after a month of dodging me. Sasha was slow to follow Lauren, which gave me a couple of seconds to hurry over closer to voice my confusion. I had to know, due to my lack of understanding the why factor of Lauren's behavior towards me! As I was just close enough to Sasha before she disappeared back into the restroom with Lauren, I asked, "What's going on? What did I do? Why is she tripping?" Sasha turned my way to hear my desperate plea to comprehend the situation. She looked more confused than me after my series of questions as if she didn't get the why in all of it either. As she was about to respond, Lauren yelled for her! Sasha had a worried look on her face as she whispered, "Cedric I'm sorry she's being this way. You don't deserve this." Then she sprinted back in the restroom to Lauren. I was on the edge of deciding if I should enter the ladies' room myself! I needed a respectable conclusion from Lauren! I hated the mind games. I didn't have the nerves or the patience to play. It was killing me on the inside after hearing Sasha say that. She gazed at me as if she was trying to alert me as if she were being kidnapped! I was too afraid to do or say anything to save her or save myself the stress. I waited by the restroom door with high hopes for about five minutes. It was a desperate opportunity to confront Lauren when she came out. Sadly, I was interrupted by some of my teammates telling me to hurry up back towards the rest of the team! They were told to round up the rest of the players to take a team photo before we loaded on the buses. We were cutting it close to our time to get to the airport. I couldn't believe I was posted outside the restroom, ready to make a fool out of myself about something I had no clue about. It took me a moment to shake out of it, as I thought about what I was about to partake in. After the craziest summer I've ever had in my life a year before, on top of the news I was about to be a father. Let's not mention the sexual attack from my old high school principal Mrs. Harris, which I thought I may have seen her! I looked like a clown, trying to address a chick about some mysterious reasons she was obviously feeling selfish about. Silly of me to assume we were close enough as friends than to treat each other like that! Sasha was right. I deserved better than to have someone I considered a good friend ignore me like that! I was fed up and after all I had been through, sharing personal details about me, she was the fool to treat a decent guy like myself that way! I was completely done with Lauren at that point. I didn't care if we ever spoke again! I marched away with my head up high, not looking back at all. I made it to the rest of the guys, took a few pictures, grabbed my things then strolled on the bus. I sat in the very back. I positioned the headphones Daniel gave me on my ears then rested my head against the window. I played some soft Rhythm and Blues to tune out the revengeful actions I could take that were trying to squeeze into my mind. I agreed with myself that

I wasn't going to let another female make me emotional about anything that didn't make sense to me.

I gave Omaha everything I had in me! We all did. We won the first two rounds and were just one game away to the championship round. We were gassed and couldn't hit anything! We fell behind quick in the series. We lost bad. They spanked our butts like we stole from them! The final game score was seven to one. We had no one to blame but ourselves although the coaches were proud of us. The rest of the players and I were torn. I felt like Daniel could have helped us well, but it wasn't time to play the blame game. The flight back to Chicago felt long. It was quiet most of the way back until I received a random call just as I turned my phone on after we landed. The number looked familiar, but I wasn't positive about who it belonged to, so I didn't answer. Finally, off the plane then on to the buses. A second call from that same number came through as I was sitting in the very back of the bus. It didn't matter who it was, I could talk freely without disturbing anyone. When I answered it, my ears couldn't deny that it was Samantha's voice! She whispered, "Hello... Cedric. How's it going stranger?" The one and only Samantha, I tried my best to forget, especially after being shut down by her. My attempt to persuade her to come with me to Chicago was a tragedy! I sat up quickly then did a double take looking at the number not believing who's voice I was hearing on the line! Of course, my heart was pumping fast as I began to sweat across my forehead as I held the phone close to my ears. "Hellooo... Are you there?" She asked. I finally replied, "Hi, I'm here. I'm here. What's going on?" I didn't hear much in her background, so I knew she was probably at home. It had been nearly a year since I heard from her. "How have you been?" She asked. I was nervous yet curious about the spontaneous call. How did I run across her mind I asked myself? "I'm good. I can't complain. I'm making it." I murmured in such a way that it didn't give off any doubts I had although I was close to losing my mind with the load on my shoulders. There was a brief silence on her end before she shouted, "I miss you!" My mouth said it before I could stop my lips from opening. "I don't believe you." I spat that out as if it was on the tip of my tongue the whole twelve months! Again, there was silence on her end for a moment then she replied, "I know it's hard to believe and it is all my fault." Although she was right, I didn't want to make her feel bad by verbally agreeing or throwing it in her face. "It's fine, I was just messing with you. I'm happy to hear from you. I'm the one to blame for not saying anything since our last encounter." I wasn't excited nor disappointed with hearing from her. I was just exhausted mentally with trying to figure out everyone's agenda. Why was I having the hardest time building solid and consistent friendships with these girls I thought really liked me. I tried not to go there with Lauren, but I didn't fight the urge. I really wanted Samantha in my life, but she wasn't with it. Rachel was kind yet I felt it was a right time right place thing with her. Charlene could have fallen dead, and I wouldn't have thought twice about her. That wasn't in my heart to hate someone as I felt I did with her. Still holding the phone as those thoughts ran through my head, I was starting to tear up. I immediately wiped my face as Samantha said, "Sorry I didn't reach out sooner. I've been busy with the store, keeping Gary in check and interning." I assumed Gary was shooting his shot daily with the money ball from all the racks, since I was out the picture. I was stuck on the interning part. "Interning? Oh really? Where?" I asked. As I waited for her answer, the thought of her being back with her ex was the only way she would have been interning anywhere in the field she was focused on. I would have not been surprised. "I started interning at a new marketing company that's only 20 minutes from my house with way more opportunities for me than the original place I was attempting to try." She answered. I replied, "Well look at that. That's nice. Good for you." She added, "Yeah I've been crazy busy with all of that. I had a minute to finally breathe so I called." I felt better knowing she wasn't back with him begging him for that kind of opportunity again. Somehow, I felt guilty for judging her that way. "Well, I'm on the bus heading back to Chicago from Omaha. We lost a huge game that would have placed us in the championship round." I said as I gave out a heavy sign at the end. "Oh no! I am sorry to hear that Cedric! I know that was tough!" She replied. "Thank you. Yeah, it was brutal, but we will be back next season with a vengeance." I said. I guess it was either hard to believe we were having a conversation for Samantha too to do the long gaps of silence or maybe she wasn't sure what to say to me. I just held the phone contemplating rather or not I should just tell her how I really felt about her decision on not being there with me. The words were right there on the edge of my mouth then Samantha suddenly said, "I hope you want to see me as much as I want to see you! I also called for a special reason... I can't hold it in much longer!" I nearly swallowed my tongue stopping the words of frustration I was about to blurt out at her! A special reason meant a surprise to me. As if I had any more capacity to store yet another compromise. I was overloaded with breaking news and quite caution as I ready myself for the next exchange. "Oh, so this wasn't a random call like you really missed me huh. This was one of those, something came up so let me call him now, phone calls?" I said jokingly as I grit my teeth with anxiety starting to take over me. As I was waiting for the spontaneous reason why she called, Lauren's number buzzed in! I was beyond dumbfounded on why she would be calling me then, but I didn't want to interrupt Samantha's big announcement. I let Lauren's call go to my voicemail as I stayed on the line with Samantha. I didn't feel bad about at all. Finally, Samantha said, "I know this is out the blue, short notice. Not to be selfish but, I'm kind of glad you'll be back at school! The company that I'm interning with, head office is in Chicago! I know for sure I'm going to be with them permanently. They're sending me there to meet with some top executives! I will be flying there within the next week. I will be there for five days!" An explosion went off in my head with a mix of fear and excitement. The phone slipped out of my hand as my palms were dripping in my sweat by then! I had to scramble to find it underneath the seat in front of me before she thought I was being rude not commenting back! I scraped the nasty floor until I felt the end of it then picked it up! I instantly asked, "Are you serious?" I sat back in my seat whipping my hands off on my shirt. I knew she wouldn't just make that all up for an egotistical thrill. I knew she was being honest. I was stunned, not knowing how to react. "Now Cedric you know I wouldn't call you to joke about something like that. I miss you for real! Things have been rolling for me, but I'm in desperate need of some time away from this place! What better way than to see you, get some fresh air and pursue my life's dream! I'm so excited!" Samantha replied as her voice elevated from the doubts I stirred up. What was I going to say, "No, don't come?" Of course, I couldn't! Maybe that was a good thing? Maybe this was supposed to happen all along? I questioned it all to myself for a minute then replied, "I like that. I think I'm in need of seeing a familiar face. I've had some lonely moments here. Don't get me wrong, I have met some super cool people so far. I wouldn't mind being around someone who knows me. You are more than welcome to come over while you're here. I'm sure I'll enjoy spending some time with you." Samantha replied, "See, I told you I had a special surprise for you. I wanted to make up for not keeping in touch. Seeing you would make my heart smile Cedric. I have some errands to run for now. I'll keep you in the loop about everything as it gets closer to the day I am coming. Can't wait to see you Mr. Smooth!" I couldn't keep the smile off my face she gave me with that news. "See you soon gorgeous... I look forward to this surprise visit. Talk to you later." I replied. And just like that, I was days away from seeing the one girl I was willing to risk it all for. I hung up the phone then laid my head down. I was going to call Lauren as I noticed the missed call notification still on my phone screen. The more I thought about Samantha, the less I wanted to hear Lauren's voice rambling about why she's been so mean to me. I drifted on back to sleep for a few more minutes until I was tapped on the shoulder by one of the coaches telling me we had arrived back at the school.

It was early evening that day with the sun setting when the buses pulled into the parking lot of the school. I collected my things as we could hear and see what appeared to be most of the student body, the band and cheerleaders welcoming us back! They were clapping, cheering and had posters with positive quotes written on them. It felt like we had won the whole championship with all the support we had from everyone as we exited the buses. I noticed Lauren right away as I was grabbing my duffle bag that was stuffed with all the giveaways we received during the series. We didn't have to do anything else at the school, our season was finished. The coaches told us to take the next few weeks off. We were free to go to the dorms or our apartments. I thanked some of the people that came out briefly as I was moving quickly passed everyone. Most of us stayed just a block or two from the school, so majority of us walked home. I shook a few more hands and gave out some high fives to people as I was strolling away from the scene. I thought for sure I would see Daniel, but he was nowhere in sight. I figured he didn't want to be around all the commotion given he was still upset with himself. Took about ten minutes to reach the front entrance of the apartments with my headphones in my ears when I heard someone yell my name! I took one of my headphones out as I turned around to see Lauren shaking her head at me as her face was as red as a Stop sign! I then took the other headphone out then ask, "What's up? What's going on?" She then walked past me as if she had been trying to get my attention the whole walk over from the school. If anyone was behind me, I made sure I didn't look back at all because I was so focused on getting to my place to lay in my own bed. We were gone for about two weeks! I turned back around as she brushed her shoulder against me with frustration. I wasn't in the best mood to chase her nor did I want to spend the rest of my night trying to pick the lock she had on the real reason she distanced herself from me. I continued behind her but didn't attempt to catch up with her as she was going up the stairs to her unit. As she was walking across the second level, she looked down shaking her head again at me. I threw my hands up at her to let her know I was frustrated with her as well from the silent treatment she continued to give me. I walked up the stairs to my place, and without a doubt, she had already gone inside hers. I was finally home with no plans to leave for at least a full day or two. I dropped my bags in the middle of the floor after I closed the door. I switched on the living room lights to make sure everything was still intact before jumping in the shower to relax. After my shower and putting my things up from my bags, it was about nine with signs of sleepiness in my eyes. I couldn't help but lay down. I connected my phone to its charger then closed my eyes.

I was on the edge of escaping my worries headed to dream land before my phone started ringing. It shook me up as I rolled out the bed catching myself from hitting the floor. I held myself up with my hands while one half of my body was still in bed with the other half hanging out. The phone didn't stop ringing as I guided myself completely to the floor avoiding a for sure concussion. I finally picked up the phone then answered it. "Can you open the door please? We need to talk." Lauren voice came whispering through the phone. Without hesitating I replied with okay then hung up the phone. I took my time flicking on the lights to my room then headed to the front door. I didn't bother turning on any other lights because I wanted her to know I was tired. I wanted to make sure that whatever she intended to say or do, I was going right back to my bed. I opened the door just enough to see her standing there as I held the door purposely not inviting her in to see how she was going to react. We stared at one another for a minute or so, until she said, "Usually you'll just open the door and walk away. Now I'm not allowed in?" I looked at her as if it was a rhetorical question. I couldn't believe she said that as if I was the one acting different! I shook my head then walked away leaving the door cracked. I headed to my bedroom. I just wanted to lay back down, refusing to give in to her mystery attitude. I sat on my bed with the light still on as I heard the door shut. It was quiet but I could hear footsteps dragging on the carpet. I gave her about three to four minutes to come to my room, but she didn't. I was irritated yet too stubborn to check on her. I laid back on the bed looking at the ceiling thinking about what she was doing in my apartment. My eyes became heavier by the second. She finally appeared at the doorway of my bedroom. I sat up again to get a better view of her to see if she had something to say. She had a confused look on her face as if she was expecting me to ask her a series of questions or something. I didn't say one word as I gave her a mirror expression of herself within my face. She slowly walked over then stood in front of me. I looked up at her still fishing for the understanding she wasn't giving me through her eyes. Shaking my head at her again as I grew more impatient with the silence poking at my brain. I finally gave her an ultimatum. "The least you can do is say something or I'm going back to sleep." I said. She calmly walked over to the light switch then flicked it off. I slid myself completely on the bed then laid my head on my pillows. I took that as she just wanted to continue to be weird and was going to leave since I wasn't putting in any efforts to interrogate her. I rolled over with my back towards her then closed my eyes. Without a full minute passing I felt her crawling in my bed.

Slowly and quietly she moved closer to me while I was laying there motionless yet curious. She pressed up against my back with her chest then placed one of her arms across me as we both laid there on our sides. She then tugged on me a few times as if she wanted me to turn over towards her. I finally rolled over for her after her third failed attempt to pull me. Our faces were aligned as she gazed into my eyes which there seemed to have been a sense of hopelessness in her eyes. I gave her time to speak before I blurted out my thoughts of confusion. She leaned upwards then placed a soft kiss on my forehead. I realized that was my signature move when I wanted someone to feel comfort or understand me without me having to say a lot. "I'm sorry Cedric." She said. In my mind I was thinking why in the hell did it take her that long to say that instead of treating me like a stranger! "Why did you have to be that way with me? I thought we were good?" I finally asked. She sat up then pushed some pillows behind her with her back resting on the headboard. I did the same. "Honestly, Cedric. I've been a mess. My emotions and feelings towards you since that day have been more than I could bare. I thought it would be cool and everything would be normal. I fought with myself trying to ignore the deeper connection I felt when you were inside of me. The more I thought about you and the possibility of us being in a serious relationship, made me scared to be around you. Not in a negative way but in way that it was something I wanted more than anything." She said as she started to break down. A tear slowly rolled down her cheek. I gently wiped it away with the back of my hand then pulled her in towards me. I wrapped my arms around her. I was caught off guard on how deep her feelings were involved causing her to react the way she did. She buried her head in my chest as I could feel her deeply exhaling. I sat there brushing her hair as she started to rub her legs against mines. I finally said, "We good Lauren. I'm sorry I didn't understand how crazy things were for you emotionally. I felt shut out by a good friend I genuinely cared about. That shit hurt. I was being stand offish as well not knowing how to handle the situation between us. I don't regret what we did, I just hate the way it played out afterwards." She lifted her head up then pulled my head towards her as we kissed. We locked lips for about a minute as I allowed her to control my tongue with hers. She sat back up after the kiss then said, "Sorry, I really needed that kiss. Your lips are so sweet and soft. You're right, it does hurts. I shouldn't have been like that. I hope you can forgive my actions." I moved to the edge of the bed because I was getting aroused from the kiss but wanted to stay focus. I wanted to avoid any physical situation between us in fear of having the same results. "Where are you going?" She asked. "Nowhere, I need to know we are being honest with ourselves about what we want from each other. I don't want to do anything that would keep us from being best friends like we have been. I like you Lauren. I don't want to lose something that was working over something that just shouldn't be." I replied. She moved down to end of the bed with me. She then stood up in front of me. She placed my head in her chest then started rubbing the back of my head. She did that for about five minutes as we both were lost in our thoughts. She finally said, "You're right. I don't want to question were we stand with one another. I'll rather have you as a best friend than to lose you all together. I want to continue what we have. Best friends forever if that's fine with you?" I stood up with her then gave her a nice long hug then topped it off with my own forehead kiss. I stepped back nodding my head agreeing with her. I replied, "Yeah I love the kind of friendship we had. Let's put this all behind us and keep it moving forward. Plus, I don't want to ever miss Taco Tuesday again with you!" We both burst out with laughter. It was late and we both needed to sleep after that. We both knew it was the best decision for us. We talked about my experience during the series and how she hated herself for not wishing me luck for about an hour until we started yawning. We agreed to have lunch the following day to get back in motion. I walked her to the door then we hugged once more before she stepped over to her place. It was about midnight, so I turned off all the lights then crashed out.

About a week had passed, Lauren and I were hanging out as normal as if nothing happened. It was a good feeling. I was glad we were able to bounce back like that. Mrs. Anthony once told David and I, "True friendship can withstand any trouble or situation. Some friendships are worth the fight and understanding. Never take a real friend for granted." I felt that with Lauren and that helped me to move on with what we had. It was working even better. She respected my calls without any awkward looks or gestures. I tried to respect our time together so I worked on talking to Rachel in the mornings since Lauren, Daniel and I would chill together in the evenings. It was a Sunday early evening, Lauren and Daniel were over with the sun slowly fading away. Everything was back flowing until I received a call from Samantha. It had slipped my mind that fast she was coming to Chicago! She told me she was getting on a plane the next morning heading my way. Lauren could tell it wasn't Rachel or Mrs. Anthony by the way my entire mood changed. I gave myself up because my voice got all high pitched when I answered the phone. I was way giggly than normal too. I sounded like I was talking to a celebrity or someone was telling me I had just won the lotto! When I hung up the phone, I tried to play it smooth and laugh about what was on the TV. Daniel was giving that nonchalant look of curiosity while Lauren got up and went to the restroom. Daniel whispered, "Who was that? You were geeked as hell my guy. Sounded like you were chatting with your first love or something?" I waved my hand at him as I replied, "Man whatever. I'll have to tell you about her later. I'm expecting a gorgeous visitor coming up from my hometown this week." Lauren suddenly appeared back in the room as if she heard me. The silence in the room was nerve wrecking. I was itching so bad to tell Daniel about Samantha that I wanted to get Lauren out of there. I was thinking of a way to get Daniel to step outside with me for a second. I stood up, faked stretching my arms in the air then winked my eye at Daniel to warn him I was about to do something sneaky. Before my little plan unfolded, Lauren marched towards the front door as she mumbled, "I'll see y'all later. I don't feel too good." Daniel and I yelled at her as she was opening the door, "Hope you feel better!" Not thinking twice about Lauren's on que act, I immediately strolled over to the door to lock it so she wouldn't interrupt the details I wanted to share with Daniel about Samantha! I sat back down then gave Daniel the scoop about Samantha. Everything from how sexy she was, our first and last dates and the reason she was coming to see me. Of course, Daniel was more excited than I was after spilling the beans to him. After about thirty minutes of me reminiscing about Samantha, Daniel apologized to me again. "Man, you have been a one in a million kind of friend to me. I hate I wasn't there for you or the team in the series. I just wanted to get that off my chest. It's been eating me up and I really appreciate you treating me the same after that whole situation with that crazy ass girl!" I wasn't expecting that from him because I was over it and it was in the past in my book. "You have a friend in me for life! We live and we learn. I hate it all went down that way too. I'm not perfect myself, things happen." I replied. We shook hands as we both stood up after that conversation. I told him I needed to do a deep cleaning of my apartment since I was expecting an incredibly special lady over soon. He volunteered to help but I declined the offer. I wanted the rest of the evening alone to get my head balanced and nerves under control. I also wanted to figure out some things Samantha and I could do when she got there besides talking. After about two hours of cleaning every inch of my place, I wrote down some chill spots we could hit up and great Chicago style food restaurants I had to take her to. I finally made it to my bedroom which didn't need much cleaning but to wash the mountain of dirty clothes that piled up in a basket near my closet. I promised myself to get to the clothes first thing the next morning because I couldn't stay up another minute. I fell on my bed, took my socks and shirt off then closed my eyes. I had my phone resting in my hands with an alarm I set to get up around eight the next morning to get ahead of the crowd in the laundry room downstairs. My phone rang. I gripped it tight in my hand as I glanced at it seeing Rachel's name pop up on the screen. I answered it quickly. She didn't want anything important. She said she was thinking about me and wanted to talk for a second. My eyes were so heavy, but I managed to keep them open to finish the ten-minute conversation with her. She told me she was going to the doctor to check up on the baby. I told her to keep me updated about any and everything about the baby's heath as well as her own. I knew that gave her a sense of comfort the more she was able to speak freely about it and I had to show my support since we both had to do our parts.

The next morning, I was up bright and early! The weather couldn't have been any nicer with the sun shining with just a few clouds passing by. My luck was rolling being that I was the first in the laundry room with my clothes. I was feeling great! After my clothes were finished, I was in my place folding them and putting them up neatly. I decided I wanted to be transparent with Lauren about the whole Samantha visit, so I went next door to talk with her. It was a little after nine that morning and I knew she was an early bird. I knocked on her door a couple times. As I was about to retreat to my unit, her door slowly cracked open. I had to take a few steps back to let the guy that had come out of her door, pass me! He had a smirk on his face as if he had hit the jackpot but wasn't going to say anything to anyone! I knew his face but not his name. He was one of the guys on the cheer team that was always cheering beside or with Lauren. It was shocking he was over at her place, yet interesting that he was over there that early. Her door was still opened. She was holding it with herself hidden from the light of the sun piercing the doorway as if she hadn't been up but a minute or so. I just stood there a little unsure of what to do. Something in me was upset and disturbed. It was an unfamiliar feeling of sadness and anger mixed. I just turned then stepped back over to my door. Lauren peeped her head out of her door. "Good morning to you too! Can I help you?" She said. There was nothing but attitude attached to her every word. I couldn't speak as if my words weren't forming a complete sentence in my head. I looked at her in disbelief as if she had slapped me in the face. I wasn't thinking straight at all, so I just went into my apartment then slammed the door! I could hear my phone ringing from the bedroom. I ran to catch it before it stopped. It was Mrs. Anthony. I was in no state to talk to anyone in that moment, but I couldn't ignore her call. I answered it. "Hello." I said as I could barely get the words out clearly. "Hi Cedric. Are you okay?" She asked. I held the phone for a minute before I burst out saying, "Can I come home! I miss you! I just want to come home please, just for a few days. Maybe a week." I realized in that very moment I was emotional and couldn't shake it off. It's like something snapped within me. "Cedric you can always come home baby. What's wrong?" She asked as she was getting worried by the second. I gripped the phone tighter trying to fix the unsettling thoughts I was having of Lauren and that guy. I kept asking myself why I am feeling this way, why do I care! Finally, I had calmed down just enough to reply to Mrs. Anthony. "I'm okay, I think I'm just home sick! I just need some fresh air from here. I guess? I'm just feeling somewhat alone here." I replied. "Cedric, I'm sorry you feel that way. We can arrange for you to come soon. I understand. I just wanted you to finish your first year there without being distracted with coming home. I didn't want to decide to either stay home or go back to school being an option. You have done a wonderful job and pretty much finished your first year without any trouble. I think you deserve to come home for a little too!" She replied. As she said that I was feeling better. She was right, I had done something I didn't think I could just a year before. I finished my first year without caving in to all the temptation that surrounded me, and I was moving forward. I felt those words were the ones I needed to hear. "You're right. I love you. Thank you for everything." I replied. "You know I love you too Cedric. You keep your head up baby. It's going to be okay. I was just calling to check on you. I know you're still upset about the series. Let's talk more about you coming home soon, okay." She replied. I smiled as I told her I'm excited about seeing her soon. We both hung up after that. I grabbed my phone then walked back in the living room. I sat on the sofa, clicking through the channels on the TV. I didn't think much about Lauren nor puzzled my brain about what went down with her and that guy. It wasn't my business to care. I watched a few funny shows for about an hour.

A few bangs on the door startled me a bit because I was so glued to the news that was on about how the weather was going to be bad for the next day or two! That was going to put a damper on the plans I had to be out and about with Samantha. I was going to have to improvise. I opened the door to see Daniel standing there with a big smile on his face. He came in as I shut the door behind him. "Is she here yet?" He whispered as he looked around. "Calm down clown. She will call me when she lands. She has to pick up a rental car and check in to the hotel she's staying at before she heads this way." I replied as I was laughing at him. I was back on the sofa and Daniel was in a chair he pulled from the kitchen. He then asked, "You check on Lauren? Is she feeling better?" Of all the questions and things, we could have been talking about, that was the last thing or person I wanted to think about it. "I guess she's okay?" I replied. Daniel leaned over in his seat then asked, "What do you mean, you guess? What kind of answer is that?" I got up then went to the kitchen to get something to eat as I tried to avoid his last questions. "Are you hungry man?" I asked him. I put some pizza rolls on a pan then slid them in the stove. He didn't turn down the food nor did he turn down his need for an answer. "What's up my guy? You went over to Lauren's place this morning?" He asked as he came into the kitchen. I turned the stove on then sat at the kitchen table. I hesitated, thinking I should just say she was fine, but the truth was in fact bothering me since he made me think of her. I looked at him shaking my head as I said, "Yeah I went over to her place. Well I knocked on the door. One of her cheer mates, partners or whatever you call the dudes that cheer, came walking out when she finally opened the door! I knew he didn't come by super early because I was up washing my clothes and didn't hear any doors opening or closing around here. I'm sure he was over there all night! So yeah that's why I said I guess her ass was okay." He smiled as if he knew something I didn't know. "That's funny to you? Am I missing something?" I asked as I looked at him with my eyebrows as high as I could raise them. "Well I thought those cheerleading dudes were on the fence you know. I thought they had sugar in their tanks! Like how manly is it to be a male cheerleader? Word is... Those guys get way more play than any of us! They low key be dating or sexing the whole cheer squad right under our noses! I heard they know everything about everyone and basically uses that to their advantage. Think about it." Daniel whispered. I did think about it and I hate I did! It only made me more frustrated. "You think that he and Lauren was messing around?" I asked Daniel. Not sure how I allowed myself to ask such an insecure question out loud. It was clear. I knew at once, I didn't want to hear his answer! Before he could reply, I added, "You know what? I'm tripping for real! Lauren is a grown woman. I'm not her dude so it doesn't even matter what him or her were doing up in there this morning or last night. Plus, Samantha will be here soon! I'm good!" Daniel nodded his head as he agreed with me. I needed some small household things for my place so I told Daniel I would be back. He had to run to the dorms to check on some things himself. We walked out of the door at the same time. As I was locking the door behind me, Lauren was walking out of her place as well. "Hey Daniel. Hey Cedric. What are y'all about to do?" She asked as if nothing had happened earlier. As if I was supposed to be all cool about it? I questioned my every thought as I tried not to look at her. I waved but didn't say anything. "We good. Are you okay? Did you have a long night?" Daniel said as he started to giggle a little. I gave him a slight bump in his back with my forearm but just out of Lauren's sight! He looked back at me wearing his apology in his eyes as he shrugged his shoulders. "Long night? Nah I feel better now. I actually had a very relaxing night." She said as she looked me up and down as if she wanted to be sure I was paying attention to her every word. I then quickly moved past Daniel, strolled by Lauren as I said, "Excuse me, I have things to do. I'll catch up with you later Daniel." I didn't look back nor wait for a reply. I heard Lauren say, "Well excuse you. Rude!" I kept my head forward until I reached the other end of the building then headed down the stairs.

I was on my way back to my apartment when my phone rang. It was Samantha telling me she had her car for the week and finally checked in. She was about twenty minutes away according to the GPS she was using. She had my address and was in motion, coming my way. I told her I was home relaxing anticipating her arrival. I hung up the phone then bolted back to my place! I had to jump in the shower after working up a good sweat from hauling my ass back! After the shower I made sure everything was fresh and in order. I lit a candle Lauren had given me since she claimed my apartment always smelled like feet and jock straps. I turned the TV on then laid back on the couch. About thirty minutes had pass as I was starting to worry about Samantha. My damn neck was hurting from looking down at my phone every two minutes anxious to see her. Finally, there was a soft knock on the door. I opened it with Samantha standing there looking amazingly beautiful than ever! She looked as if she had been working out with her hair cut short in small layers! I loved the new look. I was speechless as she stepped in and hugged me! The smell of fresh fruit floated through my nose as we embraced. She felt warm in my arms. Both of our hearts were beating rapidly as I could feel them both while she was pressed against my chest. I didn't want to let her go as we stood there for at least two to three minutes locked together. As we separated, I slowly stepped backwards more into my place as she walked all the way in. I pushed the door behind her. She had the biggest smile on her face as she looked around. "Wow! Look at you! Mr. College Star Athlete in his own bachelor's pad! I am so happy for you Cedric!" She said as she strolled around in the living room then towards the kitchen area. I was wearing a matching smile just as big as hers. I couldn't keep my eyes off her! She was wearing a long beige sun dress with white stripes on it. Every move she made I was eye balling her as her butt slightly jiggled in all the right places! "Thank you. I appreciate the love. It's unreal to me that you're really standing here in the flesh! Thank you for coming by!" I said as I followed her in the kitchen area. She was soaking it in just as much as I was which made me feel more relaxed. I was tense as hell during our hug. I wasn't sure how we both were going to react, but she made it easy for me with all the kind words and praises. "Are you thirsty? Hungry?" I asked. She walked up to me slowly and hugged me again as if she couldn't believe we were face to face. Again, it had me feeling great killing all doubts her visiting was going to be in vain! I held her in my arms tighter then placed a kiss on her forehead. She immediately looked at me then placed a kiss of her own on my lips! We kissed like never before! It was probably the best kiss I've ever had up to that point between the few lips I've had the opportunity to kiss. After we unlocked lips, she whispered, "I miss you Cedric more than you could ever imagine." Without blinking once I replied, "I miss you more." It was not what I was expecting from her. There was still a connection between us, we both didn't forget. It was surreal as we were moving away from our hug, she held my hand then looked me up and down as if she had been waiting to see me all her life! I had to pinch myself to make sure I wasn't in the best damn dream ever. We dropped our hands from one another as I shook my head at her then said, "Are you putting on or you trying to make me kidnap you! Keep this up and you won't be going back to Mississippi!" We both laughed. "Yeah I know it's hard to believe. Like I said over the phone. I have been thinking about you nonstop! I'm so glad this worked out this way! I get to do something I've always wanted to do and see a sexy guy! What more can I ask for?" She replied. I could have lifted that dress up right then and went to town! She had all the right answers with all the right curves! "Damn I'm lucky as hell! That's all I can say!" I responded. We walked back in the living room. We both sat on the couch.

We talked for at least two hours about everything! So much had happened with the store since I was there. Rachel did mention it to me, but Samantha confirmed that they expanded to two locations. She was running the new one on her own. Gary, the son of Mrs. Samson the owner of the stores, was running the original one while Mrs. Samson had given up being in the store on a regularly basis. She told me more about the internship she was involved in and how she had gained the likes of some of the top marketing executives. She bought a new car with the money she saved up plus the huge raise she received from running the new store. I was impressed with the amount of success she had since choosing to stay. I didn't want to admit it to her, but she was right. There was enough evidence to prove she made the best decision for her. I continued to listen to her success stories until a knock on the door interrupted her. I nearly snapped my neck looking over at the door as if I could see Lauren standing behind the other side! I was so engaged in the conversation that the light tapping on the door sounded like thunder to me! "Does that mean you don't have many guests at your door that often? You nearly jumped on me. Or maybe that's your little boo thang coming by to check on you?" Samantha said as she started giggling. I knew she was joking but I detected a bit of concern on the last question she stated. I played it as smooth as I could by saying, "I have a few friends. No boo thang. My place is normally peaceful. I was just savoring the moment with you as my ears were enjoying your sweet voice." I got up slowly as I headed to the door as we both smiled at each other. I opened the door while praying it wasn't Lauren! Daniel was there smiling from ear to ear. I don't recall if I've ever been that happy to see him at my door since I've meet him! He gave me the raised eyebrows then moved his eyes inward which was the nonverbal way of asking was the guest of honor there. I stepped back to let him in then said as I was closing the door, "Samantha, Daniel. Daniel this is the amazing Samantha." She stood up as Daniel walked over then they shook hands as they greeted one another. "Wow! Cedric wasn't lying when he said you make all the chicks here look like amateurs! You are on another echelon. It is nice to meet you!" Daniel said. He glanced at me as he winked his eye. Samantha smiled then said, "Well it is nice to meet you too. Thank you. Cedric said all that huh?" They both looked at me as I was smiling shaking my head wearing the guilt all over my face. "Well I was stopping through to see if you were hungry Cedric. It slipped my mind that Samantha was coming today. I'm sorry for intruding on you two. I'm sure y'all have plenty of stuff to catch up on." Daniel said as he slowly moved back towards the door walking backwards. I was starving. Before I suggested anything, Samantha said, "I am hungry too! Cedric bragged about how the food is much better up here, so. You two don't mind if I tag along?" I figured since she was here for a whole week, it wasn't going to hurt to get food with Daniel the one tagging along. "I'm fine with that. I did mention food like two hours ago! My stomach has been growling quietly." I said. They both laughed. "I need to put on some jeans and a better-looking shirt. I look like I'm about to go workout. Give me a couple of minutes to change then we can roll." I added. They laughed again but neither disagreed with my me, so I walked to my room while they sat and chatted. I finished putting on my shoes then called Rachel quick to let her know I was going to be busy. I knew she would call, and I didn't want to ignore her call while I was in the middle of a limbo with Samantha and Lauren. I didn't want to keep them waiting so I told her I had something important I needed to do. She sounded excited to tell me about the doctor visit but said it could wait. I didn't think anything of it since she was in a good mood about it, so I agreed to call her later. She made it clear that I had to call her so she could give me an update. I promised her I would call. I rushed in the bathroom, brushed my teeth then headed back in the living room in time to hear Daniel confessing his troubles that caused him to miss out on our post season run with team. Not sure how they got to that topic, but they finished that conversation with Samantha saying she understood how easy it is to get in some sticky situation if you're not careful. "Y'all ready to go?" I asked. They both nodded their heads then I made sure the lights were shut off in the rest of my apartment. "Since I'm driving, are you going to tell me where we are going?" Samantha asked jokingly. "Yeah it's a crazy good Italian place about a twenty-minute drive south of here that I know you're going to love. They also make great Chicago style pizza." Daniel smiled and added, "Yeah I've heard really good stuff about it but never been! It has a chill atmosphere and a tab bit upscale. You would usually take a pretty girl somewhere like that. I see why my guy picked that spot to go!" Samantha look at me smiling. "Oh, Cedric has always had good taste and quite the charmer. I'm sure I won't be disappointed." I walked over to get the door to let Samantha out as Daniel followed behind her. I stood there like a mannequin as Lauren was standing outside eye balling Samantha up and down! "Lauren! What's up?" Daniel shouted as he slid pass Samantha to hug Lauren. It helped me get my thoughts together quickly. "We're about to head out for food. Cedric's friend from his hometown is here." Daniel added as Lauren stared at me with curiosity. I immediately replied, "Yeah Samantha, this is Lauren my friend and neighbor. Lauren this is my future ex-wife, Samantha!" I laughed as I was attempting to ease the tension that was forming over my entire body. Daniel laughed as well while Lauren and Samantha shook hands as they smiled at one another. That may have been two of the fakest smiles I've ever witnessed. "You are more than welcome to come. There's plenty of room in the car. I have a huge SUV they gave me while I'm here so." Samantha said to Lauren as Daniel and I looked at each other with hopes she would decline! "Yeah that's cool with me if you want to go." I said not making it awkward for me not seconding her offer. Daniel also agreed it would be fun if Lauren came. We both were only being nice knowing it was a bad idea for her to be around me with the way the last couple of days went. "Well if it's no biggie, then sure I'll join the party. Thanks for the invite..." Lauren said. "Cool! Well let's go! I'm starving!" Samantha replied as she started to walk towards the stairs. Daniel followed her as he stared at me as if he couldn't believe what was happening. I closed the door and as I was locking it, Lauren whispered, "She's very pretty. Just friends huh? A pretty friend that came all the way up here to see you. A pretty friend name Samantha you never talked about. That's funny." She wanted to make sure I knew her every thought as she then walked to the stairs. I regretted the whole idea right then and there. I was hoping the truck had a flat tire or no gas when we got to it. Lauren was speed walking as she did when she was upset about something. When I made it to the truck, Samantha was already in with Daniel sitting in the seat behind her. Lauren got in the back next to Daniel, so I jumped in the passenger seat up front next to Samantha. Before we were about to pull off, Lauren asked, "So, where are we going?" Daniel quickly answered. "Cedric wanted to go to that Italian place downtown. That's by the Bears stadium." I knew she had something to say being that I took her there once. "Oh really? The place we went to a few months back?" Lauren replied. I glanced back at Daniel as he looked confused yet surprised because I never told him about that. Samantha side eyed me as well as they were all waiting for me to answer. "Yeah that's the place. The food is the best there." I replied. I would have gone somewhere on the other side of the globe than to have known that was going to play out like it did. I could tell Samantha was starting to feel something in the air between Lauren and me. I gave her the address as she put it in the GPS. Then we took off. Daniel kept us entertained during the mini road trip to the restaurant. He had jokes and we had laughs. Lauren nor Samantha said much as they both were in deep thoughts but would giggle here and there.

We finally made it to the place. It wasn't that crowded, which we were able to get a table right away. I sat across from Daniel next to Samantha while Daniel was next to Lauren with Samantha sitting across from her. We ordered drinks then I gave a quick speech on what I liked and offered suggestions. Lauren and Samantha both were still reserved with little to no talking, just observing everything. Samantha did mention the place was nice. I went ahead an ordered some appetizers for us all to share while they were still looking over the menu. I had money so it wasn't a thought about who was going to pay. Mrs.

Anthony sent money every two weeks and I was still pinching off the money Melvin gave me. I didn't do much where I really needed a bunch of money. I was doing great with saving. The drinks had come followed by the appetizers. Everyone finally made up their minds then ordered. Within minutes, all the flood gates where opened as the questions started to come. I knew the moment was going to happen. "How long have you known Cedric?" Lauren asked Samantha. Samantha finished her drink then replied, "A year and some change I believe." I continued to stuff my face trying to ignore the exchange they were having. "That's cool." Daniel said as he was all ears. He was eating yet focused on every word that was being said between the girls. "Okay... You two must be really good friends for you to come all this way to see him." Lauren said without blinking as if she was getting right down to the nitty gritty. I coughed a little not believing she said that like that. Daniel flagged down our server to request refills for everyone. "Yeah Cedric is a special person to me. He has been good to me so when the opportunity came about, I didn't hesitate. I couldn't ask for a better friend." Samantha said as she smiled at me. There's no way to hide the smile she put on my face, but I knew it was short lived. I waited to hear more from Lauren's investigation. "Aww that's nice. Yeah he's something special." Lauren replied. Daniel interrupted them suggesting dessert for us. I declined because I was stuffed. Samantha did as well. Lauren wanted a brownie with ice cream she agreed she could share with Daniel because she wasn't going to eat a whole one by herself. "Excuse me, I need to use the lady's room." Samantha said. She got up then walked off. Not even thirty seconds had passed before Lauren said she too had to go to the lady's room. I wanted to tell her to sit her ass down because I knew she about to stir up something I couldn't control if she was alone with Samantha! I just lowered my face as I rubbed the back of my head. She stared at Daniel with an innocent grin then strolled to the restroom once I looked back up at her. "Why didn't you tell me you brought Lauren here?" Daniel whispered to me. "I didn't think it mattered." I replied. "Well had I known I would have suggested somewhere else!" Daniel replied. "Yeah you right. My bad." I said as I shook my head concerned that it was taking the ladies longer than I wanted them to. "Why do you seem so worried and uncomfortable?" Daniel asked. I didn't answer as I was playing out the discussion, they were probably having about me. "Wait! Did you and Lauren ever hook up?" Daniel asked with his eyes glued to my lips waiting for my answer. I never told him, and I was looking as guilty as ever. "Noooooo... Tell me you didn't! Wow! I get it! That's why your ass is uptight! Lauren's being all slick and interested about your friendship with Samantha! Now she's in there probably telling it all! Damn...You're sitting there like a scared lost puppy!" He said as his face lit up like a lightbulb. He was right. I was going to tell him about Lauren and me, but it was never the right time. "This is not how I wanted my first evening with Samantha to go! I like her a lot, and this is not going to help me if she finds out about my thing with Lauren. I should have never allowed you or Lauren to join us!" I responded. Daniel shook his head at me then said, "It's not my fault you have all these damn secrets. I thought we were boys. You could have told me more. I could've helped! Now I'm wondering what else you haven't told me." Again, he was right. I didn't reveal any of that to him. By keeping it all to myself, it was all on me. I needed to clear my head. I wanted to just get up and leave. I knew that was the last thing I needed to do. Couldn't imagine how Samantha would have felt if she came back to the table and I was gone. "I can't explain to you how dumb I feel right now. We are boys and I will make sure I keep you in the loop about things like that from here on out. I promise." I replied. As I was finishing my plea to Daniel, the girls walked back to the table. They were both smiling as if they had become the best of friends. The dessert Daniel and Lauren ordered had arrived as the girls sat down. I wanted to ask so bad what the hell they were talking about that had them cheesing together! While the other two were enjoying the brownie sundae, Samantha was staring at her phone which had me all alone drowning in curiosity and shame! About five minutes of soft talking between Lauren and Daniel with nothing from Samantha either, I said, "I guess it's safe to say, that brownie is giving y'all life over there!" Daniel wiped his mouth as chocolate syrup was spilling down his lips. He replied, "You just don't know what you're missing!" Samantha whispered to herself, "Too bad he won't find out…" At least that's what I thought I heard from her? I flagged the waiter down to ask for the bill. Samantha insisted that she pay for her own portion, which was weird because she didn't say anything up until I had the check in my hand. I refused to let her pay. Daniel and Lauren looked on as I placed the money in the small black folder. They had no intention on paying for their stuff which was cool because I was going to anyway as I had planned. I was simply confused about Samantha's actions and silence since her restroom trip with Lauren. "Well I really enjoyed meeting you two and thanks again for the delicious meal Cedric. I am beat… I need to get some rest. I have a busy week ahead of me so if you all are ready then I can take y'all back." Samantha said as she stretched her arms out then yarning. It wasn't that late to me, yet I understood she had a long day with traveling then hanging out with us. I didn't want to pressure her to stay out any longer. "Yeah it's been a long day. I'm stuffed and feel that "Itis" kicking in! Thanks for coming." I said as I smiled at Samantha. She smiled back then stood up. Daniel and Lauren both got up then thanked Samantha for hanging out too. We all walked to the car with Daniel joking about how Lauren barely saved him any of the brownie. We all laughed. It was underwhelmingly quiet during the ride back to our apartments. Once we made it back, Daniel and Lauren jumped out with Daniel saying bye as he headed back towards the dorms and Lauren upstairs to her unit. I stayed back for a minute to say a few words to Samantha before she left. "I can't thank you enough for coming to see me. I enjoyed your company. Hope to see you again soon. Although I know you're here for business, I want to spend as much time with you as possible." She smiled then said, "That sounds good. I guess we'll see what happens. Good night Cedric." I was hoping for a good night kiss or something, but she just stared at me as if she was waiting for me to get out after that. I felt it in her energy, but I wasn't sure if I should lean in for one. "Good night to you too Samantha." I said as I slowly opened the door to get out. I was giving her time to say something else or to pull me back in, but she didn't. I was out then walked slower around the truck towards my place. She drove off before I even made it to the staircase. I walked up to my unit confused but happy to have seen her. I went straight to my room then slipped off my shoes. I wanted to wait up until I was for sure she had made it to her hotel room to call. I laid in my bed biting my fingers with anxiety wanting to call her. I don't remember falling asleep.

I remember rolling over through the night seeing the missed call light flashing on my cell phone. For some reason it felt like a dream with no energy to reach for the phone, so I went back to sleep. The sun rays where sneaking in through the cracks in the blinds when I finally woke up. I got up to use the restroom then set down at the table to eat some toast, an orange and an apple. I was unusually hungry. I sat there after I finished eating, replaying everything that happened the night before. I wanted to plan something chill for Samantha and me to do since the first night with her was a disaster. There was unwanted tension I needed to clear up. I finally went to my room to check my phone to make sure I was dreaming about the missed calls. There were fifteen missed calls! I checked the list to see that I had quite a few missed calls from Lauren and Rachel but only one from Samantha. Lauren had called about ten times that started about midnight. I wasn't too alarmed because she would do that whenever she couldn't sleep and wanted me to let her in to sleep over with me. Rachel called about four times, three times randomly through the night with one that came earlier that morning. Samantha call came through about the same time I was falling asleep. I was sure I would have answered it if I had stayed up about five more minutes. It was about nine in the morning which meant Samantha was busy with the internship business because she mentioned her days were starting around eight. I couldn't call her right away which would have been my first choice. I felt bad about not calling Rachel back like I promised. She was going to be a little worked up about that but not completely mad at me. I was still a bit salty with Lauren, so I called Rachel to check on her. I talked to Rachel for about an hour. She had a major reason why it was important I called her. She revealed to me that we were having a baby boy! The doctor visit went well, and the little guy was healthy. I was excited yet scared out my mind as the time was getting closer and closer to her due date according to her! I continued to keep my cool whenever I was talking to her because she needed more comfort and emotional support than I did. I started to see the him. I started to see a little precious human calling me daddy! I started to shed tears as Rachel went on about the things she was purchasing and how she was making it all work out. I felt that heavy load pressing down on my shoulders so hard as she spoke with undeniable great energy and faith that I wasn't sure if she was just fine or that was her way of not breaking a part. Whatever she was feeling, it was helping me see the positive outcome. She made me hopeful. With her clear understanding, there was no turning back. We were in this and whatever happened, she was ready! That conversation brought me back to the reality of my future life. I was worrying about the wrong things. Rachel had made absolute peace with it and I needed to follow her on that. I thanked her for not being hard on me for not calling her back. We laughed then hung up the phone.

I dragged myself around my place all day watching TV, snacking and napping. No word from Samantha nor Lauren until about six that evening. There was a light knock on my door that sounded like someone knew I was in there. I slowly opened it. I had to blink a few times to double check my sight, seeing that it was Lauren standing there looking like she was about to go on a hot date. She had light make up on with her lips shining like a car window reflection in the midday sun. She was wearing a skintight short black dress with black heels on. It had to have been something new because I had never seen that dress or heels before! Her hair was pinned up and she smelled like fresh roses. I was caught off guard! She had a smile of her face that indicated I was reacting the exact way she expected. She walked right in passed me. I looked around outside to see if someone was waiting for her. I was speechless as I shut the door then gazed at her sexy frame switching towards the kitchen. Hypnotized by her scent and the sway of her hips, I stood there motionless. I was aroused indeed with no fight in me to ignore the tension we still had between one another. She turned around and noticed how turned on I was then she said, "I have something I need to say to you. I know we talked before, but I can't get over how good you felt. I can't stop thinking about it and I can't go on another day without it. Don't say no." My mind was telling me to be careful, don't do it, it's a trap but my body was already on top of her, kissing and rubbing all over her! "What do you mean?" I asked as if I didn't know what she was saying. She smiled at me as if she was glad, I asked. It's like she knew everything I was going to say and do! I crept in the kitchen as she was standing there staring at me as if I was the one with the seductive dress on! She met me as I entered the kitchen with a kiss as she pulled me in to her holding the sides of my face with her hands. Again, I was no match against her lead.

While kissing she slowly stepped back towards the counter next to the stove until I had her pinned up against it. She suddenly held my shoulders as she propped herself up onto the countertop! She immediately started kissing on my neck while sliding my sweats down followed by my boxer. My erection was at full attention as she was guiding me inward between her thighs! I went straight in as I noticed she didn't have on any panties. We went on for minutes right there in the kitchen. She softly moaned my name as I continued to stroke in and out of her until I felt that eruption coming! I didn't have protection and it felt amazing but with the confirmation I was technically a father, I pulled out just in time to shoot my load all over her dress! I barely missed her face with the amount that came out! She didn't move as if she didn't care where it landed. She had a look in her eyes as if she had just pulled off the greatest scheme ever! It was an evil yet pleasing expression she had which had me regretting what had just happened immediately. I pulled my clothes back up as I took a few steps back from her. She slid off the counter then said, "Thank you. I really needed that. I knew you wanted me just as much as I wanted you! I just had to make sure I wasn't going crazy." She walked in the living room as she adjusted her dress, pulling it down. "Now I do think you're a little crazy. But... You know I like you. Our friendship... I just don't want to take things too far between us and one of us gets hurt." I replied as I followed her in the living room. I meant that for two reasons. One, it was truthful because I did care for her, although we were better together as just friends. Two, I didn't want her to try to mess things up for me while Samantha was in town. I needed her on her best behavior and not all emotional, blocking my chances with Samantha. She walked on to the door then turn and said, "I hear you Cedric. It's hard to tell what you really mean if you're so quick to give it up like that. I'll believe you when you show me you just want to be friends." She didn't wait for an answer at all. She opened the door and was out within seconds! Her words cut through me like a sharp blade piercing my skin deep to the bone! That hit hard with so much reality slapping me in the face! She was playing me according to who I was. She knew I was a sucker sexually for her and wouldn't put up a fight. She knew I was all over the place mentally, so my decision-making sense was out the window! She had me right where she wanted me, and I was guilty of not having any self-control! My only victory I could give myself was the fact I pulled out. I couldn't shake the feeling of being defeated. I went to take a shower to wash all the frustration off me. Night had come with no word from Samantha. I knew she was well done with the day handling business, so I decided to call her. I had to get my mind off the harsh lesson Lauren tried to teach me. Her phone rang at least ten times with no answer. I didn't trip or get worried, I figured she had a busy day and crashed out. It was about nine when I called. I left it alone and lay down on the couch.

Chapter 5

Take Me Home

The whole week had breezed on by! Which seemed like it was on fast forward with me spending most of my time at the gym and talking to Rachel. No time with Samantha. I was worried because it didn't feel right for her to be that close yet only seeing her that one time. I couldn't even pop up on her at her hotel because she never told me where she was staying. I asked a few times but no answers to those questions. She only managed to send me a text or two telling me how crazy the experience was but wouldn't reply after I responded. Something was clearly up yet I continued with my day to day. I knew I was going back home soon. I wanted to verbally tell her over the phone it was cool I didn't get to spend as much time with her and we could make it up in a few weeks. I didn't get that opportunity because she wouldn't answer any of my calls either. Lauren had stopped by a couple of times here and there. She didn't bring up our last sexual encounter which kept me on edge. I couldn't trust her like I use to, so I was ready for anything, if she tried to play any mind games with me when she was over. It helped having Daniel at my place during those times she popped in. She did show signs of frustration when Daniel was there, so I knew I was winning the war she was trying to have against me and my self-discipline. I made sure I told Daniel everything that was going on between Lauren and me. He made sure he didn't miss a thing. He enjoyed being over to keep tabs on all the drama. I asked for his opinion about the Samantha situation. He said, "The luck I've had with girls isn't the best, but you have all the qualification to snag a girl like her for sure! It is odd she's been missing in action with you especially with y'all knowing each other so well. I think it will work out for you honestly." I needed to hear it from someone else, that it was strange not seeing or hearing from her like I thought I should have. Which he was right about how close we were. It seemed promising from day one when she came then nothing. With no explanation other than her being busy. I was able and willing to take it further with Samantha if only she still felt the same.

It was the day before Samantha was supposed to head back to Jackson, when she finally called me! I was still in bed because she called that morning. I had to do a triple take making sure my eyes weren't deceiving me when her call came through. I answered it with silence on my end to hear her telling me to come open the door! I didn't waste a second running to the door not caring about how I looked or if my morning breathe was going to knock her off her feet. I reached door before she could place her phone in her purse. She looked as if she had been crying, which alarmed me that her visit wasn't going to be pleasant. She stepped in slowly as I waited to close the door behind her. She sat on the edge of the couch as if she was uncomfortable. I walked over but grab a chair. I could sense she didn't want me that close since she sat in the middle of the couch not leaving much room for me to join her. I sat somewhat in front of her slightly to her right. She was quiet for a few minutes then I asked, "I didn't think I was going to see you again. Thanks for coming by. I hope everything is okay. You seem upset about something?" She rocked back and forward as she scanned the room as if she were searching for the right words to say. "Samantha please talk to me. Did anything bad happen to you? Did someone hurt you?" I added as I began to get nervous about her behavior. She took a deep breath in then said, "I promised her I wouldn't say anything. This has been a long and depressing week. I imagined us cruising around downtown Chicago, you showing me a great time and spending the whole week together. After hearing about you sleeping with your neighbor, that shit really hurt! I looked like a complete fool thinking you were here being all innocent. Me thinking that I could pop back into your life to make you mines! I hate I came, and I hate knowing the truth about you! She told me everything!" I swear my heart skipped a couple of beats! I was short of breath which felt like I was about to suffocate! I started to sweat uncontrollably by the second. There was no chance to act cool or play it smooth. It was clear she had thought about it all week long. "Samantha... I'm sorry you feel that way. You have every right to. I must confess that I haven't been honest with myself yet alone with anyone. I did have this emptiness I felt when you decided to not join me. Yes, I probably could have reached out to you. But... I was being selfish. It's true I had sex with her. And... What's crazy about it? I don't have any emotional ties to her as I do with you! What I did with her was only a physical thing. It doesn't compare to the way I want you. Something way more than your body." I replied with the shame in my voice. She stood up then walked to door as I saw a few tears fall down her cheeks. I quickly cut her off from getting to the door! I wrapped her in my arms. She was unresponsive to that gesture as she stood there cold. That summed it up and there weren't any doubts she was done with me. She allowed me to hold her while she gathered herself before she found the strength to push away from me. "I can't blame you for being a guy. You have enough going for you here. I'm... I'm happy for you. Maybe, this was necessary, for the closure we both needed now that everything is out. I wish you happiness Cedric. Please be careful with who you're laying down with too. Everyone isn't worth it." She said. She reached for the doorknob without any resistance from me then walked out with no concern about my final reply. She didn't shut door as I stood in the doorway watching her rapidly wipe her eyes walking with haste to the car. She sat in the car for a moment, glancing up at me before she drove away. Calling her would have been a waste of time. I felt her words when she said them. She was torn. I couldn't figure out why she kept those serious feelings towards me bottled in. I questioned how she kept that info to herself the entire week without giving me the time to explain. I battled with the thoughts of wondering if my choices would have been altered with knowing Samantha saw a future with me by her side. I sat in my apartment for hours with all of that weighing on me. I kept looking at my phone, hoping she would call to say it's okay or had a change of heart. Then the truth sunk in on why that had happened the way it did! Lauren's big mouth! I was heated the more I tried to understand why Lauren would go that far to tell Samantha any of that! We had already had a conversation about being just friends! Then it all made sense! She screwed me over thinking there was a chance for her and me to be together. I was sick to my stomach wishing I had never crossed that line with her. I needed to confront her instantly! I jumped up then went next door to her place! I knocked on her door, but my knocks went unanswered. I called her a couple of times, but she didn't answer as well. Back in my unit I paced back and forth furious about Lauren's intentions. My anger had me wishing Lauren could suffer or face some repercussions for her actions. I went as far as thinking of other girls around campus that I could pay to punch her in the face because at that moment that's how I felt! Then my phone rang. My whole entire mood changed within a split second seeing that it was Mrs. Anthony calling me. I answered it as if I were napping so she wouldn't keep me on the phone long. "Hello, Cedric. How are you?" She asked. "I'm fine. Just laying down relaxing. What's going on?" I replied. "I was just thinking about you and something told me to check on you. My spirit didn't feel right. Something was telling me you were hurting or in danger! I know that may sound weird to you, but my intuition made me pick up the phone to call. Are you okay?" She said. I wasn't surprise about the timing of her call. I understood that things did happen for reason and I was convinced her call was needed in the moment. "I honestly don't know. Maybe I'm depressed or just need a break!" I replied. There was silence for a minute or two. "I understand... That's why it's time for you to come home to reset. It's going to be okay. I'm praying for you so don't be discouraged. I will see you soon. I love you." She said. That placed a sense of calmness over me that I needed. Her voice and her words felt the way I needed them to. "You're right. Can't wait to see you. Thank you for everything! I'm so glad you called." I responded as I started to relax more. "Also, there are some things I wanted to tell you. It can wait for now. I'll call you back soon. I must go now. I don't want to be late for our meeting at the church." She replied. Of course, that made me curious as hell. I hated when she would do that. Giving me a vague heads up about an unknown thing to have me walking on eggshells wondering what she had to say. "Okay, that's fine. Talk to you soon. I love you too." I answered. Then I hung up the phone. I had to do some soul searching. I felt I was losing in a race I shouldn't have been running in. I had put way too much effort in some things I shouldn't have given any time towards. My sexual desires had me in the most chaotic situations ever! Going home was all that mattered at that point. So, what if Lauren did it out of spite and so what Samantha was never going to speak to me again, oh well. So be it with trying to be a people pleaser I obviously sucked at. It started to make sense to me where I was failing at. No more wreck less sexual activities for me I declared! No more giving in to anyone who doesn't want to invest in my happiness. No more trying to please any and everyone that's not making the same efforts with me! I repeated that to myself as I anticipated my trip back home.

Maybe an hour into the tug of war between falling asleep and finishing the end part of a good movie, my phone was ringing as rapid knocks were at my door. My phone had Lauren's name coming through. I got up then headed to the door as I knew it was her. I opened the door then walked back to my room after seeing it was indeed Lauren. She shut door and followed me. I was still uneasy, yet I felt nothing towards her. She was looking around as if she was trying to figure out something. We made it to my room after I powered off the TV in the living room then I laid across my bed. I had my phone in my hand scrolling on it to maintain my attention, so I didn't yell out foul language at her. She sat at the edge of the bed with her back facing me. She was quiet which meant she had something on her mind. I had to get it all out right then and there. For the last and final time! "No one's here but me. I'm sure whatever your intention was, they unfortunately worked. As much as I want to hate you for it, I'm too tired mentally to even care anymore. I have been nothing but straight up with you about everything. I can't believe you would betray me like that. The damage has been done. I'm hurt but I'm a big boy." I said as calm as I could without raising my voice like I really wanted to. She turned around to me with a tear in her eye. She looked exhausted and drained as if she had been up for the last twenty-four hours straight. "I honestly don't know what my intentions were. I don't know why I told her all of that. I felt like she wasn't just a friend by the way she looked at you. It was the same way I look at you. Especially after we messed around. There is something about you that I don't think you even know about. You have this warm vibe you give out to people. You make me feel like I'm important and safe. Your respect towards women is unmatched at our age. I was beyond selfish. I know it. I didn't even know her for five minutes and was sharing things with her as if she was my best friend. Just to feel like crap now knowing it hurt someone I want to see happy. I don't expect our friendship to ever be the same. I've crossed too many lines. I hope you can forgive me at some point down the road." She said as she whipped the endless tears falling down her face. Seeing her cry, was confirmation I wasn't going about it wrong.

It also confirmed that she hadn't completely gone rogue. I thought I lost a straight up good friend in her. She was finding her way back to the Lauren I missed and needed. "Can we move towards a better friendship for real this time? No more mind games or sex tricks. I don't want to leave our friendship idle like that. We both have to control our emotions as well as our bodies. Please..." I said as I moved to the end of the bed beside her. She laid her head on my shoulder. After about two minutes of sitting there she suddenly pushed me down on the bed then climbed on top of me! She pinned my arms down then said, "Can we please do it one last time. Please!" Before I could resist or respond, she slowly rolled off me laughing hard at the look I had on my face! "Got ya! I'm sorry but I had to do it! I had to see your face! You looked as if you were in some sick nightmare. I bet you wish you could have pinched yourself in that moment. You're right Cedric, about everything. We are too tight with one another to cause a good friendship to go down the drain. I'm with you about the whole control thing. I promise to get better with that and keep it strictly about our friendship. Nothing more, nothing less than that." She said. Yeah, she really got me on that one. I was about to push her ass on the floor with frustration! I was thinking in that moment, "You got to be shitting me! I know she's not serious?" I was ready to give up for sure on being anything with her. No friends, lovers, or anything! She got me good with that. I started to laugh at myself for that. "Well I'm glad you haven't lost your sense of humor. I was going to call the police on you because that would have meant you were possessed by a sex devil or horny witch ghost or something. I'm relieved that you were joking, seriously. I know we can work it out. I don't doubt it... I'm glad it didn't get any uglier cause I would have had to move to another apartment complex to get away from you!" I replied. We both laughed. We talked for about a half an hour then ordered food. We ate and watched a movie until we were both passed out on my couch. Lauren and I never talked about what we did with each other sexually ever again.

The next week, I was packed up and ready to go! The day had come for me to finally head home for a whole week! I was excited to see Mrs. Anthony, Rachel and some old friends back home. Lauren agreed to take me to the airport with Daniel tagging along for the ride. I didn't tell Rachel I was coming because I wanted to surprise her. I didn't reach out to Samantha either, knowing she probably didn't care anyway. I had plans to just chill with Rachel since she was close to having our baby. I was going to tell Mrs. Anthony about it once I made sure Rachel wasn't lying or making it all up. I needed to see her big belly with my own eyes since she refused to send pictures of herself.

On the way to the airport I gave Daniel the keys to my apartment because I wanted him to keep an eye on the place. Lauren agreed to keep an eye on him as well to make sure he didn't get too wild. Right as we were pulling up to the drop off area, Lauren whispered, "Are you ready to see the little monster you created?" I looked at her confused because I was sure Rachel had at least another month or so before she was having the baby? "I figured that's the reason you're going home right?" She whispered again. There was nothing on my radar that alerted me before about the timing of a pregnancy. That was a conversation I had not had with anyone! Why would I? I wasn't doing anything to have needed that info back then. No one I was around ever had a child, so I was indeed clueless! I thought for sure it took about a year for a baby to be processed in the woman's belly. Then it started to hit me the more I thought about it. I had been gone well over a year, yet Rachel was feeding me information as if she was currently pregnant. Lauren could tell I was spooked and dazed by her statement. She parked then we all got out. Daniel grabbed my backpack and suitcase from the trunk. While he was doing that, Lauren and I walked in front of her car. We hugged then she said, "I didn't want to say anything about it because we were going through our hiccup. I've been itching to ask how it was going with all of that. I'm sure it's going to all work out. Take pictures please!" I nodded my head at her agreeing to her every word with no emotions. She asked, "Are you okay? Cedric... You good?" For a split second I felt dizzy then Daniel appeared with my things. "I'm good! I'm sorry. Thank you thank you! I really appreciate the pep talk and the ride! You two behave while I'm gone. I'll be back before you start missing me!" I replied with a smile as I fought back the fear, I was facing within me. They laughed as we all came in close for a group hug. I headed on through the doors of the terminal I was flying out of. They watched me through the big windows as I stood on an escalator that lead to the check in counters on the next level of the airport. I waved until I couldn't see them anymore. Within a half of an hour I was standing in line boarding my flight. I called Mrs. Anthony one last time to let her know I was on my way and everything went well with my check in. I was tempted to call Rachel to tell her I was coming. Lauren's questions about the baby situation cautioned me not to. I didn't want to be thousands of feet in the air throwing up because I was already feeling a little nausea. With the thoughts of me going home to an already born baby was not what I was prepared for! I placed my phone on airplane mode then started to pray she didn't lie or was playing me about the timing. Last time prayer was a thought it was on my way away from home! Now I'm needing it on my way back! Once we were in the air I fell right to sleep. I needed that break from the madness and uncertainty my thoughts were wrestling with in my head.

The flight was peaceful. I slept most of the way. I made it in one piece back home. I admit I was nervous, given my family's history with planes. Flying with the team was easier than flying alone. It was early evening. I heard the pilot say the temperature was around the high seventies and sunny! Once we were given the green light to turn on our devices, I called Mrs. Anthony to make sure she was there to pick me up. She was waiting for me already at the pickup area right outside of baggage claim. It seemed like it took forever getting off the plane. It's like people were moving in slow motion. I thought the people in the back should have waited for the ones up front to get their stuff and leave first but that wasn't the case. It was probably me and my anxiousness to see Mrs. Anthony. I was excited being back home. I was finally off the plane then headed to get my suitcase. I got my things then met Mrs. Anthony right outside where she parked with her emergency lights on waiting for me. She jumped out the car then gave me the biggest hug! "Well look who's gained a couple of pounds and grown about two more inches! Look at you Cedric! I'm so happy you made it!" She said as we walked to the trunk. I tossed my stuff in there then we got in the car. "So how was your flight?" She asked as she drove off. "It was cool, not as bad as I thought it was going to be. I slept most of the way so." I replied. She laughed a little then said, "Yeah that sounds about right. I remember my first flight. I recall trying to sleep the entire time too!" I smiled then said, "It was the takeoff and landing that spooked me but overall, it wasn't bad." We talked about my grades and things I did since I've been gone. She told me about all the letters that were still coming in from other schools about me transferring or considering other options. She mentioned she had to run by the store for a few things. She wanted to make me a nice home cooked meal. I was not going to complain about stopping at all for that! "I've been going to this new location that opened up recently. You should come in with me to check it out! There's that pretty, young lady you were friends with that runs the place. She's always polite to me and well mannered. I was wondering what happened between you two. Anyways, they have all your old favorite snacks you like. Come in and pick some out." She said as we pulled into the parking lot of the new store. I didn't know how to say I didn't want to go in with her! It was indeed the store Samantha took over she told me about during her visit. I did not want to see Samantha that soon after being back home for only thirty minutes. I wanted to chill for a day or two, low key and out the way before anyone noticed I was back in town. I immediately started to sweat rapidly as the moisture build up on top of my nose and forehead. Mrs. Anthony parked then started checking her purse to make sure she had what she needed as she mumbled to herself. I tried scanning the store front then staring through the large windows to see if I could make out whether Samantha was in there! I was starting to panic but I could not show any discomfort to alarm Mrs. Anthony. "I will check it out later or maybe tomorrow. I'm not feeling my best now. Maybe that flight did something to me because I started to feel a little woozy just a minute ago. I'll pass this time if that's okay?" I finally replied. That was my only answer I could come up with. She smiled then replied, "I understand. That's fine. Is there anything I can get out of here for you?" I thought about it for a second then said, "Well if you don't mind grabbing me some of those strawberry shortcake cookies I like and some of those cheesy chips you always get me. I couldn't find neither of them in Chicago! Thanks." She nodded her head then headed into the store. I let the car seat back some so no one would walk by and see me. Mrs. Anthony car was a familiar car so it wouldn't be hard for someone to know it was me in the passenger seat. I was low enough to still see the store front but would lay lower as people were walking by. I didn't notice anyone I knew although the area we were in wasn't too far from our neighborhood where the original store was. At least twenty minutes had pass then I spotted Mrs. Anthony being escorted to the door by someone I didn't plan on seeing anytime soon! It was Rico! He had on a tee shirt with the store's name on it! I was confused! Mrs. Anthony and he were chatting and smiling together as he held the door for her as she exited. She walked towards the car as I let my seat back up. As she was approaching the car, she locked eyes with me, and she could tell I was baffled. She tried glancing back at the store but her facial expression alerted me that I wasn't supposed to see him. Like I wasn't supposed to know he was working there or any of that. I was even more dumbfounded because Samantha failed to mention it to me as well. I tried to play it off as I fixed my face when Mrs. Anthony got back in the car after she placed the bags in the back seat. "I can't wait to get home and dig into those chips! I miss having them. Thanks again for getting me some." I said as I was trying to ease the load of the for sure nervousness Mrs. Anthony had. "Yes. Yes! Oh… No problem at all Cedric. You are more than welcome." She replied as she started the car then drove on to the house. She gripped the steering wheel tighter as she was trying not to seem uncomfortable. Not a lot of talking was going on. I turned the radio up a little so I wouldn't hear her heart beating. I was waiting patiently for her to say something, but she didn't. I knew the time wasn't right or she wasn't sure how I was going to respond. I acted as if nothing was wrong and I didn't see a thing. We finally arrived at home. I grabbed all the bags, my suitcase, backpack and the groceries. I declined help from her as we walked on the porch with me looking like I was competing in a world's strongest man competition. She opened the door then turned on the lights. The night was approaching with the sun setting. It looked as if she hadn't touched or moved anything, since I left. Everything was exactly the way it was when I left. I dropped my things off over by the stairs then went to the kitchen to put the grocery bags on the table. I pulled the chips out quickly as my mouth watered anticipating the taste of them. As I was crunching on every chip enjoying every bite, Mrs. Anthony walked in. She saw me hypnotized by the delicious taste of the cheesy goodness.

She laughed then said, "Couldn't wait to open them up huh? Welcome home Cedric. I'm going to start on dinner soon. Take your things up to your room. It'll be about an hour before food is ready. I prefer you stay in tonight if you're okay with that before you get busy making your rounds around town." I smiled and replied, "I don't plan on making too many moves while I'm here. I may get out tomorrow briefly but nothing that's going to keep me out too long like that. I'll be upstairs until you're finished. Do you need me to help with anything?" She shook her head as she replied, "No thank you. You can relax for now. I have it all under control down here." I went on upstairs with my things and chips. I glanced over at David's old room before I walked in mines. Just like the rest of the house, everything was still unchanged. I put my bags against the wall by the closet then stepped over to the window. I opened the blinds and stared out remembering the many times I've done it. The sun had set. A chill breeze was stirring up that crept in after I cracked the window open. I sat on the bed then called Lauren to let her and Daniel know I made it. They were both at Lauren's place watching a basketball game on TV. They both yelled through the phone they were glad I made it. Lauren had me on speaker phone which made it easier chatting with them both. We talked for about forty-five minutes then I heard Mrs. Anthony call me down to the kitchen. I wrapped up the conversation with them then headed downstairs with an anxious appetite for one of her amazing meals. I wasn't prepared nor did I have any understanding on why Rico was sitting at the table when I walked in the kitchen! I slowed down as I looked right through him wondering how and why this was happening! Mrs. Anthony immediately walked towards me after setting the last plate on the table. She had made dinner for three without warning me of our special guest! I felt betrayed! My stomach turned upside down and I wanted to turn around to head back to my room. Rico stood up as he could feel the discomfort, I had all over me.

"Maybe I shouldn't be here." Rico said. "No, it's okay. Sit down please." Mrs. Anthony whispered to him. I was just standing there numb to the idea that Mrs. Anthony was perfectly fine with his presence. Not that seeing him was hard but the fact that he was sitting in our kitchen! I wanted to ask Mrs. Anthony what kind of drugs she was on to allow that! I would have never disrespected her like that, but she had some convincing to do. "Cedric, I'm sorry to push this on you this way. I wanted to tell you over the phone. I didn't want you stressing over it. I didn't want you to worry yourself about me with my decisions. I know this comes to you as a sudden surprise, but I want you to accept Rico. Maybe, even as a friend?" She pleaded with me. As a what? I thought to myself! Like she was under some spell or witchcraft experiment to ask me such a thing. I couldn't believe my ears. I pinched myself at least ten times! He sat there barely able to look my way. I was supposed to look over the fact that David could have been the one at the table instead of him but can't because of him! I know he was set up and fed lies as I was too. I know he was acting in self-defense and I know it wasn't all his fault. I wasn't ready! I didn't want it to happen like that! I wanted it to be on my own terms. Not some kind of intervention forced choice I felt pressured to make. This wasn't fair to me. What about how I felt, what about my feelings? "Cedric, I'm sorry man. This is just as tough for me to do. Man... To be here, looking at you. I didn't want to offend you, but Mrs. Anthony insisted. I have regretted what happened every single day! Please forgive me." Rico said as he whipped his face as if he was holding back tears. This was not the Rico I was used to. This wasn't the big, bad, ruthless Rico that I remembered. This wasn't the Rico I remembered that day he stabbed my best friend repeatedly. This was some other guy. The guy that was sitting at that table was someone I had never met before. He was someone I would look at and feel sorry for. I was on guard because of the history of lies I've been told by people during desperate times yet somehow this guy I was staring at seemed hurt. I started to feel the guilt slipping in as they both looked at me, patiently waiting for me to say something. I had to search hard for the words I needed to say. I had to be honest with me and with the reality of what was to come. I was better than that to continue that hateful heart response. Something that Mrs. Anthony preached to me repeatedly. Even my real parents would have wanted me to forgive him. Finally, I said, "This is not what I expected when I came home. I wasn't sure what I was going to do or say to you whenever we crossed paths. I would be selfish not to forgive you, seeing that Mrs. Anthony has. I know her pain is deeper and more complicated than either of ours. I've never taken someone's life yet alone the thought of living with that fact the rest of my life if I had. There are things you both are feeling and have felt that I hope I never have to. I know this isn't going to be perfect, but I promise Mrs. Anthony I'm going to try. I'm going to try to move forward. I'm going to try to understand all of this. I'm going to try not to be stubborn or revengeful. I hope you are true on what you said and that you are not playing some sick twisted game with Mrs. Anthony's emotions nor mines. If you're sincere and honest, then I can forgive you." Rico stood back up as I approached him. We shook hands. I made sure I looked him straight in the eyes as I gripped his hand tightly then said, "Please don't disappoint her. I can handle it." We unlocked hands as he replied with, "Man I promise I'm being as honest as I've ever been! After all she's been through... You can mark my words. I can't afford anymore hurt, definitely not by me!" I nodded my head to acknowledge his words. "I'm not asking you two to become best friends. I just don't want you all to hate one another. It's a blessing to forgive and let go. It's not easy but it's the only way anyone can move forward. I pray you two never forget that. Now have a seat so we can eat! I'm starving!" Mrs. Anthony said as she placed hot butter rolls on the table next to the steaming hot Mac and

cheese! There was crispy fried chicken with green beans and
sweet potato casserole too! The smell alone was mesmerizing
which made it easy enough to distract us from the awkwardness
of being around each other. Mrs. Anthony loaded our plates
then prayed over us and blessed the food. She was right. I knew
better. From my parents teaching me things of that nature to
living with her. Everyone that played a major role in my life had
told me about forgiveness. Easier said than done and this was
one of the hardest ones. We sat quietly as the sound of lips
smacking and slurps of lemonade took over for about ten
minutes straight! The food was so good, Rico and I were licking
our fingers and hands. I missed meals like that! It was much
needed and satisfying with every bite. Rico and I were finishing
our first plate when Mrs. Anthony started to reveal how Rico
and she became peaceful people between themselves. "After
about a month of you leaving Cedric, I ran into Rico walking
down the street. I know we both were hesitant when I pulled up
on him. After all the time that had passed, after the brief
conversation we had over the phone, I knew I needed to do
something to help us both. I asked Rico if he wanted to talk and
to my surprise he wanted to just as much I needed to. He got in
the car and went to that burger place you like. It's always easy
to talk, understand, etc. when you have something on your
stomach. We talked for about four hours. I had to hear it all
from him, his side of the story. I needed to know how he felt
then verses now. I needed to acknowledge my frustration I had
with him. I wanted to voice my sadness and pain to him. I
wanted to hear how it changed his life as well. I'm so glad we
were able to put it all on the table. We both agreed to keep in
touch and I'm happy we did. After that happened, Rico has been
stopping by helping with things around the house. Then about
three months back, Herman came by out the blue!" Herman
was David's brother. The one that she kicked out years before
due to drug issues and stealing from them. I cut her off and said,

"Wait what! What happened? Did he do anything crazy?" Rico answered, "Well it was a good thing I was here that day! He tried to break in when it was early evening. I was fixing the kitchen sink because of a leak then I heard noise coming from the kitchen door. Mrs. Anthony was in the living room cleaning, so I knew it wasn't her. By the time I walked over to check it out, he was halfway through the door! I fought with him a little while Mrs. Anthony called the police! I was able to hold him down until the cops came." I was angry and concerned all mixed up! I was supposed to act like I didn't care about the new friendship Rico and Mrs. Anthony had had for some time with me just then founding it all out. Then on top of that, she was in danger with me nowhere in sight to protect her! I hated it all! I had to swallow my pride to not blame her for leaving me out the loop! I had to act like I was not upset nor mad as hell with the info that was forced on me! Again, I was thinking to myself how I missed all of that. "Wow! I'm so sorry you had to go through that! I hate you both had to. So, where he is now?" I said. "Well he's probably going to be gone a long time for sure." Rico replied. While wiping her eyes, Mrs. Anthony could barely say, "He finally fled back home because he's been on the run from the police. He committed numerous crimes from identity theft, armed robbery, arson to selling drugs! He's a person of interest in murders that happened in Texas and Utah." She had tears flowing down her face. I was about to jump up to go get her some tissues, but Rico beat me to it. As he gave her the napkins, he stood beside her rubbing her shoulder. All I could do was sit there and wonder what had happened! What was happening? I asked myself. My head started pounding. My heart was racing! This was too much to bear. I didn't want to hear anymore! I was seeing a picture I wouldn't have never painted with Mrs. Anthony and Rico acting as if they were mother and son. He was comforting her! Something I have done many times. The back and forth between my ability to look over it and being jealous didn't sit well. I had to go! I needed to remove myself from that strange setting. "I think I ate too much and honestly, this has been a very eventful homecoming. If it doesn't make things weird, I would like to excuse myself to my room. Please..." I said. "I'm sorry Cedric. I hope things do get better between us. I promise you I've changed! I'll show you." Rico replied. "Yeah you're right Cedric. I know this is a lot to take in. You're okay to leave. Thank you." Mrs. Anthony replied. "I hope you feel better." I whispered to her as I gave her a hug before leaving the kitchen. "I'll help her clean up down her Cedric. Maybe I'll see you around while you're here." Rico said as he started to clear the plates off the table. I didn't care what he did or what was to come while I was back. I didn't care about anything but my bed. I dragged myself upstairs then slammed myself on the bed in my room. I kicked my shoes off as I laid there on my stomach with my face buried in the pillow. I screamed as loud as I could into the pillow not caring if anyone would hear me. I was stomped! I wanted to go to sleep so that was over with! I tried and tried as I rolled over staring at the clock. Minutes rolled by then an hour as I could hear the door shut which indicated Rico had left. Still I laid there dying to fall asleep, yet the clock stared back at me as the numbers went from minutes to hours. It was close to midnight when my phone scared the hell out of me as it rang loud! I hurried to answer it not wanting to wake Mrs. Anthony! It was Rachel. I was exhausted but curious of what sparked the late-night call from her. In the back of my mind I had a load of questions that needed answers. I was in no mood to hit her with my personal survey I had for her about the truth on her pregnancy. I held the phone after saying hello. "Sorry if I woke you. I couldn't sleep. I was thinking of you. I miss you Cedric. I wish you were here." She whispered. I rolled over on my side as I held the phone while watching the night clouds float by through the window. There wasn't much intimacy with any of our previous conversations. Hearing her say she missed me was different. We talked as if we were best friends, not lovers during those times. I was trying to figure out how to reply with comfort yet not lead her on. I wasn't sure how it was going to turn out between us. Rachel was the most innocent of all the girls except the fact she cooperated with Charlene long enough to have David basically killed. She was an accomplice in my eyes if there was one thing I had to look over, that was the hardest. Other than that, she had it all as far as what I seen in her. She was gorgeous, intelligent, fun and never came off as someone with a deceitful personality. She did confess her role which she could have taken to the grave with her. I started to reevaluate the possibilities of Rachel being someone I could really be with. "I miss you too Rachel. I'm sorry you can't sleep. I'm struggling myself. Mr. Sandman isn't on our side. Can you call him to make his rounds to us?" I replied as we both laughed together. "Yes, I tried to get through, but his line has been busy for hours. Maybe you should try." She said as she giggled again. I ignored my suspicion about the baby to enjoy the moment of laughter with her. I started imagining myself with Rachel the longer we talked that night. We went into topics of sex, love, goals and day to day challenges. We were speaking more on personal levels than we have ever before. I didn't hold anything in except the fact I slept with Charlene. That was something else I was still avoiding I knew was going to need my attention. Rachel revealed that I was her first and only sexual experience passed the kissing part. It was something we never talked about, but I wasn't surprised. She didn't have but one or two guys she dated earlier in high school that neither lasted long enough to be something special she said. I remember the rumors that spread about her being stuck up because she wouldn't give too many guys a chance. She was approachable yet quiet back then. We talked for about four hours until we were both snoring off and on. The sun was peeping through the window by then and my eye lids felt like cement was layered on them. I couldn't keep them up longer than a minute. I had learned so much about Rachel I had no clue about. I felt she collected more info about me as well. It was about five in the morning when I glanced at the clock after hanging up with Rachel. It was still dark through the house when I crept to the restroom. I held my pee for the last two hours and needed to relieve myself. I slowly walked back to my room making sure I wasn't making a sound. No way I wanted to wake Mrs. Anthony this early for her to want to talk or crank up her music as she usually does when cleaning. I was beyond tired! I laid back down, and within seconds I was out like a beaten fighter that was punched by a heavy weight boxer!

Felt like the usual Saturday afternoon I missed. The sun dancing on my face as it came through the blinds of my room. The music up loud jamming from downstairs with the aroma of cleaning products and food! I was stiff from sleeping hard on the left side of my entire body. I forgot how much I used to have to switch sides through the night to avoid the pain and aches due to the mattress being on its last cushion. I was going to mention it to Mrs. Anthony back then, but I was so use to it that it didn't matter. I was feeling it with each step I made towards the restroom. I needed a hot shower to help wake me up, plus I needed to refresh my armpits. I noticed I was smelling a little tart from forgetting to put on deodorant from the previous day. Was in such a rush getting my things and to the airport that I missed that opportunity. I was surprised no one smelled my lingering musk. I laughed to myself just thinking about it while I was in the shower. I kept replaying the surprise party that Rico and Mrs. Anthony had for me that almost made me hop on a jet to zoomed back to Chicago without looking back! I was still fighting with my emotions about. I promised Mrs. Anthony I would try but I was already ready to give up! I wanted to call Melvin to let him know I needed him to take care of the issue, given he had said he would. That also crossed my mind too. I wondered if anyone else knew Rico and Mrs. Anthony was besties all of a sudden. I was sure that most people were feeling the same as I was about it. How can you be so comfortable with someone that caused so much pain? I needed to clear my head, so I decided to call Rachel with the news I was in town. I couldn't go any longer with that situation weighing on my brain either. Once I was done, I put on some shorts and a shirt then slipped on my flip flops. Before I could pick up my phone to call Rachel, Mrs. Antony called for me. I walked on down the stairs to see her with Mr. Clayton sitting in the living room! I had to do a double take! Another unexpected guest! I slowed down my pace as I moved closer to the bottom steps. "Hey Cedric!" Mr. Clayton yelled at me as he stood up. Mrs. Anthony stayed seated with an innocent smile on her face. She was throwing everything at me on my first days back! As if I wasn't under enough pressure already. At least I knew Mr. Clayton wasn't judge mental nor would he lecture me about too much. If I was going to reveal my big secret to Mrs. Anthony, I figured I could do it while he was there. I don't know why I felt edgy enough to do it then. I felt it was now or never! I wasn't prepared for any questions they were sure to ask. I just wanted it to be out in the open, so Mrs. Anthony didn't hear it first from anyone else. I owed that to her. I walked over to Mr. Clayton then embraced him with a handshake and half arm hug. "You're looking good Cedric! I see you have been pumping that good old iron up there in Chicago. I heard about your hunt for a college World Series title. I'm sure you all will get it this coming season!" Mr. Clayton said as we unlocked our hands then he sat down. I stood up to see if that was the only thing I was needed for before I walked back upstairs. I was beyond nervous and was going to abort my mission to confess my baby situation! "Yeah it was tough losing but you're right. No pain no gain. I'm looking forward to getting back out there!" I replied as I continued standing there. "Cedric, have a seat please. I invited Mr. Clayton over so he could see you and catch up. We've been praying for you and your direction. I wanted him to speak to you about forgiveness. I asked if he could add to what I was trying to get you to see last night on Rico's presence around here." Mrs. Anthony stated as she patted the open area on the couch next to her. I didn't say anything as I walked over then sat down. "Yeah Cedric, I'm only going to be brief. I have a busy day ahead of me but wanted to make sure I stopped here to see you. I know how much Mrs. Anthony loves you. She just wants the best for you." He said. I nodded my head as I then listened to him talk about why forgiving people is important. He told a few stories of his past and how hard it was to move forward with his life due to certain grudges he had with people that did him wrong. He went into the details on what happened and how it all effected his day to day life. After years of blaming others for him failing in life, he finally let go of the hurt. He reflected on how refreshed he felt and how his life instantly started to get better. He explained how he continues to work on that area of his life. He said it was even harder for him when he became a pastor. He felt like people would intentionally do things to challenge his faith. He made it his daily goal to pray for the same kind of forgiving heart he believed God had with him. After he finished about that, he added that he wanted me to try to forgive as he did. He understood the level of pain it caused then having to see these people regularly seemed as if he was being taunted. He wanted to pray with me. Mrs. Anthony and him both moved in closer to me as they laid theirs hands on my shoulders while he said a quick prayer for me. I wasn't sure on what to say after that, yet it did make a lot of sense to me. I sat there as they both stared at me while I let his words marinate in my mind. I wasn't going to win that battle of hate towards Rico. Mrs. Anthony wanted peace between us all for her to go through this much to get me to understand it. "Thank you, Mr. Clayton for the advice. I agree with everything you said. It does help knowing that it's something we all must deal with. It's something everyone goes through in life. Holding a grudge is like holding pain inside. It shouldn't be that way as much as you feel you have the right to hate that person. Nothing good will come from it. I get it. I'll be fine. Time will help I know." I finally said as they slowly moved away back in their seats. "Well I just wanted you to hear it from someone else Cedric. I only have you here for a week. I know this is a lot to deal with without any warning. If I can do it, I know you can too." Mrs. Anthony whispered as she smiled with hope in her eyes. She wanted that and I would have been a fool not to give it to her. "Well let me get on my way. It's always a pleasure to see you all. Is there anything you need from me Cedric?" Mr. Clayton said as he stood up. Mrs. Anthony and I followed his gesture. I immediately felt my knee slightly buckle as my time was expiring to announce my shocking details. He walked over and hugged Mrs. Anthony then shook my hand. As he was pulling a loose from my hand, I held his hand tighter. He looked at me with curiosity. Mrs. Anthony noticed it as well then said, "Everything okay Cedric?" The pours on my forehead opened as the moisture started to seep in. "Well I have some not so good news." I whispered as my voice cracked a little. That innocent smile Mrs. Anthony was wearing immediately turned into a worried mother's frown. As I dropped my hand from Mr. Clayton, I fell back on to the couch. I looked up at them both then said, "I'm going to be a father." No one moved nor was there a sound in the entire house. It felt as if the whole world paused in that moment to comprehend what I had said. A tear formed at the core of one of my eyes. Mrs. Anthony slowly sat back down as if she was hit with a furious blow to the head. She looked stressed as well as shocked out of her mind. Mr. Clayton sat back down too. "Oh no Cedric. Really? When? How? Where?" Mrs. Anthony asked as if she was rambling and mumbling all at once. She was shaking and reached for a few tissues that were on the coffee table. She started patting her eyes as if she was trying not to cry. "It's okay. Everything is going to be okay." Mr. Clayton calmly said. I wasn't sure I was supposed to answer all the questions she asked then or if they were rhetorical. I could see the letdown Mrs. Anthony was feeling as it was hard for her to look at me. Mr. Clayton had to walk over to calm her down as she tried to control her emotions. I started thinking to myself on how they were just trying to get me to forgive. Surely, they were able to see this one through. I didn't say anything as I waited for Mrs. Anthony to gather herself. "Cedric... My oh my. You're having a baby? I'm sorry. I don't mean to be this way. I wasn't expecting this from you." She whispered as she continued to wipe her eyes while Mr. Clayton held her hand for comfort. She started to make eye contact with me then added, "It's okay. We're going to get through this. I know this is going to be hard but it's going to work out." I could tell she was gaining more control as she started to think about it more. "I'm sorry. I didn't know how or when to tell you. I didn't want another day to go by without sharing it with you. Since Mr. Clayton was here, I thought this was the best time. I've been holding that in for a long time. It happened before I left for college." Both Mrs. Anthony and Mr. Clayton looked stunned. "What do you mean? It happened before you left for school?" Mrs. Anthony asked. "Yeah I messed around with Rachel. The young lady that had come by a few times last summer. That use to be with Charlene all the time. You remember her?" I replied. Mr. Clayton started scratching his head in disbelieve. Mrs. Anthony finally asked, "Where's the baby? Surely she's had that baby by now?" My heart skipped a beat and I was hoping she wasn't implying the same fate Lauren spoke of. "I've been keeping in touch with her. I was under the impression that the baby wasn't born yet. She never confirmed the baby's arrival date. I wasn't sure how honest she's been with me after a friend said the same thing you're saying now." I said as I rubbed the back of my head with confusion. "Don't work yourself up about it. That is big news that comes with even bigger responsibilities. I hope that young lady isn't playing a horrible joke on you." Mr. Clayton whispered. He looked like he understood the situation I was in quite well. Mrs. Anthony on the other hand looked like she had eaten something that did not sit well in her stomach. She was not comfortable at all. She was trying her best to stay calm as a few tears rolled down her face. She continued to look at me as if her world was falling apart. It was like the look she had when she heard the tragic news about David! I thought I'll never see that look on her face again. "I'm sorry... I'm sorry. I'm so sorry! I was trying hard not to do anything that would cause you to feel hurt or disappointment. It's all my fault! I apologize for letting you all down. I don't know what to do." I cried out as I fell to my knees. Seeing Mrs. Anthony as she was struggling to keep herself together because of my decision hit me harder than I expected. It wasn't fair that she had put in so much time trying to keep me focused. She took some more tissues then handed them to me. I wiped my eyes as Mr. Clayton pulled me back up by my arm. "This is not the time for weeping eyes son. This is another part of life that we all must face day to day, week to week and so on. Dealing with the results of our everyday decisions can either make you or break you. You are blessed with people that care. There's no need to break down now. Stand to your feet and hold your head up. You will get through this. You have to believe it!" He said as I stood back up looking at the fearless look, he had written all over his face. I felt his every word. It cut deep within without any doubts. He was speaking facts. He tapped into a mindset I hadn't explored myself. It was giving me the confidence I needed. Mrs. Anthony added, "I am disappointed but I'm not mad at you Cedric. If everyone and everything was perfect, we would never learn some of life's most important lessons. What you're facing is one of life's greatest challenges. It's ultimately up to you to decide what are you going to do about it. Living and learning is a blessing that seem like curses at times. Certain decisions are nonreversible that will make you dig deeper than ever to find the courage to go on. I will never stop teaching you nor ever stop loving you. You don't have to do this alone. We will get through this together." My heart rate slowed back down to its normal rate. The tears stopped falling. I felt lighter as so much of the weight had been lifted off me in her caring words. "This means more than you all know to me. I needed this support and love. I felt like I've been in a bad nightmare for a long time. I can't see myself dealing with this alone. Thank you." I said to them both. "I will continue to pray for you two as well as the truth being revealed about the baby. No need to fear what God has his hands in. Blessings and strength are the way. I must leave now to keep my other appointments I have for the day. Feel free to call me Mrs. Anthony if you all need me. I will keep this information between us until further notice from you two." Pastor Clayton said as he rubbed Mrs. Anthony on the shoulder then shook my hand again. We all walked together to the door. Mrs. Anthony opened the door as Pastor Clayton walked out. "Thank you for coming by. I will keep you updated with how things are going. Thanks for understanding we need time to figure this out before anyone else finds out." She said. I stood in the doorway with her then added, "Yeah I do appreciate your time. Thanks for stopping by to check on me. I need all the prayers I can get!" We all laughed a little as Pastor Clayton walked to his car then drove off. Mrs. Anthony hugged me as tight as she could after she shut the door. We both needed that. She wanted me to call Rachel immediately to get to the bottom of whether the baby was here already, and if she was lying the whole time! I ran upstairs to get my phone then I met Mrs. Anthony in the kitchen. She told me to call while the phone was on the speaker phone so she could hear exactly what was being said from Rachel's end. I was sweating as Mrs. Anthony was biting her nails. Something I haven't seen her do for a long time. That indicated she was just as nervous as I was. The phone rang slowly for about five rings. My heart was back racing that felt like it was about to erupt through my chest. "Hello..." Rachel's voice softly came through the phone as I was just about to hang up. I hesitated for a moment then Mrs. Anthony nodded her head to me for me to say something. "Hi... How are you?" I replied with my voice sounding choppy. "I'm okay... You don't sound to good yourself? What's going on?" She asked. Again Mrs. Anthony nodded her head as if she wanted me to get right to the main reason I called. "Yeah I'm trying to understand everything. I know we've been talking about the baby and all. I called to ask you something and I'm hoping you will be completely honest with me. This is hard for us both which I'm aware of, yet I can't seem to put it all together." I calmly said. "Yes... I had the baby already Cedric!" She yelled out as if she couldn't hold it in any longer! Mrs. Anthony shook her head in disbelief as if she was upset. "Why would she not tell you that?" Mrs. Anthony whispered to me. "Wait what? Are you serious?" I asked as I tried to keep my voice from cracking with sadness. There was silence from Rachel's end of the phone followed by sounds of her sniffing and sobbing. Mrs. Anthony grabbed the phone from me then said, "Rachel... Sweety... It's okay. I'm here with Cedric right now. He told me about the news, and we wanted to know the truth." I sat back in the chair waiting for Rachel to reply. "I know this is tough on you right now. I understand. Please let us know what's going on with you and the baby. You are not alone. Cedric and I can come by right now if you're home." Mrs. Anthony added. She was quiet long enough for us to hear soft crying in the background. "Hold on please." Rachel whispered. She must have sat the phone down upright as we could her hear speaking cheerfully to a little one trying to calm them in the background. There was indeed a baby over there with her! I don't know how she managed to keep the baby quiet during all the talks we had. She returned to the phone then said, "Yes I'm here with Mr. Cedric Mason Jr. He's just a little fussy but we're doing fine. I'm sorry Cedric for not being completely honest with you about it all. I didn't want to mess up what you had going on with your baseball hopes and dreams. My family has been incredibly supportive through this. They're the only ones that knows you're the father." She said. My eyes lit up as my ears were tuned in to the sounds of my son! I felt an instant mental push to want to get up immediately to get to them! I heard my real parents telling me, "You will do whatever it takes to be a great father to that child. You were raised well. It's your turn to take care of someone who needs you." All doubts left from my thoughts. I knew my parents as well as Mrs. Anthony wasn't going to let me walk away. I could never ignore my responsibilities under Mrs. Anthony watch, then or ever. If my parents were indeed still there, they would have been excited to have their first grandchild regardless of the circumstances. "Aww I can hear him. I can't wait to meet him! We are on our way!" Mrs. Anthony said as she had the biggest smile on her face. She too was hypnotized by the innocent baby melody he was putting out through the phone. "Yeah I can't wait to see Junior too! Wow. This is unbelievable... I mean. You know. It's believable but ummm. Yeah. Well anyway. Y'all know what I mean!" I said as they both laughed at me for my rambling of words. "I know what you mean Cedric. It is crazy. Again, I sincerely apologize. You know where I'm at if y'all want to come by." Rachel said as she sounded more at peace with me knowing the truth finally. Mrs. Anthony nodded her head at me as she raised her eyebrows for me to say we were on our way. "You don't have to keep saying you're sorry. It's okay Rachel. We will be over in about a half an hour. See you two soon." I replied. "Yeah it's no need to feel any more pressure or blame for anything. Things are going to be okay for sure." Mrs. Anthony said then I hung up the phone. I wiped the sweat off my forehead as I shook my head in amusement on how well that conversation went. Mrs. Anthony wasted no time jumping up heading to her room to get dressed. "I'm going to freshen up. Don't have me waiting on you Cedric. Get to moving! Let's go see our precious little man!" She said as she hurried through the hallway to her room. She sounded as if she had been waiting for something like that for a while. It was odd from the sense of me thinking she was going to yell at me or even break down. She was overjoyed about it all. She was more enthused than I was. I finally got up then my knees buckled a little due to the nervousness that was controlling my entire body! Felt I had to force my legs to walk up the stairs to change my clothes. The bright side of having Mrs. Anthony in good spirit eased me enough to tell myself I could do it.

It barely took Mrs. Anthony fifteen minutes to get ready! She yelled for me to come on downstairs! I slipped on some jeans and a clean shirt to make sure I looked presentable since I was not only meeting my son for the first time, but Rachel's family as well. I rushed to the bathroom to brush my teeth then threw some cold water on face to double check that I wasn't dreaming! I dried my face then picked up my shoes as I had to juggle myself putting them on while heading down the stairs. I looked like I was performing a side show stunt trying to put my shoes on each foot while hoping down the steps. I didn't want to give Mrs. Anthony any reason to have to ask me to come down once more which would have led to her growing more impatient. I wanted to keep her in the best mood possible. There was no way I was going to allow her positive energy to leave when she had enough for the both of us! "Now don't kill yourself before we get there Cedric. I'm ready but not that much in a hurry to have you doing that. Take your time to make sure you have your shoes on good. I'll be in the car. Please lock the door behind you." Mrs. Anthony said nearly laughing at me as she walked out the front door. I sat at the bottom step shaking my head at myself thinking about how crazy I was acting. She was right so I caught my breathe while slipping on my other shoe. I was tripping and overthinking everything. I was starting to sweat again. I hurried in the kitchen to grab a few paper towels. I made sure all the lights were off then walked out the house. I locked the door then on to the car.

As I walking to the car an all-white SUV slowly crept down the street then stopped right next to Mrs. Anthony's car. This wasn't your ordinary SUV. Something a president or celebrity would be rolling in. It was spotless with all white rims that were trimmed in gold! I paused as I was reaching for the door handle to get in with Mrs. Anthony. I stared at the driver's side window but couldn't see anyone due to the heavy dark tint on the windows. The window slowly came down and my eyes lit up light a firework show! "Well well, look who's in town! Our local superstar, Mr. Baseball himself. My guy Cedric! I did not plan on seeing you on this fine afternoon." Melvin said as he had his usual evil grin on his face. I could only imagine the look on Mrs. Anthony's face as I stood there motionless. Melvin waved at Mrs. Anthony as he glanced at her waiting for me to say something. She didn't say or do anything to his liking by the way he frown at her. "Yeah man, just back home for some fresh air. Trying to stay out the way. Good to see you Melvin. I have to go now." I said, hoping he understood that it wasn't a good look nor the time for me to be caught having a conversation with him. "Oh okay, I see. Well don't leave without saying bye. I have something I need to talk to you about anyways. Glad to see you back home superstar." Melvin replied then rolled his window back up staring at Mrs. Anthony as if he knew she didn't want me to have anything to do with him. Melvin then peeled off with his music blasting. I immediately got in the car shaking my head as if I had never seen Melvin in my life. Before I could defend myself or come up with a believable explanation,

Mrs. Anthony said, "As if you don't already have your hands full. That's the last person on earth you need to be talking to, seeing yet alone around. I don't have to say it twenty times for you to know how I feel about Melvin and the evil that he does around here. I need you stay as far away as you can from him while you're here Cedric. Let that be the last time I tell you that! Okay?" I nodded my head at her agreeing with her demands. She was right but I knew I was going to have to see him. I wasn't worry because he took care of me before leaving. I was just hoping I wasn't going to regret spending all that money he promised there were no strings attached to. "Good... Now let's go see our little prince charming." She said as she refocused on where we were going. As the music played during our ride over to Rachel's, I found myself replaying good times I had with my dad. I knew how I felt knowing my dad was there with me, working and providing, teaching and directing me, loving as well as disciplining me, gave me the confidence I was seeking. Mrs. Anthony didn't say much as she hummed the tunes of the songs playing as I gave directions. There were a few cars outside when we were pulling up to Rachel's home. I didn't recall seeing that many cars in front of her place on a regular the one or two times I came by. I was starting to feel the nerves acting up as the sweat resurfaced. Mrs. Anthony looked over at me then said, "We are going to do this together. You are my son and I love you no matter what. Don't be afraid or worry yourself. You can do this." She rubbed my shoulder then got out of the car. I took a deep breath then followed her. As we walked towards the house, I could see the curtains were opened as figures moved through the house. My heart began to race a bit as we made it passed the white fence surrounding the front yard. The door slowly opened as we approached the steps to the porch. Rachel stepped out with a curly haired cutie. Rachel was wearing a light-yellow dress that matched the navy blue and yellow short set our handsome son was wearing. Mrs. Anthony instantly started tearing up as she held my hand to step up on to the porch to meet them. I admit a tear appeared briefly in one of my eyes when I saw my handsome baby boy! It was love at first sight. A lady came out of the house to join us. "Don't be shy daddy, I won't bite you." Rachel whispered as if she was speaking for our baby. I couldn't do anything but smile. She moved in closer to me as she then raised him upward towards me to place him in my arms. I was beyond scared out my mind! The tiny guy looked at me as if he knew exactly who I was. Mrs. Anthony helped position my arms and hands to hold the precious cargo up right. I only held him for about two minutes as I feared he was uncomfortable due to him moving about in my arms. For a second, I thought he was about to jump out of my arms! Mrs. Anthony then took him from me gently to calm him. She was in tears, smiling and talking in baby language I didn't recall learning from anyone. "Hi Cedric. Hearing you were home was nerve wrecking, but I haven't been this happy in a while. This is so priceless to me. Thank you for coming." Rachel whispered why everyone else was focused on the baby and Mrs. Anthony laughing together. Junior was giggling like Mrs. Anthony was telling him all the funny baby jokes. "All of this is crazy yet amazing. I wouldn't have guessed this in a million years to happen or unfold the way it has. I'm happy to be here." I replied to Rachel. "Oh yeah this is my mom." Rachel said as she turned then pointed to the unfamiliar lady standing slightly behind her. Rachel stepped to the side as her mom walked up then hugged me. "Nice to finally meet you Mr. Cedric Mason. Wish it was on other terms but I'm not going to act like things don't happen this way. I fought with her through the years about this very thing happening sooner than any of us wanted it to. I love her and I'm going to support her no matter what. From what I've heard about you, you're not a bad guy. Let's keep it that way." Rachel's mom said as she stepped back and smiled at me shaking her head. I still thought I was dreaming after she said that. One of the hardest things I was facing in life was turning out to be one of the easiest things ever. "Thank you for accepting our mistake and not punching me in the face. I know this is life changing for all of us. I'm going to do my best to be here for my son. I owe Rachel nothing but respect and support. I hope I make us all proud." I replied to Rachel's mom. They all smiled and even giggled at the punching me in the face part. "Y'all have no doubts I'm going to ensure he stands by his words and his duties as a father. It takes a village to raise a child and this village looks committed from my perspective. I don't ever want to put you down, cutie." Mrs. Anthony added then rocked Junior in her arms slowly. "I agree with that. We all can make this an opportunity to grow together. I know what you mean. I held him for hours this morning knowing he's going to be spoiled rotten." Rachel's mom said. There was no more sweating from me. "Please, come in." Rachel's mom said as she walked over to the front door then opened it. I waited to enter before all the ladies went in the house as I insisted on holding the door for them. I followed behind looking for another manly figure besides myself to balance out all the emotions and tears flooding the place as I was outnumbered by the women. I pushed the door up behind me quickly as I noticed the trail of ladies disappearing down a hallway off to the left of the living room area! I was playing catch up when a man just a tab bit taller than me stepped out from a side room! I nearly crumbled in to a thousand pieces as I was thrown off guard on how sudden he came at me from out of nowhere! "Oh damn!" I said then immediately apologized for my foul language. "I'm sorry, I didn't mean to jump out at you like that son. I was heading out because they said you were coming by. I was trying watch the end of the ball game! Hey man, I'm Rachel's dad." He said as he reached his giant like hands out at me. He locked hands and gave me a firm squeeze like the way Pastor Clayton would shake my hand. I was positive he could have crushed every bone in my hand if he wanted to with ease. He looked as if he used to play on a pro football team in his early years. Rachel never told me her dad was the hulk. "Yeah I was so focused on keeping up with them women I didn't see the door you came out of! I'm Cedric Mason. Nice to meet you. Mr. umm?" I felt embarrassed because Rachel's last name did not find its way to my tongue. "Just call me Darryl. That's fine with me. I'm sure they're going to be glued to the little one. Come have a seat in here if you like. My favorite team is trying to make a comeback in the top of the eighth inning. I've heard a lot about you. You're a baseball guy yourself, right?" He said as he slowly limped back in the room. I looked down the hall hoping someone would come save me in case he was being polite just to get me alone to strangle me for knocking his daughter up! I didn't get that vibe from him being an aggressively overprotective dad, but I was on high alert just in case things went downhill. There was a dark brownish couch that looked like it was their first then the house was built around it that sat along on one side of the room. A coffee table sat between two fresh looking recliners facing the big TV that was on a stand. The blinds were opened that gave the room the only light allowed with the flashes from the TV. He picked up the remote then lowered the volume some as he sat in the left recliner that looked more worn than the other one. He waved me over to sit in the other chair. As I was sitting, Rachel popped in and said, "There you are! We were looking for you. I see you two have met." Rachel said as she looked surprised and somewhat worried. "Dad, Cedric...Cedric my dad. Junior had us in a daze. Mrs. Anthony had him giggling up a storm! We are in the kitchen Cedric, down the hall then make a left if you're looking for us." She added. "Oh, we're fine. Just chilling, watching the game. I'll be in there shortly." I replied looking as if I wasn't worried at all. She smiled then said, "Okay then. Glad you two have finally met. Behave daddy." Her dad raised his eyebrows with innocence shrugging his shoulders. "Yeah I'm going to kill-'em! At least not yet. We just met! Let's see who's his favorite team before I decide which way to go on that." We all laughed together then Rachel magically disappeared into the hallway before I could glance back at her. It was a must I got familiar with her dad to get his official opinion of me. I wanted to show him I wasn't a bad pick to be the father of his first grandson. Although it was never planned to have happened that way, I'm sure for all of us! "Now I'm a home team kind of guy. You can't go against your own city! There are players I do enjoy watching but team wise, I can't cheer for any other team. Sorry but that's my opinion and how I was raised." I said. He nodded his head thinking and agreeing with my logic. "Yeah that makes sense to me. I can't argue with that. I was born in Columbus, Georgia. I was a huge Braves fan forever until we moved here about ten years ago. Atlanta traded too many of my favorite guys which pissed me off! I wouldn't let myself watch another Braves game after that! I somehow found a liking for the Cardinals which made sense because they acquired a few players I loved. It was an easy transition and I haven't thought twice about it since!" He replied as he shrugged his shoulders as if he didn't care for anyone's opinion if they had one against his ship jumping reasons. We talked about the game for about twenty minutes nonstop. He admitted he knew of me before he found out about my ties with Rachel "Now that you're a father, you will understand this statement one day. As hard as you try to keep your kids from making some of the same mistakes you've made, they'll find a way to make them." He said. I knew what he meant. I started to think over some of the choices I had made that matched some of the similar choices my dad told me he had made when he was young. I remember my dad saying to me over and over, not to make the same mistakes he made. He would tell my sister and me to be smarter than he was. "I know what you mean, believe or not. I've experienced it before. I guess we all do. Maybe it's something in our genes that makes us do it unconsciously. The bad part is not having any control or choosing which mistakes you can deal with verses the others. That would be nice if we all could." I replied after my detailed memory lane visit. "Well if we had a real choice, I don't think we would want them to make any of our mistakes at all. What a perfect world that would be huh?" He said. It was the truth. In a perfect world we wouldn't be in any unwanted situations or dealing with any conflicts if our parents could have chosen our every decision. "Yeah you're right. Didn't think about it that way. Makes sense." I replied. He offered me some refreshments as water was needed because my lips were feeling dried out. He passed me some pork rinds that he was munching on as he got up to get me some iced water. I wasn't a fan, but he swore that they were the best in town. I took a handful then sat the bag back on the small table between our seats. I took my time in fear the snack was going to cut through my dry throat. He didn't take as long as I thought he would, so I grabbed the glass of water with pleasure. I sipped from the water a few times before eating the pork rinds. To my surprise, they were delicious! I went on to eat the rest I had in my hand as he smiled with confidence, he knew what he was talking about. "You don't have to say it, I already know how good they are. I told you so! Have more if you like?" He said as he sat a can of beer down on the table, he had gotten for himself. I couldn't resist the offer, so I took some more from the bag. While crunching on them he told me about his past that removed the last of the remaining tension I had about meeting him yet along being all alone with him. "I remember when Rachel was first born. Well, let me say this. I remember when my wife, Gloria, first told me she was pregnant. I didn't know what the hell I was going to do! We were still babies, ourselves. Just about the same ages as you and Rachel are now. As much as I hate it, I can't beat you down when I've been in your shoes before. I had just started my third year in college. I played football with a full ride. I was good. One of the best with a for sure spot in the Pros. When Gloria told me, she was getting an abortion, I couldn't sit back and allow it. I had to make a tough decision that I'm glad I made! I quit school then started working. There wasn't any support from neither of our families back then. We had a hard time getting by on our own. It has made me the man I am now. By no means I'm suggestion you follow those steps son. I said that to say, the situation is going to take some work on your end if you want what's best for your son. He's going to need his father in his life. I'll make sure he has the best granddad he can have. I promise you that!" He said as he lowered voice as if he wanted only me to hear it. I guess it was his way of making sure no one was ease dropping during that moment. I understood his sincere statement and respected it. He was looking out for his daughter and grandson. I agreed with his every word. "Thank you for being open with me like that. If you had the courage to handle your business the way you did, so do I. I cannot express to you enough how lucky I am to have such a caring family accepting me. I appreciate you for understanding. I have no doubts you and Mrs. Gloria will be the best grandparents ever." I said without getting too emotional or too loud, making sure I kept the same tone as he did. "You're okay with me Mr. Baseball. You sound like you have your head on right. You have my blessings to marry Rachel." He replied with a serious look on his face. That was probably the most awkward silence I've ever had between someone after he said that! We stared at each other for what felt like 30 seconds until he finally burst out in laughter! "I'm messing with you on that marrying her part Cedric! Sorry but I had to get ya." He said with a smile as big as the sun. I shook my head as if I was on a hidden camera show. "Yeah you got me with that! I didn't know what to say or how to answer that one. Don't get me wrong, obviously I like her. We'll see what happens now." I replied in relief that he was joking with me. "No pressure at all. You don't have to marry her to be in your son's life. It does make it easier. Please don't feel like we're going to hate you if you don't." He said in a more serious voice to make sure I understood he was just joking. "Thanks. But yeah, I get it." I replied smiling to ensure he knew he didn't offend me with the joke. Again, Rachel appeared out of thin air! It startled both of us that time. "Cedric, someone wants to see your face! I'm sure my dad will have plenty of time to interrogate you. Come join us in the kitchen please!" She said as she took a few steps in the room. "You need shoes with bells on them or a bull horn to announce when you're approaching! You're like a pretty ninja!" I said as I stood up smiling. "Yeah he's something else that little handsome monster. Nice talking with you Cedric. Go ahead, daddy duties are priority! Look forward to seeing more of you around. Enjoy him now, because when they get bigger, you're not going to be able to tell them anything." Darryl said as he laughed while eye balling Rachel with his last words. "You're right. Thanks. See you around." I replied then followed Rachel out into the hall. We took a few steps then she immediately turned then hugged me as tight as she could! I wrapped my arms around her as we both stood there together as if we needed that embrace just as bad as the other one. She then looked up at me once she pulled herself off my chest. I lowered my head to her, placing a kiss on her forehead. "I need more than a kiss on my head Cedric. I miss you like crazy." She whispered. Without question, I kissed her on her sweet lips. Before I could detach myself, she grabbed my head with both hands on the sides of my face then pulled me in for a long passionate kiss. I was nervous the whole time thinking her dad was going to walk out of the room or someone was going to pop up in the hall we were in! We kissed for at least a full minute. It was the kind of kiss you would remember for a long time the way it felt and everything that had happened that lead up to the kiss. Something in that kiss hinted that Rachel wanted me more as her man then just the father of our son. She kissed me as if we had both just said, "to death do us part." We were interrupted by what we both thought were footsteps coming our way from the kitchen! We disconnected ourselves then hurried down the hallway. We held hand as Rachel led me to our son and the others sitting together in a small opened circle. Mrs. Anthony still had junior in her arms as her eyes were filled with happiness. "There's daddy!" Mrs. Anthony said to junior as she pointed him in my directions as if she was trying to get him to see me. I walked over then sat beside her with Mrs. Gloria sitting across from us then Rachel sat next to her mom. "Let's try this again daddy. You can do it." Mrs. Anthony said as she passed junior over to me. She made sure my arms were positioned correctly again before laying the little man into them. He was yawning and stretching as if he had been working all day. It was a good sign for me because he wasn't as active like he was during my first attempt to hold him. "See, you got it daddy. I'm just a precious little prince. I'm sleepy now." Mrs. Anthony added in her baby's voice. I sat all the way back in my seat as I locked in on his every move. He looked up at me a few times as he blinked his small light brown eyes at me. I kept telling myself that it was all real. Not a dream, not a nightmare, as real as real can get. I moved my arms in a way that he was cradled in one of my arms as I moved his fingers from his face. He was starting to get aggravated with his hands scratching himself. He was back calm heading to sleepy town after his hands were under control. "I'm so glad this happened. You all stopped by. I can't stress enough how refreshing it is to know Cedric has someone in his life that cares about him, to see him be all he can be as a young man. Thank you, Patricia." Mrs. Gloria said to Mrs. Anthony. I haven't heard anyone say her first name in so long that I almost looked around to see who she was talking to! Mrs. Anthony nodded her head agreeing with Rachel's mom. Junior was out cold, basically snoring within minutes. He looked so peaceful and innocent. The emotions I felt were beyond my imagination watching him sleep in my arms. "Let me get him to his crib. It's past his nap time. I'm surprised he lasted as long, as he did. Guess he was excited to see daddy and his other granny." Rachel said as she walked over to get Junior. "Yeah he's sleeping good." I replied as I lifted him up to her. She then took him to her room where she said his crib was as she walked out the kitchen. "Well we have some shopping to do. We need to talk about some things as well with Cedric being in school and all. We need to figure out the next steps. We will keep in touch and will be back over soon. Thanks again for having us." Mrs. Anthony she as she stood up. Mrs. Gloria hugged us both then escorted us down the hall to the living room. We did pop our heads in the room Darryl was in as Mrs. Gloria introduced him to Mrs. Anthony. They both spoke then said they looked forward to spoiling Junior as grandparents. Rachel met us as she opened the front door. We all walked out on to the porch. "See you all soon." Mrs. Anthony said as she stepped down the stairs from the porch then headed to the car. Mrs. Gloria said the same then headed back in the house. I felt like they did it on purpose the way they immediately went their separate ways once we were all outside. I waited until both ladies were clear from our presence then said, "I can't lie like I'm not still in shocked and confused on why you kept it a secret that Junior was already here. It's not important now. We must push forward with it. That kiss was something special. We need to figure out what we both want. Although your dad said I didn't have to marry you, I found it hard to believe he would be disappointed if I did." I whispered. We both laughed softly. "Well things have been crazy, but my family has really stepped in. They were in their feelings for about a day or two, then it was all about preparing for the arrival of the little guy. My mom took it the hardest during those two days. I think she was shocked that I had sex without talking to her first. It was weird but we had a three-hour talked, that brought us even closer. We both revealed some things we needed to one another. My dad was more concerned about who was the father. He suspected someone had forced me to do it, so I pleaded with him that it was a choice I made. Of course, he could barely stomach the truth, but he came around after him and my mom talked. Well... To be honest... Never mind... But yeah that's how that all went down" She said. Something sounded off when she talked about her dad. That slight hesitation had more info imbedded in it. Like her tone was off. I rubbed my head just thinking how much courage that took for her to confess all of that to her parents. Yeah, I did it too, but I knew it wasn't as stressful as it was on her. If there were any doubts about Rachel being tough, that was one of those moments I didn't question her character. I noticed a shadow by the door that indicated Mrs. Gloria was investigating the conversation we were having on the porch. I glanced at Mrs. Anthony as she was eye balling us as if she was trying to read our lips! That was a sign for me to wrap it up with Rachel. "I'll be seeing a lot of you. Especially since I'm only here for just a week. I'll call you later tonight if that's cool, baby momma?" I whispered then laughed at myself. The look on her face was priceless. She didn't see that last comment coming. "Oh, so that's my name now huh? You got jokes. On a roll I see. Yeah yeah." She said as she was starting to get louder with every word. I stepped closer to her as I grabbed both of her hands in mines. "I'm playing, I'm playing. I'm just messing with you. I had to say it." I whispered again with a big smile on my face. She rolled her eyes then smiled. "Oh, I know. You good, baby daddy." She whispered back then giggled. "So, you funny too? I'll give you that. Are we good now?" I said as I let her hands go then stepped back again. "Yeah we good. Talk to you soon Cedric." She replied. "I will never address you that way for real. You're the mother of our child. Junior is lucky to have you as his mom." I said then I leaned in and gave her a soft kiss on her cheek. I didn't want to go too far with the noisy conversation monitors watching and listening to everything. "Thank you. I needed to hear that. This has been tough yet amazing. He makes my heart smile. Okay... Bye Cedric." She replied then stepped over to the door. I nodded my head then went on to the car.

"You good?" Mrs. Anthony asked me once I was in the car. "I'm nervous, happy, surprised, anxious and scared if you want me to be honest." I replied as I fastened my seat belt. "Good. It's exactly like that all the time as a parent. Those feelings will never go away. Doesn't matter how long you've been a father or mother. I can confess that it is a world of all sorts of emotions mix all together coming at you at random." She said while smiling. She then drove off. I waved at Rachel as she was looking at us riding by. "Well, day one of many is done. We need to do some serious shopping and praying!" Mrs. Anthony said then burst out in laughter. I couldn't help but laugh with her. She could tell I needed all the laughter I could get. "I may have to get a job huh?" I asked. I was thinking about how I wasn't prepared financially to support Junior. I had school to go back to, but I didn't have a single clue on how it was going to work out, money wise. "No baby, you don't have anything to worry about that right now. That's my grand baby and I need you to stick to school. We need to continue as planned. It's going to be fine." She said with a determined look on her face. "I can go back and finish this year out. I'm thinking I could transfer somewhere closer. I don't know. I just want..." I said then she cut me off. "Cedric, it's going to be okay. Please don't worry nor stress yourself out now! Please trust me." She nearly yelled out to me as we were pulling back up to our house. She was right. I was in way over my head with the endless cringed worthy thoughts! "Okay. I won't. I do trust you. I'll try to relax."

I replied as I held my head up. That was my way of letting her know I had hope.

After we parked the car, we both got out and slowly walked on to the porch. Before she put the keys in the door. She turned and said, "I can't say it enough. These are the things we try to teach as parents because we too know the struggle and stress that follows when you're young having a baby. You're basically still a baby. You are blessed beyond your imagination and I need you to understand that. This is not the time to give up on your hopes and dreams! You are loved, Rachel's loved, and that precious baby is loved by us all! With that kind of circle, none of us will fail! Okay..." She didn't wait for a reply. We went on into the house. She stated she needed to make a list of things Junior needed from her conversation with Rachel's mom. She asked me to give her about thirty minutes before she headed out to determine if she needed me to come with her. I didn't want to go upstairs, knowing I would doze off. I sat on the couch then flicked on the TV. It seemed it was at the right moment as a breaking news alert came through on the early evening news! It was the latest update on Ms. Harris! The city and state issued warrants out for her arrest as more young men had come forward with graphic details about inappropriate touching, she committed with them! They had a few parents on there, pleading with the news reporters about how sick and angry they felt with the news from their boys. Most of the guys she had these encounters with were of senior classes from about the last three consecutive school years! Ms. Harris had been working at the school for at least seven years. I began to tear up a little as I listened to the report! I immediately changed the channel when I heard steps coming my way from the kitchen! I wiped off my face with the bottom of my shirt then leaned back on the couch as relaxed as I could. "I'm probably going to stop by a few places. I don't want to drag you around unless you really want to go. I'm sure you'd rather stay here and chill out after the day you've had already." Mrs. Anthony said as she entered the living room. I sat upright as I pondered my options. "To be honest, I don't mind going but you're right. I need a chill pill and a never-ending head massage! I'll take a rain check if you're okay with that?" I replied as I smiled. Mrs. Anthony giggled a little then said, "I'm okay with that. I figured you needed some time alone to get yourself together. There's plenty of leftovers and other stuff in the fridge if you're hungry. I left twenty bucks on the kitchen table if you wanted to walk somewhere close for something else. I'll be gone for a few hours so please call me if you need me or anything." I slipped my shoes off then laid back on one end of the couch with my legs up facing the other end. "Thank you for being a super mom. Thank you thank you! I'll try not to bother you while you're on your mission for the little monster." I replied. She shook her head and smiled. "See you later. Don't leave here and get lost. I don't know what's going on up there in your head, but I hope you're going to trust that you can get through this. We all can." She said as she opened the door with her purse and jacket tucked in her arm. "I would never leave like that. I trust you. I trust that this will be okay. I promise. I get it. Don't you worry." I replied then got up. I walked over and gave her a hug then held the door for her. "I'm okay. I'm just making sure you're not about to fall apart. Believe me, I'm fine." She replied as she stepped down the steps. "Yes ma'am. I'm good. Thank you again for everything. Now be careful. I'll be here when you get back. I might be sleep but I'll be here." I said while laughing. She smiled back as she got in the car then drove off. There was a nice breeze out complimenting the sun set. Traffic was slow on our street. I decided to sit on the porch to take advantage of the quietness and perfect weather. I pulled the door up but didn't shut it completely. I stepped over to the chairs on the porch, sitting down in one then pulled another in front of me to prop my legs up on it. I had my phone with me when I noticed a missed call from Lauren as it vibrated to alert me. I ignored it because I wanted a moment to myself. I sat there laid back in the chair watching the sun set and the few people out strolling. I was slightly nodding a bit but kept my eyes opened from the loud cars that would pass by.

Chapter 6

When it Rains, it Pours

The night lights were coming on and from my clock on the phone I was out there for about an hour. From a distant I could zoom in on the infamous white SUV buzzing speakers coming down the street! I instantly slipped out my chair as low as I could without being notice. I was thanking God I didn't have to use a key or anything to slide in the door! I crawled into the house as quick as I could. I slowly closed the door as I stood up. I peeped out the front window as the truck passed by the house with Melvin and his entourage. They were blasting the music and I could see someone hanging out the window laughing with a bottle of alcohol in his hand. Look like they were just riding around through the neighborhood looking for trouble, straight wilding. They slowed down at the end of the street before burning rubber on the tires turning the corner towards the next block. I locked the door then headed to the kitchen as my stomach felt hollow as if I hadn't eaten in days. Leftovers was a perfect idea. Didn't want to leave out the house for anything different after that close encounter with Melvin.

The house phone rung as soon as I was getting my plate out the microwave. I carefully sat the plate on the table then grabbed the phone without thinking twice about who was calling. "Hello... This is Cedric." I said. For about fifteen second, I stood there patiently waiting for a reply. Finally, I heard a cracking voice whisper, "Is that you Cedric?" I clutched the phone even harder as the voice hit clear to my ears. I couldn't get the words out as I started to mumble. Every word was on top of one another. I pressed my back to the wall as my knees started to weaken. I slowly slid down the wall until my butt was sitting on the kitchen floor. "Cedric... I'm sorry..." My sister

Tammie's voice came through the phone. My heart felt like it was being squeezed by someone with gloves made of needles! The immediate pain I felt hearing her voice could have taken me completely out for good. I started to cry uncontrollable as I rubbed my head in mystery. How did she know this number? Has she been calling or keeping up with me all this time? How long has she been calling? Questions after questions ripped my head apart as if I was being tortured! "Cedric... Please... Say something." Tammie begged. I couldn't breathe! I was speechless. The words were there but I couldn't get them out. I held the phone sniffing and sobbing to myself. "I know. I know I was wrong to leave you like that. It's been too long. I take full responsibility for it. Cedric, please say something to me." She continued to plea with me. About another minute or so I finally calmed down good enough to speak a complete sentence. "Please tell me I'm dead. Please tell me this is not happening. I know this is not my one and only sister. I don't get it..." I whispered loud enough for her to hear the confusion and frustration in my voice. We both held the phone for another minute or two before I heard the front door suddenly open! I tried to wipe my face with my arm trying to dry the tears! I rushed up on to my feet then hung up the phone! I ran over by the sink and grabbed some paper towels from the roll sitting on the counter! I patted my eyes then sat at the table to eat the food I had warmed up. "Cedric, are you still here? Are you up?" Mrs. Anthony yelled as she was walking through the house towards the kitchen. I started eating then said with a mouth full of food, "Yes ma'am. I'm in here!" She came through the kitchen doorway with her hands full of stuff. I jumped up to help her as she seemed to have stumbled a bit with the bags. I put some of the things on the table then she told me to go get the rest out of the car. I walked outside then grabbed the last of the bags that were in the passenger seat. The night had come, and it was still quiet out. The porch lights were on down the entire block which was unusual. I noticed a patrol car cruising slowly down the street coming my way. As I stood up looking around, I noticed no one else was outside. That was another red flag. I started to feel something weird was happening that I was clueless of. As I slammed the door shut on the car the officer had made it to me. He stopped his car then signaled me over. His window was down as I could hear him asking, "You're Cedric, right? Baseball guy!" I replied, "Yeah that's me. Just home for a few days." He nodded his head then leaned over and asked, "Everything's good? Have you seen anyone or anything out of the ordinary since you been out here tonight?" I looked around again as I started to get extra nervous as I saw he had a shotgun in his lap! Something had happened seriously, but I didn't want to ask too many questions. He was staring at me with anticipation of my every motion. He waited patiently for my answer too. "No sir. I just ran out to get the rest of these things. I've been in the house most of the evening sir. Other than a few cars zooming down the street earlier. I haven't seen a thing." I said as I leaned down a little to make sure I saw his every move as well. "Okay then, well it's best to be inside tonight. There's been a bad accident that involved someone being shot over a road rage dispute a few streets over. We have information that some of the suspects fled on foot. We don't have much more than that. Keep your doors lock and call us immediately if you all see or hear anything around your house. Thanks." He said with a more frustrated yet concerned look on his face. "Wow! That's crazy. Has things gotten that bad around here?" I replied. "To be honest with you, we know who's been causing the problems but can't catch him in the act. People are living in fear or cooperating with the wrong side of this mess. If you know what I mean? Sooner than later we hope some people will be brave enough to help us stop the criminal chaos that clown has been causing around here for too long." He said as if he was baiting me in to give him something to go on. He knew I was aware of who he was talking about. The way he said it and the tone he used that he was indeed desperate for anyone to help them put Melvin away. A load of guilt fell upon me suddenly. I tensed up a bit as the thoughts of telling the officer about what I saw earlier. I figured someone must have cut Melvin off in traffic or looked at him funny that probably caused whoever the innocent person was to have had that altercation, resulting in him or her getting shot. Melvin didn't discriminate with his hate. Male or female, if you disrespected him in any form, there were violent repercussions. I could see it all happening just like that like every other story I've heard about Melvin over the years. Then the guilt of taking that money from Melvin hung itself over my head as well. I was dancing with doing the right thing or staying quiet. As I was about to force myself to speak up, Mrs. Anthony voice pierced through my reaction! "Is everything okay out here Cedric? Hey Officer... Is there something we can help you with?" She said as she started to come down the steps. "I better let her know what's going on. We will stay inside tonight. I hope you all get to the bottom of it. Thanks for the heads up!" I said then quickly walked back onto the sidewalk then towards Mrs. Anthony cutting her from reaching the patrol car. "Thanks!" The officer said then slowly crept on down the other end of the street randomly flashing his spotlight between the houses. "What was that about? What is he looking for?" Mrs. Anthony asked as I walked past her to get her to come back into the house. "Let's get in the house. We need to be inside right now." I said as I pushed the door open, letting her enter before me. "What's going on?" She asked as I shut the door then locked it. I walked in the kitchen and sat the rest of the bags on the table. "Someone got shot. They're patrolling the area because the fools who were involved ran away on foot. They have a good clue on who was involved. They're just making sure no one's hiding out between houses or in backyards." I finally said. She shook her head and gave a deep sigh. As soon as she opened her mouth and started talking about her worries on the crime rate rising during that past year, it was as if I had an out of body moment. My body was standing by the table with one of my hands leaning on it while I was listening to her but another part of me was pacing around her as if I couldn't recognize who she was! As she talked, I was wondering what happened to the Mrs. Anthony I once knew? Something had changed! Things were different as if I didn't trust the person I was looking at. I kept replaying the chain of events and truths that had been revealed to me over the couple of days I had been back home. Her mouth was moving but I didn't hear one word she was saying. I stepped back into my body after circling her then shook my head in disbelieve. I finally snapped out of the hypnosis I was under when she yelled my name! "Cedric! Are you okay?" She said as she snapped her fingers at me! I nearly fell from coming back under control of my senses. I felt numb a bit and lightheaded. "Yeah I think I am. I think I need to lay down. I'm sorry I blanked out." I said as I slowly moved towards the doorway of the kitchen. "Yeah, I see. I was saying, I have noticed the spike in offences and that's why I'm glad you're not around it all. I'll put your food away if you're done eating." She stated as she went over to the table. My appetite was deceased. I was beyond miserable yet curious about more than what I was willing to ask at that moment. I had to rest my brain. I didn't want her to know about my sister calling nor the level of betrayal I felt about everything that had happened. "I am done with that plate. I'm sorry for wasting the food. I'm going to my room to relax. I may try to eat something else later." I said rubbing my stomach as if it was aching. "Well don't wait too late to try to eat again. You don't want to go to sleep on your food like that since its already getting late." She replied. I nodded my head agreeing then made my way upstairs.

I was starting to feel so much anger towards Mrs. Anthony. In all the years she's been taking care of me, since day one, I have only felt love, peace and appreciation for her. I made it to my room and slumped down on the bed. I felt defeated as if I had given my all to an unbeatable situation! It was beyond my understanding on how all of it was fine with her. She's been smiling, laughing yet quiet as a mouse about some significant information! The how's and why's had completely taken over me. I was paralyzed by the thought of the answers she would give me if I asked the questions that were hunting me! What made it worse for me was that she wasn't alone with the secrets! Everyone was in on it as if I was a complete outcast. I turned my phone off. I laid on my back in the bed then closed my eyes. I wanted to fall asleep and never wake up again! My whole world seemed as if I was being pranked with no one jumping in to tell me it was all a bad joke. I glanced at the clock on the desk and it was close to nine o'clock. With about five more days there at home, I wanted to sleep the rest of the week! If there was a pill or drink, I could have taken to do just that, I wouldn't have hesitated to take them. My stomach started growling but I fought with the hunger as I refused to be in Mrs. Anthony's presence. I was done with being around her or anyone else! I even thought about barricading myself in the room just to make sure no one else could let me down with more terrible secrets or painful truths. My eyes were closing more and getting harder to open by the second. I heard footsteps coming up the stairs. I immediately rolled over onto my side with my back facing the door of the room. As the sounds of the steps reached the doorway, I kept my eyes shut. "Cedric are you still coming down to eat something. Cedric... Cedric?" Mrs. Anthony whispered. I was still and breathing heavily as I pretended to be sleep. She waited by the door for a few seconds then I heard the door slowly being pulled up from the bottom of it brushing against the carpet. Her footsteps were heard going back down the stairs as I rolled back over to see the door pushed up some. It wasn't closed completely but up enough where I could only see just a crack through the hall. I then laid back on my back then powered my phone on. I wanted to set an alarm to wake up early to work out. I needed to relieve the stress and anger that had built up. After turning my phone on, there were some notifications that buzzed through. There was a text from Lauren, a missed call from Rachel and a missed call from an unknown number. I went ahead and texted Lauren as she was checking on me from what I read on her message. I told her that things are going well but nothing exciting and that I would call her the next day. After I sent that message, I found myself contemplating on calling Rachel back. It was late. I didn't want to call back in case she was sleeping with the baby close by then waking him or her. Lauren texted back right away saying that was cool and to make sure I call her. I placed my phone back on the nightstand then closed my eyes.

It was another restless night. I slept a total of about four hours until I found myself sitting up in the bed staring at the window as the sun started to peak itself up from the night sky. It was close to six in the morning. I sat there scanning the room as I reminisced about all my accomplishments looking at the trophies and awards that were on the dresser. There were some pictures and newspaper articles about some of my best games I played in high school. I was thinking deeply about how things had turned out since I went off to college. I heard a few voices in my head telling me I had failed! I was feeling the guilt settling in with the doubts I had of myself. My confidence was questionable, and my attitude wasn't the same as before. I was starting to believe the voices until my alarm went off! The alarm scared yet triggered me that it was time to get up! I took that as it was redirecting my thoughts to somethings, I knew I needed to do. I had to work out as I have done for so long. I had gotten away from some of my morning routines. I was thrown off track by a land slide. I used to get up early and put in the work to better myself every day. Early morning workout gave me a peace of mind. I was focused back then without a care in the world. I needed that more than ever. I had to build myself back up mentally. I had to regain that same determination I once had. I just had to transition it towards being a young father and a student-athlete. I had work too hard to get there to have it all taken away due to self-doubts. Mrs. Anthony was right! I had a great support system with her, Pastor Clayton and others.

       I jumped up feeling inspired! I couldn't let myself down nor those few that still believed in me. I had some gym clothes I could still fit in the dresser, so I put them on. I laced up my running shoes I brought with me. I wanted to run about three miles away from the neighborhood then back. It was early enough where most people were still in bed or just getting up for work. I crept down the stairs then out the door without making too much noise. When I shut the door behind me, I waited a couple of minutes to see if Mrs. Anthony heard me leave. I didn't hear anything or see any moving through the windows. I took off on my run with my headphones on and my phone strapped to my arm. I received an arm band from Mrs. Anthony when I first went off to school that I left behind. I started my run with the music blasting! I was watching only what was in front of me while the tunes drowned out all the rest of the sound around me. I ran for about thirty minutes before my phone started to ring. I glanced at the screen while still cruising down the street. I started on the sidewalk, but people had their trash cans out, so I moved in the street. I ran towards the traffic side in case someone was still sleepy and swerved on me if I was running in front of them on the other side of the road. I've heard too many stories about runners getting smashed by distracted drivers. I didn't want to take any chances like that. Jackson didn't have the best drivers at all. I was finally able to hold my arm still long enough to see that it was Mrs. Anthony. I could have just stopped, but I was feeling great, so I managed to swipe the phone while I was running. My phone could receive the call which made it easier for me to talk to her while still in motion. "Are you okay Cedric? I wasn't sure if you had left or someone had come in the house. I was scared to come out my room. I was still worried about the shooting from last night." She said as I could tell she was disturbed. "Yes ma'am, that was me leaving for a run. I didn't want to wake you. I'm sorry to have gotten you worked up like that." I replied as I slowed down to catch my breath. "Okay. I just wanted to be sure no one was in here but me. I jumped up then locked my bedroom door! You must have run off the porch fast. I peeped out the window but didn't see you." She said. "Yeah I wanted to get out early before everyone else started their day. I wanted to avoid the traffic and crazy drivers. I'll be heading back that way in a few." I replied. "Okay. You be careful. I don't think they ever found them boys who caused all that craziness last night. Keep your phone close and watch yourself." She said. I knew what that meant. She wanted me to come back right then and there. I had forgotten that quick about the trouble from the night before myself. I didn't want to worry her for too long, so I crossed over the street as more cars were starting to hit the streets.

The sun was up as the heat was making its presence felt. One of my shoes came untied as I was about twenty minutes from the house. Not trusting the drivers, I ran onto the sidewalk that was at an intersection with a traffic light. I was drenched in sweat as my hands were slippery trying to grab my laces quickly. I fumbled a few times but finally got them tied back together. My calf muscles were feeling tight, so I stood up then bent over to give them a good stretch. I stood back up then glanced at the light before I crossed over but was frozen in my movement. It felt like I was under some sort of spell. My entire body had suddenly shut down and I couldn't move my feet nor my arms. Melvin was sitting in his all white luxury car right in front of me! We locked eyes as he had on his devilish grin. He was alone which was surprising given the police was on a manhunt for him and his entourage. He pulled his car over out of the crosswalk then parked a few feet away. If I had any chance to survive the rest of my days in town, running would have increased my danger. That would have pissed him off. I wanted to run so damn bad. The sweat was not letting up as I wiped my face with the bottom end of my shirt several times. He then got out of his car wearing his usual all white linen shorts and button-down short sleeved shirt. He had a kango hat with some shades on with white frames. I wasn't even bothered with the fact he had a huge silver gun in his waistband with the handle hanging out. I was more cautious about it slipping out because of how low it hung in those thin linen shorts. Last thing I wanted to happen, was being shot yet alone by accident! He waved me over but didn't say a word. He leaned on the back of his car as he waited for me to come. "Cedric... Cedric. Cedric! This is God's work right here. Blessing me to seeing our local superstar on this beautiful morning." He said as if he had hit the power ball! I was indeed nervous because he was happy to see me. "What's up Melvin?" I immediately asked to get right to whatever business he had with me. He then hopped up on the trunk of the car to sit. That was a horrible sign that this wasn't a normal hi and bye interaction. He seemed somewhat uneased himself or the sun really was starting to heat up! He was sweating just as much as I was. If he was spooked or on the edge, he played it off smooth regardless of the drenched hat he had on. He kept his ugly smile on his face but couldn't ignore the drips rolling down his forehead. "I just wanted to have a word or two with you, young future millionaire. If you don't mind. I mean, only if you have time to for little old Melvin." He said with heavily noticeable sarcasm. What else did I have to lose other than my life? I stood there patiently waiting, giving him my undivided attention. I wanted to be sure he knew I wasn't brushing him off or rushing him in any way. "I got time Melvin. Just out here trying to get it in man. Just home for a few. I'm just trying to stay low key and out the way. I heard things have gotten crazier around here?" I replied. I wanted to hear it from the horse's mouth personally, that he was without a doubt the main one causing the crime rate to shoot up, literally. He hesitated for a moment before he replied. That was a factor in how he wanted to be careful on what he said to me about it all. I could tell he wasn't trusting me as much as I thought he would. It was strange because I thought I gain some points for not snitching or saying anything about that night they stomped them guys near death for me. Guess it's easier putting your faith in the hands of those around you that have probably done the actual crimes for you. "I'm sure it's not as bad as many are saying that it is. To me, I haven't noticed a thang." He replied. He was lying through those busted teeth he had as if I was as naive as he may have assumed. I played the role well with Melvin. I knew that was one of the reasons he continued to pursue me the way he had. I believed he had this imagination of me being just another big dumb athlete, that my only purpose in life was going pro. "I know better than to ask you like that. It may be cool to you but for some, it's a living nightmare around here. Mrs. Anthony like many others have claims towards a different story than you have. I wish things were better. I'm glad I got away." I said with more confidence. I didn't want to come off too sure. He would have taken it personal had I said anything more than that. "Speaking of Mrs. Anthony. You know… That's exactly what I wanted to speak on. I still owe you that favor. You do know I don't make promises I can't keep. I noticed Rico and her, have been spending some time together. They threw me way off balance with that. I been keeping a close eye on him you know…" He whispered as people were walking by. The looks I were getting from the passer byers was a huge indicator I was in cahoots with the enemy. The subject had shifted to a forbidden place I didn't want to go. Word spread fast around there. I had to find a way to get Melvin to get to the point. My thinking cap was on tight searching for a master plan to shake him from holding me hostage! I guess he sensed it. "I'm going to handle that Rico boy for ya like I said. I just need you to get involved a little." He said once the people were far enough for his comfort. I started backing away in fear of the worst. He slid down off the trunk of the car that made me stop. My eyes were attached to the gestures he was making as he gripped the handle of the gun! He held it in place then said, "I've been itching to get that boy. This is the perfect opportunity to get rid of him for good. I'm not asking... I am telling you to cooperate. Let's not forget you owe me a return on that little change I gave you." I feared that day would come when he asked for a favor or demanded me to do something because of that money he gave me! The days are always short numbered when someone has something, they can hang over your head. I could feel the strings being attached as if I was becoming a puppet for him by the way he plotted his evil plan in his head. Mrs. Anthony had a sincere forgiving heart to welcome Rico into her personal life the way she did. As much as I wanted to hate that fact, it wasn't much I could do to stop how she felt. I didn't want to take that from her nor did my hate simmer up enough to want Rico dead! "I need you to get him to meet up with you at the old skating ring near the tire shop off Russell street tonight. Tell him y'all need to talk some things out to get it off your chest or tell him you need to meet up with some pretty honeys or whatever it takes to make sure he comes! I need to clear him off my check list of problems that must be erased." He said while looking right through my soul! My skin crawled from the look he was giving me as if I was his slave. He knew I wouldn't decline nor reject whatever he said. I still had to try. I tried to plea my case. "Melvin man, I promise I don't want to get involve like that.

There must be another way. Please don't make…" I was saying until Melvin stepped upon me closely then whispered, "There isn't no other way, you feel me. I'm not repeating myself either. Don't piss me off Cedric. See… I like you… Don't let it be both of y'all… Okay?" I had to rub my hand across my face and nose area to keep from fainting due to the aroma of his foul cologne he was wearing mixed with under arm musk and his cigar breathe! I was relieved that he headed back towards the driver's side of his car. He didn't care what my answer was. I spent the next few minutes trying retrieve my tongue because it was like I swallowed it! He gave me a long stare then nodded his head at me as a sign that he knew he had my cooperation. I stood there as he pulled off down the street trying to gain feeling in my legs as they had become numb from anxiety. I waited until he was well gone out of my sight before I walked across the intersection towards the house. As I made my struggle stroll on the sidewalk, I didn't notice my phone was still lit up in my arm ban! I took it out then glanced at it to see that Mrs. Anthony number was still on the call! I thought I hung it up, but I guess I was too big of a rush to get back to her before she came looking for me that I didn't hit the end call button! I hesitated to put it against my ear. My headphones where disconnected which too was brought to my attention as I held the phone in my shaky hand! I sped up until I started to jog. I ran with the phone still in the palm of my hand. I didn't want to say anything to throw the fact that I knew she may have heard the whole conversation. I wanted her to believe I was unaware that I left her on the line. I was within feet of the house when I noticed Mrs. Anthony sitting on the porch! She was in one of the chairs off in the corner of the porch. She didn't see me as I slowed down then walked in the direction of the steps to the house. She was looking off in the distant with a bothered look on her face. I knew for a fact that she had heard it all. I was doomed for sure! What was going to happen to me when

Melvin found out? How was I going to explain my way out of that one? Would she warn the police as well? Those were among the questions that darted through my mind as I dragged each foot up the steps to the porch. She suddenly zoomed in on me as I moved swiftly to the front door. I was going to pretend that I didn't realize she was there. That was my instant game plan in my attempt to avoid the interrogation she was going to perform with me. "Cedric, so glad you made it back. Your old coach is on the phone! You're here right on time!" She yelled at me as she stood up. I was speechless as I immediately looked down at my phone seeing that it was still counting the seconds of the ongoing call I was in with her number! I quickly pressed the end call button as she approached me. I slipped my phone in my pocket as she handled me her phone. I had to catch my breath as I was overjoyed with the triumph feeling of escaping a near disaster! "Hey Coach Thomas. What's going on?" I said with a smile on my face. Mrs. Anthony silently went in the house as she waved at me that she would be in there. Guess she wanted me to have some privacy. "My guy Cedric! Just know I'm in the loop with your success up there in Chicago! That was a hell of a freshman year I'll say! I'm so proud of you man!" He said loudly through the phone! I could hear the loud revving of his engine in his old pickup truck he had. "Thanks Coach! I appreciate that. I'm trying my best to represent!" I replied as I stepped over to the chairs. "Yeah I'm headed out of town now. I really hate I missed you coming down this time! We will have to catch up over some of that good fried chicken Mrs. Anthony cooks over there the next time you're home! Keep your head on right! I'm proud of ya!" He said. "Sounds like a plan to me! I'll do better to reach out to you before I come back." I replied. "Well take care of yourself. Don't do anything dumb while you're home, okay! I'll talk to you soon." He said with emphasis on the "dumb" part. If only he knew the role I was recently asked to play in a planned killing! "Yes sir. I'm only here a few more days then back to business. It's understood Coach." I replied while contemplating on telling him everything Melvin requested of me. It wasn't any use since he was heading away. As bad as I wanted to, I didn't want him to get involved. "Good. Okay then. Take care son." He said then hung up the phone. I sat in the chair for a second before going in the house. I was slouched down in the chair as low as I could without getting too uncomfortable. The morning was in full motion as more traffic and people appeared through the streets and sidewalks. I didn't want anyone else to see me or approach me until I pulled myself back together. I sat there going over every single possible way I could get out of the jail or death sentence I had to choose between later that evening! I was out there at least fifteen minutes before Mrs. Anthony finally popped back out onto the porch looking for me. With my one hand over my face sitting low in the chair, she had no doubts something was bothering me. I couldn't adjust anything in time before she whispered at me, "Tell me what's going on. Something has you out here looking like a broke down car." She smiled as she sat down next to me. I sat up in my seat as I laughed a bit at her comment. "I'm good. I'm good. Not broke down..." I replied. She shook her head as she gave me the side eye. I gave her the phone back as she was looking at it as if she wanted it. "You probably need to keep it to call to check on our little prince. You need to spend as much time as you can with that baby before you leave back out." She said as she stared at me as if she wasn't asking me to. I was starting to inhale the flagrant odor that was suffocating me from the much-needed fresher air outside! I promised her I would call Rachel once I had properly cleansed myself of the reeking musk before it settled in my bones. She threated to cancel phone service on my cell if I didn't hold up my end of the bargain. I would have rather taken that punishment than the one Melvin was offering in any lifetime. I repeated to her about thirty times that I would not forget to make the call before she allowed me to walk past her into the house. I needed to soak my bones, so I decided to sit in the tub for a bit. I had to shake some Epson Salt in my bath to help because I didn't stretch as good as I needed to after the run. The water gave me a great deal of relaxation. I had to lay my entire 6'3 frame in with my feet propped up on one end and my head tilted back on the other end of the rim of the tub. My habit of dozing off at random when I'm nervous or exhausted did not help that situation. If there ever was a time, I needed to utilize an alarm clock, that was the perfect time to! I guess it was the undoubting impression I gave Mrs. Anthony about calling to check on the baby was the reason it took her two hours to realize there was no sound or moving upstairs before she came to check on me. Falling mid dream then suddenly being awaken by the screaming of your name while in a water filled tub is one of the worst experiences I've had in a bathroom! No words could express the amount of pain I suffered in so many areas of my body from jumping up attempting to grab something to pull on to find myself slipping, hitting every elbow, arm and legs I had on the solid tub shell! Mrs. Anthony banged on the thin wooden door as if she was the FBI! In agony half sleep mixed with confusion at its highest form, I scrambled to reach the towel to cover up. I bit my tongue trying to keep myself quiet from revealing how much trauma I caused myself! Had I not said a word any faster than I finally did, she was a millisecond from tearing the whole damn door off the hinges! "I'm okay! I must have fell asleep!" I'm getting out now!" I yelled through the door as I finally had control of my footing. I stepped slowly out the tub onto the floor mat we had to keep from tracking the water through the house. The sounds from feet dragging with her pacing around outside in the hallway gave me more of a reason to dry myself quickly. "You can't be falling asleep in the tub Cedric! That's not smart at a..." She was saying when I cracked the door open cutting her off. "I know... I'm fine. You're right. Sorry..." I whispered to her as she then turned with relief that I was okay. I waited until she was down the stairs before I limped over to my room. It dawned on me after my clothes were on that I didn't take a real bath. I laid there but not once did I apply any soap to my body. I was too worked up yet too lazy to go back at it, so I made sure I applied plenty of deodorant under my arms. My phone notification light was beaming at me as I picked up my phone. The sun was sending high temps of heat waves throughout my room causing me to sweat. I had to turn the ceiling fan on as I stood by the window with it pushed opened. I didn't notice the new neighbors that had recently moved in across the street were looking at me until one of the older ladies coughed as if she was choking on something! I was trying to cool off. I was giving the neighbors a real show as one of them were glued to my every move. I quickly slid over out of their sights! I laughed at myself thinking about how they must have questioned themselves about the choice they had made moving in across from a young amateur nudist! I was embarrassed, nonetheless. I had to hang my head out the widow to yell how sorry I was for flashing my man boobs at them. I was thrilled that they all had a sense of humor. They could tell I wasn't being a perv from the ashamed childlike look I was wearing on my face. I monitored them from the opened spaces of the blinds after I disappeared from their view.

After they went inside their home it was safe for me to walk about as I kept the window open welcoming the windy breeze to circulate through my room. I used the towel again to wipe my face and back until they were completely dry from the water and sweat. I sat at the edge of the bed finally calling Rachel to check on her and our little gremlin. I had to double call her because she didn't answer the first time. I gave it about five minutes between my second attempt. It rang about four time. It appeared she answered it but there was no hello or hi or anything from her end. There was complete silence. I was hesitant to hang up. The longer I held the phone the clearer the voices in the background started to become. I was hearing a conversation that sounded like Rachel's voice and her dad's. The only words that I was able to make out was, "He believes it, I promise…" It was said more than any other statement that was made between the two. In fear that she was going to pick up her phone at any moment, I hung up my end. The last thing I heard was, "You can never undo this, okay?" I didn't think long about it as I put my shirt on. I was starting to feel the bottom of my stomach. I ignored the thoughts that kept the curiosity lingering from the words that were said on the other end of Rachel's phone.

I staggered down the stairs as my vision started to lose its focus which was a first! I was met with the sounds of chatting from the kitchen. It was Mrs. Anthony on the phone. She did not look happy when she saw me entering. It wasn't a look of anger. It was more of inconvenience as if she needed to say something, she didn't want me to hear. The way she hurried off the phone was the proof she wasn't going to let me decode whatever she was rambling about. "Hey, what time are you seeing the baby today?" Mrs. Anthony asked as she walked over to the fridge. "I called twice but no answer. I'll try again in about twenty minutes." I replied as I sat at the table scoping what she was about to get out the fridge. "Oh okay. That's fine. Are you hungry? I'm sure you are." She said. "I could eat a whole horse right now." I said as I smiled with my eyes still glued to her. She pulled out some eggs, bacon and a few other things. "Does breakfast casserole, biscuits and gravy sound good?" She asked as if she knew I wasn't going to object. I nodded my head then helped with getting the pans out for her. I sat back down while she cooked. We talked about the baby, me going back to school, plans for the upcoming holidays and more until she was done. We ate together and out the blue, I asked, "You haven't mentioned anything else about Rico since that first night I was here. Is everything okay with him?" I guess my nerves were hinting that I should put my plan in play if I wanted to live. All I could see was Melvin's stained teeth smiling through those crusty lips while he dangled his gun in my face. "Well we agreed to give you more time to process your emotions about him being around. After thinking about it, I do apologize for not forewarning you. I was too caught up in my healing that I ignored yours. I promise to consider your opinion before something like that again." She said. Even that was a surprise. She seemed to have mastered the sense of shock and aw. I didn't want to be stubborn with my reply although I felt she would find a way to do it again without understanding it from my perspective that she had done it. I started a mental countdown on when she would do something like it again. "I get your intentions, after I thought about what you said. I know you've taught me about forgiving and finding peace. I want to have that kind heart like yours. It's just taking me longer." I replied as I smiled. She took a moment to think to herself as if she wanted to go somewhere else with the conversation, but my cell phone rang derailing whatever she was about to say. I quickly answered it seeing that it was Rachel's number showing on the display screen.

"Hello." I said. Mrs. Anthony signaled to me that she was going to go to her room. I gave her a thumbs up then covered the mic of the phone with my other hand to whisper to her I would clean the kitchen. She nodded her head then walked out. "Hey baby daddy! How are you?" Rachel said as she burst out with laughter. "I see you have the jokes on deck early today huh. I'm good. I can't complain. And you and the mini me?" I replied. "We have been up rolling. He's an early bird. Not a big issue because he doesn't fuss that much in the mornings. I saw where you called. I think I was in the shower then. Sorry." She replied. I sat down to hear the little man's precious voice clearer in the background. "Yeah I did call to check on you two. I got up for a run then called when I was done." I whispered. "Oh, did you? Yeah, you must keep that body tight. Don't want you to get lazy on us." She replied then giggled a little. Everything seemed normal with our conversation other than her voice. I kept hearing her say those words. "He believes it." It rang out louder as we continued to talk! I wanted to admit I overheard her talking somehow earlier, but I didn't know how to say it. I felt I missed the opportunity to say it at the beginning of the call rather than to spring it out the blue. After about ten minutes of talking she said, "I can bring the little goblin over if you all want to see him today? I was going to take him out in his stroller to let him get some fresh air. He loves being outside. If we can come by there that would save me the never-ending stroller ride." I looked around the kitchen as if I was waiting for someone to oppose the thought. I didn't have any issues with that suggestion. I was for sure Mrs. Anthony would approve so I replied with, "Yes, you two are more than welcome over here. That would be nice. I'll let Mrs. Antony know in case she had plans. I don't want her to miss seeing him if y'all are coming over." She told me she was gathering his things and baby bag. She told me to give her about a half an hour then they would be on their way. I agreed with that then hung up the phone.

I immediately cleaned up the kitchen as if the president of the united states were coming by. I guess I was so focused with haste that I didn't see Mrs. Anthony creep back in the kitchen. She yelled out at me, "Cedric! Can you slow down please? I don't want you breaking anything. Why are you in panic mode?" As she said that, I nearly dropped one of the plates as I was loading it in the dishwasher! "Oh, sorry. I was just trying to tighten up since Rachel is bringing Junior over in a few." She walked in closer to me and said with a worried face, "What? Why didn't you tell me right away! I need to finish cleaning. I need to make some refreshments too! Cedric, you

should know better about inviting guess without warning me."
As much as I was tempted to blurt out that it wasn't a big deal
since it was just Rachel and the baby coming over, she was
right. There was never a time she didn't do a little extra
sweeping, spraying and wiping whenever she had company
over. Also, I don't recall a time she didn't cook or have
something to snack on for anyone that was over. There wasn't
much time for me to be stubborn. I apologized. "Take that
chocolate chips dough out the fridge and set some lemons out.
I'll bake some cookies and make fresh lemonade for you all to
have while they're here. I'm going to go freshen up myself and
please make sure you wash your hands. We don't want to get
the baby sick from any germs or what not." She said as her
voice faded through the hall while heading back to her room. I
sat out the things she asked me to then ran in the living room to
fix the pillows on the couch, vacuumed then headed upstairs to
wash my hands. My stomached rumbled a little which wasn't a
good sign. I had to drop a deuce! It wasn't a quick one either. I
finished my business then lathered my hands and forearms with
soap until I washed and rinsed them several times. I brushed my
teeth then fixed up my room before being called back
downstairs by Mrs. Anthony. That was probably the fastest
thirty minutes ever! The smell of fresh cookies gave off the
sweetness aroma of walking through a bakery. I entered the
kitchen to see Mrs. Anthony unloading baby toys, clothes and
pampers on the table! She had out did herself I'll say! She must
had spent a fortune on all the cool things she brought. I never
checked the bags she had from the night she went shopping.
She had it all in presentation form like at a babies store. It was
positioned on the table as if it was a grand prize a lucky
contestant was winning on a game show. I was thankful and
amazed at the effort she had put in for me as well as Junior. I
couldn't have been any happier seeing that kind of support

from her. I walked up and hugged her tight then whispered, "Thank you."

As I was stepping back as we smiled at one another, my cell phone rang. It was Rachel telling me they had just pulled up outside. Mrs. Anthony flapped me out the kitchen as she knew who it was while she finished her surprise set up for the baby. I went out to help Rachel get everything to bring Junior in. As I was making it to her car, Samantha's car droved passed! She was rolling as if she was trying to get somewhere in a hurry. She glanced over at me then did a double take not knowing if it was really me, she had seen! It was weird overall because she kept driving then turned the block. I had to keep my cool while helping Rachel. I grabbed the bags while she unfastened the little guy out of his car seat. I was holding the bags waiting for her before heading up to the house while in a state of emergency mentally! Every car sound or person walking, I was eye balling hard. Finally, Rachel had him and we were on the porch heading in the house. I looked over my shoulder once more but no sign of Samantha coming back down the street to verify what she saw! I nearly slammed the door behind me as we made it inside. Mrs. Anthony appeared as she greeted them with a big smile. Junior's eyes were as wide as they could stretch as he stared at Mrs. Anthony hovering around him. I sat the baby bag on the coffee table then locked the door. I must have done it with force by the way they both looked over at me as I turned around. "Oh sorry, it was hard to turn." I whispered as I walked over towards them. "Let me see our little giant. Grandma Gloria has something special for you." Mrs. Anthony said as she reached for him. Rachel carefully placed him in Mrs. Anthony's arms. She then slowly walked him in the kitchen. Rachel glanced over at me as if she wanted to ask about the special surprise from the look on her face. I pointed to the kitchen for her to follow Mrs. Anthony. She turned towards the kitchen and proceeded with cautious as I followed as well.

"Wow! Oh my God! Look at that!" Rachel said as she saw all the things for Junior that were on the table. "Look what you have my cutie pie. I had to get some things for you to play with when you're over here. I had to make sure I was prepared when you spend time with Grandma Gloria." Mrs. Anthony said as she started to pick up some of the colorful toys, she had for him. "I can't thank you enough for doing this! I really appreciate it!" Rachel said as she smiled at Mrs. Anthony. "Well, all you have to do is bring him by whenever. You can just drop him off. I have everything he needs now. You don't have to bring him a bag or wrestle with all of that. I know with babies that young, you have to pack so much. They are so needy. I wanted to make it's as easy as possible for me to spend time with my little guy." Mrs. Anthony said to Rachel. I then offered Rachel a seat at the table. We sat down while Mrs. Anthony continued to whisper to Junior showing him everything. "I did not know she bought that much stuff. I'm lucky to have her." I whispered to Rachel as she was staring at me as if I knew what the surprise was but didn't tell her. "Yeah that was so sweet of her. I tell you, that it has been an unreal feeling I've had since you've been home. I hope things adjust accordingly without any stress for both of us." She whispered back. I felt that unreal feeling as well. I knew things would get extremely stressful if I didn't do something to get Melvin off my butt! Something hit my thinking cap like a lightning bolt! I thought about that cop and the frustration he had, being unable to pin anything on Melvin. I envisioned a scenario that would make both of our lives more peaceful. The clock was ticking so I had to excuse myself for a second to make a phone call. I remembered the officers last name from staring at his badge when he pulled up on me. I stepped out on to the front porch then sat at the first step then made the call. I was able to get a hold of that same cop within minutes then unfolded my idea. We talked for about ten minutes then I hung up with both of my knees bouncing with uncertainty! I stood up slowly hoping I didn't just commit suicide on what I agreed to do with him. I wiped the sweat off my face until it was as dry as I could get it without anyone noticing I was a nervous wreck walking back in the house.

I walked back in the kitchen to find Rachel munching on some fresh hot chocolate chip cookies that I had to get my hands on! Mrs. Anthony was still entertaining the little guy walking through the house. I sat beside Rachel after grabbing a of couple cookies. I was in a daze enjoying the warmth and tasty cookies when Rachel leaned in then asked, "What are your plans with me?" Nearly choking I hurried sipping the cup of lemonade I had poured! She sat back in her seat then shook her head as if she knew exactly how I would respond. She even smirked at me as she waited patiently as I wiped my mouth off with a paper towel. I was about to laugh it off as a joke, yet I sensed the seriousness in her tone. The last thing I wanted to do was piss off the mother of my child to have her storm out with our baby, in tears from not choosing the right words to say to her question. I was too smooth to allow myself to miss the opportunity to put a smile on her face. I admit I couldn't keep my eyes from dancing all over her sexy body. The post baby weight she was wearing added a few pounds in the right areas to her already gorgeous frame. I allowed the words to come together in my thoughts while giving her my innocent puppy dog eyes. "What do you mean? What I'm going to do with you? Hmm... It depends? I know what I'll like to do to you." I whispered back at her while cutting my eyes to scan the doorway to the kitchen making sure Mrs. Anthony didn't catch me carefully rubbing my hand down Rachel's thigh. I slowly brushed my hand against the top of her leg as I then waited with curiosity to see her reaction. I could see goose bumps forming on her arms as she sat there breathing deeply while I continued to get closer to her inner thigh. She suddenly placed her hand on mines then said, "You have no idea how much I would enjoy you. I haven't been touched or looked at this way since the day we did what we did." Not once did it cross my mind that she could have or would have been with someone else sexually besides me. I immediately took my hand away as the guilt started to fill my thoughts. I felt selfish. My body didn't care because I wanted what I wanted in that moment.

Mrs. Anthony appeared with Junior resting peacefully in her arms as she cradled him. He was snoring with a smile on his face like there was no better feeling than that. "I wanted to lay him in my bed if that's okay. I'll be in there with him keeping a close eye on him if you're fine with that Rachel?" Mrs. Anthony whispered to her. "Yes ma'am, that'll be fine. It is about that time for his afternoon nap." Rachel replied. "Let me know if you two need anything. I'll be in my room with the little angel." Mrs. Anthony said as she walked past us heading towards her room. We both said okay. The imagination of being inside of Rachel did not leave my thoughts. I stared at her the same way she gazed at me. From the look on her face, she was giving me the same vibes. I wasn't sure how long nap time was going to be and I didn't want to waste another second trying to count the minutes. "Want to go in the living room?" I calmly asked while observing her nonverbals. I wanted to see if she was going to just follow my lead or she was going to block the lust that had stirred up. She got up without saying a word then walked slowing out of the kitchen. Looked like she wanted to lead instead. I followed her as I hesitated to make sure I didn't hear any moving about from Mrs. Anthony down the hallway to her room. It was enough silence to keep me walking without worry. I was catching up with Rachel as we entered the living room. She didn't stop to sit on the couch, she walked over by the stairs! She waved me over to her. "Isn't this what you meant? You want to show me your room, right?" She whispered with a playful smile on her face. I nodded my head as I eased past her then up the stairs quietly without giving us up. She did the same as we both tip-toed upstairs. I held her hand as we entered my room. I was glad things were somewhat in order. Would have hated if I killed the mode with the room looking like a tornado hit it. There were some clothes scattered on the bed that I placed in the laundry basket by the closet. Rachel sat on the bed once I cleared it off. I pushed the bedroom door up just enough to still hear anything that was coming up the steps. The blinds were down and closed but the sun rays shined through bright enough where I didn't have to flick on the light switch.

I stood in front of Rachel then she grabbed a hand full of my shirt pulling me down to her. I maneuvered myself towards her as she spread her legs. We both laid back on to the bed with me between her legs. We began to kiss one another repeatedly. Soft and slow pecks that turned to tongue-wrestling and lip biting. I caressed her breast as she rubbed her hand against my chest. I started to kiss her gently on her neck until she whispered, "Have you been with anyone else since me?" Like a grenade was thrown at me! BOOM! The blood that was flowing down below my waist immediately made its way back up towards my head. It was an instant headache! My arms began to shake a little as I had to retreat, rolling over on the side of her! The air in the room left as if I started to gasp for oxygen from the decision of telling her anything but the truth. "What? What's wrong?" She whispered as she stared at me with innocence. She had made it clear enough that she hadn't been doing anything sexually, physically and none of the above with anyone. How was I going to go on with the guilt that time as I thought hard before replying? I didn't want to continue with the naïve image I painted of myself being clueless to her question. If there was any other question, I could have chosen for her to ask me in that moment, that wasn't on the list at all! "I have to be honest but I'm not sure how it's going to make you feel." I replied. She suddenly sat up on the edge of the bed to embrace my next words. I raised up next to her as well as my skin crawled with nervousness. If I was going to do anything physical with her, the best solution was to be transparent about everything and everyone I had been with. The mood had been compromised already, but I wanted to clear my conscience once and for all. "I'm sorry but I have been with someone else since then." I finally said as I exhaled before suffocating in stress. She didn't say anything for a few minutes. That gave me time to add, "I do like you. I know we're going to have to be at least casual with one another to raise Junior together. I just want to start by keeping it real with you about everything I have done or have going on. I'm not currently in any relationship with anyone but I have been with someone else physically." No words from her as she stood up then paced the floor as if she was thinking long and hard about what I said. Shaking her head as if she didn't want to believe any of it, she said, "Has it just been one girl or more girls?" Another question she tossed at me I wasn't prepared for! I could feel the temperature rising in the room as I again struggled to find the words to answer her. I was already in deep waters so there was no holding back. "Since you... There's only been one girl. Someone I met at school." I mumbled, although she heard every word as clear as she needed to. "You sure?" She immediately asked. I looked at her as if she was being funny, yet her expression was of a drill sergeant commanding an answer! "Yes, just one. We're not together, just friends now. It was something we both shouldn't have done. We agreed to keep it strictly about our friendship, nothing more than that." I replied. She stood by the door still with her thinking cap on as if she searched for more questions and understanding. "I promise there's nothing to worry about with that. All of this is new to us both. I just want to make sure I don't do anything to cause you not to want to talk to me or keep me from seeing our son. I've heard of crazy things happening that makes parents hate one another that puts confusion on the child that's not healthy. I hope for something better for us. I don't want him to experience anything like that if we can find a way to trust one another and do it for him. I won't hide anything from you if you do the same. That's the truth with that." I whispered as I had to lower my voice as I was starting to elevate it because of the emotional connections I felt with what I was saying. I started to relax after those words. I had said those things from my heart. I was ready for whatever she had for me. Whatever respond she gave. It didn't matter because I had reached the point through that confession that made me satisfied. After a few seconds she looked up at me as we were standing in front of each other. "If that's how you truly feel, if you want what's best for Junior then I won't hold anything against you that's in the past. I'm not and will never depend on you to be with me, but if we're going to be physical at any time going forward, I prefer us to be in a relationship. You have so much going on right now. I will give you time to figure some of it out. I can't express enough how much I would love for this to work out, but I know it's going to take time. I really like you and I'm thankful we have a precious baby boy together." She replied. I stepped to her then gave her a big warm hug. We held each other for a few minutes until I heard Mrs. Anthony calling my name! "Cedric? Are you all up there?" She said as I could tell she didn't want to talk too loud from the way her voice carried itself. I knew I would've been explaining why we were up there all night, but I was relieved that we didn't take anytime walking to the top of the stairs. I motioned Rachel to hurry over with me because I knew if she saw us, she would have assumed that we couldn't have been doing much if we appeared with that much haste, fully dressed. "Yeah we're up here. I was just showing her some old pictures and awards I had up here. Is everything okay? Is Junior up now?" I said followed with those questions for her to think about as we started our way down the stairs. "Yeah he claimed he was a skinny guy when he was younger, so I wanted to see the proof." Rachel added as she giggled. That was a nice assist from her without a que. I loved how she played the part with me. It was clutch because Mrs. Anthony was giving me the doubtful eye as I was stepping down past her but gave a smile when Rachel backed me up. She gave us both a good looking up and down that Rachel didn't notice. I was side eyeing Mrs. Anthony while she examined our body language and clothes as we lead the way into the kitchen. "Yeah he was a little joker back then. I'm glad he has some meat on those bones now. I don't know how he would have made it this far without putting on a few pounds." Mrs. Anthony finally replied as we all entered the kitchen. "Where's Junior?" I asked. "Oh, he's fine. Still resting. I got up because I thought I heard knocking at the door. I was coming out to see if you all answered the door?" She replied. Rachel and I both looked at one another with curious faces as neither of us heard any knocking. "Oh, well I don't think we heard it?" I said. I offered them both something drink. They decline while I poured me some water. "Okay. I'll go check on Junior." Mrs. Anthony replied then went off to her room. Rachel and I sat at the table. "Look at you, saving the day with the quick cosign! She wasn't going to believe my words. Thank you!" I said to Rachel smiling, feeling impressed. She smiled back then said, "You didn't sound too convincing. I knew how sketchy it looked for us to be up there like that to her. I wanted to make sure she didn't think we were wilding, being that disrespectful."

It was wrong on many levels to praise Rachel for helping me with lying for us to Mrs. Anthony. To a degree it was necessary in my eyes if I wanted to ease back over to getting her to start trusting me more. I was being stubborn yet needed to gain control over my actions and desires. I needed to survive those next two days to leave so I could regroup to get better. About twenty minutes went by while Rachel and I talked before Mrs. Anthony walked back in with Junior in her arms looking around as if he was on a scavenger hunt. His little eyes widened when he noticed Rachel standing up to greet him! "There's my man! Well rested… You took a nap with Grandma Gloria?" Rachel said to him in a cute funny voice. She picked him up from Mrs. Anthony's arm as she held him, giving him kisses on his big cheeks. "Say Hi daddy! I see you!" Rachel said as she swayed him over towards me as I stood still for him to get a better view of me. I'm wasn't sure if Mrs. Anthony was giving my cues that it was time to go or if she had something she had to do? "Let me get all his stuff together for you Rachel. There's only a couple of these toys I will keep here. You can take everything else back home with you." Mrs. Anthony said as she pulled out two giant bags. She started to place the things she bought Junior neatly in the two bags. Rachel placed Junior in my arms as she signaled me to get him so she could help Mrs. Anthony. It was too weird for me to hold him with care and attention to detail with his every move. His tiny hands and feet swinging and kicking all over the place. My nerves where getting better the longer I held him. I was overthinking it the whole time. I was focused on not dropping him instead of just resting my arms enough so he was as comfortable as he could be. I was getting the hang of it by the minute. He didn't say anything as he looked up at me. His eyes, his nose and those small shaped ears were all mines as I examined him. He couldn't have been anyone else's! The minutes felt like hours as I strolled around in a figure eight through the kitchen while the ladies sorted the things out. I guess time had sped up or something because it didn't feel like almost three hours had passed since they had arrived. "I really enjoyed coming by. Thank you all for having us over." Rachel said. She looked as if she needed a nap herself by then. She looked as if she needed that break from Junior as well. "Thank you for letting him rest. He's a night owl sometimes. I'm trying my best to get his sleeping schedule in order. I hate for my mom to have to get him from me because I haven't figured out the trick to get him to sleep at night."

Rachel added. "I think that's about it... Cedric will you help her carry these bags to the car?" Mrs. Anthony said as she was anxious to exchange Junior for the bag, she was holding for me to take. I gave her Junior then took the bag to the car after Rachel handed me the keys.

I stepped out to the car putting the bag in the back seat. As paranoid as I was, I was moving like a sleepy snail. I was having a difficult time getting the big bag in the back because a part of the bag was caught up on the hook part of the door. I kept trying to force it, but the bag started to rip a little! I pulled it back out to readjust it. I finally got it in there without anything catching onto the bag. I was bent down struggling with that bag longer than I should have been. Time had played a trick on me as the devil's chariot rode up on me once again! I nearly peed my pants as Melvin was parked right next to Rachel's car staring at me! The only thing that was okay about that situation was the fact that she had parked a way off and not directly in front of the house. The ladies would have had to come out the house to see what was going on outside. I thanked God they didn't! "Hey there daddy Cedric! Word spread fast around here you know. I wonder if they told you about the packages, I've sent them on your behalf. See I told you Cedric, I got you and that's what I meant. What's mines is mines and what's yours will be mines. You know how the saying goes or whatever." He said as he laughed at himself as if he had said a hilarious joke. I wanted so bad to correct him on that saying as he quoted it wrong. I also knew that wasn't best because I figured he was smart enough to have known that and that's why he laughed at himself I guessed. Looking over my shoulders every five seconds as I stood there trying not to piss him off wishing I was invisible. "Hey Melvin. What's going on?" I asked to get to the reason why he pulled down on me as if I didn't know already. "Tick tock, tick tock... We good? Just want to confirm our arrangement." He said as he leaned over closer to say to me while one of his arms were hanging out the window. I wanted him to believe me without the slightest doubt. "You right, I need him gone! I'm still not cool with him being around Mrs. Anthony like that. I need him out of the picture! I think he will be over in a few. We will be where we need to be tonight." I replied as I had the best poker face I've ever had in my life! He immediately started smiling nodding his head as if he had won me over to the dark side. "That's all I needed to hear. It's already done! I don't have to remind you that you better be there or else." Melvin said as his truck started to slowly roll away. I nodded my head agreeing with him that I understood the severity of the consequences if I was a no show. He disappeared up the street as I leaned against the car for a second. I wiped the sweat from my face then walked back in the house without anyone seeing the interaction with that menace.

I was opening the door just in time to catch Rachel coming towards to check on me as Mrs. Anthony had directed her to, she said. I explained to her about the bag fight I had. We both laughed as we walked back in the kitchen. I look to the sky thanking God for sparing me the headache of trying to explain why I was conversing with the enemy. Mrs. Anthony didn't say anything, she just pointed at another bag for me to take to the car. There was more enthusiasm with that second bag to the car trip. I didn't waste a second fumbling with the bag to get back in the house in record breaking time. That didn't matter as the ladies were coming towards the front door. "Thank you for bringing our little angel by to visit us. He is so adorable!" Mrs. Anthony said as she gave Junior a kiss on his forehead before walking to me with him. She motioned for me to get him. I reached for him as she guided him in my arms. It was my turn to say goodbye as they both watched me carefully. I rocked him in my arms saying how much I loved him and looked forward to spending more time with him. I was imitating the kinds of things I imagined my dad doing when I was as young as Junior. He never shied away from telling me he loved me. I reflected on those feelings and the fact of being okay to cry around him because he would tell me that if a man cries that means something is truly bothering him or he's passionate about it. He would say things like, expressing your pain, frustrations and emotions in the form of tears isn't a bad thing as a man. It shows that you're just as human as anyone. Never be afraid to vent in that way. He mentioned that I shouldn't do it too much around a lady too often because she'll think you can't protect her if you're always sitting around crying. He joked heavily about that part but never made me feel ashamed if I cried. Most of my tears came from disappointment with myself, my performance or actions surrounding baseball. I guess that too helped with him understanding. I never cried about something I couldn't get if my parents declined a request or over spilled milk as my mom would say. It helped overall as I teared up a little as I started to walk to the door. I didn't want them to see me. Not that I felt weak or childish. My emotions were getting the best of me as I held him. He just looked up at me the whole time. I saw myself in his eyes. The reflection was unbelievable. I was enjoying every second with him in my arms while we had our moment of searching for each other in our eyes. "Let me get the door for yawl. Thank you again Rachel. Please bring him back anytime. I'll make sure Cedric gives you my cell number if you ever miss me on the house phone. Please don't hesitate." Mrs. Anthony said as she opened the door for us. Rachel had the rest of Junior things.

We walked out on to the porch as we were suddenly greeted by Rico! He was hesitant as he crept up the steps to the porch. It made sense now as I thought about how Mrs. Anthony seemed a little hurried with getting Rachel and Junior home. Rachel as well as Mrs. Anthony both looked as if they wanted to say more than what came out of their mouths. "Oh, hey Rico, how are you?" Rachel said as she kept walking past him to the

steps. "Hey Rico." Mrs. Anthony said then looked at me with
caution. For me to convince Rico to go or do anything with me, I
couldn't act like the aggressor. It took a lot not to naturally want
to kick him in the chest. This was not only about his life that was
in jeopardy but mines as well. I took a deep breath then got in
to character. "Hey Rico, how's it going man?" I asked as I
continued walking following Rachel. I wish I had a picture of
Mrs. Anthony and Rico's faces after I casually went about it as if
I didn't have any reason to not say one word to him! Rachel and
I waited at the top of the porch for a reply to our greetings as he
was trying to make sure he wasn't mistaken for someone else.
"Oh, I'm fine. I'm okay. Was just stopping by to check on Mrs.
Anthony. It's a habit and I hope I didn't intrude." He finally
replied. "That's nice of you. Take care. Thanks again Mrs.
Anthony." Rachel said as she went on down the steps. I nodded
my head agreeing with what she said then added, "No intruding
at all. I'm glad you came by. If you're hanging around for a
minute, I wanted to catch up for a few if that's fine?" Again, the
looks they were giving each other were priceless. "Yeah, I'm
finished with my shift at the store. I do have time to stick
around for a little." Rico replied with uncertainty of my kindness
towards him. I went on to the car with Rachel. I helped with
putting Junior in his car seat and made sure she had all the
things she brought with her. I then walked over to her while she
stood at the driver's side. She turned the car on to run the air
conditioner for Junior to stay cool while we chatted. "You good?
I know you're making some serious adjustment right now with
all of this." Rachel said as she motioned with her hands pointing
at Junior, herself and towards the house with Rico and Mrs.
Anthony heading in. I had only one thing on my mind. I had to
get focused on my approach with Rico to gain his trust. I kissed
Rachel on her forehead then said, "Everything is going to be
okay. I can feel it. We have things to figure that are bigger than
my feelings towards something I should be getting over you

know. I'll call you later to check on you two." She smiled then said, "I hope we can figure it out." With a hint of sarcasm in her voice. I stepped back on to the sidewalk as I watched them pull off down the street.

Chapter 7

A Life for a Life

I plotted during the short walk back to the house as the vision of my plan locked in my sight. My intentions were to guilt trip him just enough to get him feeling like he owed me whatever favor or request I had for him. I replayed the answers he would try to give me and my counter questions or statements to make sure he didn't try to swivel out of what I needed him to do. I felt bad but I didn't have a choice. I thought about it as much I could, yet the time had come. I was still amazed on how it worked out with him dropping by that kept me from going on a wild goose chase to find him. I finally walked in knowing they were in the meeting room which was the kitchen. I could hear them speaking softly as I slowed my pace a bit to tune in to their whispers. Guess the wax was too thick in my ears or they perfected the ability to say things in code at the lowest volume! I heard voices but couldn't make out one word. Frustrated with not ease dropping good enough, I rushed in to see if I could throw their conversation off. They were sitting across from one another as if they knew I was going to come in at any time. What a waste of energy. Thinking I had the upper hand or the element of surprise, but they were good. "Hey Cedric, they make it out okay?" Mrs. Anthony asked without batting an eye as if she wasn't having a whole secret conversation with Rico. I had no time for the charades! I needed to get Rico alone to get to the point. "Yeah, they're good. I told her I would check on them later or to call me sooner if she needed me." I replied as I stood at one end of the table. My patience was challenged as they both looked at me as if I was supposed to make an announcement or start giving them reasons why I was standing in their presence. Mrs. Anthony had taken a liking to him that almost made me question her concern for me over her friendship with Rico. "I hope you're in a friendly mood. If I would've known Rico was coming, I promised I would have told you. Please don't be angry at me Cedric." She said. I sat down thinking something weird was about to happen or be said. "I'm okay. I have no issues right now with you nor Rico for him coming by." I replied as I started to get nervous with the unknown. "Well Cedric, I wanted to come by to see you. Talk, maybe hang out for a little to clear the air more if possible." Rico finally chimed in. I pinched my leg under the table without them noticing to make sure my mind wasn't toying with me. It couldn't have been real! I was thinking they were about to confess some awkward love they felt for one another that they were tired of hiding. I couldn't have answered him quick enough. "Well that's what I was about to say myself. I need to get an understanding between us. I don't want to leave here with questions unanswered nor do I want to make things uneasy for you, me or Mrs. Anthony. If this is what things have come to." I replied. Mrs. Anthony gave him the go-ahead nod that he could trust my word. He was expecting some push back by the way his eyes squint as I sat there with my serious face on. "Are you sure we good? I can give you more time if needed." Rico asked as if he wasn't sure himself if he was ready to move forward. "If you two are making it work, so can I." I answered. "I'm happy this is happening! It takes courage and patience. You two young men are displaying the kind of growth many take longer in life to achieve when it comes to forgiveness and redemption. It's a blessing I tell y'all. I'm going to let you two make amends. I'm going to run to the store before it gets too late. Don't break anything." Mrs. Anthony said as she was about to tear up until her joking comment at the end. She got up then hugged us both then kissed us on the cheeks before walking to her room for her keys.

Rico and I sat there as we both look around as we waited until Mrs. Anthony walked back through and on out the house. As soon as the door closed, the energy in the house shifted as I stood up immediately! Rico flinched for dear life with fear as if he knew he had made a bad decision to think we could get passed the past! "I'm sorry, please Cedric man, please! I'm sorry! I'm sorry!" Rico shouted as he slowly rose from his chair while I walked over towards him! I kept quiet while the suspense sat in until I was face to face with him. The once bad ass bully had become the gentle giant as he shivered, embracing for whatever I was going to do to him. He stood there hopeless with the innocence of a small child in fear. I lifted my arm just waist height then extended my hand to him. He looked as if he was a contestant in a prank show as he released a huge sigh of relief. He took a step back to catch his balance as he nearly tipped over from thinking he was about to be punched or pushed. He shook his head in embarrassment thinking we were about to brawl. I finally smiled at him shaking my head as well then said, "You good man?" He grabbed my hand as we shook them as a peace treaty. It didn't last but a second as I pulled my hand back looking at it after it was wet from his sweaty palms! "I'm better now! Yeah, I know my hands are drenched. You had me on the edge! I didn't know what was about to go down. I should have wiped them for you." He said as he continued to shake his head in pure joy that things didn't go sour. He rubbed his hands on the side of his legs to dry them. I walked back over to my seat then sat down as he did the same. "I realized that no matter how much I wanted things to be, the world finds a funny way of making it another way. I can't hide the fact I still have bitterness about losing David, yet we know what really happened and why. I'm in a much better place with Mrs. Anthony leading the way with her forgiving heart. She makes it hard for me to find hate in mines. I can't go anywhere farther in life if I stay grounded with the same hurt, doubts, frustrations and complaints. Something my dad would say countless times until it rang in my head after I had a dispute with my sister Tammie back then." I said. He looked confused as if I had said something wrong. "Wait, you have a sister?" He asked. It didn't hit me until then that no one knew about her here! Or was he lying like Mrs. Anthony was about knowing her and her whereabouts? I was thrown off with the memories scattering my mind of missing my sister and hearing her voice! It came down heavy on me as if I button was pushed. I was drifting away with sadness into a dark place of loneliness then I remembered we had a date with Melvin! I snapped out of the daze I was in about Tammie then said, "Yeah I have a sister, but we haven't seen each other in years! I'm used to it now so..." He couldn't believe it but didn't press the new information by the way I switched subjects. "Oh okay. That's crazy." He said before I suggested we go walking for some fresh air. He didn't hesitate, which gave me the opportunity to guide us where we needed to be.

I made sure all the doors were locked then grabbed my keys as we both existed the house. It was nighttime with the wind giving off a nice evening chill. The humidity was still roaming around but nothing that had us sweating. I knew it was going to take us about twenty minutes to get to the old abandoned skating ring about two miles from the house. I needed to keep him engaged with the conversation. I started off by sharing a little of my past as far as about my sister. I mentioned how that whole situation went and the reason why I ended up living with David and Mrs. Anthony. It was funny how no one never questioned that as he explained that he thought David and I were blood brothers. "I'm for real man. I apologize about everything. There are no words that can explain the depts I would go if I could bring David back. I just wanted to put that out there. I know we haven't had the real talk about it face to face. I just wanted to apologize again." Rico said in a very calm and sincere tone. I was quiet after he said that, thinking hard on how I wanted to respond. As we cruised down the street, getting closer to the spot, I noticed several cars slowly approaching then sped up once I looked back at them. It wasn't unusual at first until I seen the same car circle the block three times during our trek. I stayed chilled as I didn't want to alarm Rico on my true intentions. I continued with getting deeper about how I felt after David's death. I knew the day would come and if things went as planned, I felt that there was no better time than then to tell Rico. "I hated you and wished it was you laying there dead instead of David! I wished you were never born or ever lived anywhere near us. I wanted to pick that blade up to stab you too! You made my life a living hell from that! I had no sympathy for whatever time they were going to give you in jail. I was hopeful that you would spend the rest of your life behind bars. I had no emotions for weeks after that. I felt empty like someone had taken a huge chunk of me without caring how it left me. I questioned everything about life and my purpose. I even wished that it was me instead of David that died that day. He was the good guy! He didn't deserve that!" I said as the anger built up with every word. It was quiet as if everything were on pause. Rico's face said it all. He looked as if he was afraid of what was coming next. I had to catch my breath as the area was like a ghost town as we walk slowly across the parking lot of the old skating ring. I looked around trying to see if we were too early or too late. It was just Rico and I standing there as he started to get suspicious. "Cedric, I don't know what else to say. Every single word you said, I felt them, and you couldn't be more truthful than you are about it all. David was a good guy. I don't know what else to do to get you to forgive me. Whatever happens from this point on, I hope it works out in both of our favor. I pray things get better between us. Again, I apologize man!" He pleaded.

The wind had gone away with clear skies with sounds of traffic in the far distance as we stood there. I shook my head stalling as if I had to think about how I wanted to reply to him. I wondered about us just leaving to head back home to avoid the mayhem. I waited a minute too long to decide. Melvin's SUV crept up towards us as we both turned towards it with the headlights shining on us! I had to act my part which was beyond heartless of me when Rico asked, "Cedric, what's going? Is that Melvin? Why is he pulling up on us like this?" It took a lot out of me to lie to him as he was scared by the way he positioned himself slightly behind me. Melvin drove his truck right up on us within a foot or two with the lights blinding us that we had to place our hands over our eyes! If he had come any closer, he would had run us over! Once the truck stopped, we both took a couple of steps back then removed our hands from over our eyes. Three of the four doors of the truck opened, with Melvin and two of his workers getting out. As soon as Rico saw them, he tried to make a run for it, but I grabbed a hand full of his shirt tail to warn him how it wasn't a smart thing to do! He had the look of someone who knew things were about to get very ugly. He didn't want to have any part of it. The only way I could get him to chill out before Melvin made it to was to tell him, "Don't be afraid. It had to happen this way. I didn't have a choice. Trust me, you don't have to be scared." He relaxed enough for me to release his shirt as we stood waiting for them to get to us. My palms were sweating, my heart was beating a thousand times a second, as I stood there nervous as ever. "Christmas has come early for me once again! Cedric my boy, you came through for me!" Melvin said as he walked upon us with his evil smile on his face as he was excited like a child on Christmas morning. Rico immediately looked at me as it started to add up. He looked as if he wanted to say something. He already knew the answer. "I'm sorry..." I whispered to him. Melvin wasted no time pulling his big chrome revolver out of waistband with his two goons following by pulling their guns out too! "Don't make this harder than it needs to be. Bring your ass over here boy!" Melvin yelled to Rico as he waved his gun at him! I kept asking myself what I had done and was it worth it as the seconds felt like hours! Rico just gazed at me with tears in his eyes. He was mumbling as his lips were shaking like his legs were. Maybe he was praying or cursing me. I looked over at him as the tears were rolling down his face. "I said get your ass over here now before I splatter your brains all over Cedric! I know he doesn't want that! I've been waiting to get your ass for a while now! Thanks to Cedric here, I can finally make you pay for what you did!" Melvin said as he pointed the gun directly at Rico's head! Melvin's fingers were itching to pull the trigger as his partners laughed. I was getting dizzy from the hundred ways I thought I could have jumped in the way of Rico and saving him. Feeling like I had more to live for, all I could do was nod at him to move away from me. "Please Cedric! Please don't let him kill me! I wouldn't have done that to David if I knew! You know it! Please! Cedric... Help me! I'm sorry..." Rico begged through the tears. I looked over at Melvin then back at Rico. I felt cold. I couldn't respond to Rico. I held my head down. "Come on... You can do it!" Melvin said as he was toying with Rico.

As soon as Rico took his first step towards Melvin, lights from everywhere popped on shinning on all of us! About four police cars pulled up on us from all over the parking lot in all directions! "What the fuck is this?" Melvin said to himself as he looked around at all the cop cars that had surrounded us within seconds! His two goons slowly lowered their guns as they were shocked and confused on what to do. I pulled on Rico's shirt to step back with me while Melvin was distracted by all the lights and cars! "Melvin put your gun down man, we good." One of the guys with him suggested. The cars had all stopped with officers out of the cars with their guns drawn. They were all standing behind their car doors for cover. "Oohh, okay... I see what's going on. Y'all think it's over huh? Y'all think I'm going down like this!" Melvin shouted! He had forgotten about us as we were able to slowly run off towards one of the cop cars! We duck down low until we made it out of harm's way with one of the officers directing us behind his car! Melvin was tuned in to the fact that the cops had finally caught him in the act. "Ced... Cedric? Oh... You set me up motherfucker? Where that rat go? Cedric!" Melvin yelled when he finally noticed we slipped away! It seemed as if it happened in slow motion, how it all unfolded with us running away, I could see the look of madness in Melvin's face. After the cop made sure we were safe, he got back in position with his shotgun pointed directly at Melvin! "Drop the gun and put your hands above your head! Now!" One of the officers yelled at Melvin. Melvin looked disgusted at his boys as he seen the look of defeat in their faces. It was like a scene from an old western movie my dad used to watch on Saturday evenings. I watched every move Melvin made while the cops held their guns steady and ready. Even some of the officers were nervous as some of their guns were shaky as they waited for Melvin to comply to their commands. "Put the gun down now! Put your hands up!" The officers yelled at Melvin again giving him time to think about his decision. Melvin swayed back and forth with his revolver in his grips as he looked bamboozled about how everything had suddenly changed to his disadvantage. I was peeping from an angle from underneath one of the car doors as Rico and I laid flat on our stomachs in fear of the worst. I couldn't make out the words Melvin was saying to the two with him, but I could tell he was getting angrier with them by the second as he began to wave his gun at them! "Melvin! Put your gun now! Don't make things harder than it has to be! Please drop your weapon!" A familiar voice rang out at Melvin! I scanned the other cop cars best I could to get a view of the officer I had called earlier that day. I thanked God they had finally showed up as I laid there thinking that I made the right sacrifice that night! I decided that Rico and my lives were more important to me than Melvin's. I couldn't allow Melvin to walk around our neighborhood like he owned everything and everyone. Who was I to give him such an evil request as to killing someone while I sat back and watched? Without a doubt that if he killed Rico in cold blood like that, there was no chance for me to walk away knowing the truth. I was for sure we both were going to die that night. I did what was best for the community. If calling the police and setting a notorious nuisance up by lying to him to take the bait he asked for, so be it. I was scared I was going to get a lot of heat from Melvin's entourage if they ever found out I dimed him out. The officer made it clear that I would never be mentioned as an accomplice in any report with helping them catching Melvin committing a crime. I felt like a proud snitch with no guilt or regret. If trying to do what was best for the whole made people look down on me then I was all for it. The decision was done, and we were witnessing the fate of Melvin with every second he continued to hold his gun in his hand! "This is the way it's got to be then so be it! If you want me to drop my gun, you drop yours first!" Melvin finally said as he continued to play chicken with the officers. More officers started to arrive with a few random people approaching. Some of the cops had to keep the people from getting too close as I seen them flapping people away from the scene! "This is your last warning! Drop your weapon now and put your hands up!" The officers shouted at Melvin! The two guys with Melvin looked as if they were going to pee their pants. They pleaded with him from the look on their faces as they kept themselves a few feet away from Melvin! The tension was at the highest stress level as the officers showed unbelievable patience with Melvin until he went from waving the gun at the two with him to pointing it at a few officers as they were getting closer! Again, it all slowed down even more as if I was given seconds ahead of it all. Seeing the way, the two guys with Melvin raised their hands as soon as Melvin turned his gun at the police! The two rushed in the opposite direction from Melvin with their hands straight in the air! I was able to get a glimpse of that same evil grin on Melvin's face right before I heard, Bang! Boom! Bang Bang! Boom Boom! The shots rang out repeatedly! I immediately covered my ears and tucked myself in to a small tight ball! It sounded like about fifty shots were fired until one of the cops yelled out, "Hold your fire! Hold your fire!" My entire body trembled with terror as my heart felt like it had beat completely out of my body and laid in my ears as it pounded piercingly! Rico had rolled over to me as he too was shaking uncontrollably as our backs pressed against one another! Dust and smoke covered the area! I carefully turned over towards Rico as I placed my arm on him to check to see if he was okay. It was the slightest touch of my hand on his shoulder that caused him to tighten up even more with horror! I had to whisper to him, "Rico, it's me. It's me man. You good? It's me Cedric." He gasped for air until he was able to tame himself before he could finally turn towards me. He looked as if he been awakened out of a deep sleep, saved from a crazy nightmare. Suddenly voices yelled out, "Melvin! Let go of your weapon now!" I popped my head up to see a few of the officers moving in closer to Melvin with their guns still pointed at him as he laid on the ground slumped on the front bumper of his SUV. Smoke from their guns and Melvin's body could be seen as they kept their eyes glued on him. I slid over to zoom in on Melvin's bloody body as he still had a grip on his gun! He was coughing up blood struggling to catch his breath! I for once in all the encounters I had ever had with him, finally saw the same fear he caused now planted deep in his eyes! He looked around as if he were searching for help or for the two guys that were with him. "Let go of the gun now! Drop it now!" The cops continued to scream at him! They stalled as if they were waiting for him to respond to their commends. I could see in his face he was not there mentally nor physically. He was in disarray clinging to the last seconds of his life! I knew that look. I've witness that look before. It was the same look David was wearing when death was taking over him. As bad as I wanted to yell out that he is dying, I knew it wasn't going to matter! All the officers looked as if that's exactly what they were waiting on. They did not call for an ambulance nor did they hurry to check him out as it was clear that he didn't have the will or strength to lift his gun anymore. The threat was for sure over yet not one cop budged. Melvin had just enough in him to say his last words! "Officer Jackson! You won!" He yelled as the ending breaths left his body as the motions of his chest declined in normal rhythm. The gun beyond doubt fell from his palm as a sign of confirmation that Melvin was gone. A couple of the officers rushed over to the two other guys as they were both laid on their stomachs with their hands above their heads. They were then handcuffed. Finally, one of the officers strolled up to Melvin's lifeless body as blood dripped from the countless holes that were deeply embedded in him. The officer swiftly kicked the gun away as if there was a chance Melvin would be able to do anything after that.

I could not feel my arms or legs as my ears echoed the gunshots while I was trying to sit myself up. "Are you fellas okay!" The one cop asked us that was the closest to us. I examined myself carefully as I rubbed my hands all over my limbs to triple check, I didn't get hit with the flesh piercing ammo they fired off. I felt fine but Rico was trenched with tears as he could not stop himself for shaking. "I could've died! I almost die! I was supposed to be dead right now! I was supposed to be dead... Right now!" Rico cried out as he looked at me with confusion! "Son! It's okay... You're fine! The right person died tonight. Don't you worry about anything. You guys did great!" The officer I made the call to said as he walked over to us. I checked the name badge to be sure it said, "Jackson".

His name was Officer Jackson. Him and another cop near us both helped us up on to our feet. Rico was a complete mess as he couldn't catch his balance as the other officer escorted him to another car to have a seat. I couldn't help but stare at Melvin until they placed a sheet over his body. The crowd was getting bigger as more sirens sounded from the distance. The other two dudes that were with Melvin were drenched in sweat as if they had been through a terrible storm! They were yanked up on to their feet! The officers then placed them in two separate cars which drove away in opposite directions. I was distraught about how I was feeling as my hands started to shake with anxiety as the blood soaked through the sheet Melvin's body was underneath! It hit me harder and harder that I saved one life in exchange for another! My stomach boiled with remorse as I had to hurry to the side of one of the cars to hurl up everything, I ate for the last two days! Dark clouds could be seen in the distance as an ambulance final made its way on the scene. Officer Jackson appeared behind me then grabbed my arm with so much force that if I would have resisted in the least amount of effort, he would have for sure snatched it out of the socket! "Come now Cedric! I need to get you two out of here!" He said as he pulled me to the car Rico was sitting in! He placed me in the back beside Rico as he was still shaken up. I wiped my mouth with my shirt as the smell of puke lingered. Officer Jackson shut the door as he walked over to a few other cops and whispered to them then pointed back at us. "I'm sorry I got you in this for real. You may not understand it now. I had no other choice." I whispered to Rico. He wouldn't look at me. He even slid as close as he could to the other side of the car away from me. He just stared out the window as if I was contagious with a life threaten disease. I didn't press him about his reaction towards me. I didn't force any conversation with him from that point on.

We sat there in complete silence as the sounds of the officers scrambling around trying to control the crowd as a news truck finally pulled up as well. Rico's knees shook repeatedly as he was pressed against the door on his side of the car that made me want to plug my ears as it gave off an irritating ticking sound. After about five minutes of the quiet sitting session with Rico, Officer Jackson jumped in the driver's seat then demanded us to lay our heads down without being seen! It wasn't the most pleasant ride as we both balled up in the back on the very stiff and uncomfortable hard plastic seat. It was way too tight for two six-foot dudes to be sitting yet along crouched down back there. I placed the side of my face on top of my hands avoiding touching the seat with my face not knowing what kinds of asses had been sitting in the car before us. Don't know why I was more concerned about getting some sort of rash on face from the unsanitary seat than the fact I just helped our local police department in the murder of Melvin! He drove slowly through the parking lot away from the bulk of the people waiting and watching what happened. Office Jackson continued to whisper to us, "Stay down please. Don't move. We're almost in the clear." Rico was out of commission as well as furious with me as he began to mumble to himself while trying to keep the top of his head from touching mines as we laid there. Thunder echoed from the clouds as we rode away from the scene. "You guys okay back there? You two can come up now." Officer Jackson said. Rico popped up before Officer Jackson could finish his statement. He wiped the tears and sweat off his face with the sleeve of his shirt as he stayed as close to the door on his side. "I don't know what to feel to be honest. I can't believe what happened. Was that supposed to happen? I mean... I didn't think y'all were going to kill him!" I said as my voice cracked up pushing the words through. Officer Jackson didn't reply to me as we ended up in front of Rico's house. He then got out of the car then walked over to Rico's side. He opened the door then signaled for Rico to get out. He closed the door back once Rico slowly pealed his body from the seat. I wanted to say some encouraging word to Rico, but I had a feeling it would fall on deaf ears. Rico and Officer Jackson walked together to Rico's porch. They talked for about five minutes as I could see Officer Jackson had his hand on Rico's shoulder whispering in his ear the whole time. After that Rico shook his head then went into his house.

Officer Jackson returned to the car as raindrops started to fall on the front windshield of the car. More thunder sounded off as it began to rain harder as we drove away. I waited patiently for a response to my statement as we rode through the neighborhood as I could tell something wasn't right about the direction, he was heading in. I began to get impatient as he made a few turns down some streets away from where I should have been going! We ended up at a dead end surrounded by some abandoned houses that looked like a good place you would dump a dead body! No one would know for weeks! I was beyond cautious and nervous about his intentions of driving me at that location after what had just happened. He turned the car around then backed it in where we were facing any approaching person or vehicle. He then turned the car off as I was trying to figure out the best route to run in if he opened the door trying to get me out the car! He sat there for about a full minute before saying, "First off, I have to thank you for your bravery to do what you did. Secondly, I know what happened is something that you'll never forget. Cedric, I want you to know that it isn't your fault that Melvin's dead. Please... Under no circumstances should you feel any sense of guilt for that. You know just as well as I do, that if anyone deserved to be shot, he was number one! I wanted to talk to you about what's going to happen now." I processed his words as I shook my head still unsure if it was the best thing for me to have gotten involved in. What he was saying was true. I hated I had to be the one to set it up like that.

I did make the call. I thought they would just lock Melvin up for good while. At least long enough to clean up our neighborhood. I guessed wrong. I had to live with that fact for the rest of my life. "Yeah it's tough knowing I was a part of it overall. I can't imagine what people are going to say or even the retaliation from his crew when those two other guys start talking." I replied. He immediately followed with, "No, no worries at all about them two. This is classified information I'm about to give you. Do not let this leave this car! Okay Cedric. I'm serious." I hesitate for a moment. I thought that I probably shouldn't know it just to not give him any more reasons to want me dead for knowing too much as I felt I had reached that threshold already. "As if I don't know enough already that'll put me high on your list to take out if this thing blows over. Shoot me now then." I replied with the deepest concern about my life and safety. "Those two guys were a part of an ongoing investigation we've had open on Melvin for the last two years. You don't have to worry about anything. There won't be anyone looking for you nor will anyone find out." He said. My mind was blown as the questions rushed in trying to figure out why I was needed in the first place! I threw as many of them at him as they were coming in! "But why did I have to be involved then? Who else was in on this? How many people suffered during this long investigation? Why did it take so long to put something together? How can..." I screamed at him! He yelled my name cutting the load of questions off as he became frustrated with my interrogation with him! "You have no clue how hard this decision was. We did not want to get you involved! Remember, you called me! We've had many officers working countless hours trying to find the right time and enough evidence to take Melvin down for good! It was a blessing in disguise that you reached out to us. Especially under the circumstances and the planned murder that was going to take place! You didn't have the best choices I understand. It was either assisting us to take down Melvin or you were assisting him to kill an innocent guy! I apologize son but that's just how things happen. I too wish things could have ended a different way, yet you wanted us to ignore the fact he was literally pointing a fully loaded pistol at us! Let's keep the facts straight jack!" He said as I could feel the heat coming from his anger towards the doubts I riled up. I took a second to compress my emotions on everything. The choice was made way before I got involved. Melvin's destiny was coming to an end either way. The life he lived was heading nowhere fast. I couldn't blame myself nor the officers for doing what needed to be done. Melvin chose his expiration date. There was no need for me to hold my head down with shame or ignorance to the divine cycle of reaping what you've sowed. "You've made your point... I apologize for my reaction. Melvin fate was already aligned with a tragic ending one way or another. Thank you. I appreciate you all for having our backs! Things could have been the other way around with Rico or me laying there stretched out with a hole in us. I apologize for not seeing the bigger picture." I said as I rubbed my eyes to keep the tears from falling. It hit me suddenly on how real that situation was! Melvin wasn't going to leave there without someone dying! Guess he didn't know that it was going to be him.

We both sat there as I noticed Officer Jackson had wiped his face too as if he were holding back something. I leaned forward in my seat then asked, "Hey man! You okay?" He tried to stiffen his posture but couldn't keep it together as smooth as he intended. He started slamming his hand on the steering wheel with hard blows! I thought he was having a nervous breakdown! "Officer Jackson! Please say something! You're scaring me back here man!" I yelled at him trying to get him to shake out of it! "I've been trying for years to get him to change! For so many years! We weren't raised that way!" He screamed to the top of his lungs as I could hear the hurt in his voice! I had never until that moment seen or heard a police officer cry yet alone with that much passion! I stuck on the "we" part like a fly on a turd! That was more surprising than hearing what Melvin's last words were! "Wait, what?" What's going man?" I lowered my tone to get him to a calmer level mentally. It took about three to four minutes to finally get it out. "Melvin was like one of the most honest, thoughtful guys I knew! He treated me like family! We grew up next door to each other. We were both raised by our grandmothers. We played pee wee football, ran on the same track team and went to the same grade schools coming up." He said as his voice forced every word out with pain. I was speechless! I didn't have any come back or motivating words to say as I sat there listening. "Melvin got caught up with the wrong group of guys. Innocent kids were shot, one guy died that day and the rest was history! Melvin was locked up for about 10, maybe 11 years for being in that car! I stayed in school, determined to become somebody. Once I finally graduated high school, I moved here to Jackson. I became an officer because I was scared. I ran from a situation that still hunts me! When Melvin was released, he found us... I had begged and pleaded with him that he could become someone better. Instead he was mentally gone. The life he lived in jail, had taken over him! He was never the same! No matter how many passes I gave him, he became worse beyond my imagination! A few years back once all the evidence pointed at him for robberies, murders and drug trafficking, I drew the line! The last conversation I had with him, I told him that if we both had to take each other out, I wouldn't hesitate." Officer Jackson said. My mind exploded again! I thought it was going to be hard for me to move on! Not a second went by that I had put together anything linking the two of them together with that kind of history! I felt selfish for trying to take the credit for feeling like a monster for what happened to Melvin. Officer Jackson was dealing with it all on a deeper slope than I was. "Wow! I had no idea whatsoever that you two were like brothers! Man, I'm so sorry you had to do that! I know it's tough as hell to witness the downfall of someone you knew personally." I replied as sincere as I could voice my words. He didn't respond. He cranked the car back up then slowly drove up the street. Before I sat on back in the seat as we turned on the streets leading to my house, I noticed a picture of Officer Jackson, a lady and a little girl I thought I've seen with Melvin years ago. It wasn't strange as he had just told me they were like brothers. I figured she was probably like a sister or someone close to them both.

Lightning flashed like fireworks in the night sky as we got closer to my house with the smell of fresh rain breezing through the front car windows. As we arrived at my house, we both sat there as the rain started to ease up. "You don't have to say anything to anyone about anything that happened or that was said." Officer Jackson reminded as he turned around towards me. I looked around as I noticed the window blinds of the front window to the house started to move. Mrs. Anthony was going to come out soon! "It's understood. I didn't see no evil, didn't hear no evil! Got it." I said as I pulled on the door handle nearly breaking my hand! He started to laugh then said, "I can tell you've never been in the back of a police car. Let's keep it that way, okay..." He then got out of the car then pulled the door open for me. "You're only here for another day or two, there's something else I need your help with before you do your disappearing act. I'll be back tomorrow afternoon when we get everything under control with what happened tonight." He whispered as I stood up from the back of the car shaking my legs to regain the blood circulation in them. Another surprise I didn't have the energy to question or address. I just wanted to get to my room and lay down to sleep for the last two days I was there. "Okay. I don't think I'll be leaving the house until it's time for me to catch my flight out of here!" I replied as I slowly edged my way towards the house. "I can't say I'm sorry enough about what you had to see. I trust we both understand the effect it will cause if you mention any details about this anyone." He said making sure he gave me his serious face one last time. I nodded as I stared at him with my poker face to confirm I understood. I kept walking until I reached the steps then turned to thank him once more. He nodded then sat back in his car. I went up the steps as the front door cracked open. Mrs. Anthony was waiting patiently for me to enter. I wanted to run back to his car to tell him take me anywhere but there! I didn't think I was mentally prepared to talk to her so soon about the hundred questions she had. I hesitate long enough to generate a few quick answers in my head before I stepped in the house. "Oh my God Cedric! Are you okay? Please come on in!" She said as she shut the door behind me once I walked in. I headed to the kitchen as she followed me. "I'm okay." I replied. "I just hung up the phone with Rico! He told me everything!" She said with a worried tone in her voice that made me cough nearly choking on my tongue! I fumbled with the water pitcher as I grabbed it out the fridge. My toes tingled as my feet started to cramp up from being jammed in the back of the squad car. I was about to panic until she continued with, "He told me y'all were out walking and talking. Seems like you two crossed paths with the wrong group of guys. Rico said you had some words with some guys that weren't being nice. I'm so glad Officer Jackson was patrolling the area. I appreciate him for offering you two a ride home! Who knows what would have happened to y'all?" All I could do was agree with her on what was said. I didn't second guess any of the story. I added my two cents. "Yeah... I wasn't sure what had them guys harassing us. We tried to overlook them. They kept talking smack to us. Officer Jackson definitely saved us!" I replied as I faked yawning hoping she would get the hint I wanted nothing to do with a detailed summary of what Rico and I talked about. I feared she was going to ask by the way she sat at the table looking like a curious toddler. "Are you tired?" She asked. I drank the full glass of water without stopping then sat it in the sink. "This has been another eventful day for me. Tired is an understatement. The bed has been yelling my name for the last hour at least." I replied as I stood there waiting for her to take the bait to release me from her web of curiosity. I finally regain the feeling in my toes as I looked at my hands and noticed how dirty they were. A sharp pain formed through both my wrists as I started to slowly swing my arms without alarming her. "That's fine. I understand. Get some rest. I want to hear about your little conversation stroll with Rico tomorrow, okay." She said as she stood up. The was my que to go. "Thanks. I will tell you all about it. Good night." I said then eased out the kitchen.

I walked faster once I made it to the stairs. I made it to my room then push the door up a bit before crashing on the bed. I balled up both fists a couple times as I was trying to figure out why they were sore. It hit me as I replayed the scene from earlier of Rico and I dropping on the ground face first! I remember catching myself with my hands as we pasted ourselves on the dirt and gravel. I jumped back up then went to the restroom to wash the dirt off as I ran my hands under the cold water. After I dried my hands, I start patting for my cell phone but didn't feel it! I ran into the room then searched all over the bed before sliding back downstairs to look in the kitchen. I looked everywhere! My phone where nowhere to be found. I went as far to call it from the kitchen phone, but I didn't hear it anywhere in the house! I was mad as hell! I kept quiet about it as I walked back upstairs. The last thing I wanted to do was to tell Mrs. Anthony, for her to ask me even more questions about what we were doing for me to have lost my phone. I made it back up to my room then kicked my shoes off followed by throwing my shirt I had on over towards the closet door. It was well after ten with the rain starting to pick back up beating on the house. I laid in bed retracing where I was to see how my phone could have come up missing. Nothing was pinpointing my thoughts to the exact time or place. I added it to the lost column.

Chapter 8

A Priceless Reunion

It wasn't that I hadn't gotten enough sleep, it was the fact that I was in the middle of seeing Melvin dropping his gun before they started shooting! I was awakened by sounds of my name being called! It felt so real that I started to smile when I saw the gun laying on the ground right before Melvin put his hands up! I tossed and turned as I blinked my eyes realizing it was all a dream. "Cedric! Get up!" Mrs. Anthony yelled from the top of the stairs. I looked over at the clock to see that it was passed nine in the morning. I sat up wiping the sleep crumbs from the corners of my eyes. "I'm up! Okay, I'm up!" I replied loudly back at her. "Officer Jackson is here! He needs to talk to you! Freshen up then come on down please!" She said. "Okay! I'll be down there!" I replied. Forgetting some of the many words during the conversations I had with everyone had me guessing his prompt early interview with me. I replayed the spotty interactions but remembering every second of Melvin being shot to death! My nerves started to dance through my body as I could barely hold the toothbrush while brushing my teeth. Didn't even wash my face as my anxiety got the best of me to seek the reasons of his visit. I stepped carefully down the stairs knowing that he was in the kitchen with Mrs. Anthony. They both were sitting on the couch as they spotted me from the noise of the steps as I was trying to cruise down them. "Hey! Cedric, morning to ya! I'll try not to take up too much of your time if you don't mind." Officer Jackson said while giving me an awkward stare as if he was concern with how I was going to respond. It was clear on what not to say although I was skeptical on what to say as I reached the bottom of the stairs. "Good morning Officer Jackson. How can I help you?" I said as I stepped over to them. I stood in front of them blocking the TV they were pretending to watch. What alarmed me the most was the silence from Mrs. Anthony as Officer Jackson did all the talking. She looked like she had heard I was involved in a mass killing spree and there was nothing she could do to help me out of the arrest he was about to make! "Have a seat." He said as if I was the guest. I sat down in the love seat that was to the right of them which put me next to Mrs. Anthony. There were tiny sweat bubbles forming along the top of my nose. I took some long deep breaths trying to stay relaxed. "Well Cedric... I don't know how to put this. We need your help. I don't want you to feel embarrassed or ashamed. Please be as truthful as possible. For us to help you, you need to help us. Okay..." He stated as he leaned in taking a note pad out of his pocket that had an ink pen attached to it. "Please Cedric! If anything, I mean anything, happened to you, tell him everything! Tell the truth Cedric!" Mrs. Anthony finally said with a passionate worried voice. She too leaned forward as she started to fan herself with some old mail, she picked up off the coffee table. I felt more confused than a baby twin seeing his or her identical sister or brother for the first time! There were no special signals coming from Officer Jackson for me to decode. There was no warning from Mrs. Anthony to prepare me. I was on a deserted island all alone with zero hints to what was about to be asked of me! "Yes ma'am. Okay... What do you want to know sir?" I replied to them. Officer Jackson clicked the top of his pen then asked, "Did principal Ms. Harris, at your old high school ever do anything that was inappropriate to you or around you Cedric?" Those words stomped on me out the blue as if I had been jumped on by ten dudes! They had me trapped for sure! I shook my head with my mouth hanging opened as if I was unsure about the question. "What? Say that again." I asked as I tried to give myself a second to think. "Mrs. Anthony and I spoke for some time about it this morning. She said she had asked you about it. I had to come ask you again because there's an ongoing investigation that involves up to eight former students. We need the truth Cedric. Please take your time. I'm in no rush." Officer Jackson said with sympathy as if he knew more than he was suggesting. I had tried for quite some time to erase what happened to me from my memory. I thought it wasn't a bad thing overall since we didn't go all the way. Since she only rubbed my chest and legs. The fact we didn't kiss or anything else, it wasn't anything I needed tell. I didn't know how far she went with the others. It made me uneasy thinking how she was seriously taking advantage of us all. I was being selfish especially if more guys were confessing. I was scared to change my story because I had lied to Mrs. Anthony. I do remember my mom telling me that the truth helps as soon as you tell it. She said the longer or the more you lie the more you'll start to believe the lies. She would tell us that a lie doesn't care who tells it. I had to get it out my system! "I... I don't remember everything but... Well... She did come on to me in her office weeks before I graduated." I whispered as if Ms. Harris was standing in the next room listening to me. "It's not easy sharing something like that. I understand. We have been going through tons of school surveillance videos. We came across some footage of her walking you to her office after a fight you had with Rico I believe. What grabbed our attention was the amount time you two were in there alone as well as the actions we saw from you the moment she left her office. We noticed the discomfort and fear you displayed sneaking out of her office. I hate to ask but I need you to think hard back to that day to give me as many details about what exactly happened to you in her office." Officer Jackson said. I glanced over at Mrs. Anthony as tears fell from her eyes as she looked at me as if she had failed. I told them both everything I could remember. I told them how I ended up with her alone, how she had me pinned down on the chair to when she tried to pull me between her legs while she was propped up on her desk. I explained how I was able to get away because of Rico. That's when I realized how significant Rico's actions were! He caused Ms. Harris to be needed in the main office. If it weren't for that, I would have been raped! Rico saved me from some serious mental trauma I didn't foresee at all. Then I felt the first tear fall from my eyes. Officer Jackson grabbed some tissues from the table then handed them to Mrs. Anthony and me. "Thank you for being brave enough to share that. This is not normal nor okay for young men to experience this type of behavior from any adult. We have been working extremely hard to get all the evidence, statements while trying to track her down. We have had two of her victims try to commit suicide because of the shame they've felt! I hope and pray Cedric that you say something to someone if you ever feel any pressure that will cause you to want to harm yourself because of what happened to you! Please reach out! I'm so sorry you had to go through that..." Officer Jackson said as he walked over to me then gave me a pat on the back. I felt this huge load lifted after it was all out. The tears didn't let up, but I was okay with that. Mrs. Anthony came over to me as I stood up and we embraced one another. She whispered, "I'm sorry baby. I'm so sorry... I'm sorry... I'm sorry you went through that... I should have asked more questions. I didn't know. I wish there something I could have done. I'm sorry." The tears that fell from my face weren't for me. They were for the other guys. I learned that day that no matter who it is or how it was done, wrong will forever be wrong. It was clear that I could be as opened as needed with Mrs. Anthony or anyone when it came to anything that was illegal, offensive, inappropriate or downright sinister. Speaking up about it not only released tension within myself, it instantly created an even closer bond between Mrs. Anthony and me. It also gave me hope that justice would be served for me as well as anyone else that fell into her sick, nasty grips! "'I'm okay. I needed to get that off my chest. I'm so lucky to have your support and love. It's not any of our fault what happened to me or those other guys. I hope she pays for what she did." I said as I slowly took a step back looking at Mrs. Anthony while wiping the last tears from my cheeks. Again, Officer Jackson handed us more tissues as we dried our faces. Suddenly, a call came into his walkie talkie like device he had fastened to his shoulder area that was slightly hanging near his chest as he grabbed it then turned a button on as he placed his ear to it. It sounded like it was an emergency by the way he stepped back a couple steps to hear it better as his entire facial impression changed from relaxed to intense. He walked back over then said, "I need to leave! People are starting to gather to protest about what happened to Melvin. Can you believe that? Not sure if you all have heard it yet, but he was shot dead by us late last night. I hate to run off, but I'm needed! I have all the information I came for Cedric. Thank you for your cooperation. We have a special counselor that will contact you all within a few hours. It's a good idea to speak with him Cedric, just in case there's more you need to say. These types of things can really take a toll on you mentally. It can cause discomfort for the rest of your life. I want to make sure you have access to the right people. I'm here for you, Mrs. Anthony, and the ears of the therapist. Please contact me if there's anything else you remember or want to say. Take care Cedric. Thanks." Officer Jackson said as he shook my hand then gave me a pamphlet that had, "You Are Not Alone" on it. He gave it to me carefully. That's when I noticed it had my phone tucked in it! He gave me a look that meant, it was a close call and be glad he found it before anyone else did! I gave him the nonverbal eyebrows raise agreeing with his gesture then I thumbed through it quickly as it was for the sexually abused. I nodded at him agreeing to his words. Mrs. Anthony thanked him for coming by then seen him out the house. They whispered among themselves as she walked him out the front door. I was sure she was asking about the Melvin news. She came back in with a shocked look on her face then shut the door. She walked back over to me then asked, "Are you okay?" I shrugged my shoulders as if I couldn't think of anything to complain about. I was interested in what they were talking about. I didn't want to slip up with my words. "I apologize for lying to you." I said. "I understand why Cedric. It's okay…" She replied. "I think that was best. I do feel much better now. I needed that. Thank you." She hugged me once more then asked, "Are you hungry?" I smiled instantly as I could feel my stomach smiling too. "You know it!" I replied. She returned the smile then said, "There's a new restaurant with an amazing breakfast buffet about twenty minutes from here. Let's go there." My smile got even bigger! "Sounds good to me!" I replied. We both laughed because she had no doubts, I was all about some all you can eat. "We will leave in fifteen minutes." She said before heading to her room. I shook my head then strolled up the stairs to get ready.

We went on to the breakfast place and it was indeed amazing! It had everything you could imagine eating on its tasty buffet line. From fresh biscuits to pancakes. It had meat for days! Country fried ham, sausage links to steaks! The French toast with some of the best honey maple syrup I've ever had! We must had been there for about two hours until Mrs. Anthony made me stop! I was going in on the deep end of pigging out! I was in breakfast heaven! I guess she drew the line when I rolled a piece of steak up in a pancake with eggs and cheese then dipped it in a small bowl of that delicious syrup. I was eating like I hadn't eaten in weeks! The manager of the place stopped by our table several times to cheer me on to have as much as I could handle. I almost had to crawl back to the car. I was full to max capacity with a huge smile on my face with a few crumbs on my lips Mrs. Anthony had to tell me about.

During my breakfast adventure, Rachel called. Mrs. Anthony suggested we stop by to spend time with Junior on our way home since I was leaving back to Chicago the next morning. As we made our way to Rachel's house, we approached an intersection about a mile away. We could see a large crowd gathered. It looked as if they were yelling and clashing with the police! You could see them yelling at the officers as the cops stood in a single line beside each other with their patrol cars behind them blocking the road towards the police station! "Please stay away from this nonsense Cedric. I don't know what's going to happen here, but I know it's not going to end well if you have a bunch of fools going after the police about something that's good for the neighborhood." Mrs. Anthony said as we both stared down the street. She paused for a moment realizing what she was saying then added, "I mean. Lord forgive me. I'm not saying someone's death is a good thing. It's the fact we don't have to worry so much about a well-known problem anymore." I nodded my head then said, "I know what you meant. That's crazy people are so upset about it. Just about everyone I know with all the worries they've had with Melvin, I thought people would be celebrating! Not upset about how he died. Plus, it's a lie anyway." She immediately turned to me as if she were curious about my certainty of the details on what really happened to Melvin. "I mean... I just can't imagine the cops would just walk up to him and shoot him dead in cold blood. You know?" She sat there as if she was trying to make sense of it all. She wanted to talk more about it, but we were holding up traffic as a car blew its horn at us to go through the light! We were caught by the light at the next intersection as the car behind us swirled over in a speeding rush almost cutting us off the road! Mrs. Anthony slowed down so that car could go on through the light. While sitting at that intersection I had to do a double take, wipe both of my eyes with my hands and blink a few times as I couldn't believe who I was seeing! There was

Charlene standing off in the distance! She looked like she hadn't bathed in days as her hair looked dry, all over her head while wearing some cutoff jeans with a dingy t-shirt. She looked lost as if she wasn't in a rush to go anywhere. She looked as if she was having a conversation with someone but there was no one there! I bit my tongue as we had the green light to go. I noticed a small box with a blanket laying inside of it. First thing came to mind was a baby! The stress of wondering why she was out there like that burned a hole in my head! I even pressed down on the imaginary brakes on my side of the car to stop to go check on her, but I kept quiet. I turned slightly as we drove on watching her hoping there wasn't a baby in that box! "You okay? You look like you're about to fall asleep in a food coma?" Mrs. Anthony said as she broke my chain of thoughts about Charlene. I sat back up right in my seat as we were pulling up to Rachel's house. "I'm good. I'm sure Junior's energy will shake me out of the idea of sleeping any time soon. I wish we had one of those buffets in Chicago! That food was super good!" I replied. She laughed at me as she parked the car.

"Well I'm glad you enjoyed it. I need to run some errands if you're okay with me coming back to get you. Just call me if you want me to leave any sooner than me coming back after the stops I need to make. I wanted you to get more time with Junior instead of me stealing my little precious prince from you." She said as she smiled then waited for me to reply. She was right, I needed to get that extra time in with the little guy. "Yes ma'am, that's cool. Thanks. I'm sure I'll be fine. Take your time." I replied. I had to check my pockets for my phone before she pulled off. I walked up to Rachel's porch as she was opening the door to greet me. Mrs. Anthony blew her horn at us as she was driving away. Rachel invited me in as I noticed there was nothing going on in there. It was noticeably quiet with no signs of Junior. We walked in the living room area then sat down together on a couch. "Where's our little monster?" I asked. She smiled then said, "He's taking a nap. My parents are gone so I'm enjoying this peace. I have the baby monitor over there on the table to hear him if he gets up." She said then pointed at the device on top of the self by the couch. "If you listen closely you can hear him snoring. He's fighting off a running nose but it's clearing up." She said as we both tuned in to hear him sleeping. I didn't want to admit he probably got that snoring from me since I've been known to get the whole house up at night a time or two. We both laughed as she offered me something to drink. We sat there for about an hour talking more about Junior, my plans the rest of the year as far coming back home soon, how I feel about school and the people I've befriended since I've been up there. She seemed somewhat anxious about hearing all about my return. She kept asking questions about my options if things didn't go well with school and baseball as if I needed a backup plan. She danced around that thought the longest during our conversation that forced me to seek ideas for my future beyond baseball. I had no other alternative as it was clear to me that I was going pro. From the moment I hit my first home run to stealing my first base, the potential I possessed as every coach I've had since has always praised me for. I saw myself in a major league uniform traveling across the country making big money, enjoying life! In the back of my mind the mystery of life without baseball started to sink in as she wasn't satisfied with me settling for that one and only dream, I've embraced for years.

The "what ifs" were endless as if she had written them down and studied them to interview me with. I began to get frustrated because my answers were thin compared to the thick, heavy load of hypothetical situations she was pouring on me to respond to! In all that time, I don't recall anyone, not even Mrs. Anthony ever caring enough to speak of my dreams or goals beyond being an athlete. Rachel hit a soft spot I didn't think I had when it came to my determination in knowing my destination in life. "I'm just being curious Cedric. I mean… Since Junior has been here, there's not a day that goes by where I'm clueless about figuring out what I'm going to do with my life. I need a plan now more than ever to ensure that I can support and raise my child. Sorry, I mean our child. I want to make sure I have some sort of direction or goal in place. Every day of not getting closer to those ideas or directions scares me." She said as I felt the sincere concern in her voice. I needed something else to live for. If baseball let me down, I needed something else to pick me back up to make sure I could take care not only myself but my responsibilities of being a dad. "Damn… You got me thinking. All I know is baseball. I need a plan B, C and D basically. I'm glad you're picking my brain." I replied then tried to lean in to kiss her but was blocked by her forearm! "I'm serious Cedric! I don't want to fail, nor do I want you to. I need to know that you have your head on the right! I'm sorry but we need to figure some of this out." She said with an overly aggressive look on face. It was another reality check by Rachel as she demanded me to visualize my goals to make it work. It was understood that she wanted me to choose to do what was best not just settle for whatever happens happen. We sat there in silence for a couple of minutes. I visualized the obligations I had as well as the ultimatum she demanded for me to be intimate with her and to tame her doubts of me being a responsible baby daddy. Sounds of Junior crying altered my thoughts as we both jumped up! We both high stepped through the hallway to Rachel's room to him moving his tiny arms and legs as if he was trying to roll over. She coached me on picking him up as she directed me to get him. I had him in my arms within seconds as I patted his little booty like she told me. That quickly calmed him down like magic which I wouldn't have guessed that in a thousand years. "Yeah for some reason that's the go-to comfort he enjoys the most. It works most of the time with everyone else but me. Go figure. As if I don't have the right method or rhythm that's up to his standards. Looks like you have the touch. Yes, I'm jealous." Rachel said then rolled her eyes at me. All I could do was laugh as I could tell she was really disturbed about not getting the butt pat to his satisfaction. "Well, I can't speak for everyone else, but its nature for me. I'm so smooth with it." I replied with a smirk on my face.

My phone started ringing with Mrs. Anthony's name blinking on the screen. Rachel took Junior from me so I could answer the call. I stepped into the hallway to talk. Rachel signaled me that she going to change him because she made a face as if he was stinky while holding him close to her nose. "Mrs. Anthony, hey… What's going on?" I said once I was halfway down the hall. My skin started to crawl a little as I could tell she was in a hurry to answer me from the heavy frantic breathing I could hear through the phone! "I need to come get you now! Your sister is here, and she wants to see you!" She said loudly through the phone as I could hear keys rattling and what sounded like her cranking up her car! I nearly dropped the phone as my mouth and throat became dryer than sandpaper! My hands were shaking as I tried to keep the phone up to my ear. "Cedric…" Mrs. Anthony said as I hadn't responded yet to her. Rachel popped out the room holding Junior as she looked like I was a stranger. "Are you okay? What's wrong?" She asked. I was stuck there like my feet were glued to the floor and my body was frozen all over! "Cedric I'm on my way!" Mrs. Anthony said then the phone call disconnected. "Cedric… Is everything okay? You look like someone died!" Rachel added. I slowly lowered the phone from my ear. I was hoping to be long gone back to Chicago before I questioned Mrs. Anthony about Tammie. I finally answered Rachel, "I have to go. I'm sorry I can't stay longer. Something came up and Mrs. Anthony is on her way to get me now." The disappointment showed as clear as a sunny afternoon sky on Rachel's face. She didn't want to hear that. She walked past me with a stone-cold attitude.

"Rachel. I'm sorry. Please…" I pleaded with her as I followed her back into the living room. She sat down on the couch then started to whisper to Junior. "It's okay baby. Daddy has to get things in order. Daddy keeps making boo boos. Daddy needs time to figure some things out. He loves you. He just can't spend time with you right now." The way she said it, to our son just loud enough for me to hear after me telling her I had to go, really pissed me off! It stung deep within me that she would do that. I knew she was upset. That was beyond selfish to say that like that which made me even more stressed out. I kneeled to give Junior a kiss on his forehead. Rachel immediately moved him out the way of my attempt. I stood up quickly in shock she would take it that far. "Wow! Are you serious right now? Please don't make this harder for me." I said as I took a step back shaking my head in disbelief. Without hesitation she said, "Don't make this harder on you? Really Cedric? Is this all about you? Everyone has to make sure you're okay huh. Whatever you want? Oh no Cedric is upset because things aren't going his way. Boy please! You don't know what I've been through!" She started to tear up a little. I reached for Junior so she could wipe her face but again she rejected that! It was as if I had hit a switch on her or pressed the wrong button. She went from an innocent queen to a wicked witch within seconds!

I swear Mrs. Anthony must have had her whole damn foot on the gas! The honking of her horn came within minutes! It was good she came on over as fast as she did because I wasn't sure where things between Rachel and I were heading. I was hurt how all the negative energy came full speed without any warning. "I don't know where this is all coming from, but I have to go. I'll call you later to check if I can see him again before I leave since I only have one more day here. Thanks for being a great mother so far. I hope we can get past whatever this anger or misunderstanding is. Talk to you soon." I said then gave her a second or two to respond. I feared it wasn't going to be pleasant by the way she stared at me as if she wanted to slap me. She didn't bother to say a word as I walked out the door. She has never looked at me in such a way. I truly didn't know who Rachel really was. It started to make sense on what I had in my mind of the kind of girl she was verse me not really spending any time with her to get the know the real her. Yeah, we had many conversations over the phone but that face to face energy was different. I felt guilty leaving in the way I did as I realized Rachel probably needed me more than my heartless sister did. The older sister I had that magically appeared from the pits of the darkness, she left me in! Mrs. Anthony was parked in the middle of the street as if she were waiting to drive off in a dash like she was a getaway driver! I glanced back at the front door, but Rachel had already closed it. I guess she was too upset to say or even wave bye to Mrs. Anthony or me. I jumped in the car with jumbled feelings and defeats. On one hand I was figuring out who Rachel was and who she required me to be. On the other hand, I had a mountain of questions for my selfish ass sister.

The closer we got to our house the louder my heartbeat became! Mrs. Anthony was unusually quiet as if she wanted to say something but didn't want to say the wrong thing. I had to hold my knees down with my hands to keep them still from all the shaking and bouncing they were doing. They were worse than Rico's the night we were in the back of the squad car! It had been too long to act like I didn't miss her as well as not long enough for her to every forget she had a little brother! I wanted to scream out how cold it was that Mrs. Anthony knew more than she was telling me. That would only complicate things for me. The sun was setting as a breeze of air circled itself throughout the car from window to window keeping the sweat under control. I noticed a small funny looking dingy blueish van with long rectangle windows on each side out front as we parked behind it. It had California license plates on it. As we got out of the car then walked past it, I noticed it had bags and items stuffed in it as if someone had moved or was throwed out. There was no order on how it was packed in the tiny shaped van, that looked like a hipster's ride from the early 70s. I had no doubts that that was Tammie's. "I apologize Cedric. I know this is coming to you so randomly. I don't know what to say. I've prayed that this helps you." Mrs. Anthony said as we walked on the porch. She was feeling some guilt as far as my thoughts were about what she said. She knew way more than she had told me or whether not told me. It was probably killing her on the inside. I suddenly felt a sense of relief. Something came over me that reminded me that the thoughts I used to stay up with worrying about my sister's wellbeing were being answered. I did for weeks and months at a time, wondering if she was alive, safe or alone somewhere lost. That was the one positive thing I had to hold on to before I walked in the house to see her. "It is what it is. Don't be sorry, it's not like you did anything wrong." I replied as I started to step in the house after her. I shut the door behind me then turned around to see Tammie sitting as she had her head laying on the arm of the chair in a deep sleep. She looked cold and tiny! She wasn't big or out of shape. She was way more fit compared to the boney lady I was staring at. I stepped over towards her as I examined her from the messy hair to the rough looking shoes she was wearing. She had on some very wrinkled baggy clothes. She had sores that looked like bruises on arms! At first, I thought to myself that that wasn't the Tammie I last seen or if that was even my sister at all! I moved in close enough to spot the small scorpion tattoo that was behind the top part of her neck slightly behind her ear. That was the only confirmation I had that she was indeed my big sister. I wanted to shake her to wake her, but she looked like she hadn't slept in days if not a week. I grabbed the thin blanket Mrs. Anthony kept in the recliner then laid it on her. Mrs. Anthony had tears falling from her face as I finally turned to her. I had the questions on my tongue, but the tears wouldn't let me get any words out. I nearly fell into Mrs. Anthony's arms as she held me up before walking me in the kitchen! She guided me to one of the chairs then I sat down at the table. All I could do was shake my head in anger and sadness. Mrs. Anthony stood over me as the tears poured down my face while she rubbed my shoulder. I sat there with my head laying on top of my arms as they were folded on top of the table.

For about twenty minutes I sat there completely dazed at the fact my sister was sitting in the next room. Mrs. Anthony went from the kitchen to the living room checking on us both. I was torn apart at the condition Tammie was in. Finally, Mrs. Anthony moved a chair closer to me then sat down beside me. She looked at as if she didn't know where to start with what she was about to say. I wiped my eyes with some of the tissues she placed on the table for me. "Cedric, I believe that God has placed so much weight on you because he is going to bless you beyond your imagination. I know you may not understand it now but soon you will. I feel it in my soul that you were placed in my life for many reasons. I hope that you can go on to seek your purpose in life. I know when God is using someone for a greater purpose than their own. The things you've been through and are going through will only continue to make you stronger in areas others are weak in. Your ability to push through the storms will be a living testimony of how great God is. Your sister has been through a major storm in her life and as hard as its going to be, she needs you more than you need her. I know it may seem unfair but right now, your love for her is all I'm asking you to give. She's your sister, family and she need her little brother to be a big brother." She whispered to me as she went on rubbing the top half of my back. The load did get heavier after she said that! I wanted to whine about the fairness of it all, yet she was right. Tammie looked like she was in worse shape than me mentally and physically. All this time I've been holding on to the lashing I was sure to give her whenever we crossed paths. I would have looked like a low life bully had I addressed her about any of that. "I don't know what to do. What do I say?" I whispered back confused about how I should approach my sister. "Don't worry about what to say, maybe she just needs you to be a good listener. When it's time for you to speak, I'm sure the right words will be there." She replied then walked towards her room. I got up and went back into the living room then sat next to Tammie as she slept. I managed to flick on the TV without causing a scene with the volume down. I watched about fifteen minutes of the news reporting on the story behind Melvin's death. People were confused as to what exactly happened. The police captain gave a report and what he described wasn't anything close to the truth. I didn't even raise an eyebrow about it. I sat there quiet as a mouse until I found myself nodding off. Tammie shifted herself in the weirdest positions on the arm of the couch as if she were fighting something or someone in her dreams. I gave her a light nudge on the shoulder. I looked on in case she was close to falling off the couch, but she managed to stay put. That helped her to get more comfortable as she went back to sleep. I couldn't get as relaxed as I wanted to, so I placed a blanket on the floor next to the couch then laid down. I grabbed one of the pillows from the couch then rested my head on it until I was out cold.

Vibrations from my phone had me lurking around on the floor looking like a scared mouse! It was dark with the tv glaring in my face that made things blurry for me as I fished around to find my phone. Whole time I was moving my hands in small circular motions thinking it was hidden amongst the pillar and blanket, until I finally realized it was deep in my pocket. I immediately remembered how I ended up on the stiff carpeted floor. I pulled my phone out of my pocket to see eight miss calls from Rachel, Lauren and one from Officer Jackson. The time said it was close to midnight. I didn't believe it until I looked up to find the living room empty with just me and the tv staring at one another. I jumped up as if someone had taken something from me while I was knocked out! I surveyed the room as I slowly walked over to the light switch. It was pitch black outside as I could see nothing through the small creases of the curtains. I decided not to turn on the light because there wasn't a need to. No other movement nor sound was made through the entire house. I was too curious on the whereabouts of my sister to lay back down on the floor. No one in the kitchen as I quietly went in there then peeped down the hallway towards Mrs. Anthony's room. Her door was closed which meant she was sleep. I went back to the living room then on up the stairs to finally find my bedroom door pushed closed slightly. I peeped my head in there but didn't see her in there. I glanced over to David's old room and saw that the door was pushed up as well. I stepped over to see that she was laying peacefully in the bed snoring louder than a lawn mower! There was no way I was going to endure that the rest of the night across the hall from me, so I decided to go back downstairs and finish my night sleeping on the couch! At least that proved to me that women do snore in their sleep. It was once an urban legend that women were too lady like to snore, but Tammie killed that myth! She could blow! I made myself comfortable on the couch as I turned the tv off before going back to sleep.

I felt cold slightly damp fingers graze against my ear a few times before I rolled over to see who would wake someone like that! I felt violated a little because it gave me the wrong kind of chills. "Cedric... Hi... It's me, Tammie..." Tammie said as her voice met with my eyes seeing her face as I turned over. Her hair was wet as if she was fresh out the shower. She was wearing one of my old shirts with some loose jogging pants I assumed were hers. She looked as if she was struggling to stay still as if she were cold and shivering all over. I didn't think it was that cool in the house. It was a very noticeable shake she had. It was hard for her to look me directly in the eyes as well as it was for me to look in hers. I slowly raised up to give her room on the couch to sit down. I tossed the blanket over on to the chair next to me as I gave her time to sit before, I said anything. There were so many words that formed all at once at the tip of my tongue as I held them all in. I was hoping Mrs. Anthony was up and was going to walk in to mediate the reunion. After a few awkward silent minutes, Tammie whispered three words that crushed me like an empty soda can. "'I'm sorry Cedric." The sound of those words traveled straight to the center of the softest part of my heart. Whatever anger or vengeances I had set for that day were thrown out the window! The tension I felt in my shoulders down to my toes suddenly disappeared! I didn't hesitate for a second to wrap my arms around her as she pressed herself close to me. We both squeezed one another exactly the way anyone would when you see a loved one you thought you'll never see again! I didn't care about the time or the how that kept her away from me. I cared about that moment! She took long deep breath as if she needed every second of that hug from me. I exhaled that same sensation. My whole mood flipped, I felt in charge of my emotions as I remembered what Mrs. Anthony had said. Tammie needed me. The light bulb lit up as I started to crave some answers. My approach was at ease, less aggressive as I had planned for some time. "Where have you been? What's going on with you?" I asked in the sincerest tone. She slowly ran her hand through her hair as she finally looked into my eyes for more than two seconds. Tears came flowing down her face as she shook her head as if she couldn't believe she was sitting there next to me. I had chills and goosebumps on my arms as I waited to hear her story. She took a deep breath than said, "I don't know where to start... I don't want to be short but the things I've been through wasn't what I signed up for. I have never felt as low as I do now in my entire life. I didn't know what else to do! I had to see you! There was nothing else I cared about anymore but seeing your face." I know what I heard but it sounded like there was some deeper darker life changing experiences she wasn't tapping into. I felt sorry for her because she looked like she had been though a lot. "I'm glad you're here. Whatever happened is done. I hope we can move forward, together. I'm so happy to see you!" I replied. I leaned in and hugged her tight again. She continued to cry as I held my tears back. "There's things I want to tell you... I just don't think it's the right time. As crazy as that sounds. I need some time to get my head on my shoulders. I'm a hot mess. I know there are so many unanswered questions you have. I just need you to be patient with me Cedric. Thank you." She said then suddenly stood up excusing herself to the restroom.

The timing was in sync as Mrs. Anthony came into the living room. She quietly said, "Give it time. She's going to need some serious help. I will make sure she's okay while you're gone." I wanted to tell her there was no way I was going back to school. Seeing Tammie in the shape she was in gave me all the reasons I needed to stay home. We needed each other. I didn't want to abandon her in a time of desperate need for support and comfort. I wanted Mrs. Anthony to tell me what to do so I asked, "What do you think I should do? I'm leaving in less than 24 hours with a baby to take care of and now a sister that hit rock bottom! Please tell me what I need to do?" My head was spinning with blame! "I've already made it simple for you! I told you I'm going to make sure everything is okay. I will take care of our little angel and I'm going to help Tammie with whatever support she needs to get her back on her feet. You will go back to school and finish what we started. There's not a damn thing you should worry about. Okay!" In all the years I've been living in that house, I had never heard Mrs. Anthony use the slightest cuss word whatsoever. The look in her eyes with the clear-cut authority of her voice, I knew I needed to go back to Chicago with no worries about anything. I wished I could have replayed her saying that as a reminder that she was indeed human with a passion for my wellbeing! I wanted to hear it over and over whenever I felt down or discouraged. Tammie walked back in as Mrs. Anthony played it off as if she were asking me about my travel arrangements for my departure the next morning. It was slick of her to do because she didn't want Tammie to know we were talking about her. The last thing we needed was to do anything that would alarm her or push her away during her time of need. Tammie sat back down next me. "I'm sorry I left like Cedric. I'm trying hard to hold things in because I've cried out for so long on deaf ears. I honestly have been dealing with a very abusive brick wall! My life has been in shambles. I tried for way too long to love through the pain, the verbal and physical abuse! I turned to weed then to alcohol then to the harder stuff searching to feel alive again. Rodrick, my knight in shiny armor, well... He was the worst thing that happened to my entire life! I regret the day we met! I thought we were going to live this fun filled love adventure together. Boy was I wrong! Young and dumb! To think that I left my one and only brother behind for him! I can't apologize enough Cedric! I'm so sorry! I haven't been high, nor have I had a smoke or a drink in three days! I couldn't drop in on you unannounced with that poison in me. I need help badly. All I have is my life, that beat up van and my rags." She said while the tears poured from her eyes. Again, I was enraged yet heartbroken. A tremendous force of anger came upon me with the image of seeing my sister being hit by that punk! I wanted to find him and drive my whole fist through his head! She basically answered every question I thought of.

A tear fell from my eye as I leaned over to her and placed my arm over her shoulders. Mrs. Anthony didn't give any reaction like I expected which made it clear that she had heard the story before. I questioned my insanity as I couldn't gasp the connection of why all these things were happening like it was around me. "I hate that you left me just as much as I hate what you had to go through. No one deserves that kind of life. No one does! I won't lie... Rod, Roddick, Rodney... whatever his name is... Is on my list of people that needs a personal beat down from me. I'll throw in two broken legs and I sore asshole after I get my shoe out of it! I'm pissed but there's nothing I could do to him to change the hurt he caused." I replied. They both smiled a little at my name miscue and wanting to smash his face in. "We will all get through this for sure. You two have the right to be free from worry. Whatever it takes to see to that then I'm a part of it." Mrs. Anthony added. "Can I see my nephew already please!" Tammie asked as she smiled through the tears before whipping her face. "Yes, I need to call Rachel to see if we can arrange that. She may let you two see him. You know this is my last night here? I hate to leave with this much excitement going on, but I know Mrs. Anthony is going to take good care of you. She's the best in the world and I wouldn't trust another soul with you other than her." I said. "I hope she lets me see him then. I know you have to go back to school. I'm so proud of you Cedric! I apologize for missing those special moments! Seeing you graduate as well as seeing you off to college! You have become your own man I see. I'm so glad you have had Mrs. Anthony in your life through it all! I can't thank her enough for loving you and supporting you the way she has." Tammie replied. We all went to freshen up as I called Rachel to have her to bring Junior over for a little to see Tammie. She didn't answer my first call. I left a long voicemail about why I left and apologized if I seemed incentive to what she's had to deal with overall. Minutes later she called back and said she would. She only agreed to bring him because of Tammie and Mr. Anthony. I was okay with that. I took a shower then put on some fresh clothes. It was indeed weird yet refreshing to have my sister back as well as her meeting my son. I would have bet money she was going to be the first one with kids the way she was moving so fast with her dumb ex-boyfriend.

About an hour later after we were all back downstairs in the living room chatting about the college life so far, Rachel called and said she was outside pulling up. "The little prince has arrived!" I said as I hung up the phone. Tammie didn't wait a second as she ran to the door then out of the house to greet them! Mrs. Anthony and I smiled at one another as we followed Tammie out on to the porch. I didn't have to help as Tammie was at the car getting Junior out of his car seat. Her eyes glazed with tears in them stunned at the handsome fella. Rachel was giving me the stare of anger and curiosity as she knew of Tammie but had never seen her. "Hi Rachel! How are you?" Mrs. Anthony said to Rachel. "I'm fine. Just fine... How are you all?" Rachel replied as she came on to the porch behind Tammie and Junior. "Rachel this is my sister Tammie. Tammie this is Rachel and the Prince of Jackson!" I said jokingly as Tammie couldn't unlock her eyes off Junior. Tammie looked up for a split second to say hi to Rachel. We all went back into the house as I held the door for the ladies. After about an hour of talking, laughing, playing with Junior, Mrs. Anthony made tacos and baked brownies for us since neither of us had breakfast. It was around noon time. We talked more and ate at the kitchen table for hours. While the ladies were chatting and Junior being passed around like a precious diamond, I had another out of body experience! I saw happiness and love with me right in the center of it all! It felt so good too! I needed every second of it and by the looks on everyone else's faces, they did too! Rachel was the only one looking a bit uneased which I understood her concerns. It was a priceless moment overall I could live with for the rest of my life! I had not one complaint. Another two to three hours later after junior had played himself to sleep and all the brownies were gone. It was time to call it a night. I gave my little guy all the kisses I could give him without waking him as

Rachel was packing their things before, we walked to the car. Tammie had fallen asleep as well and Mrs. Anthony looked like she needed some rest as she yawned before she went to use the restroom.

I promised Rachel several times I wouldn't miss a day without calling to check on them. My flight was leaving exceedingly early the next morning. I wasn't going to see them for a while. Rachel wore her frustration well with the reality setting in of my departure as she wrestled with the straps on Junior's car seat. I grabbed her hands then turned her towards me. I looked in her eyes then said, "Everything is going to be fine. It will get better. I'm not leaving forever. I want this to work out okay." She held her head down as if she didn't want to hear any of it. She was pouting to herself. I lifted her head by placing my hand under her chin. When she looked up at me, I placed a soft kiss on her lips. She didn't fight me or move out of dodge. "I mean it. I want all of this to work out. And it will." I whispered. She tried to hold back the smile that was pushing through as she couldn't keep her eyes locked on me. "I hear you. You better come back!" She replied as she then pulled me in for another kiss. Just as we were untangling our lips and tongues from one another Mrs. Anthony walked back in. She gave Junior a little stuffed animal she tucked under his tiny arm without waking him then kissed him on the cheek. "Thanks for bringing our handsome guy over here Rachel. I will be in touch. Take care sweetie." Mrs. Anthony said then walked back in the kitchen. I assumed she was going off to her room. I helped to make sure Rachel had everything she came with before I picked up the little guy in his car seat. After getting the little guy in the car, I walked over to Rachel's side of the car. We talked for about five minutes, but not once did she say anything about Tammie or how I felt about the whole surprise party we just had. I joke about not knowing how I got myself in all of that with the ladies in my life. Then said I could handle it. She finally started up the car as Junior was moving about in his seat. She wanted to get him on home because she said he didn't like to ride as much as she thought he would. He didn't like not seeing anyone as he was faced backwards in the car. He was either sleep or crying the whole time whenever they were riding. We smiled and I leaned in once more for one last kiss. It felt good to see Rachel from a different perspective as far as in her mommy duties and expressing her desire to be a family. I was lucky she gave me that much action after her hate speech with me the day before. We both said bye then she slowly drove off down the street.

I stepped back in the house. Mrs. Anthony told me to double check my things to ensure I wasn't forgetting anything to take back to school with me. It was just late enough where we both needed to lay down since my flight was super early. Tammie had made her way to David's old room where she was crashed out. As I walked up the stairs peeping in to check on her, I realized I didn't hear from Lauren at all that day, so I decided to call her. Her phone rang about eight times before I decided to give up. I went through my bag and backpack to make sure I was ready to go as soon as I got up for my flight. It was warmer than usual upstairs. Maybe it was from the moving I was doing packing or maybe from the thoughts chasing one another through my head. I wanted to wake Tammie to have a few more words with her before bailing on her but she looked so peaceful. I pulled the door up after leaning in to see her balled up in a blanket then went back to my room. I was good to go with about four more hours before it was time to head to the airport. I laid down with my phone in my hand as I scrolled through the few contacts I had. I stared at Samantha's name for a couple of minutes as I played out the kind of conversation we would have had if she would have answered the phone if I called. I didn't think it was a great idea especially not reaching out to her while I was in town. I still felt like she saw me or heard I was here but didn't want to see me. It made me hesitate long enough to just sit my phone down next to me as I rolled over to take advantage of the few fours I had to rest.

Chapter 9

Close Encounter

My flight back to Chicago was nice and chill. There wasn't a big rush as I arrived at the airport well in time to check in. I was up in the air and back on the ground after a relaxing morning nap. Lauren was there on time to pick me up after I double checked with her before taking off to make sure she was going to be there. She ran up to me and gave me a big hug as if she hadn't seen me in months! I looked around for Daniel, but he wasn't there. We jumped in the car and was off to our apartments. "Sooooo how was the big trip back home sir?" Lauren asked with a curious grin on her face. I replayed everything that happened that past week as if I were reliving it all. I eliminated the worse of the worse because I didn't want to go into any details about some of it. "I saw my little guy! I spent most of my time chilling with him and Mrs. Anthony. It was crazy! I didn't know holding babies required some much focus and skills." I replied. She laughed at me as she shook her head. "Aww that's so cute Cedric! Mr. Dad over here becoming a real man huh. I can see you holding a baby and trying to act all fly with it. Like "yeah I'm a dad and all but I'm smooth." I can hear you saying that!" She said as we finally pulled into our apartment complex. I smiled and thought about how I was trying not to look goofy when I was holding Junior. She was right. "Yeah yeah but I am fly. I make anything look cool." I replied. "Whatever you think Cedric. You make some things look okay." She replied as she continued to giggle.

We parked then got out as I looked around sensing the quietness of the place wasn't an accident. I got my stuff out of the back then we headed up the stairs. "What's going on around here? What has that damn Daniel been up to the past week. I knew for sure he would have called about something?" I asked jokingly. We kept walking with no answer from Lauren. We made it to my front door as that smirk she had on her face turned into a worried kitten. She opened the door for me with the same key I gave Daniel to keep an eye on the place. She walked in first as I followed with butterflies dancing in my stomach. To my disgust, a few things were out of place and slightly trashed! I couldn't even make it all the way in the apartment as I was mad as hell about what I was seeing. Lauren suddenly pulled me all the way in then shut the door! I didn't say a word as I started to walk through my apartment seeing that my TV was missing, the video game console was gone, as well as some of my nice shoes and two watches I loved! After seeing the mess, I knew someone had been in there looking for anything of value. I dropped my bags on my bedroom floor then sat on my bed feeling violated. Lauren looked at me as she waited for me to say something. I was speechless as I tried to understand the how part. "If you know something please say it now." I demanded from Lauren. She tried hard to dress it up as she stumbled with her words. "See, what had happened was... You know I wouldn't have let anything happen to your place like this. It's sad. I didn't think it was bad but... I tried stopping him but..." She mumbled which frustrated me even more. "Stop trying to explain yourself. Just tell me who did it! Please!" I screamed at her! It wasn't her fault I guessed so I had to apologize as my voice leveled up to a tone she didn't deserve. "I'm sorry for yelling at you. If you know who done it, just tell me. It's that simple. Okay..." I said with a calmer voice. She nodded her head but looked worried about giving me all the facts. She took in a deep breath then exhaled. "Daniel did this. I know it's weird and strange for it to be him but yes, he isn't the same." She whispered. I didn't say a word. I walked right past her towards the door. I didn't care to know why and how. I wanted to see him face to face immediately! Lauren rushed after me then swiftly propped herself in front of the door not giving me the access to leave. As bad as I wanted to pick her up and move her out the way, her stalling me did give me a moment to think about why he did it.

I could feel the pressure in my head starting to split my skull apart. "What excuse would anyone have to do their friend like this? There's nothing I can think of that would make this an acceptable situation. I need answers right now!" I yelled again! She wouldn't move an inch for me as she looked at me with concern. "Cedric. I'm sorry to tell you. But... Daniel is in the hospital." Lauren said as she started to cry. I went from wanting to bash his head in to realizing how none of the stuff that was missing outweighed my worries for Daniel's health! "Wait! What? Say what! He's where?" I asked as I walked back over to her. My head felt heavier! I couldn't take all the breaking news. Once I was close enough, she hugged me tight. She had her arms around mines as I stood there unable to loosen my arms to hug her back. "It's okay... I hope." I whispered to her. She looked up at me then said, "I'm not sure what's the update on him. His family rushed up from his hometown to check on him. It's that bad. I think someone slipped something in his drink at the party we went to a few days ago." I pushed away from her aggravated and puzzled. "What party? You were there with him?" I asked. "Yeah there was party up the street by that old motorcycle bar. He begged me to go until I gave in. He told me some of the other baseball guys were going with some other people from the school. Everything was chill until some random group of guys started to make me feel uncomfortable when I didn't want to dance with them. Daniel had had a few drinks in his system which caused him to approach the guys aggressively. At first, we thought they were intimidated as they didn't challenge Daniel's threats about finding someone else to mess with. After that I was ready to go but Daniel insisted on staying longer. All I remember was Daniel ducking off for a couple of minutes from me then reappearing with a cup in his hand with a macho man smile on his face. He bragged about how scared those guys were, that one of them gave him a drink to apologize for the misunderstanding. Maybe about twenty minutes of him sipping the drink and me trying to convince him to leave, he suddenly became wildly belligerent towards any and every one that bumped him or said one word to him. It was like he transformed into an evil maniac right in front of my eyes! Lucky for me a couple of the baseball guys were there to force him outside. He fought them off then ran away!" She said as she had to sit down for a second to catch her breath. The way she said it was if she was reliving the night again. She was visibly shaken. "Damn! That's crazy! You okay?" I asked as I sat down by side her. "I'm better now but Daniel mind is off the tracks big time! After I made it home that night, I went straight to bed. It was a little after one in the morning. Maybe about an hour after that, I heard a bunch of noise coming from your apartment. I knew for a fact you weren't home, and Daniel was the only one that had a key. I peeped out the blinds first to see if I could see anything or anyone. The sound from the movement had stopped. I cracked my door opened to step out to check on your place. Suddenly Daniel ran past me as soon as I walked out my door! He had a bunch of stuff in his hand not looking back with not one care in the world! I knew he saw me! I was expecting him to turn around or be thrown off guard, yet he was rushing with a great deal of focus! He disappeared down the stairs as I slowly went on over to your door. The darkness filled the living room area with just a crack of light from the door not being closed completely. As I pushed the door all the way opened as I feared for the worst, I stepped in to be greeted by a ram shacked place! I wasn't sure how long he had been in here or what was missing exactly. I immediately called the cops because it was beyond wrong for the mess he made! It had to have been some serious drugs he had in him because he wasn't the same Daniel that we know! He was himself before that drink he had!" She replied. I sat there looking at my apartment, wondering if it was my fault for leaving him during hard times for him. I was starting to blame myself for not being there for him and having his back. Lauren could see the guilt forming on my face so she immediately jumped up then said, "Now don't think for one minute that you could have saved him again! Yes, I agree that this was some messed up stuff! Daniel once again, is reaping the consequences of his own actions. Had he not tried to be a tough guy and handled that situation in a less aggressive way, maybe things would be different. I'm not looking over what someone did to him like it was cool but... I'm just saying Cedric. Please don't blame yourself for something that someone else must face because of their own ignorance to their choices! Daniel is learning the hardest way. You know what that feels like." She called me out on everything I was trying to pin on myself. She knew it too. I was trying to come back with some facts that would plead my case of taking the wrap for why Daniel was in the trouble he was in. I had nothing.

She started to pick up some of my things with no care about what I was going to say after that. I finally stood up to help her get things back in order. She had me thinking. We cleaned up in silence until my place was back in reasonable shape. It was only right for me to offer her food although I didn't have an appetite. We decided to hit up one of our favorite sandwich shops. Halfway through her smashing some cheese fries and a turkey club I started to feel the emptiness of my stomach. She had me ordering myself a meatball sub from all the lip smacking and crumbs falling all over the table. We joked a little then I asked her about what hospital Daniel was at. "I tried to go see him but the people at the hospital couldn't give me any details. I wasn't a family member or anything, plus he was in too bad of shape by the look on the nurse's face. She wanted to give me more info, but she couldn't. I left because I wasn't sure if it mattered once I overheard his parents had made it in. I guess he had enough sense in him to provide those details to the doctors." She said as she sucked down the rest of her soda. "Yeah I want to go see him. If it's that much of a challenge, then I'll wait to hear from him maybe. If I don't know anything by tomorrow afternoon, I'll go up there to try my luck." I replied. We finished our food then headed back to our place. I didn't want to be in my apartment because of the thoughts racing through my head every time I looked around it not seeing certain things as well as not seeing Daniel. Lauren was cool with me crashing at her spot.

The next day at the crack of dawn, I was awakened by Lauren telling me that some guys were knocking on my door. She said she heard them knocking loud enough to wake her to see who it was. I rolled out of the bed then went to the door. I stepped out as the two gentlemen were walking away from my apartment's door. "Hey! You guys looking for someone?" I asked as I wiped the crust from my eyes as the sun beamed off the windows. I could barely make out who they were from the glare of the sunlight. "Cedric! It's Coach... We need to talk. It's about Daniel." Our head baseball coach said. "Good morning Coach. Yeah, I heard he had some serious stuff going on. You know he trashed my place and stole a bunch of stuff." I added as they walked back towards me. "I'm sorry son. I hate that happened. We need to figure some things out about what exactly made my boy do those things." The guy standing with Coach said. It wasn't a puzzle figuring out who he was by his timing and his words. It was Daniel's dad for sure. He looked like Daniel about twenty years older. "I'm sorry sir. I didn't mean it like that. Daniel is my guy. We are good friends and I just got back in town with news of his unfortunate events. I want to help as much as I can. My neighbor Lauren knows way more than me about what happened. I'll get her." I said. Lauren walked out of her place as soon as I said that. She gave me a frantic look as if she didn't want to answer any questions but knew I had already given them the green light to talk to her. We all went into my place as Coach and Daniel's dad looked around as they shook their heads. I pulled up some chairs from the kitchen for them as Lauren and I sat next to each other on the couch. Lauren didn't waste a second with going into all the details about the night of the party as well as the witnessing of Daniel running from my apartment with my stuff in his hands. After about thirty long minutes of Q&A between them, they had enough information to go on. Coach and Daniel's dad apologized again for the trouble that was caused. I asked about Daniel's health and was he okay. His dad told me that he was recovering from a near overdose of something he described as an underground drug that causes people to see things and hallucinate. He didn't know the name, but he told us that it almost took Daniel completely out. He was recovering but we may not see him if we didn't go by the hospital soon. He told us he would make sure we were cleared to say our goodbyes before he took Daniel back home for good. I told him thank you and that we were going to go as soon as possible as they were leaving. He called over to the hospital to inform them that we were coming by to check on Daniel. He gave me a thumbs up when they got to the bottom of the stairs before getting into Coach's car.

It was a series of unfortunate events that took over Daniel's life. He was in the same boat I was in when we first started out our freedom away from home. We both had high hopes! I hate his came to a dramatic end. Lauren and I jumped in her car to go see Daniel. I couldn't stop thinking how the roles could have been reversed with me laying in a hospital bed and him coming to see me. It wasn't fair I thought. It all sunk in when we made it to the room, he was in. We walked in after being briefed about his condition from one of his aunts that were there. She was heading to get some fresh air when we approached the room. She looked sad with red eyes as if she had been crying. She warned us that Daniel wasn't very responsive to anyone and his memory was a bit off. Lauren stepped in first as I pushed the door open for her. We announced ourselves as we crept in making sure we weren't too alarming. It was dimmed lighting in the room with only the brightness of the sun from the window blinds which were slightly opened. There was a TV on with the volume lowered that you could barely hear. There was snoring traveling throughout the entire room as we strolled past the restroom then up closer to the bed. My heart was pounding as we finally stood beside each other at the foot of the bed while Daniel laid there asleep. I coughed to see if he would notice that he had visitors, but he didn't budge. The way he was laying, I couldn't really see his entire face. We moved around on the side to make sure it was really him. As I came upon the side of the bed, my hip bumped the end of it which caused him to open his eyes suddenly! He glanced around until we made eye contact. I tried to smile but his uncertainty of who I was or where he was, confirmed he wasn't the same. "Hey man... It's me. Your guy. Cedric..." I whispered. He stared at me as if I were speaking in tongues or a different language. "Cedric? I once had a friend named Cedric. We were good friend in preschool. We climbed the monkey bars together. We held on so long that once we let go, we were in college. I don't like college. College make me sick. I like when the lady in the white suit brings me treats. I want to go with her, but she can't take me away." He said calmly with the most confident tone I've ever heard from him.

A tear rolled down my face as Lauren grabbed my hand as she was shaking all over! She looked as if she was about to run out the room! I coasted her to the seat that was along the wall by the window. I couldn't believe what he said and how calm he was about it. "Daniel... It is me, Cedric. Your Northwestern baseball teammate from Mississippi. I'm back man! It's me! Damn man, I feel bad you're here." I said as I walked back over to the bed. He didn't say anything for about two minutes as he looked at the TV as if I wasn't even there! You could see it in his eyes that he was on another planet. I went as far as to waving my hands in front of his face. That did not faze him. It was like he was soulless. "I have a TV for sell! Might work and it might not! I found it! Do you know how to dance? I got some moves! They say I'm sick, but I don't believe them. They're the ones that's sick. All of them. Y'all must be careful. They can see us right now. All the sick people watching." Daniel said as his voice descended from loud to a whisper. The tears fell from my face. Lauren in fact did run out of the room! I was stuck standing there looking at him hoping he would snap out of whatever mental block that held him captive! "Daniel it's me! Daniel please! It's me Cedric! You're from Louisiana and one of the best athletes I know! We're friends! I need you to try hard to remember something! Please!" I said as I was nearly touching his face with my face. I got as close as possible. It was like a nightmare! Suddenly I felt two hands grab me by the shoulders. "Cedric. It's okay. Calm down. I know it hurts. But he's not there. I'm sorry son." Daniel's dad said as he pulled me off Daniel. "What is wrong with him! Why is he acting like that! That's my friend! He doesn't deserve this!" I yelled with frustration with a face full of tears! His aunt was back in the room as well with her and his dad walking me out the room whispering to me that they understood everything I was saying. "We know baby. We are all sick to our stomachs. Daniel is a good boy." His aunt whispered to me. We all walked to the waiting room. Lauren was sitting there with another lady with her head in her hands shaking uncontrollably. I quickly sat on the other side of Lauren then held her hand for comfort. I tried to breathe as I could feel myself nearly having a panic attack! Daniel's dad gave us some tissues. I was dizzy, sweating with snot starting to mix in with the tears. We had to use so many tissues that they gave us a whole box. Lauren was really disturbed as it was harder for her to get a grip on herself emotionally. They gave us bottled waters as we continued to sit there in total shock. The lady next to Lauren was Daniel's mom. His dad told her to go check on their son.

That's when I straighten up completely. I realized that my reactions and how I was taking it was not even close to how they must have been feeling. I didn't want to be a burden on them. I cleaned my face. I immediately whispered to Lauren about us needing to leave so they could be with Daniel. It was clear that Daniel was gone mentally and as hard as I wanted to keep trying until he remembered me, it would have been a waste of time. His family understood that by the way they were calmer than us by then. It took us another ten to fifteen minutes to talk to them before we left. Daniel's dad thanked us for coming and said they are staying there for another two to three days then leaving once they get more word about the investigation on who did that to Daniel. They were also waiting for the doctors to give him medication that may help him come back around to his normal self. He told us he didn't think we should come back. As bad as I wanted to say one more thing to Daniel, I understood that it wasn't best. That was the last time I saw him. We headed back to our apartment.

About three months had passed with Daniel gone, everything became routine for me. I was up early checking on Junior with my morning calls to Rachel. I would call Mrs. Anthony as well to see how she was doing. I would go to the weight room before classes then study hall afterwards. Lauren and I spent a lot of time together but nothing more than just hanging and studying. I took Daniel's misfortunes to heart. I recalled the advice Mrs. Anthony gave me about how easy it was to get in to trouble and distracted from the real reasons I was in school. I didn't care to go to any parties whatsoever. They never found out who the guys were that drugged Daniel. Nothing was worth losing my direction nor my sanity. I found myself resisting all temptations when it came to me choosing between what some called fun verses my kind of fun. When it came to being around anyone that was drinking alcohol to smoking weed, I got out of sight in hurry. I didn't want to be in any situation that was going to add any unnecessary pressure or stress on me. Lauren too separated herself from it all. That made it easier on both of us because we were able to hold each other accountable when anyone else was trying to persuade us to go out or do any of that stuff. Ashley was finally kicked off the cheer team and expelled for lying on Daniel. That was the closure I needed because I didn't let it be swept under the rug. Lauren, Sasha and I stayed on it until it was final. The craziest part about it, so many students were falling into that trap every weekend! As soon as a story would get out about someone getting kicked out of school or losing a scholarship or found abandon somewhere due to drugs or sexual misconduct, it's like it never happened! It made me more focused on how passive everyone were about the seriousness of how it was affecting so many during that time. I even went as far as to remind some of our classmates about how Daniel's life was ruined because of the same mistakes they were making. It went in one ear then out the other. The results were the same for many. Only a few did listen.

I continued down the straight and narrow as my mom would say when she was trying to convince us that doing things differently from others was rewarding. It was all work and no play overall for me in a positive way! Well, until we were cut off in traffic coming from the mall! It was a Saturday afternoon. It was like this lady came out of nowhere as she drove right in front of us nearly hitting us head on! She was turning at the same light we were going through! Lauren blew her horn several times as we pulled into the gas station lot that was just a block up. We were both breathing hard as we looked around shocked that we were still alive. It would have taken us out for sure had she hit us. I ran in the store to grab something to drink because we both needed to hydrate from all the moisture pouring from our pores. Lauren stepped out the car for some fresh air. Thinking how rude and dumb that was for the lady to turn in front of us like that as if she was trying to do it on purpose. I bought two sports drinks. I was exiting the store when I saw a car that looked identical to the one that almost smashed us driving slowly pass the gas station. I walked faster back to the car to alert Lauren about the suspicious driver. She was already on it. We both got back in the car. We drove off watching every direction making sure we weren't being followed. We drove about a mile down the road closer to our apartments when Lauren noticed the crazy driver following us about two cars back! "What the hell is wrong with that lady! Is she really following us?" Lauren said as she kept checking the side and rearview mirrors. "I have no clue! Maybe she thinks we're somebody she knows. I definitely don't need her ass behind us all the way to our apartments! Let's make a block towards the police precinct. Let's see if she'll follow us there!" I said as I kept looking back to see if she was still trailing us.

We drove about five minutes heading by the station. After a couple of lights, she turned off down another street. We doubled back to make sure she was gone before driving on to our complex. "I don't know what that was about. I think she was following us for real! Especially after she nearly ran us off the damn road." Lauren said as we finally pulled into our apartment's parking lot. She parked then we got out slowly with both of us looking around near the entrance. "Yeah I feel the same way. Some people are just off their meds or something. I don't know why she looked so familiar?" I said as we walked up the steps. "Looked familiar! Wait... You knew who that was?" Lauren asked as we reached my door. "No! I'm not saying I knew her. Just saying she looked like someone I may have seen before?" I replied. "Seen where? Here? At school?" Lauren added. "I'm not sure where. You know. Don't worry about it." I said as I opened my door. "Yeah yeah. Don't worry about it? Okay. Let me find out you have stalkers." She said jokingly before stepping over to her place. I shook my head at her then closed my door.

We talked about making homemade pizza earlier. She was coming over to my place later that evening. I had to tell someone else about the scare we had with the looney driver, so I called Rachel. Plus, I missed a day without hearing from her. Junior was crawling and pulling up on everything! She sent me videos and pictures through the phone of him in action. I hate I was missing those moments. I had work to do at school. I couldn't let him or myself down. I was doing it for us as well as Daniel and David. I was on a mission! Everyone was doing fine from Rachel's statement once she answered the phone and we talked for about thirty minutes. She sounded exhausted. She said it in many ways without coming straight out with expression how tired she was dealing with Junior on her own. I understood that from her words, "I wish you were here to spend time with the little monster because he is quite a handful." And "If only you were here to be with him sometimes, I hate I didn't take advantage of all those nap times when I was younger cause lord knows I need them more than ever now!" We both laughed together for a second, but she was really venting about how she felt. I did my best comforting her during the rest of the conversation. It had become a norm by then she would throw in the need to tell me she wanted me back home with them.

I took a shower after I got off the phone with her then realized I didn't bring up the crazy driver during our conversation. Lauren made it back over to my place right before I nodded off on the couch. I was glad she was there because my stomach was barking louder than a junk yard dog! Guess she was just as hungry as I was because she brought over all the stuff to make the pizzas. I knew for sure we were going to have to go back out to get something. She was well prepared. We joked while we both made our own personal style pizzas. Once we put them in the stove, we chilled out waiting patiently in the living room until they were done. We were eating, watching a show with the volume up a bit when the first knocks on the door happened. Lauren had surprised me with a new TV because she felt bad about what happened. We both thought it was from the program that was on. About ten minutes had passed with the knocks sounding louder that made it clear someone was at my door! I turned the TV down lower then walked to the window. It was late which was weird because I wasn't expecting anyone. By the time I made it to the blinds to have a look, there was no one there. I looked back at Lauren to make sure I wasn't going crazy as I asked to make sure she heard the knocks too. She agreed she heard something but wasn't sure where it came from. I was nervous about opening the door. I was too curious not to. My fingers were tingling as I turned the knob slowly as the door cracked open. I poked my head out looking both ways down the entire apartment's walkway. No one in sight which made me hurry back in. I was scratching my head trying to come up with an explanation on how I heard what I heard but didn't see anything or anyone outside. Lauren gasps as if I were joking as she stepped around me then out the door. She walked to the railing looking down both ways of the walkway. She came back in looking just as confused as I was. I shut the door then went back to the kitchen table where we were eating. Lauren glanced once more out the blinds to see if she would catch someone playing or running by. There was no one out moving about around our apartments.

She came back in the kitchen shaking her head then asked, "Is there something you need to tell me?" I nearly dropped the food out of my mouth trying to answer her because of the serious look on her face. "Huh? What are you talking about? Me? Tell you something like what?" I replied. She started back eating as if I was supposed to confess. She was quiet as if she were giving me more time to think about it. "You assume I know what that was about? I promise you I am clueless." I said looking innocent. "So that wasn't one of your fans or should I say, some eye candy that was doing a pop up?" She finally asked. I couldn't keep from laughing at her conclusion. I was slick scared. No one had ever played any pranks on me or any of us since we lived there. I heard about the wild jokes they did on one another at the dorms but never at the apartments. "You know I've been too busy to be messing around with anyone. Hell, I'm surprised you haven't felt sorry enough for me to give me a little loving by now." I replied with a big grin on my face. "Please, you know you don't want to go there. We've been doing good. Don't ask for anything you know you don't want. Please believe I understand. I haven't been doing anything with anyone my damn self. Don't tempt me, please Cedric." She replied with frustrations. It was better distracting her with that then her thinking I was fooling with some other chick. "Yeah you're right. My apologies. I was just playing. But for real. I don't know what that was." I replied in a calmer voice with my sincere face on. She put her plate in the sink then decided to call it a night. It was earlier than she usually would leave which meant she was in her feelings about my comment. I didn't press her about leaving so soon because it was best for the both of us. I walked her to the door and peep out to make sure she got in her apartment okay. I shut my door then finished cleaning things up in the kitchen and in the living room. It was a little depressing not having my game to play. I didn't replace it because I didn't have the time to. I settled with just going to my room.

The one thing that did keep me balanced was masturbating. I remember our coach telling the team once about it when we first joined the team at Northwestern. He would say, "If you get to the point where you need sex that bad then my advice is for you all to rub one out. It would give you a better thinking head than a better feeling head. I don't want you guys caught up in lust, making bad decisions because you have so much testosterone built up. It's okay to relieve yourself or wound up in a bad situation because the head upstairs let the head downstairs think for you." If only I had heard it sooner that way earlier in my life, I may not have had Junior. I hated to think of it that way given he was such a precious mini king. I kept some X-rate magazines hidden deep down in my sock drawer that Daniel had brought from his hometown he gave me. I knew it would help me sleep as well as getting my mind off the urge to call Lauren back over to get busy with her.

I was about to get comfortable to get to my hand to hand combat with myself, but I heard tapping on my bedroom window that scared the crap out of me! I was laying there like a rat in a mouse trap, thinking that if I laid there as still as I could, no one could see me. It felt like someone was watching me the whole time! I had goosebumps all over me! I finally jumped up thinking it was Lauren goofing around with me. I slid the magazine back in my drawer then tip toed over to the window. I peeped out the edge of the blind as I tried my best to open one of the flaps slowly. I squinted with one eye closed as I scanned the outside walkway area fishing for a shadow or something. Nothing in sight again. It was too late, and I was too tired to walk to the door to check again. I made sure all my lights were out then waved the white flag. I wasn't in the mood to do anything as I was puzzled to who or what was entertaining themselves by aggravating me. I checked the window once more before retreating to my bed. I didn't care if anyone was kicking my door down by that time. I wanted to sleep by any means possible. I gave that round to the clown or dummies playing around outside, with my eyes weighing themselves down. My need for the jerk session was canceled. I turned my back to my window then placed my pillow over my head. I didn't care to see anything nor to hear it. I was sleep within seconds.

   I started to feel movement or something sliding itself underneath my blanket I was wrapped up in! I knew for sure I was sleep as I was tossing a little. It felt like a dream as the movement increased from my feet upward towards my crotch area. I kicked my legs around before swiping my hand down there thinking I could knock whatever it was off me or out the bed. I swung my arm hard enough to hit another hand! It wasn't my other hand either! I could have just left my skin in the bed then ran for my life with just my bones when I flipped over to see an older lady standing over me! I wanted to scream for help which was pointless because she was holding a large blade in her hand! I thought my eyes were deceiving me as the silhouette of the mystery woman filled in with a sharper site of her. I wanted to wipe my eyes, but I didn't want to get stabbed. She had on a loose dark colored dress with a jean jacket on. She didn't say a word as she directed me with the motions of the huge shiny knife. She moved it in a gesture that I comprehended was for me to slide back towards the headboard. My vision was becoming better as I looked around calculating the method of how I was going to make my move to get away from her if she got any closer with that blade. My heart was beating insanely. I couldn't wrap my mind around how it was happening. With all the lights off in my place, I only had the brightness pressing through from the outside porch lights and lights from the parking lot. I was avoiding all eye contact. My focus was on whatever the knife was directing me to do. That was the only thing I cared about at that moment. What was she going to do with the knife if I was insubordinate to her commands? I played out the superhero scenario where I reasoned with her, but I wasn't going to push my luck.

"Please don't hurt me... Okay... I'll do whatever you want me to do. Just don't stick me with that knife, please..." I whispered as I forced every letter of every word out my mouth. That triggered her to drop the silent treatment! "Now why would I hurt my Cedric. I've been waiting too long for this opportunity baby." Ms. Harris said in a very seductive way. I nearly fainted when her voice hit my ears! She said it in the same exact tone she used the day she tried to rape me in her office! That's what it was back then now that I understood her intentions. I was past the questions on how she was in Chicago and how she knew where I lived! I had to get the hell out of there! She stuck the knife directly in my face as she started to climb on top of me! She straddled me as I could feel her cold thighs touching mines. I gave myself only one chance to do it right. I told myself I had to fight her off me! I was counting to ten before she went any further. I was going to grab both of her arms then try to shake the knife out of her hand! One, two... "I wanted you so bad for too long Cedric. Why would you do me this way!" She whispered to me. Three, Four, Five... "I want to feel you deep inside of me! Finally, I have you again... All to myself!" She said as she started to lean in towards me. Six, seven... "I've been so patient. Watching you from the shadows. Completely torn. Now give me..." Boom! The lights were as bright as the sun that came through my bedroom door! I guess she must had closed the door as the voices followed the lights after the bedroom door was kicked off the hinges! It was so loud and frightening that somehow, I pushed her off me then balled up in a knot covering my eyes from the blinding lights!

"Get down! Get down now! Drop the knife now! Put your hands up!" The voices yelled out to Ms. Harris as she was completely disoriented! The voices were of cops dressed in all black as I finally caught a glance at them! One ran up on her while she was in disarray then stepped down on the hand that was holding the blade! She was no match for that pressure as her hand weaken immediately unclutching it! I turned my head enough to witness the take down before another guy moved in on me then grabbed my arm! He told me to hurry out as he led me passed two other guys until we were outside my place! There were three cop cars parked directing down in front of my apartment that he walked me downstairs to. I saw lights starting to come on in the windows of the other units of my building. I knew it was going to draw some concerns from all the yelling and door kick! I was nervous, embarrassed and happy too! All types of emotions. I was saved! I was at knife point by a psycho sex driven rapist! Some students were either looking out their blinds or standing in their doorways watching.

One of the cops opened the door for me then asked me to sit in the back of the car. I was sweating as my hands were shaking trying to sit down. "Man, I'm sorry you had to go through this... We finally got her ass! This woman is bat shit crazy! Man, was she obsessed with you buddy!" The officer said to me as he stood by the door. They didn't shut it, one guy hung around by the car as the other officer went back up to my apartment. I sat there for about ten minutes with my head down. I finally peeped up towards my apartment as Lauren was walking past my door looking scared. She saw me in the cop car as she scrambled down the stairs then bee lined to me. The officer jumped in her way and warned her that it was a profoundly serious matter. She didn't go down without a fight to get to me, but I had to say something to keep her calm. "Lauren I'm good. It's okay... Just wait on me at your place. I'll call you soon! Please go." I said as I poked my head out the car.

She was crying and worried. She slowly walked away on back to her apartment confused and sad. I wanted to say more. I couldn't bring myself to do with all the eyes and ears out guessing what had happened. "Do we need to take you to a hospital son? Are you hurt?" The cop asked as he sat in the front seat of the car. I rubbed myself all overall to make sure I wasn't sore or she if she did poke me during the take down. I was physically fine. My mind was turning flips with uncontrollable emotions bouncing from sadness to anger. I was starting to feel unusually violent with a sense of wishing I had slapped that knife out of her hand then punched her in the face! I was confused all together after all I've been through, I wasn't expecting to be a victim of sexual abuse again! She had her opportunity, yet I thought I had put that experience behind me! What would make someone do another person like that I kept thinking to myself. I would have bet anyone a million dollars I had ran far enough away from my hometown to never have to go through anything like that! "I'm fine for the most part sir. I don't think I need to go. I want to get as far away from here as possible. I'm just lost and shocked. I can't believe it was her. I hate I know her!" I finally replied. I held my head back down.

"Between me and you, she is a sicko like all the others. I hate anyone the preys on the young. We have been following her for months and wanted to be sure she was who we thought she was. I personally apologize for it going to this extreme. You did absolutely nothing wrong son. It's very unfortunate that this is a common thing all over the world. We are having to arrest more and more adults daily for things of this nature." The officer said as he turned towards me. He said it with sympathy and disappointment. All I could do was shake my head. He was right. She was disgusting! I started thinking about all the other young men back home that were sexually violated due to her sick pleasures! His radio went off that was attached to his shoulder that made him step out the car. After a couple of minutes of waiting, he shut the door then hopped back in the car. He said he wanted to take me around the block, so I didn't have to see her when they brought her down. I agreed as we drove around for about five minutes until she was out and, on her way to jail.

He wanted me to go get examined anyway for evidence sake. I agreed to do that. I was able to call Mrs. Anthony as well. i didn't know how to tell her what happened. I asked the officer to help me. She wanted to drop everything and come right away! I finally got on the phone to let her know I was fine. I was shaken up mentally but physically, nothing happened. She cried hard for me as she was devasted to hear what occurred. We agreed she would come the next day. She didn't want to get off the phone. She talked to the officer for about twenty minutes as he asked her a bunch questions about me and Ms. Harris. I was seen by a medical examiner who asked me more questions about the event and how I was feeling. They sent another person that said they wanted to talk more about my mental state which he too asked about the situation and more about my emotions towards everything. It didn't seem like I was there for hours. I noticed the sun had come up. I was extremely exhausted and wanted to sleep. Another hour after all the tests and questions were asked, the same cop drove me back to the apartments. I called Lauren before we headed that way to make sure it wasn't too crazy outside for me to slip in without too many people seeing me to ask me anything. I was dropped off with a bunch of paperwork I had to keep. The cop apologized several more times before I got out of the car. I went straight upstairs to Lauren's place. She hugged me tight as I could feel her tears soaking into my shirt. We stood at the door inside her place after she shut it embracing one another. After about two minutes, I broke down! I had held too much in. I fell to the ground as the tears poured from my face. I wanted to scream as loud as I could! There was a load of pain that stung me deep to my core as if I were being stabbed in my chest! I wanted to give up on everything! I wanted to lay on the floor and just die! I could see myself walking out of the door trying to go on like nothing happened as I normally would. Something felt completely different. It was a strange feeling I had never felt before. I felt weak and hopeless as if my life was worthless. Nothing had worked out for me I thought. Going back to school wasn't the best choice. All the decisions I made up to that moment were all toxic and heavy. I had run out of gas with nowhere to go. None of the advice anyone had given me had any effect on me as I had hoped for! Not only did I want to blame everyone for where I was mentally, I wasn't looking in the mirror to give myself any recognition for my mishaps. I needed something or someone to tell me this was just a test or none of it mattered. Lauren tried to comfort me the best she could but there wasn't enough faith even in her to comprehend the kind words she was saying.

There were a few minutes where I felt deaf to her voice and the room started fading to black. I couldn't move nor catch my breath. I felt like I was being held captive in a blank space of life. There was only emptiness surrounding me with my heart thumping slowly as the sound of my pulse rang in one ear then to the other. I thought I was falling asleep until Lauren stood up over me as my body drifted on down to the floor. She was crying as she ran off in the distance. I didn't move due to the numbness of my entire body. The cadence of my heart slowed down with each exhale of the short breaths I was taken in. My eye lids closed slowly as I caught a glance of Lauren's return. She had her phone in her hand in complete panic. I stretched my eyes back opened as I felt her feet kicking me. The oxygen rushed up my nostrils with a shockwave traveling through my veins as I could feel every nerve, I had in me! I shot up to my feet like a rocket. I was sure that the apartment was on fire by the way Lauren was holding the phone stomping in place in a frantic! "What's wrong? Are you okay?" I asked her as she stopped immediately, then hung up her phone! "What the hell? I thought you were having a heart attack or something! Are you okay?" She yelled! I nearly stumbled back down as she caught me then walked me over to her sofa. "Damn... I don't know. I thought I was daydreaming. I didn't feel like anything was wrong until you came back panicking." I said as I sat down wiping the sweat from my face. "Oh my God! You had me bugging out! I was calling the paramedics! Scared me crazy!" She said then headed to the kitchen. I kicked my foot up on one end of the couch then laid back sideways. My head was pounding. She came back with a glass of water. She made me drink it after I refused it. "You look stressed as hell Cedric. Drink it and try to relax please." She said as she forced the glass in my hand. I sipped the water repeatedly because she wasn't moving from in front of me until I finished it. After sitting the empty glass on the table, she placed her personal fan she kept in her bedroom on the floor next to me. She saw the sweat and wanted to keep me cool.

I needed to call Mrs. Anthony again to make sure she was indeed coming to get me. I couldn't call her quick enough. Something kept whispering to me to go back home. It wouldn't stop echoing in my ears. Once I had my phone, I called Mrs. Anthony. She was already on the road. "Hello... I want to come home. I don't want to be here anymore." I whispered. I didn't want Lauren to hear it that way. I knew she was going to flip out. She read my every word as she crawled to the floor then placed her head on her coffee table. "I'm on my way Cedric. I'm so sorry. I understand. Just stay put and pack up your stuff please." Mrs. Anthony replied. "Yes ma'am. See you soon." I replied. We hung up the phone. I sat there waiting to hear an ear full, from Lauren. She didn't move or say a word. I stood up for a minute or so then sat back down fighting with how I should tell her what she already knew. I waited another five minutes hoping she would just tell me to leave or something out of sadness. Finally, after heavy breathing and sobbing, she said, "I know you think leaving is best. No matter what I say, you're still going to leave. I don't want to be selfish about it. I was sitting here thinking about what this means to our friendship. First Daniel, now you? Two people that has been straight up with me since day one of this crazy college life. I want what's best for you. You've been through hell Cedric. For the life of me, I can't comprehend how you're still in your right mind! The load you have is demanding. Go and do you..." I helped her up off the floor as she was getting her words out. I hugged her tight. It wasn't going to mean anything, but I said it anyway. I leaned down and whispered in her ear, "Come with me..." She instantly pushed away from me! She was aggravated with my lack of compassion. She read right through my immature thought. "You know you can be so selfish at times. What makes you think I could just drop everything and leave. Why would that even come out of your mouth. Are you serious right now? What, you want me to come be a stepmom or side piece or just a cool little friend? I will never lose feelings for you, you know that. I've been more than understanding with your dealings but that is too much. I would never do you that way. I'm sorry but that just did something to me." She replied as she looked at me with fire in eyes. "My intention was not to offend you I swear! I apologize if it came off that way. No disrespect... I meant it! I don't want to leave you like this. I don't want to lose someone like you seriously. I swear I be trying not to make everything about me. I didn't know what to say." I replied. We both stood there looking at each other puzzled about what to say next.

Suddenly my phone rang with Rachel's name flashing on the screen that Lauren saw as well. "See what I mean. I can't be caught in the middle of that. She needs you more than me. Go home Cedric. I'll be fine I guess." She said then walked to her room. I answered the phone disregarding what Lauren had said. "Cedric! Are you okay? I'm so sorry! I'm riding with Mrs. Anthony. She asked me to. Junior is okay with my parents. I wanted to hear your voice." Rachel's voice came rumbling through the phone! It was like Mrs. Anthony didn't even talk to me just minutes before. Not sure why she did it again, but I wasn't going to stress about her not giving me any clue she had a passenger with her. "I'm fine, I guess. I need to get away. Not sure if coming home will help. I know I don't want to be here anymore." I said as I walked to Lauren's front door. I twisted the doorknob aggressively while yanking the door open in hopes Lauren would hear me leaving. I stood there with the door cracked opened while tuning it to the quietness of Lauren's apartment while the words Rachel was saying were fading in and out in my ear. I stepped out the door then slammed it shut! I paused for a moment to see if that would trigger her to come rushing to the door to confront me about it. Still nothing. "Cedric... Can you hear me? What's going?" Rachel's voice became louder as I was pushing my apartment door opened. "Yes. I'm fine. I'm about to shower so I can hopefully get some rest. I'm over this day for good." I replied sounding frustrated "I'm sorry. You're right, I'm sure you need to rest. See you soon." She responded then hung up.

     I packed all the things I cared about thinking about calling my coach the whole time. If he knew what had happened, I was sure he would have come over by then. I figured that was a good sign not too many people were aware of my stalker's attempt to put another W in her win column. Although reaching out to him was the best thing to do. He wouldn't accept the fact I was leaving if I told him. I even went as so far to dial his number. I held the phone playing over our exchange. I never pressed the call button. After I made up my mind, I plugged my phone up then finished gathering everything before sitting my bags by the door. I sat on the couch trying to force down some leftover pizza as I doodled a letter to my coach about how sorry I was for leaving like I was. It was short with words of my appreciation for the opportunity as well as the life lessons about better decision-making behaviors that I promised to work on for the rest of my life. I took another sheet of paper out to write my goodbye to Lauren as it seemed she didn't want to speak again after I announced my departure. I wanted it to be something to help her move on. I wrote out some of our most memorable moments not excluding our intimate times. I wanted her to know she meant more than she could imagine to me. I wrote how our friendship will forever be, regardless of the time if we didn't see one another for fifty years. If somehow, we crossed paths again later in life, we would pick up where we left off. I needed her to know she was one of kind with being one of the most down to earth, funniest and respected people I've ever been around. I ended that letter with expressing that I loved her. I placed both letters in separate envelopes I had from the times I wrote Mrs. Anthony.

I had time and didn't mine getting the fresh air since it was late enough not to be noticed for me to walk over on campus to slip coach's letter in his inbox. It was a much-needed stroll to admire the campus one last time. Ran into two other people for a quick chat which was crazy that everyone was clueless about something so serious happening right across from the campus with no breaking news alerts or warnings! I made it back to my apartment to find a note on my door from Lauren! That read: "Where are you? I called and knocked! I hope you're fine. I'm sorry for being selfish. Enjoy the rest of your life." I forgot to grab my phone before I left. I was glad I didn't have it. It allowed me to inhale that last day in Chicago alone during my walk. I stood there between her door and mines tugging myself both ways to either knock on hers or just go in mines. There was way too much tension built up for me to say anything to her. I needed to go to sleep. I took the same tape she used to tape the letter I had for her on her door. I did it all as quiet and quick as I could. I opened my door then shut it the same way. I didn't want her to notice that I was back home. I kept all the lights off then went to my room. Finally showered, not checking my phone made it easier for me to get right to sleep.

Knocks on the door had me rolling out the bed wiping the slob from the side of my mouth. The sun beamed straight through the windows which was a good sign that my ride back home had arrived. I opened the door to be rushed with hugs and sighs of relief from Mrs. Anthony followed by Rachel! It was real that I was heading home when I saw their faces. Once they were in and after the hugging and small talk about me being okay, I wanted to get out of there! "Thanks for coming. Can we go now?" I said after I double checked my bags and they had both used the restroom. "Yes honey, sure. Have you said anything to your coach, teammates or anyone else? Did you let them know you were leaving?" Mrs. Anthony asked as she walked upon me staring me in my eyes with an overly concerned look on her face. She knew I hadn't done any of that. She only asked because she wanted to make sure that I was ready to leave like that. My mind was made without a doubt. Rachel looked around as well then said, "I know this is tough. I know how it feels to be violated. It's hard to move on. You can do it Cedric. We are here for you." Mrs. Anthony and I squinted our eyes at one another when she said that with a strange curiosity energy moving between us. I immediately replied, "Thanks. I appreciate that. But... Yeah... I'm ready." I gave them a second to say something then I went to make sure I had my phone and charger. I used the restroom myself once more. I was cornered by Mrs. Anthony as I was coming out of the restroom! "What do you think she was implying? What's her real story Cedric? Is there something you need to tell me?" She whispered as she occasionally looked over her back making sure

Rachel was still in the living room. I shook my head looking just as inquisitive as she was. "I have no idea where that came from. Rachel has always been soft spoken and reserved honestly. I'm sure I'll find out soon. I'll let you know when I know more." I replied. "Well that sounded interesting. She may be trying to tell you something. Please follow up with her about that. I would hate for her to be going through something that would cause complications for herself, Junior or you. When a woman says certain things in a certain way, you have to read between the lines." She said before rushing off back to the living room.

We gathered my bags then headed to the car. I kept glancing over at Lauren's apartment to see if she would have been peeping out the windows or opened the door to wish me well. There were no signs of her. Once the car was all loaded up, I went back up one last time to leave the keys on the coffee table then turned off all the lights. I left the door unlock so the property manager could get in once they knew I had moved out. I was back down at the car looking around again, taking in the scene before ducking in the back seat while the ladies sat up front. "We're all loaded and buckled up?" Mrs. Anthony asked. "Yes ma'am. I'm good." I replied. "Me too!" Rachel replied with joy. She was excited about my impromptu return home. "Well let's go home!" Mrs. Anthony said as she started up the car then pulled off slowly. Right before we turned out of the parking lot, Lauren stepped out of her unit staring down at the car as we drove away! I wasn't sure if she could see me as I gave her a wave goodbye. She looked heartbroken as if she had been crying with her hair all over her head wearing one of my baseball shirts, she borrowed but never returned. She stood there with her hands on the railing as we kept moving on. I didn't want to stop. I didn't say a word as we headed off the property, down the street then on to the highway. I wiped the one tear that formed in my eyes then used my backpack as a pillow to lay my head on it as I leaned to the side. "Thanks again for doing this for me." I said to the ladies. "You're welcome baby." Mrs. Anthony said. "You know I got your back." Rachel added.

Chapter 10

Secrets Revealed

Two weeks after being back home I found myself trapped in the house most of the day and night. Due to all the news and reports about Ms. Harris's arrest in Chicago then being prosecuted with all the lawyers and officers either coming by the house or calling, left everyone in our neighborhood doing the same. Everyone knew I was the only one from Jackson that was in the Chicago area. It wasn't hard to put two and two together. Mrs. Anthony was working overtime managing all the attention which made things easier for me. Rachel was doing an amazing job with getting Junior over every day as well as keeping the information she had on the low. It was working out for the most part, but I still wasn't happy overall. Not a word from Lauren within those two weeks. I finally talked to the Coach from Northwestern. He was saddened by the news. He didn't pressure me about quitting the team to come home. He wanted to make things right. He told me there will be an opened scholarship for me if I ever decided to return. I made a promise to him I would take that offer if he were still coaching there or wherever he was coaching when I did make that decision.

Officer Jackson was coming around more often as he was given some authority on the Harris case. He told me that they had information he couldn't reveal until she was caught. He made it clear that there where an enormous number of tips that came in around the time, I left for college that she was seen in Chicago. It was all connecting her to me as she was being spotted around the university and surrounding areas up there. About a week before she was arrested, they had officers following her daily. I was basically the center of the case as they used me as bait to finally catch her in the act. Mrs. Anthony was looking into a lawsuit against the high school, the local police and anyone that was involved with using me the way they did. She kept questioning me about how I felt almost every day because she could see the events affecting me mentally later down the road that I couldn't realize at the time. I didn't notice any major changing with my thinking or how I was acting. I did question the method they used to catch her. Officer Jackson continued to say that they have always had to make tough decisions like that. To convict someone at the highest level possible, especially someone that deserved to be. They had to take unfavorable risks. Because I wasn't a minor like some of the other victims, it was a call they had to make to get undisputable evidence to seal the case on her without any cracks or loose ends.

After all the scenarios they laid out, that was the for sure win for the greater good. I was the sacrificial lamb that all would have a for sure victory and justice was served. Mrs. Anthony had a different way of seeing it overall. I didn't get too involved with what that outcome was or where that outcome was going. Either way I was happy she was going to spend the rest of her life in jail. Rachel was the one that had some hard moments when it came to ask me about how I was doing emotionally. Her biggest concern was trying to understand how it was taking a toll on me to just talk about it. She would bring up how easy it was for me to not let it bother me as much as she or anyone thought it would. I guess most of them thought I was going to freak out and be stand offish or something. Even Tammie was worried a lot about me. She was there as well with the random questions whenever we were alone. Some things were similar to the talks I had with Tammie that matched the questions and concerns Rachel had.

Many times, Tammie would bring up when she was being forced to do sexual acts that she was uncomfortable with. Feeling powerless because she didn't have anyone to save her from that darkness, she was stuck in. She would wake up days and weeks at a time, wanting to run away to escape what felt like enslavement by someone she once loved. It went on for too long until she built up enough courage to talk about it with a coworker she had when she was working at a bar. They told her the more she talked about it, the easier it became obvious that that wasn't the life she deserved. She couldn't look herself in mirror until she got there with us. Seeing how Mrs. Anthony and I saw her as a real person, welcomed her in with love and support, gave her the hope she needed to move on. She slipped some things out that I didn't think she meant to say. She mentioned a conversation Rachel and she had, about being a victim without a voice. She was going on and on about being around people, looking like you're happy and peachy but no one has a clue the suffering you've buried deep within.

"Yeah cause Rachel was saying how she's dealing with trying to keep a smile through her pain but I didn't want to dig too deep with it after she switched it up by saying she was just thinking, not that she was going through anything. You never know how people really feel until you have that heart to heart uncomfortable conversation with them. Everyone's going through something. Some people just need someone to just ask how are they really doing in life? You know…" Tammie said all nonchalant. I took a second to process what was said in their exchange and how Tammie went about explaining it to me as if it wasn't a big deal. It was weird because she was saying what Rachel was doing. Tammie thought it wasn't a red flag for her to ask more questions about Rachel's potential cry for help? I was confused. I went on about my day as if it weren't important. I didn't want Tammie to alarm Rachel before I had the opportunity to have a sit-down conversation with her. I gave it a few days as I started to talk more with Rachel about her past. It's funny how you can grow up around a person but still not know one real thing about them. That's how I was starting to feel about Rachel. We had a handsome child together. We only knew basic and general things about each other.

Another week had passed with the attention on me dying down about the Ms. Harris case. I decided that it would be cool to take Rachel out alone. I wanted to spend some time with her to start my research on the real her. Mrs. Anthony and Tammie were all about it because they got to spend time with Junior. They loved Rachel so that was a bonus for them that I was focused on trying to work things out with my questionable relationship with her. It was a Friday evening. I wanted to go downtown away from the normal close spots to try something new with her. There was a hibachi restaurant Mrs. Anthony thought we should try since she heard great reviews from some of her friends from church. She wanted us to try it so bad that she agreed to pay for it. Who would say no to that?

Rachel arrived with Junior around six that evening looking quite easy on the eyes! It was something about her walking up the steps in heels holding Junior that made me smile thinking to myself that I did a damn good job picking the mother of my first born. She looked like a grown woman on a mission with a smile that lit up the house when she walked in as I held the door opened for her. "Wow..." I whispered as she passed me. She had a black top with straps on the shoulders that matched her black skirt that came right above her knees that ruffled at the end. Never seen her in heels. I was amazed at how she moved so elegantly with precision. I was glad I had on a nice button down with some khakis and loafers. Mrs. Anthony suggested I look like a gentleman and not a street dude when I was taking a lady that has class out on a date. Boy was she right. Tammie and Mrs. Anthony both were just as pleased with

Rachel's attire as I was. "Well look at you ma'am!" Tammie said with a smile on her face looking at Rachel up and down. "Now make sure y'all keep it at just dinner and nothing else. Junior is enough for now." Mrs. Anthony said as she smiled, followed with a serious eye stare at Rachel and me. "No ma'am, Junior has made it clear that he needs all the attention and every cent we got to survive. I'm not trying to create another crumb snatcher anytime soon!" Rachel replied as she laid him down in the crib, we had that was in the corner of the living room since he was asleep. "Yeah yeah. Ain't nobody trying to play like that. We good on that. Although she is looking scrumptious, I'll do my best to stay off her!" I said jokingly. Mrs. Anthony didn't find that too amusing with that same look on her face. "See, look at him. He plays too much... Y'all enjoy!" Tammie said as she walked off to the kitchen. "He can say whatever he wants to. We just going to eat then back to our little monster. I'm ready when you are Mr." Rachel said. "I'm just messing around. I know better... I'm ready too. See y'all later." I grabbed a jacket because Mrs. Anthony told me that it was a good gesture when going on a date. She said it wasn't for me, it was for Rachel. She explained how ladies like to look cute but not have enough on when going to places like the movies and restaurants. Having a jacket or something she can cover up in to stay warms helps more than I could imagine. Especially when you're taking her somewhere, she's not familiar with. Ladies like to look their best for themselves as well as for you. And sometimes if they must wear their jacket or coat depending on the weather outside, it doesn't complement their dress or whatever they have on. We left the house after Tammie snapped a picture of us with her camera she came from the kitchen with before stopping us at the door.

Did my gentleman thing the whole night with opening the doors for her to letting her seat back once we were seated at the huge hibachi grill! The place was packed so I was glad we called ahead and made reservations. We made it there fifteen minutes early as we were told to. Funny thing about the whole time we were there talking amongst ourselves, occasionally chatting with the others around the flaming food show, not once did I think about anything or anyone else but Rachel. She held full control of my every thought. Her smile was different. The way she flowed with every topic. I was in tune with her. We would lock eyes between the conversations as our looks gave off more than what we were saying. Two hours of great food and resisting the nerve chilling attempts to slide my hand down on to Rachel's thighs to signal her I wanted to express what our eyes were telling. We parked close to the restaurant which was a block from a river walk park. Rachel loved the idea of us walking off some of that food we ate. It was my chance to ask the serious questions I couldn't shake. It was the perfect weather for a nice stroll along the water line.

People were out, walking, jogging, sitting on the park benches as a light breeze from the water kept us all cool. Good thing I had that jacket! Rachel needed it right away. She smiled at the gesture as I helped her put her arms in it. Mrs. Anthony was right! The stars were out shining bright in the clear sky with sounds of airplanes echoing in the distance. Other than the few questionable homeless gentlemen that were a bit aggressive with the whole pan handling competition they were having when we first approached the walkway, the evening was winding down peacefully. They were a little too well-groomed to be out begging the way there were. Once we had a clear lengthy stretch of privacy along the concrete trail, I took advantage of that moment to drop my concerns on her. "You said something maybe a few weeks back, that hasn't sat right with me. I was trying to avoid it, but curiosity isn't letting me leave it alone." I said as I tried to give off a not so offensive look on my face. Sort of like a look you will give when you honestly forgot to ask someone something that has been eating you up on the inside, but you know its hell of risky to say. She slowed the pace down as she kept looking over at me as if she was scrambling with wonder to what it was that had me feeling a way about something she said. "Umm, okay. Hope I didn't say anything that upset you. Cause if I did, you should have said something sooner. Sorry." She replied as we continued our walk. I had to wait before I could reply as a lady trotted passed us with her golden dog. I wasn't a big dog kind of guy, so I pulled Rachel over closer to me, just in case it snapped at us. "Really Cedric? Someone's afraid of dogs I see?" She said as we continued our walk. "Let's just say old man Jenkins' dog gave them an unforgiving rap with me." I replied. "Old man Jenkins who lived across from the high school?" She asked. "Yes! It was around freshman year. David and I was messing around, horse playing, and I ended up falling by the opening of the gate of Jenkins' house. That damn dog must have mistaken my shoes as a T Bone steak! He came charging at me as I slipped on the rocky driveway he had! That dog locked on my shoe with his mouth like some pilers! He shook my leg so hard that my shoe came off! David ran him off with a stick with my shoe stuck in his jaws! I never got my shoe back nor did I ever walk pass that house again!" I said as I got chills reliving that attack. She laughed without hesitation as if it was a joke! "Wait a minute... I'm sorry but... You're talking about old man Jenkins' dog, right?" She asked as if she weren't sure if she could believe my story. "Umm yes! His dog!" I replied shaking my head at her. "That little chihuahua took your shoe? That dog was harmless! It was too small to be taken that serious Cedric. You must be talking about another dog. I'm just saying... You were afraid of that tiny thing?" She said as she couldn't hold back the giggles. "Say whatever you want, that dog was out for blood or starving or something! You weren't there! That little thing almost took my whole foot off! That's why I'm not too fun of any of them. I rather have a cat. Or even a fish before I ever own a dog!" I replied. "I hear you. I love dogs. We're going to have to work on that. You have to give them another try. Dogs are man's best friend remember." She said then laughed again. I didn't reply. I just kept on walking.

We were running out of time before we needed to head back to the house to relieve them before Junior got too fussy. I needed to double down on finding out what Rachel was struggling with on the inside. We turned to head back. Before the words could form properly in my mouth to ask again, there was some commotion going on back near the start of the walkway. There was a voice of a young lady that started to sound more and more familiar as we approached the area. There was a female officer and another lady restraining the girl while another male officer walked to the car with something wrapped up in a blanket! "Give me back my damn baby! You can't fucking tell me what to do with my baby! There's nothing wrong with me or my baby dammit! Give her back to me!" The voice screamed as people were gathering around the scene! That voice became clearer as we were about thirty feet from the tussle. My stomach rumbled as if I had eaten a raw chicken stew! Rachel elbowed me in the side so hard that I nearly fell! Both of our eyes stretched in disbelief as we witnessed Charlene cuss and fight with the officers! "Oh my God! What happened to her! Baby! What baby? That's Charlene Cedric!" Rachel said as she pointed. I slowed my pace as I could only hear Charlene's voice echoing in my head, "I'm pregnant... I'm pregnant..." I scanned my eyes over towards the police car to find the other officer standing by the front of it carefully holding a crying baby in his arms! All the sound left my ears as my vision was blurry while I was trying to feel the sidewalk as my legs started to wobble! For about a full minute I wasn't there! I could feel my body slowly shutting down until Charlene's voice called out my name! "Cedric! There, he is right there! I told you the father of my baby was a famous baseball player! He's going to be so pissed when he hears about what you all are trying to do with our child! Cedric! I knew you would come back to save us! I knew it! Tell them!" She yelled as we were within a few feet of them! Felt like something was crawling through my body then up my throat choking me as I couldn't say a word! Rachel had tears falling down her face as she stared at Charlene as she was making sense of everything. The female cop managed to place handcuffs on Charlene as she escorted her to another cop car that was pulling up. Most of the crowd looked at Charlene, while some people had their eyes on Rachel and me. I grabbed Rachel's hand to get us out of the spotlight! She pulled her hand away from mines as we started to walk away! The screams died down as they placed Charlene in the back of the car. I looked back a couple of times to see the cars drive off.

We made it back to Rachel's car as she rushed to open her own door! She jumped in as I walked to the passenger side. I had to stand there worried and embarrassed while she refused to unlock the door for me to get in. I was going to beg her to let me in but the way she looked at me when I leaned down to make eye contact with her through the window wasn't a welcoming sight. I stepped back away from the car then sat down on the curb as I waited for her to process her thoughts. I had some things I was struggling with to understand myself as I planted my head in my hands. The facts were there just like they were there when Rachel admitted that she was pregnant. There was no denying it. Charlene wasn't lying nor did she take care of whatever she was insinuating on the phone that day. That baby looked like Junior as far as the size and age, if indeed that was a baby girl. Was I supposed to had said something to the cops then? Was I supposed to acknowledge that was my baby? Too many questions came piling down on me as I sat there then looking up to the sky as if someone up there was playing a trick on me. Sat there so long I lost the feeling in my butt. I was there at least twenty minutes planted on the side of the car. Hadn't prayed since I left for school. I made a desperate effort to say I needed a miracle! I asked God to give me courage to stand up to all responsibilities I had created for myself. As I was begging to God underneath my breath, Rachel appeared out of thin air, then sat next to me! Maybe someone was listening because she placed her arm around me. I lifted my head to see her tears all wiped away. I shook my head giving her every nonverbal defining how sorry I was for not saying anything sooner. She didn't ask me anything. She just looked at me as if she needed to help me or if I was a lost soul. I took my phone out my pocket to check the time to see that Mrs. Anthony had called several times. It was passed the time we agreed to be back! We both jumped up to get in the car to head back to my house!

I called back to let her know we were running behind and was making sure it wasn't anything wrong with Junior. She said she received a called from a neighbor who was down by the river walk! She was worried about what she had heard! She asked us to get home right away! I told her we were almost there. After I hung the phone, Rachel asked, "Is everything okay? Is Junior alright?" The traffic was moving slow as we tried to weave through it. It gave me time to come clean with Rachel. "Junior is fine. I'm going to be straight up with you. I apologize if this comes as a surprise. I know we have been talking things through since Junior was born. I do like the way things are going for us. Please believe me. But… I must confess… Charlene is telling the truth. There's a high possibility that the baby is indeed mines. I can't deny it at this point. There were rumors that she had a baby. I guess I didn't care enough to check on her like that. With all the mess I've been in and juggling, I didn't know what to do. I understand if it makes you hate me. I don't deserve you. My baggage continues to get heavier. Don't want to drag you down with it. Sorry…" I whispered as I got choked up trying to keep myself from sugar coating the truth any longer. I gazed out the window at the downtown lights and buildings as we finally got on a cleared street. I didn't mind her taking her time to think about the load I put in her lap. I cracked my window in need of some fresh air because I felt like it was stuffy from the hard breathing I was doing. "I haven't been completely honest myself. My life isn't as great as some would believe. I need to tell you something but... I need you to promise me you won't say anything to anyone about it. I want to trust you. I haven't said this to anyone else... It's something that has been haunting me for years now. With the unexpected and crazy chain of events this past year or so, you of all people need to know. I don't know what to do to save myself from the pain I've suffered, but I need help. Can I trust you to help me?" Rachel finally said as we were then turning on my block. I was speechless and scared shitless as to what I had to do to help her. It didn't help that she was concerned about me keeping her words to myself. I was sure it couldn't have been as bad as my mess.

"Your secret is safe with me. I must warn you, I'm nervous about what you're about to reveal. I had some questions about a couple of comments you've made recently. Maybe this is about to answer them. I won't say a word. What is said in this car right now, will stay in this car. Cool?" I replied as she parked the car. She turned off the car then unfastened her seatbelt as she moved facing towards me. She couldn't get a word out without tears falling down her face. I gave her some baby wipes I found in the glove compartment. After padding some of the tears away she finally said, "It started when I was about eight years old. It was after a Christmas eve dinner we had that year. Once everyone was gone, my mom had to drop one of my aunts off at her home. I was there getting ready for bed when my dad called me in his room. I didn't think twice about it. He asked me to sit on his lap then asked me what I wanted for Christmas. At that age I was excited to tell him all the things I could imagined I wanted. I filled his ears up with the things I seen from the TV commercials to whatever I didn't get the previous Christmas. About halfway through my long wish list, he began to brush my inner thigh with his hand. He went on with that as he inched up closer and closer until he was touching my private part. I jumped off him feeling uncertain of what was going on because he had never done anything like that to me! He grabbed me by my wrist with total control of me as he guided me back on his lap. I inhaled the lingering smells of alcohol all over him. He whispered to me that I was the prettiest thing he'd ever seen. He told me he didn't want me to miss out on getting those things I named for Christmas if I told anyone about what he did. He promised me he would make sure Santa brought me all of it if I let him touch me again. I was scared, shocked and naïve to his words and actions. I let him do whatever he wanted to do because I didn't have a voice. I literally couldn't put together any words to say to let him know how uncomfortable I was! I closed my eyes while he touched me. It felt like an eternity, sitting there while he had his way with me. I started to cry as it became too painful to hold in! He finally stopped then told me to go wash up before my mom made it back. I couldn't look at him anymore after I slowly stepped up stairs to my room. Once I was in the shower, I cried the entire time. The water couldn't get me clean enough to wash away the filth I felt I had all over my body! I... I..." The porch light came on suddenly that caused her to stop! We both glanced over to see it come on then the front door opened. Mrs. Anthony came out on the porch then looked over at the car to see if we were in it. I quickly gave Rachel more wipes for her face. "I'll let her know we're coming in. Take your time." I whispered to Rachel before I got out the car. I yelled up to Mrs. Anthony, "Sorry! We're coming in now! Traffic was crazy downtown. Too many people down there tonight!" She waved at me in relief that we had made it. She then went back in the house leaving the porch light on. I walked over to Rachel's side of the car. I stood by the door as she was looking in the mirror making sure she didn't look like the hell she described to me. I was sweating with anger as I kept struggling with the images of her dad being all nice and cool with me. Not for a split second I would have guessed he was a devilish pedophile! My hands were shaking as I had to take deep breathes in order to keep calm. She too had to calm herself down as she closed the visor mirror then sat there for about thirty seconds talking to herself. I didn't interrupt a damn thing as she needed way more comfort than me!

I pulled the door open as she was pushing it to get out the car. "I had no idea. Damn... I can't imagine how you feel, nor can I change any of that. Please believe me, I wish I could change what he did to you. I want to blow your dad's head the fuck off right now, if you just say the word." I said as I had to bite my tongue before spilling out more of the hate I was feeling towards her dad. I hugged her as tight as I could. "Please don't mention it to anyone. There's so much more that happened but I don't have the energy to go into it right now. I don't know why I told you that now, I just wanted to get that out of my system finally. Thanks for listening to me Cedric." She whispered after I unlocked my arms from her. I gave her a very discouraged look as if I couldn't believe that there was more to the torturing, she had already been through! I could believe it! I was getting even madder by the second. Unfortunately, I had to defuse my emotions as we were about to head in the house! How could she live the way she did without giving any signs of any trauma she had? That made me look at her as one of the strongest women I've ever met! Tammie then stepped out on the porch holding Junior in her arms as we were walking towards the house. "I don't know what to say. I'm glad you trusted me enough to share that. I know that wasn't easy." I replied before we made it to the steps of the house.

"Someone was looking for his mommy and daddy. He's been up playing for the last hour. He's a busy bee! I've had a nice workout for the evening I'll say." Tammie said as she held him swaying back and forth. We both smiled as Rachel grabbed Junior from Tammie. Tammie gave me a curious look as if she could see the trouble in my eyes. It caught me off guard as I tried to smile again. We all walked in the house. While Rachel was collecting and gathering Juniors things, I just looked at her as a fragile diamond in the rough. I wanted to say so much, but I knew I couldn't at that moment. She was smiling and talking with Mrs. Anthony and Tammie as if she were the happiness person in the world. I directed my attention towards our son. I held him while Rachel went to get his extra bottles from the fridge. I felt selfish as hell as I examined him. I looked at his facial features and for a second, I questioned if he was really my son. I felt like shit after that! I couldn't believe I was taking everything to the extreme when I wasn't even the one truly effected by anything. I kissed my little guy on his cheeks and whispered, "I'm sorry. I know you're mines. Daddy will never do that again."

Rachel returned to the living room with everything packed up. She thanked Mrs. Anthony and Tammie for allowing us some free time together. She mentioned that it was worth it then she walked over to the door. I followed not thinking about anything but getting her on her way before I said something stupid in front of everyone. Mrs. Anthony and Tammie both gave Junior cheek kisses before we walked outside. After getting Junior strapped in, I said, "Are you okay? I can't say how sorry I am about all of that. Please call me." She got in then looked up at me then replied, "It's okay. I will call you before I go to sleep. Please don't worry yourself Cedric." I closed the door for her then asked, "Do you want to stay here? I mean, how do you still live around him? I mean... You know... damn... I hope that doesn't offend you. I'm just saying." She sat there thinking about it as if she had to respond a certain way. "I'll call you about it. Please don't say anything." She answered then turned the car on. I stepped back then she pulled off. I went on the porch but didn't go back in the house. I sat down in one of the chairs. Tammie pulled back the curtains then leaned in tapping on the window. She gave me a thumbs up as her voice muffled through the window asking me if I was okay. I gave her the okay nod and return the thumbs up.

I sat out there for at least twenty minutes before Tammie came out to check on me again. I had slid my loafers off to allow my toes to move freely. I wasn't thinking about anything. There was too much to focus on than just one situation. Tammie sat next to me. She knew I wasn't being myself. "Are you sleeping outside tonight or there's something that heavy you're holding in that it won't let you get up? Y'all sat in that car for a good minute before Mrs. Anthony decided to go out and check on you two. I'm sorry for spying on y'all but Rachel looked like she was venting some deep shit to you. Are you sure everything is okay with you? With her?" Tammie said as she kept her eyes glued on me. I didn't budge or give in to her invitation to say or mention anything. She was right but I had a promise to keep. "Yeah she was just having a moment. Scared of what's to come with trying to be a good mother. I mean, we talked about us. Nothing too crazy." I replied. The way she looked off while I was talking was a sign, she wasn't buying my whole story. She wasn't in the car, so I didn't care. I started rubbing my eyes then yawned a huge one out. "I hope everything does work out with you two." She said then started yawning herself. "See, look what you done started with all that yawning. You are making me sleepy!" She added. I stood up then grabbed my loafers. "Everything is going to be alright. I don't doubt it. In due time, it'll be fine. All of it." I replied then reached for Tammie's hand to help her out of the chair. She pulled up holding my hand then said, "Well if you say so. I'm here for you if you need to do any venting. I've been there and done just about everything. I know through experience. Okay?" I smiled at her then held the door opened for her. I said good night to her, and Mrs. Anthony then shot up the stairs to my room. I took a cold shower that night. Felt like my whole body was over heated. I finally had the chance to shed a few tears while I stood in the water. I promised myself I wouldn't cry over things I couldn't control anymore. Rachel's story was an exception. The mother of my child had been molested and I was clueless to it! I cried because I wanted to save her back then as well as now! For about fifteen minutes I let it all out then got out of the shower. I checked my phone several times to see if Rachel had called before I laid down. I waited until almost one in the morning for her. Her call never came through.

Chapter 11

Can't Ignore That Itch

Over the next few weeks, I continued to have Rachel and Junior over as much as I could. It worked out because I didn't shy away from the thoughts of kneeing Rachel's dad in the face if I saw him again. We agreed it was best for me not to go over to her place unless there was an emergency. Rachel opened up more and more about her past by telling me that the touching lasted all the way up to her high school days! It never crossed over to him having sex with her but more so of her waking up to him removing his hand from underneath her covers while she was sleeping. It became so norm that she would fake sleep for him to do whatever it was he needed to do to please himself. She said she used to fall asleep in their bed but on her mother's side which placed her mother in the middle of the bed so he wouldn't bother her! Days after telling me more I needed prayer and a restraining order to keep from losing my shit that would have giving me a life sentence for murder! She went on and on about how Junior was the best thing that has happened for her. After she told her parents she was pregnant, her dad tried to disown her, but she threatened to say something to her mom about their secret. She said as hard as it was, she forgave him. She said her mom would have had a nervous breakdown if she found out. She cared more about how it was going to affect her relationship with her mom than to say anything to cause pain for the family. For me it was too much to think about at times! I would find myself drifting off in a daydream about the kinds of torturing I would perform on her dad. I would imagine myself cutting off his filthy hands as well as removing his dirty genitals. Rachel caught me a few times zoned out with an angry look of revenge I had whenever I was plotting about how to make her dad disappear. Only thing that tried to distract me from carrying out my plans was Samantha!

I was sitting on the porch with Junior playing with him on an early afternoon. Felt great outside which was perfect for him and since the ladies were all busy with other stuff, Junior and I kicked it outside. I had just given him a bottle and as I was burping him, I heard a car horn, blowing in the distance! I didn't think twice about it as I continued to pat Junior until he burped in my face. I laughed at how he smiled at me once he got it all out of system. He had a look on his face as if he knew what he had done to daddy. The horn sound was gone but then my phone started ringing. I repositioned Junior in my arms then grabbed my phone. I answered so fast I didn't glance at the number. "I know I don't see you sitting on your porch right now!" Samantha's voice shouted at me through the phone! My stomach hit the floor as my neck almost snapped looking around while clutching Junior tighter in my arm making sure he was secured. I looked at the phone to make sure it was her number before I responded. It had been so long since I thought about her or cared to. "Hello. Cedric... You know who this is! Are you really not going to answer me?" She said. Everything in my body was telling me to get up and walk slowly into the house. Nothing good was going to come from it, I kept thinking. "Hey... What's up with you stranger? It's been a minute huh?" I responded as I continued to monitor the street and sidewalk. "If I weren't running late, I would get out my car to pinch you to make sure it is really you! What the hell Cedric. It's been well over six months! Why did you ghost me the way you did? Then you pop back up for like a visit or for good? I guess it's like that..." She yelled at me again! I was relieved that she was in a hurry. I eased back in my chair as I smiled at Junior while he stared at me as if he were glad, she wasn't coming by too.

"Do you really want to have that conversation right now? We're not going to say who ghosted who. I've had so much going on and I haven't really talked to too many people since I've been back. Sorry if you feel a way about it. I'm here... I don't think I'm leaving anytime soon." I said without sounding too uneasy about being back home. "Oh... Okay... Well, I wasn't expecting to see you anytime soon. Wait! Who baby that is someone trusted you with? I mean... That was a baby, a toddler, you were holding up right?" She said. Rachel came out on to the porch as I held the phone to my ear. It would have been perfect if I could have ended the call two to three minutes before she came outside but it was too late. She walked over then took Junior away from me as I looked for any signs of attitude or anger as she walked back in the house with him. She didn't say a word as I sat there debating if Samantha needed to hear the truth or if it even mattered. "Hello... Cedric..." She said. "I'm sorry. My bad... I was giving my son back to his mom. So... Yeah... I have a son now. Hate you have to find out like this but... Yeah, I'm a dad..." I said as I stood up anticipating her to hang up in my face. "I know..." She replied within seconds without any arrogance or worry. "You know?" I immediately asked. "Yeah... I knew you had a child. I must admit that this wasn't the first time I've seen you with your child. I don't want to sound creepy but... I've seen you many times. I wanted to knock on your door like a week or two ago just to let you know I'm still here... You seemed happy or at least focused on doing the right thing. I didn't want to add anymore complications to your life. Things haven't been the best with me overall but I'm surviving." She said with a lower and more embarrassed tone. I couldn't believe my ears! As if I haven't had enough of the creep stuff already. That wasn't that bad to hear it from her. I'm glad she didn't show up unannounced.

"Wow! I had no idea. I've been putting more things under a microscope when it comes to the decisions I've made in the past. There are things that happened that led me back here that I would have to explain later. For right now, I don't know what to say. I gave up on trying to make something more than what it truly was between us. We were good as friends. I've made some naïve choices I'm dealing with as we speak. Now I understand what my mom meant when she used to say, "What goes around, comes around." Funny thing about it all, I'm not sure if I feel any regret now. I hate you're not doing too well yourself. Maybe we can catch up or something? Put it all out there you know. I've been coming clean with a lot of stuff and I think it's what's really helping me handle everything." I replied. "I understand. I'm fine with that if it doesn't get you in any trouble you know. The baby has a mother and if I know you, I'm sure you two are getting along just well." She replied with curiosity. I knew what she was fishing for with that reply. "I don't think it'll be any issues for me to see you or talk with you. Maybe later this evening when you're off I guess if that's not too soon?" I suggested. "As long as there's no trouble with it, that will work for me. Please don't be upset with me when you see me. There's a lot that's been going on. Somethings I don't know how to explain. I'll see you later Cedric. Bye..." She replied than hung up the phone.

     I wasn't prepared for any more surprise. I put my phone in my pocket then walked in the house. Junior was laying in his crib sleeping like a log while Rachel was on the couch looking like a lioness ready to protect her cub if anyone got near him. And by anyone, I mean me! I could feel the tension in the air by the way she was clicking through the channels on the TV. She wasn't looking for anything to watch, just scrolling without a care. I walked past her to the kitchen to get a snack. My nerves weren't at ease enough to say anything to her in that moment. I had to get my game face ready. She didn't waste a second coming in right behind to get the answers she was patiently waiting for.

She was slick with it. She tried a sneak attack, but I was mildly prepared. "I'm glad you keep your phone handy like that. That way I know if there's ever an emergency, you'll answer it quickly. I have so much stuff going on, I'm always misplacing my phone. I need to super glue it to me or something?" She said then giggled a little. I laughed with her then said, "Yeah it's a habit now. I guess that is a good thing. I mean, it's not like I get a bunch of calls or texts from anyone." I replied. I put it out there like that to see if she would jump on it. To get her to get right to the point. "Ummm, well.... A few people must have your number. You weren't just talking to me or Mrs. Anthony just then so. I'm sure you gave it out. Well... No... Never mind... That's none of my business. Didn't mean to say it like that." She said then started to walk out. "Wait! It's okay... You're good. No need to apologize. I get it. I know how it looks." I replied as I grabbed her by the hand pulling her back. She exhaled as if she was hoping I would have an explanation. "I don't want it to be like this. I know we're still trying to figure it all out. I don't want to be all up in your business like that. I'll do better." She replied as she looked innocent as if she had made a big mistake. I wasn't going to lie about who it was. "That was Samantha. She lives here. She's a friend I've had for a little while now. We've hung out a few times. She saw me on the porch as she was driving by then called me. I haven't talked to her for months. I might catch up with her later this evening. She's a good girl and friend." I replied as I continued to hold her hand. She stood there thinking about what I said as I could tell she was fighting with how she wanted to respond.

A knock on the door interrupted her before she could say anything. I walked to the door then opened. It was Rico standing there looking half scared like someone was after him! I stepped out the way to let him in. "Hey man. Where have you been. I haven't seen you since that, ummm you know." I whispered to him. "Yeah, I know... I'm sorry. I've been trying to forget about that night. I've been having these crazy nightmares. I had to come over to check on you too. How's Mrs. Anthony?" He replied as I shut the door. "Everything is good over here. Glad to see you're okay. Nightmares? Really? Damn that's crazy. I had a couple some days after it all happened too. Nothing else since then. Let me tell her you're here. Let's go in the kitchen. My little guy getting his sleep on." I said then we headed to the kitchen. "Hey! Rico... I haven't seen you in a while! How are you?" Rachel said as we entered the kitchen. I kept on going to get Mrs. Anthony from her room. Rachel and I had several talks about Rico. We both found that it was a good thing that we put everything behind us. She was all about forgiving and moving forward. It wasn't odd at all that we were all together. Mrs. Anthony jumped right up.

For about thirty minutes we all stood in the kitchen talking and trying to make the best of what may have been an uncomfortable setting just over a year before. I found myself mentally moving back and forward with the thoughts of how life makes the ugliest things turn full circle to some pleasant situations. There was no anger or hate yet along any doubts clouding my emotions. "Looks like a great day for some good eating. I'm sure no one is going to disagree with that right? Rico are you staying for dinner, Rachel? It'll be nice if we could be together. I'm thinking some friend chicken, mac and cheese, green beans, corn on the cob and some banana pudding! I need to run to the store." Mrs. Anthony said with a glowing smile on her face. She wasn't lying about anyone objecting that idea. We were all just as excited about the menu as she was. I needed to get Rico alone for a few to ask some questions. "Only a man without taste buds would turn that down! I know that delicious smell would have him eating it anyways! Sounds like a plan to me." I replied as we all laughed. She received the go ahead nods from Rachel and Rico as well. "I haven't had one of your soulful meals in a good minute so I'm in need of one! My mom can cook but not like you Mrs. Anthony! Please don't quote me on that!" Rico said jokingly as he was trying to adjust after being missing in action. "Great! I'll get Tammie to go with me to the store. Are there any special request or anything I left out?" Mrs. Anthony said. We all looked around at one another confirming that we didn't need to add anything else. The fat kid in me wanted to suggest adding another side and desert but I needed to watch myself because I was determined to play baseball again, somewhere. "Dinner should be ready in about two hours once I get back from the store. Junior's little voice came echoing through the kitchen. Rachel went to check on him as Mrs. Anthony headed to her room.

"Hey man, can we go for a stroll down by the park? Maybe shoot around for minute since we have a couple of hours before dinner. I need to talk to you." I whispered to Rico. He looked a bit worried. "Man, it's nothing crazy, I promise. I need to know if you have seen or heard anything about the position, we were in." I added. "The last time I strolled with you, I almost got shot! I know we are in a better place and working on keeping the past in the past. I've been laying low for real! I'm going to try to trust you again man." He whispered back. "We good man. I'm not on any funny stuff or anything that's going to cause any stress for any of us! You can trust me. Straight up." I replied just before Mrs. Anthony came back through the kitchen. "You two behave. I'm happy to see y'all together like this. God knows we all need a break! I pray that you two can continue to push forward. I'll see y'all in a few." Mrs. Anthony said as she walked past us. We both smiled. I told Rico I was going to let Rachel know what was up before we headed out too. It wasn't the first time Rachel stayed there with just her and Junior.

Rico and I went in the living then he headed out to wait on me on the porch. Rachel was sitting on the couch rocking

Junior in her lap. I leaned in and gently rubbed Junior's cheek with my thumb. Rachel side eyed me as if I was leaving her out on the affection giveaway. "I'm about to walk to the park with Rico for a minute. Y'all good?" I said. She gave me a curious look as if I was up to something more than just going to the park. "It's not like that. I'm good. I just want to ask him a few questions. Catch up, you know." I added as I gave her a guilty grin because she wouldn't stop staring at me. She shook her head as if I was hiding something from her. "Well I guess we'll be right here chilling. I'll make sure the kitchen is clean since he's about to tap back out in a second." She replied. I told her thanks. Before I went out the door, she mentioned Samantha. "Are you still going to have time to go see your friend? I mean since we're all having dinner and you're about to kick it with Rico now. Maybe you should invite her over?" She said. Awkward and stunned wasn't even close to the thoughts going through my head. I had to take a second to make sure I heard her right. "Umm... Well... I guess I forgot about that. Maybe I would ask her over. Since you suggested. Maybe?" I replied then walked out the door. I paused for a split second about to poke my head back in to ask was she serious. I didn't but I wish I did! I grabbed the basketball that was sitting in the corner on the porch. As much as I wanted to ignore the signs Rachel was throwing my way about her feeling a way about us being more of a couple, I still found some hope that maybe talking with Samantha may help cut any lose ends if any were still there between us.

Rico and I headed to the park. We talked about not hearing anything from Officer Jackson in a while and how everyone quietly forgot about what happened. There was an uproar about it for about two to three weeks then nothing. He said he's been trying to find something else to do other than working at the store. Most people feared he was a bad pick to hire. People were still uneasy about Rico's past. No one else would hire him so he did yard work for those that weren't holding what he did over his head. "What I wanted to ask you was about Charlene." I said as we shot around once we reached the court at the park. He didn't look too interested. "What about Charlene? I haven't seen her. Have you?" He replied. He didn't sound as convincing as he may have thought. I heard some cracking in his voice with a bit of attitude. He shot the ball hard at the goal causing it to bounce off the rim then rolling halfway across the park. I ran after it then walked back over as he had his hands on his hip looking impatient. "Is there something you want to say or get off your chest? You seemed a little uptight about me asking about Charlene. What's up?" I asked as I stood right in front of him. He tried to play it off by trying to steal the ball from me. I moved in time to keep him from getting it as I stood there. "Come on man. Be real with me. I've seen Charlene a few times and I'm worried that she's not herself." I said. He walked over to the bench then sat down. He started tying his shoes since one had unfastened when he reached for the ball. I went over then sat beside him. I drippled the ball under my legs while I waited on him to say something. "I did see her. I've seen her more times than I should have. It was hard every time. You know she has a baby... I mean... Your baby." He finally replied slightly under his breath. I picked the ball up sensing he knew way more than I thought.

"Yeah man. I don't understand it. It's hard to even talk about it. She hates me. I mean really despises me. I've tried so many times to talk to her. Her sisters have tried to help her as well. It's like she is stuck. She only talks about you and the baby. She calls me the killer and have even called the police on me. I had to stop going over to their house." He said as he became choked up. "Damn. I didn't know you had seen her like that. Yeah, I've seen her and the baby. My baby. I just don't know what to do. I mean if she's bad like that and that's really my child. I have to do something." I replied. "Yeah you may be the only hope she has left. Her sisters are about to put her back in a place that's for people with mental challenges. They said they're probably going to have to take the baby from her. Not sure what that means but it didn't sound good how they were explaining it to me. I tried man. I really did. That's why I came over today. I had this feeling of frustration with you about that night as well as not understanding why you're not trying to help Charlene. There are too many questions with not enough answers. She needs you Cedric. More importantly, that baby needs you." He said then stood up. He grabbed the ball from me then went back on the court. As he started back shooting around, I was glued to the bench. I couldn't lift the ton of bricks that kept getting heavier and heavier the more I took in what he said. He painted the clearest picture I needed and answered the questions I feared the answers to be.

I watched him shoot as I pictured myself trying to take care of myself and two children. The only person I wanted to talk to was Lauren. I was hoping time healed whatever wound I caused leaving like I did. I needed to vent to someone, and Rico wasn't going to cut it. God knows Mrs. Anthony would have had a stroke and Rachel had her own personal concerns with it all. I pulled my phone out to call her. It rang about six times with no answer. I was about to call again but Samantha's number showed up calling me. I answered quickly! She said she was following up with me to make sure we were still going to meet up soon. If I ever needed a voice of reasoning, my answer should have been approved by that voice. Without even giving it just a second of thought, I suggested for her to come by for dinner! I told her that Mrs. Anthony was having a few people over. I failed to disclose who those people were. I told her it would be nice and maybe we could hang out afterwards. She was super excited to come over and see Mrs. Anthony. I told her about what was on the menu which made it an easy yes for her. I told her the time she should head over and to call when she pulls up. She thanked me for caring enough to invite her over for dinner because she needed a break from her normal day to day routine. I could tell in her voice that she had a lot on her mind but was saving it for when we saw one another. I hung up the phone not noticing Rico was standing right in front of me with the face of a shocked child.

"Wait a minute... I'm sorry man, but did you just invite some chick to dinner with us? A chick to a dinner that the mother of your child will be attending. After hearing news that you very much indeed have another child that needs you. Are you sick or insane? I'm not the brightest at all. But what I do know is that's some dumb shit you're doing! Who does that?" He said then threw the ball at me! My natural reaction wanted to rush him, tackling him to the ground then punch him in the eye! Lucky for me I had quick hands to deflect the ball from hitting me in the face! "You mad at me because Charlene lost her damn mind! You don't think I know that I have enough shit on my plate! I don't have all the answers! I don't know what I'm doing! I don't have the luxury of watching someone else deal with their mess while I stand around making them feel bad about it! I don't need your bullshit about what's going on with my responsibilities!" I yelled at him as I stood up, slowly approaching him! He kept easing backwards as I got closer.

I snapped out of my rage at him questioning my behavior and choices when Officer Jackson walked up on us out of nowhere! He looked curious to what was taking place between Rico and me. I went mute as if he had pressed a button to close my mouth when he walked up. Rico looked around to see who was approaching because of my sudden silence. "What the hell? What's he doing here? Please tell me you didn't know he was coming up here." Rico whispered to me as he turned then walked back beside me. "Hell no. I didn't know he was coming. Just be cool. We good." I whispered back to him. We were standing side by side as Officer Jackson stepped up then said, "Fellas! It's been a minute. What's going on? You two good over here? I was making my rounds and saw y'all having a disagreement or some sort? Anything I can help y'all with?" He looked as if he knew we weren't going to say too much of anything. "We're good. Nothing serious at all. We were just arguing about the game last night. He didn't know enough so I had to school him about how amazing it is to hit a walk off home run to seal the game." I replied before giving Rico a chance to say something that would keep Officer Jackson around for too long. "Oh yeah! That was a good game. That's a great feeling too! Cedric, I know you racked up on walk-off homers during your senior year here. I remember witnessing a couple myself. But anyway, have anyone said anything to you all about anything?" He replied glancing at Rico. He could tell Rico was nervous. "No one's said anything to me. Nothing..." I said then coughed to get Rico's attention. He looked over at me as I widen my eyes for him to speak. "Umm. No. Nothing at all." Rico mumbled out. Officer Jackson stepped in closer to us both then said, "There are some rumors floating around town about our little secret that shouldn't be floating around. I'm not saying it's a big deal, I just hope whoever started them will see that they are stopped. I can't control what any of the other officers will do if they found out who put those rumors out there. I just thought I should let y'all in on what's going on." He looked us dead in our eyes with a sterned look. I was curious yet had to do some investigating myself. "That's crazy. I don't have a clue how or who would do that. My mouth has been sealed since that night!" I replied. Officer Jackson and I then directed our attention towards Rico. "I don't know anything about anything. I hate I was there and that's that." Rico finally said. He didn't sound convincing. Officer Jackson shook his head then walked off. He uttered, "Just be careful out here. Keep your mouths closed please."

Once Officer Jackson was in his car, I pushed Rico then said, "What the fuck man? Are you crazy? You been talking about that night to someone? But you are pressing me about my baby mothers like you Mister innocent over here. I don't think you understand the level of, I don't want the police to shut us up if we tell people about that night!" He didn't react to me pushing him or my statement. I grabbed the ball then started to walk off. He followed close behind me mumbling to himself. I could hear bits and pieces of his words. Before we made it to the steps of the house, I had to get him to shut his mouth going forward. He was unraveling with personal anger towards me and it was started to jeopardize both of our lives.

I turned around to him then stood in his way on the sidewalk. I had to be calm and careful with my words not to trigger him. "Look Rico, I'm not going to act like I don't have very crucial responsibilities I have to take care of. I promise I'm trying man. I don't have anyone to talk to. I just been doing whatever and hoping for the best results. Everyone can see that my decisions haven't been at their best. I'm going to make things right. Officer Jackson was basically warning us that we shouldn't bring up that night ever again with no one. I think we need to agree that that's best for both of us. I also want you to please not say anything to Mrs. Anthony or anyone else right now about Charlene. I will go see her to check on the baby first thing tomorrow. Please man, I can't snap my fingers to make everything happily ever after. I'm asking for your help man. Please, let's keep this all between us. I just need a little more time to make sure I want to go the way I think I need to go with everything that's happened to me." He scratched his head as he started to rock side to side as he was wrapping his brain around what I said. I stood there waiting not trying to walk off not caring because he acted like he was dealing with some troubles himself. As the cars passed by and the evening sky dimmed darker, I was playing out how the night could go with everyone over for dinner and how I was going to be as charming as I could be to the ladies. I didn't want anyone to think I was doing it out of spite as I promised myself to be transparent with my intentions.

"I know you think I'm being selfish with the way I've handled things with you and your business with the ladies. It seems as if you're in need of someone else's opinion on how you move and make decisions. Yeah, my past hasn't been perfect but who's has? I'm wiser than people think. I know when things are being pushed too far. I learned more than I could have imagined after what I did to David. I promised myself I would never let anger, or my emotions get the best of me! You need help Cedric. You don't have any control of yourself. It shows. Whatever you have in your head about how tonight is going to be, I promise you it's not going to go down that way. It won't have anything to do with what I say to anyone. You're doing too much. You don't know which way to go now. I actually feel sorry for you." He said as he pushed past me. That hit harder than what he said about Charlene. That hit harder than being afraid the cops had a hit out on us. That grabbed me by the throat with a strong grip. I dropped the ball then quickly chased it down the sidewalk before picking it up in front of the house. Rico went up the steps then stood on the porch waiting for me. We could smell the food cooking coming through the front door and windows. He stared at me as if he didn't have anything else to say. He had made his point to the core. All I could do was whisper to him, "Thank you. I needed that. I have to do better." He gave me a forced smile as if he knew I wasn't going to change anything anytime soon. He was right if that's what he was thinking. There was an itch I felt that only got worse the more I wanted to see how much I could take. That's how I was living. I needed to see for myself. That behavior was taking me deeper down the rabbit hole. I needed to live it moment to moment to get the real results.

We went in the house. I hurried on in the kitchen to see if I could be of any assistance to the ladies cooking. Rico had to use the bathroom. Everyone was in the kitchen when I walked in. Tammie was playing with Junior at the table while Mrs. Anthony was at the stove sprinkling spices in a pot with Rachel beside her taking notes. To my surprise, Pastor Clayton was coming in through the back door with an empty trash can. This was a real deal dinner Mrs. Anthony orchestrated. All the cards were on the table while I was playing with the worst hand for the hundredth time! I started to wonder about the conversations that were about to take place. "Hey! Looks like a family reunion or something up in here! Smelling good, everyone looking good, okay I see what's up." I said as I slowly walked over to Tammie and Junior. Everyone smiled and greeted me. Pastor Clayton nodded his head as he put a garbage bag in the trash can then washed his hand before walking over to me. I reached for Junior, but Tammie wasn't having it. She was enjoying their play time together as Junior was giggling up a storm. I managed to sneak some soft pinches on his thick thighs before turning my attention towards Pastor Clayton. We shook hands as he said, "Brother Cedric. How are you? Glad to see you!" Rico came in then greeted everyone. "I'm good, Nice to see you too. I can't complain. Trying to get myself above it all." I replied. He still had my hand in a tight grip then pulled me in closer to him as he leaned in. "Son I know you are fighting some of the worse kinds of demons. I need us to get together as soon as possible. Don't try to do it all on your own. You'll be left empty and defeated. God wants to fight these battles for you, okay." He whispered to me. I wasn't ready to share it all with him, but something was telling me he could help. "Yes sir. I'll make sure it happens soon. Thankyou." I replied. He smiled then walked in the living room. I caught Mrs. Anthony glancing over at me then gave me a look as if I needed to follow him to listen to what he said.

I was throwed off when my phone started ringing. "Hey Rico, can you put some plates out? The food will be ready in a few minutes. Please wash your hands." Mrs. Anthony said to Rico. She then looked at me again as if me still standing there was making her upset. I lifted my phone up to let her know I had a call. I walked by the back door to answer it as I could see that it was Samantha's number calling. She was telling me that she had just pulled up. I told her I would be right out to let her in. I hung up the phone thinking if I really want to go through it. Nothing urged me enough to deny Samantha's invitation. Everyone was in a good mood. I figured it wouldn't change that too much. I washed my hands quickly then walked past everyone as they all were moving about in the kitchen with setting up the table and placing all the food on the table. As I entered the living room Pastor Clayton was sitting on the couch with a bible in his lap. He started to slide over to make room for me with a smile on his face. "Cedric, son I wanted to talk to you for a quick minute if you don't mind. I hope that's not too much to ask." He said as his face looked worried when I kept walking towards the door. "Maybe we can talk after dinner. If that's cool with you." I said before I reached the door. He paused for a second trying to understand why it wasn't a good time then. I can tell Mrs. Anthony and he had spoken about him having a conversation with me for the millionth time by the way they both were acting. I hate I had to disappoint them. He stood up then said, "Okay son. Whatever works for you. I'll hang around for a little after dinner for ya." He slowly headed back in the kitchen. I thanked him for his patience then opened the door.

My eyes were latched on Samantha as she walked up the steps to the porch with her hair straighten, light orange fitted skirt that hugged her thighs right and a cream-colored tank top looking shirt on. She looked dressed to impress. I almost wanted to tell her to take the cream-colored wedge heels off because she was over dressed. She looked like she wanted to make sure she had my attention all night! "Well damn, someone has a hot date after dinner or something? You look gorgeous as hell." I whispered to her as we hugged before she stepped in. "Thanks. Are we going on a date?" She said without hesitation with a serious look on her face. I closed the door as she walked on in as my mouth watered looking at her from head to toe. She moved with confidence as I couldn't keep my eyes off her sexy frame that was looking perfect in that skirt. "I tried the date thing with you. We know how that turned out." I said jokily as she smiled then shook her head. "Yeah, well things change with time. You're not a quitter, are you? You never know what can happen if you try again." She replied. She was throwing me all the right vibes in the most convincing ways. I wasn't expecting it to flow like that. I was doubting the decision to invite her to the dinner had I known she was feeling like she was about me. Like when she dropped in on me in Chicago. I was becoming a believer with the whole time does change and heal wounds for real. "Well let's see what happens after dinner. Thanks for coming." I said as I started to walk towards the kitchen. That was probably the best time to tell her who was all there but again, the itch was getting unbearable. I needed to see how it was going to play out organically. "No problem. It smells delicious in there! I brought my appetite with me too." She said as we both started laughing then flowed into the kitchen.

You would've thought I walked in with a celebrity the way they were looking at Samantha! Everyone stopped what they were doing for a nice long second or two when they looked up to see us standing there together. "Hey, this is my friend Samantha everyone, Samantha this is everyone. You know Mrs. Anthony and I'm sure she remembers you. It's been a minute. That's Rachel, my sister Tammie with my little man Junior, Rico and Pastor Clayton." I said pointing at them as they all either waved at her or said hi. The table was set with the food ready to be served. "Hi Samantha, how have you been? I wish Cedric told me you were coming! Let me set out another plate for you. There's plenty of food." Mrs. Anthony said as she made room on the table for Samantha. "I've been fine. Busy at the store. Thanks for having me." Samantha replied then looked at me as if I was rude for not notifying Mrs. Anthony of her coming. I got that same look from Mrs. Anthony as well. I didn't want to look at Rachel or Tammie for nothing in the world. I knew the two of them were giving me the looks of death. Rico didn't say anything as he knew what was going on. He was sitting beside Tammie with Pastor Clayton at one end of the table. I didn't have a choice but to sit next to Rachel as Samantha sat on the other side of me. Mrs. Anthony sat at the other end of the table.

Before any questions were asked, Pastor Clayton prayed over the food. He decided that holding hands was going to make it more holy or something which of course Rachel made me hold her pinky finger. She wouldn't lock her whole hand in mines while he blessed the food. He indeed prayed over the food then inserted words of the direction for our young minds. He prayed that we all find the best oath for ourselves. He prayed about us making decisions that were pleasing to God and not of the flesh. Samantha squeezed my hand after he went on about that. He finished his prayer asking God to give the weak courage to take care of all their responsibilities. That gave Rachel a reason to move her hand as if she were testing my grip. I continued to hold on to her finger until he finally said Amen. "Thank you, Pastor Clayton for that! Yes, finally we can eat! Please help yourselves with passing the side dishes around. Can you serve the chicken Cedric?" Mrs. Anthony said. I got right up then washed my hands again! I started placing chicken on everyone's plates with the big shiny tongs. Everyone requested two pieces except Rachel and Samantha as if they weren't as hungry as everyone else. The sides were floating around the table with some chatting between everyone as Samantha was making sure I had some of it on my plate. She didn't let the sides pass my plate without putting a little on it. The looks from Tammie and Mrs. Anthony was a mixture of shock and understanding. Tammie was giving off the look of, 'who do she think she is.' But on the other hand, Mrs. Anthony was looking like, 'someone taught her well.' I'm glad that Pastor Clayton started to choke up a little that he needed something to drink. That directed their attention towards him. Mrs. Anthony asked me to get the strawberry lemonade, she made out the fridge while I was still standing. She jumped up as well to grab some glasses for everyone. I quickly poured him a glass before he coughed out a lung! Mrs. Anthony took over the serving of lemonade as she told me to have a seat so I could start eating.

Rico was stuffing his face without a care in the world. He didn't look up for minutes as he continued to throw down on the chicken. Tammie started to eat as Rachel and Samantha slowly started to eat as well. I got right to it once I sat down. I was going in like I hadn't eaten all day! Everything was so damn delicious. I was on my way to a for sure food comma. Once the drinks were poured Mrs. Anthony sat down and started back eating. It was quiet for about three to four minutes before the jabs started. Lucky for me that was enough time for me to put plenty of food in belly. "Shaa... Shalonda, Shanda... Excuse me. I'm sorry, what was your name again?" Rachel asked as she leaned in looking at Samantha. I looked over at Tammie to see that she was all for it. She had the evil grin on her face pretending she was focused on her food as if nothing was said. Rico coughed a little as to make things even more awkward. I was confused on how Rachel got any of those names mixed up with Samantha, but I didn't say anything. "Oh okay. It's Samantha. Or you can just call me Sam if that makes it easier for you. I'm fine with either way." Samantha replied with a smile on her face. "Yes, that's right. Samantha. I apologize. Got it. Are you from here? I thought I may have seen you at the grocery store not far from here. I'm trying to remember where have a seen you at?" Rachel said then took a bite of mac and cheese staring at Samantha.

Pastor Clayton wanted no part of the twenty-one questions as they were heading that way. He started to talk with Mrs. Anthony about updates at the church. They started their own side conversation that helped take the spotlight off the two ladies going back and forth. Tammie and Rico even started to talk between each other as well. It helped me say a few words to clear the tension between the ladies I could feel breathing down my neck. Rachel knew I gave her that info, but I guess she was verifying it for herself. Samantha did answer Rachel question. She told her she recalls seeing Rachel a few times at the store and where she was from. That led to me interrupting them to go down memory lane. I don't know if it was the prayer or me being stupid again, but I just put it all out there between them two. I was able to slide my chair back just enough to have both seeing each other clearly. "I met Samantha when I started working at the store. I liked her probably more than she liked me. It became clear when we went out. I had this crazy idea about being with her and her coming to Chicago with me. Obvious that didn't work out. I felt it was best for us to just be friends. Samantha did visit me in Chicago for a little. Things went south because of a situation I didn't handle well. We haven't really been in touch until as of today. We don't have anything extra going on or anything like that. Rachel is the mother of my child. We did some things that lead to Junior being here but never really took things further than trying to co-parent. I respect you both because I do have feelings for you both. I didn't mean any harm by inviting Samantha over but with nothing serious going on between anyone, I didn't see what the fuss would have been. I appreciate you ladies for hearing me out. That's what it is and there's nothing more to it." I said then took a sip of my lemonade. It was obvious everyone had tuned in to my words because no one else was talking. Everyone was pretending to eat while the ladies were thinking about what I said. Finally, Rachel responded, "Oh... So, she came to visit you at school. Interesting... I understand. I'm good. Unbelievable... Nice to meet you Sam. I'm sorry it didn't work out for you two. I wish y'all the best." She then stood up, picked up Junior out of his play bin then walked in the living room! I was confused as hell. I thought that was fair and straight forward. I thought being real about what things were and how I felt was the best way to put it out there. Boy was I wrong. Rachel was double down on her true intentions.

"You better go after her! Please Cedric. You need to make sure she's okay." Mrs. Anthony said. "I'm sorry. I would have never come over if I knew more about some things. Thank you all for having me. I'll just leave." Samantha said with tears in her eyes as if she was holding more in than she wanted any of us to know about. She walked in the living room too! "Son go in there now!" Pastor Clayton demanded. I jumped up then followed the ladies! The door front door slammed shut as I walked in the living to see Rachel on the couch with Junior's bag, putting his stuff in it. She was tearing up but not crying. She was struggling with holding him while collecting his stuff. She was visibly frustrated as she was mumbling to herself. Junior started to get a little cranky, so I rushed over to get him from her. She refused to let me touch him! "Please leave me alone Cedric. Please!" She said with exhaustion. She got up adjusting Junior on one side of her on her hip then pulled the strap of the bag over her other shoulder. She started searching for her keys that made her even more impatient. I found them on top of the TV as she was declaring she would walk home if she didn't find the car keys. I gave them to her as she quickly walked over to the door. I hurried over to stand in her way. "Please Rachel, help me understand. I'm sorry. I didn't mean to upset you in any way." I pleaded with her. "Can you please get out my fucking way. Please! Just move Cedric. See... You have me cussing in Mrs. Anthony's house. Lord help me!" She said as the first tear fell from her face. Junior was crying reaching for me while Rachel didn't care if I dropped dead right there in front of her. I finally stepped out her way to open the door for her while whispering to Junior that everything was okay.

She walked on to the car as I tried to open the doors to help get Junior in safely. She nearly slammed my fingers in the door when I tried to hold it open to talk to her once she was in the driver seat! She just stared at me as if I were a toxic soul making her life miserable. I could it feel it in her eyes she hated me in that moment. "Move Cedric. I don't want to run over you." She whispered as she started to weep with frustration as I tried to hold on to the door after she missed my fingers with it. "Please don't go like this. Not like this. Rachel I'm sorry. Let me kiss Junior at least." I begged her. She didn't say anything. I started to walk behind the car over to Junior's side then she sped off down the street! I was left in the middle street watching them ride off.

For about minute or so I stood there looking like a damn fool. I looked around wondering if Samantha had taken off too. I spotted her in her car on the other side of the street. She was just sitting there looking straight ahead out the window with a blank face. I slowly approached her car trying to see was she crying or if she would even speak to me. "Hey, I'm sorry to get you in the middle of my mess. You didn't have to go through any of this. I feel dumb as hell." I said when i reached her car. She had the windows down with her keys in her lap. She looked over at me as if she couldn't figure out why I was talking to her. She looked as if she lost all hope with me as she started to bang on the steering wheel. "You want to know my truths. Since you know, you're being all honest. I was ready to be with you again!

When I came to Chicago, I wanted to see if it could work. I wanted to spend time with you. I was hurt but it was partially my fault. Even after that, I told myself, maybe he needs time to get some things out of his system. Seeing you back home, seeing you with a child, I still wanted to be with you. I knew you had a genuine care for me, and time would bring things back around to us possibly trying again. I admit I did get back with my ex. It was hard but I was lonely. I had no one! He hit me Cedric! Can you believe that shit! I was selling myself short again to find myself being abused by someone I knew didn't deserve me! Getting an invite to be around you, I thought the time had come. I wasn't going to make any excuse for me nor was I going to let you slip away. I was going tell you I was ready to try. I was ready to be with someone I knew that would never put their hands on me. I trusted you enough, knowing that something like that would never happen. I didn't care about you having a baby. I wanted you. Now I honestly regret not leaving with you. Maybe we could have had it all. It's undeniable that we'll ever know. Thanks for letting me know where I stood with you." She said as the tears came rolling down her cheeks. She then turned on the car. No words could reach my tongue to make any difference from the way she felt. I stood there watching her cry.

About twenty, maybe thirty seconds went by then she slowly shifted the car gears then rolled off. I had to back off the same way Rachel pulled off on me avoiding getting my toes smashed or dragged down the street. I lifted my hands in the air then slammed them against my side with disappointment. I didn't want to go in the house. As I started to walk on to the porch Pastor Clayton came out glaring hard at me to make sure it was me due to the porch light being off since it was pitch black outside. Rain clouds decided to join us. A storm was approaching as Pastor Clayton called out to me as he closed the door behind him. I met him once I got up the steps. He stepped over on the side of me throwing his arm across my shoulder.

We walked over to one side of the porch away from the windows in the corner. He didn't say anything to me directly as he began to pray. We both stood there in the shadows of the porch. He went in deep on the levels of guidance and forgiveness I needed to move forward with my life. He prayed that I wouldn't follow the flesh. He prayed that from that day, that I would be even more patient with making decisions than I've ever been before. He prayed for me being a better father and fearless. The more he prayed the tighter he gripped my shoulder. I was at the edge of shaking loose from underneath his arm because I wasn't sure if he understood how much pressure he was applying to my shoulder! I knew that would have been disrespectful not only to him but God too. He finished up with a moment of silence to offer me an opportunity to say some words myself. After about a minute of nothing from me, he concluded the prayer with asking for peace and protection for Junior, Mrs. Anthony and Rachel. Once we both said Amen, he shook my hand then headed to his car. Again, he didn't say anything to me. He went straight to his car then pulled off slowly down the street.

The rain came pouring down. Thunder sounds were closer as a gust of wind blew on to the porch to give me a chill to force me in the house! I was greeted by Tammie once I was in the house as she was walking in the living room. "I've done my best to let you breathe little brother. You really showing your whole ass! I wouldn't have guessed you've been living this crazy life with the way you're doing these girls. You know better than to do some shit like that! Come on now Cedric! Seriously… You thought that was cool or you really lost your damn mind? Please explain to me how something like that made any sense to you!" Tammie yelled as she walked closer to me! Her voice was loud enough to bring Rico and Mrs. Anthony in the room to see if things were going to get physical! Mrs. Anthony ran in looking at Tammie and me as if we were about to go at it. Tammie didn't get but within two to three feet of me as she stopped once she heard the footsteps enter the room. She didn't want to hear me out or cared to understand my madness. I stood there quietly as Rico said his goodbyes to Tammie and Mrs. Anthony then walked out the house. Mrs. Anthony offered him an umbrella as she caught him before he closed the door. He said he rather take his chances with the storm than to stay in the house around me. I had taken enough verbal bashing that I headed upstairs but was held up by Mrs. Anthony's voice. "Cedric Mason! I'm embarrassed as well as disappointed in your actions to allow the things that took place here tonight. Why Cedric? Why do such a thing?" She said to me as Tammie babbled to herself with irritation. I just looked at them both for a few seconds then continued to my room. "Really Cedric? She is talking to you! Don't do that!" Tammie yelled at me as I didn't break my stride up the stairs! "It's okay baby. Let him go. I've prayed about it and I'm letting God deal with Cedric from now on." Mrs. Anthony replied to Tammie. I went in my room then shut the door. I put my phone on silence then plugged it up to its charger. I kicked my shoes off then took off my shirt. I lifted the window up just enough to let the smell of the fresh rain come in. I felt I was going to suffocate in that room if I didn't allow some extra air in. I laid down and was out. I didn't give myself anytime to reflect or contemplate my next move. Resting was the only thing I felt I needed.

Chapter 12

Try to Make Things Right

Two whole days went by. Two days were too many without hearing from Rachel as well as checking on Junior. I wasn't talking to anyone. I guess it was the other way around. No one was speaking to me. I was like a ghost moving in and out the house. Mrs. Anthony was only speaking because of her conscience I assumed. She only greeted me in the mornings and maybe before bed. I didn't mind being alienated by them. I was able sleep great, as long as I wanted to. I was able to move about my day without being questioned by anyone. Tammie gave me looks that looked so mean, you would have thought I stole something from her. As much as she wanted to, she kept her opinion to herself. I stayed away from everyone as well as I could until I saw Rachel walking with Rico!

I was heading to the store which was a few blocks past the one I used to work at avoiding any run ins with Samantha. The sight of seeing them together casually strolling down the sidewalk, talking and laughing set me on fire! Before I knew it, I was running over to them at full speed! I was nearly hit by a car crossing the street to reach them! The car's horn alerted their attention to my fast approach towards them. I slowed down because I was confused about where Junior was! I was within a couple of feet of them before Rico started yelling at me! "Whoa Whoa! Cedric! What's going on? Please don't trip!" He tried to stand in front of Rachel as if I was going to do something violently to her. Like he was trying to protect her from me. "I honestly don't give a shit about what y'all doing, what y'all talking about or why you two of all people are together walking around like this. I will say this! My concern right now is… Where is my damn son?" I said while zooming in on Rachel as I was eager to hear her response. She fixed her face as if she wanted to bash me for being concerned about Junior as if I haven't been a good dad so far. It was all in her nonverbals that had my blood boiling. She was very nonchalant about responding to me. I had to restrain myself from calling her unforgivable names because I was beginning to get angrier by the second. She knew she was getting to me because I couldn't be still long enough for her to look me up and down like I didn't deserve a reply. "Why does it matter? He's fine. He's in good care." She said as she tried to walk off before any other words could be exchanged. Rico was close enough to tag along right behind her. I was pissed because everything she told me about her dad started to resurface when she finally mumbled that he was at home with her mother and father! I think I lost it! I don't remember if I blacked out or I was being controlled by some evil spirit!

All I remember from that point was, I started running as fast as I had ever run, to Rachel's house! Rachel and Rico must had waited a few minutes before they came after me or I was just that much faster during the spell I was taken by. I don't know why so many images of her dad touching on Junior in places he shouldn't popped up in my head! Doing similar things to him Rachel confessed to me about what he did to her. At no point did I want to turn back to comfort Rachel about her dumb decision to leave Junior around her dad. I was damn near in tears as I arrived at Rachel's house! Again, I don't remember it all but recall banging on their door so hard I bruised the sides of my hand! I then had my head glued to the door listening for footsteps to come open it. My heart was pounding as well as the images I had of what I was about to do to Rachel's dad.

The door opened slowly with Rachel's dad holding Junior in his arm! "Put my baby down now!" I demanded as I walked in forcing him back into the house. "Say what? What's going on son?" He replied. "You heard me! You are fucking filthy pedophile! Rachel told me everything! I don't trust you! Give me my baby before I drop your ass!" I screamed at him! I didn't see Rachel's mom until she spoke. "What? Wait a minute! Cedric, honey. What are you saying?" Mrs. Gloria said as she stood up from the couch that was to the left of the front door. I was caught off guard for a second when I heard her voice. The guilt started to take over Darryl as I could see it in his eyes.

He gave Junior to Mrs. Gloria then stood there shaking his head. "I'm sorry for whatever happens after this! You know it's the damn truth and I hope you suffer as much as she has!" I said to him as I balled my fists in case, he wanted to shut me up. "What is he talking about? I'm so confused. There must be a mistake. Oh Lord! He loves Rachel! He wouldn't harm a string on her head." Mrs. Gloria said as she started to step in between us while rocking Junior to keep him calm. "I... I don't know what you're saying... I don't remember... I..." He mumbled to himself as he started to sway back and forward wiping the pouring sweat from his face. Mrs. Gloria started to fear for the worse as she had to sit back down. "Wait what? You don't remember what? Did you do something to Rachel?" She cried out to him! "Yes, he did! He molested her for years!" I yelled at him! "Baby, It's not true. I don't know what he's talking about." He pleaded with her as he tried to move closer to towards her. I blocked him from getting too close. "Get away from my child! You are a monster! How could you do an innocent little girl like that? How could you take advantage of her! I hope you rot in hell!" I said to him. Mrs. Gloria had tears forming in her eyes as she could see the guilt building up all over him. He stood there looking around at me then back to his wife as she began to cry.

"I don't remember. I'm sorry..." He whispered for about a minute to himself until he started to frown up in pain! It's like a light went off in his eyes! He suddenly leaned against the wall hitting his back on it hard! He immediately reached for his chest! I changed my entire mood! He was in total agony as he began to slowly drop to the floor as his body slid down the wall! "What's wrong! Are you okay?" I asked as I rushed over to him! "Oh my God! What's wrong Darryl?" Mrs. Gloria asked as she stood up quickly watching him hitting the ground uncontrollably! He was short of breath as his eyes searched for help! He laid on the ground as we both kept calling out to him, asking him what was wrong, but it was soon nothing but silence! "Call 911, please!" She shouted! She laid Junior down on the couch then she crawled over to him. He was lying on the floor motionless! I immediately pulled out my phone then called 911! I walked over to the couch and set on the edge to make sure Junior didn't roll off it. I had to confirm the address and what the emergency was between the operator and Mrs. Gloria.

Seconds turned to minutes as there were still no signs of breathing or movement coming from him! She tugged on him a few times with no reaction from him. She sat there beside him as the cold reality started to sit in. He was gone! The door slowly opened as Rachel walked in with Rico right behind her. Rachel looked around in total shock and clueless to what happened. "Mom! What's wrong? What happened to Darry? Cedric! What did you do?" Rachel yelled as she hurried over to her mom then looked over to me! Rico didn't know what to say or do as he was locked in on Darryl's stiff body lying there. Sirens were coming as the sound became louder by the second! It didn't hit me on what had just happened until the paramedics came rushing in then cleared us out the house. Rachel and Mrs. Gloria remained in. I had Junior as Rico and I stood on the porch listening in on what was going on. Sounds of counting between the two guys as they performed CPR was heard loud and clear. For about five minutes they were scrambled trying everything to bring Darryl back!

Then there was a long pause of quietness followed by questions of what Darryl was doing before he started to grab on his chest, and if he had any medical conditions. Then finally one of the guys said, "I believe he just had a massive heart attack. He's been out too long. I'm sorry there's nothing else we can do." A loud scream came ringing out the door loud enough that the neighbors on the next two blocks could hear! It was Mrs. Gloria's voice. "Noooo! Please! Noooo!" She cried out at the top of her lungs! Moments later Rachel came out the house holding on to her mother. Neighbors were standing around looking on as she fell to her knees on the porch. I went on down the steps as I didn't want Junior to see or get too riled up from the emotions of his granny. Rico and Rachel tried to help her up, but she didn't want to get up. Rachel wasn't too pleased with the sight of me nor was she sad about what she witnessed. She had a chilling look on her face. As if she was pleased that his time had come. She didn't leave her mother's side as a couple of cop cars pulled up. Finally, Mrs. Gloria was able to stand to her feet to be escorted to a chair that was on the porch. The paramedic guys and then the cops asked her more questions. I was just focused on Junior. The hate and frustration I had was starting to fade away the more I was looking around at everything and everybody. I wrestled with the fact that Darryl had just died right there in front of me. I blamed it on the guilt and not my threats that caused the heart attack.

Mrs. Gloria couldn't look at me nor in my direction. I needed to get out of there. I was able to pull Rachel to the side to let her know I was taking Junior with me. I believe she only agreed because of the circumstances and she needed to be there with her mom. Rico stayed behind with them. "You may want to use his stroller. He gets heavy, especially if you're walking with him that far. Just a smart thing to do you know. Since you don't think things through." Rachel said then tried to go back in the house before she was stopped. After explaining to the officers what she needed, one of them walked with her. She came back out with his stroller. I strapped Junior in then told Rachel thanks as I walked away. No one else asked me anything. No questions about if I did or seen anything. It's like I was never there. I expected to deal with some sort of consequences when the truth hit the fan, but it never did.

I made it home with Junior with Mrs. Anthony and Tammie wondering what was going on. All I said was Rachel asked me to get him because something bad had happened to her dad. I mentioned that he may have had a stroke or a heart attack or something. Before Mrs. Anthony ran out the house, I told her that everything was under control and the best thing for us to do was to stay put until we got an update from Rachel. They both were concerned but Junior started to get cranky as they turned their attention to him. For hours they played with him while I sat by the window upstairs in my room. I zoomed in on every passing car and anyone that was walking by. I was nervous with the feeling of uncertainty on my mind. The why and how and the for what questions came flowing in about my relationship with Rachel. If there should be a friendship with Rico. Tammie return hasn't been the most pleasant and my relationships with Mrs. Anthony was on the edge. I was daydreaming about how I could sneak out the house, find Charlene and our baby to try my luck with that. Junior was going to be alright with them, but my little girl needed her father. It seemed right until Tammie came running up the stairs screaming my name! "Cedric! Come listen to this. You have to hear it!" She yelled at the top of the stairs before running back down! It scared me for a second as if she were referring to the news or if someone was on the phone. I wasn't sure as I crept down the stairs trying to catch a clue before getting all the way down there. I went on into the kitchen where Mrs. Anthony and Tammie had the biggest smiles on their faces. As soon as Junior saw me, with his little cute voice, he said," Da da! Da da! Da da!" I didn't know how to respond because I've never heard him say anything other than giggles or cries. It nearly brought tears to my eyes because when he saw me, he was excited and was reaching for me while saying it! My dad's voice started to echo in my head, "If a man doesn't take care of his family then he can't be rich. There's no true happiness than being there for your kids. The joy a man gets when his kids smile at him, love him and appreciates his hard work and dedication he has for them. Don't ever be a coward and walk out on your kids. They are a blessing to the world and a blessing to you!" I walked to him then lifted him in the air as he continued saying it! I was there forever in his life. That poured the cement for me to be stuck with him for the rest of my life. That feeling he gave me was so special. It cleared up more of the doubt that was clingy on to me.

I looked to the sky thinking about my parents. Wondering about how they would respond to me if they knew how I was acting. I was embarrassed. I immediately turned to Mrs. Anthony then said, "I love you for everything. I apologize for how I've been lately. I've said it many times, but I'm for real this time! I must take things more seriously. Please keep praying for me and my mind. I need it! More than ever right now. Please don't ever stop praying for me." Before she responded, I turned to Tammie then said, "Thank you for being a better big sister. I can't imagine going on without you in my life. We must move forward from our past and I know I have to do better. We both been through it. I promise to be a better little brother. Continue to check me. Call me out on my wrong. I need it. Thank you." I embraced Junior vowing to love him unconditionally as our parents had done so for Tammie and I. Mrs. Anthony and Tammie both just smiled and hugged me. They nodded their heads with high hopes that what was happening would last. "Cedric, you can be the man, the father you truly need to be. Stop fighting it! We can't make you do it. I've been praying for you to see how blessed you are. Be brave enough to do the right things. We all want what's best for you. I've said it before, and I'll keep saying. You're better than that other stuff. Let's get it together." Mrs. Anthony whispered to me. Tammie added, "Come on now. You know we know better. Mom and dad wouldn't have accepted any of the things we've done! Let's focus on making them proud of us. Mrs. Anthony as well!" They put a smile on my face. They were being patient with me. I needed that commitment they had to me. We all sat around the kitchen table. We had food and played with Junior until he was played out.

After laying him down we all talked in the living room for another hour or two. The sun had set then finally a knock on the door. That awkward moment when you open the door and it's the person you didn't ever want to see again standing there. "The man I wanted to see! Are we becoming best friends or something? I'm starting to see a pattern here. Can you help me out?" Officer Jackson said with a grin on his face. I didn't care to let him in. I stepped out on to the porch. "It's just Officer Jackson. Nothing's wrong, I'll be on the porch for a second." I leaned in the door and said to Tammie and Mrs. Anthony without seeming anxious or curious about his unexpected visit. "No invite in I see. Oh okay. I see where this is going. Trust... I thought that's what we were working on Mr. Mason. I thought that maybe... If something happened and you were there, just maybe you would call me. Give me a heads up. It's funny finding out about someone dying and you were right there? Got a second to include me on the details now or did I catch you at a bad time?" He said as we both walked over to one side of the porch. "Come on man. It's not like that. Everything happened so fast. I had to get out of there. I was talking to him then suddenly the guy fell to the floor! I didn't do anything wrong. I promise!" I confessed to him. Of course, the blinds were moving behind us as I could see out the corner of my eye. He shook his head as he walked over to the steps then back over to me as if he were moving in a circle. "It's strange that no one else is saying you where there besides one officer. It's not in any reports or anything. He only said something because I asked. Said, it was another guy there with a baby that walked off. Said you were the baseball kid that won the state for us a year or so back. I knew exactly who he was referring to. I guess someone's been doing some praying for you. You're always around the trouble but never in it? You're one lucky son of a bitch I tell ya! Sorry... I just wanted to hear it from your own mouth. Try not to say any of this to anyone else." He said. He hesitated for a second as if he wanted to add more but he waited for me to reply. "The more I try to run from shit the more it finds its way to me. I'm laying low I promise! I don't want to be involved in anything other than taking care of my responsibilities. My life has been a nightmare for too long. I need some peace! This is not what I had in mind when I wanted to be an adult and out of high school! Can I have a do over please." I said jokingly to ease some of the tension between us. He shook his head then said, "You and me both. If it was that easy, man how life would be for us. Sounds good. Then again, we wouldn't learn anything. We'll just keep making the same dumb choices and end up right where we are. Honestly, Cedric, I really hope I don't have to see you again. Okay..." I understood the message he wanted me to get. "Yes sir." I replied. He slowly walked to his car then drove off.

Within seconds of him pulling off, Tammie came out on to the porch. "Hey... Everything okay. Looked like y'all were having a serious conversation. Y'all did well with keeping your tone down. Which has us even more curious about exactly what were y'all secretly talking about." She said. She knew right away the answer I was giving her was watered down. "He wanted to be the first to tell me that Rachel's dad didn't make it. He knew I needed to hear it before everyone else did." I replied. She gave me a mysterious look. "Wow... I'm so sorry to hear that. But I thought that's what you told us already? Or maybe I heard you wrong. Just seems weird for him to personally deliver that kind of information when you're not part of their family. I mean, you're just her baby's daddy." She said then walked back in the house. She left the door open for me to follow her inside. I closed the door as she continued to the kitchen. Junior was still sleep so I sat down on the couch. I looked at my phone to make sure it wasn't on vibrate or if I missed a call. Still no word from Rachel or Rico.

Mrs. Anthony came in the living room as if she wanted confirmation to whatever Tammie had said to her from the chatting I heard in the kitchen. "Rachel's dad is dead? Oh, my goodness! You sure you don't think we need to head over there? That's heartbreaking to hear that." She said as she stood in front of me blocking the TV. "I honestly don't know what to do. Rachel and I aren't on the best of terms and are barely speaking to one another. I only have Junior with me because I went to confront... I mean... I don't know what to do. I hate that happened to him." I said. She took a step closer to me then leaned in. "You confronted who Cedric? What are you not telling us? Please... Tell us what happened? Don't you care more about how she's feeling than whatever happened between you two before this. Her dad's passing is more serious than anything right now. I need you to go and check on her." She replied. Tammie walked back in while Mrs. Anthony was talking to me. She didn't say anything as she looked worried about the way things were being handled on my end about hearing the news on Rachel's dad. It took so much concentration to not blurt out how the sick bastard deserved to be dead! No one is going to miss him. I wanted to so bad, but it was only going to draw up more questions from them.

I got up then grabbed a jacket out the closet. I didn't know if they were at Rachel's house or at the hospital. I headed to Rachel's house not wanting to call first because I figured she would just tell me not to worry or come where they were. I was getting closer to Rachel house about a block away when my phone started to ring. It was Samantha. I was far enough to answer to talk for a second but too close to have a long conversation with her. It rang about six times before I answer it. "Hello... Samantha. What's going on? You good?" I said. The usual pause and heavy breathing when I knew she wasn't sure if what she was doing was best. "Am I doing something wrong?" She asked. "You? Never... I'm Mr. Wrong himself. Like we've talked about before. Timing is everything and that's the case here. I mean even at this moment. I'm headed to Rachel's house because her father just died. I don't think she cares about my presences, but I guess it's the thought that counts. I'm sorry if I can't talk as long as you may have intended." I answered. "Oh wow! I'm so sorry to hear that. I don't know why I called. I'm all over the place and I can't seem to shake how things are between us. Maybe I'll call later or if you're ever free enough, you'll call and help me settle my mind about it all." She replied then hung up. I was in front of the house appreciating her politeness of not giving a second or opportunity to give her my thoughts. It was best since the door opened as I was putting my phone back in my pocket. Rico stepped out followed by Rachel. I was amazed by his persistence. I exhaled the selfishness I wanted to speak on about his volunteered time he was comfortable with giving Rachel. I coughed loud enough to be noticed as they were coming down the steps, not paying attention to anything with their heads down. "Oh shit! Cedric! Man... You scared the hell out me! Like a damn black ninja out here!" Rico said after nearly stumbling down the last few steps. "My bad, wasn't trying to be creepy or anything. I came back over to check on you Rachel. Haven't heard anything from her.

How are you? Your mom? I'm sure I'm the last person anyone wants to see." I replied as I stepped up to make sure they could see me. "Is that right? You should've stayed. I guess coming back helps. Funny thing was…" Rico said before Rachel cut in. "You have altered my life in so many ways, it's not even funny. I don't want to be a bitch right now because I don't have the energy. You revealed things to my mom that I am finding it hard to see a common ground we can both stand on together. I will give you time with your son, as much as you want. But don't call me or come by here unless I ask you to. I need time away from you and your negative energy you carry." Rachel said as she was having a hard time looking at me.

There were no lies told. She was speaking from a hurt place that I drove her to. I didn't need to say much more after that. She turned then ran back in the house. I think Rico thought it was his que to run behind, but his access was denied. I win for me I thought. He looked just as desperate as I did when his knocks went unanswered. He turned back around then came down the steps. "You're like a superhero of fucking up. I mean I can't lie, Rachel is a sweet, innocent and straight up chick. You know that! You been too damn lucky with your choice of ladies. I haven't been Romeo myself, but the amount of shit you've displayed, I know my stats are looking nice compared to yours." Rico said as he walked past me. I didn't find any of that amusing. "What kind of shit you're on? My patience is starting to run really thin with you! You think this is the best time to swoop in and save her. Since you struck out with Charlene. You think, how Charlene was done, you'll just try your luck with Rachel. Trying to piss me off or something? This your way of getting even. Speak on it. Tell it like it is. Man, the fuck up to it since you have plenty to say!" I said as I caught up with him walking down the street. He didn't say a word, he ran off across the street as if he was running from an attacker or a kidnapper!

I wanted to chase him, yet nothing made sense for me to do it. I knew it wasn't going to end good for neither of us.

I mumbled to myself as I made a turn on my street heading to my house. Careless thinking had me walking in a huge circle street to street as I avoided going home. I was careful because it was late. I didn't want to look lost nor vulnerable. I walked for about an hour and a half until my legs felt drained and the shirt, I had on was sticking to my back drenched. I had run out of real estate with nothing but unwanted trouble surely waiting on me if I stayed out any longer. I had no choice but to go on home. It was well after ten when I made it in the house. Most of the lights were off except the porch light. I walked in to see the living room TV still on with Tammie wrapped up in a blanket sleeping. I glanced at Juniors baby crib to find him not there. Tammie didn't move a muscle when I closed the front door. I walked in the kitchen then down the hall to Mrs. Anthony's room to see that the lights were off in her room as well. I wasn't going to wake anyone as I assumed Junior was still there in Mrs. Anthony's room. She didn't call to tell me otherwise.

I went on upstairs to my room right after I took some chips and cookies up there with me as my stomach begged me to hush it up. How did I go from prayers and feeling great to being banned from communicating with the mother of my child to feeling hopeless? Snacking helped with the headache I had. I promised myself I wouldn't let another day go by without speaking with Charlene so that was my future until things got better between Rachel and me. Samantha wasn't going to hear from me anytime soon. I didn't want to be her crutch. Stop thinking with the wrong head, I kept telling myself as I laid in the bed. An hour went by. Then another one and another one. I was still up staring at the ceiling squeezing every thought and best-case scenario on reaching out to Charlene. Flashbacks of how beautiful and flawless she was. More flashbacks of her hair all over her head walking around town like she hadn't bathed in weeks. I remembered her innocent smile, I remembered how I felt when we first kissed, and I remember what it felt like when she looked me in the eyes down by the Riverwalk. No one had any answers for me about her sanity. No one could explain why she was so irate. Not even Rico would give me any solid details on why she was this uncontrollable maniac. I felt sympathy for her until I glanced at a picture of David and I on my dresser's mirror. I started to feel some sort of anger that made me want to get up right then and there in the wee hours of the night to go confront her about her madness. I imagined myself yelling at her, calling her bluff about the attention she was surely seeking with her circus side show. I had made my mind up to try the tough guy approach to see if she would be more responsive to that since she had given Rico the cold shoulder with his nice guy stance.

Chapter 13
The Disappearing Act

I was up before everyone when I quietly came down the stairs fully dressed heading out the door. Tammie was snoring with a whole face full of dried up slob. I laughed to myself as I thought about snapping a quick picture. I would have been able to black mail her for years with that sight. I slipped out the house undetected by anyone. I walked swiftly with a purpose. Took me about fifteen minutes to get to Charlene's house. I wasn't sure who was going to open the door as I knocked lightly. I was going to knock until someone came to the door as I saw some cars parked out front.

Didn't take but a few seconds before one of Charlene's sister answered the door. "Can I help you sir?" She said with an attitude that indicated she didn't want to be up answering the door that early in the morning. Being that it was a Saturday morning didn't make it any better. "Good morning to you too. Is Charlene home ma'am?" I replied. I said it with the same energy she gave. I looked at her as if I didn't want to be there, but I didn't have a choice. "And who are you? You do know it's like eight in the morning, right? What do you want with Charlene?" She replied as she leaned out the door looking around to see if I was alone. "I wanted to make sure I caught her before she got out. My name is Cedric." Her entire mood changed! She went from the sleepy mean chick to a violent fighter within seconds! She stepped closer to me then landed a punch to my forehead as I was trying to duck it! Bam! "I know damn well you didn't just pop up over here out the blue like everything is all sweet over here!" She screamed at me while trying to scratch me in the face! I restrained her arms by grabbing them both! She twisted and yanked from me until she was out of breath! "What the hell is your problem? You need to chill out! Damn! Please chill!" I yelled back then lowered my voice trying to ease the sudden hate she had with me! "No, fuck you! My sister is dead because of you! I hate you!" She screamed! She became weaker as she started to cry. "Where have you been! This shit is like a nightmare right now! Get the fuck away from here!" She yelled through her tears as her fatigued arms barely touched me. She tried hard to hurt me as she kept trying to swing her limped arms. She couldn't stand on her own as she leaned in on me. "What? I don't understand what you're saying. Please calm down. Where is your sister. Where's the baby?" I asked as she was trying to stand up straight pushing my arms away. I was trying to assist her with her balance. She continued to refuse any help from me.

Another woman finally appeared at the door! She was in shock to see me when she rushed in to catch the other girl from falling. "Liz! What are you doing? What's going on?" She asked as she looked at me up and down confused on who I was. "That's Cedric! Can you believe that! Like... Of all the people that showed up on our porch today. It's him! And then have the nerves to act all clueless about our damn sister! I can't believe this shit!" Liz shouted! "Wait... What? Are you serious? You're Cedric?" The other sister asked. "Tricia! Who else you think it is? Don't be dumb! Yes, that's him!" Liz said to Tricia. "This has to be some sort of game you're playing or you both are playing? Why did you show up now? Haven't you been back home for months now? You do know you have a child with our sister, right? Where is our sister?" Tricia asked me as she stepped out the house. She looked at me with anger as well as curiosity to understand how much I knew before she did or said anything else. "I promise y'all I don't know what's going on with y'all sister. Yes, I heard from several people that something overly concerning was going on with her. I also heard she had my baby. I've been going through more than I can explain. I'm here now so I'm trying to figure out a lot. I didn't come over here for any trouble or cause anymore complications. Now, you said she's dead?" I said to them both. "Well, we don't know for certain. She left us a detailed letter insinuating she may have been heading that way. We don't know if she went to kill herself, ran away or what? She stated some convincing things to have us to believe she didn't want to live anymore. You are at the center of this letter and why she doesn't care about living anymore." Tricia explained.

        "I believe everything she wrote so I know she is dead! I hate you!" Liz screamed at me before Tricia grabbed her as she tried to swing at me again! "Stop it! We don't know that! Stop saying that please! I'm just as upset and worried as you! We can't put that out there like that! We need to go to the police now!" Tricia said as she was holding both of Liz's arms standing in front of her. "Where is the baby. Did she take the baby with her?" I asked. "She is here. Thank God she didn't take her. Come in." Tricia said. She then pushed Liz in the house first as I followed them in. They both disappeared down a hallway as I was standing in the living room. Liz came back first with papers in her hands. I was bracing myself to defend her off again, but she then threw the papers at me! "You tell me what you think she did. Just know if my sister did kill herself, I'm going to kill you! I promise!" She yelled to me! I crotched down to pick up the papers. Shaking my head as I replied, "I promise I didn't know things were that messed up. I would have said something or came around sooner had I known. I'm sorry."

        I stood back up to see Tricia walking slowly with the baby wrapped up in a pink, white and yellow blanket. I folded the papers then placed them in my pocket as she was close enough to hand me the baby. My first official encounter with my princess had me speechless. The most beautiful, innocent and precious person I had ever seen in my life! She had light brown eyes that glowed as she looked up at me. I had never seen a baby with that much hair on their head. Her hair was black and shiny. I thought I knew how to hold her, but she was so adorable I was scared to touch her. She was quiet yet observing everything that was happening around her. She was just as big as Junior was. I finally had her in my arms, and I was in aww. I was mesmerized by her presence. Tricia had tears in her eyes after handing her to me then stepping back. Liz didn't care for my special moment with my daughter. "If only you were here like two days ago. Maybe Charlene would still be here to see this. I'm not going to pretend like I'm okay just because you're here now. I know you could have done something sooner." Liz said before she walked away back down the hallway. Neither Tricia nor I said anything to her.

I held my little lady with a heavy heart. I knew the feeling Rachel had when she saw me holding Junior. Liz was right. I know things may have been different if Charlene was there to witness it all. "I want to read this letter if you don't mind?" I said to Tricia as I gave her back the baby. I wanted to know what had them upset and worried. "You probably want to sit down and read that. I'll give you some time to yourself. I'll be back in a few." Tricia replied. She too went back down the hallway. That only made me more cautious about what I was about to find out. I was thinking about telling them to just give me the summary of the letter instead of having to look at it myself. I didn't want to deal with Liz's response. I pulled the papers out then started to read them carefully.

The letter said: "This is not the way I wanted things to end. Not for me... It brings me to tears as I write this. I know no one is perfect yet I tried my best to be that way for so many years. I wish I had control of the things I've done in the past. I wish I could have stopped myself from doing so many things. There are decisions I made that I can't live with anymore. I caused an innocent person to lose their life based on my selfishness. I lost my mom and felt like it was the end of the world! That caused me to seek attention in ways I will forever regret. I took my frustration out on people that didn't deserve it. After it all happened, I was in a very dark place. I wanted to feel alive again because I thought I was dead inside. Cedric was someone I thought I could trust since he fell victim to my lies. I wanted to make things better between us. I thought that if I could give myself to him, he would forgive me. I thought he genuinely liked me. I realized that too late. He got what he wanted then turned on me. I guess I deserved it. I thought the pain I caused could be forgiven. He didn't want me, especially after I told him I was pregnant. I was crying out to him, but he didn't care. I played tough because I had to for too long. He left to go live his life. He didn't want anything to do with me. That meant he didn't want to have anything to do with our child. How am I supposed to raise a baby when I don't know what I'm doing with myself? How am I supposed to raise a baby alone? I promised myself that I wouldn't bring a child in this world if I didn't have my shit together. I lied to myself and I can't do that to her. I thought I had everything under control. I thought it could never happen to me. It did! I don't think Cedric will ever admit that this is his child now! I don't think he'll ever come to save me. I know he doesn't care about me or his child since I found out about his other baby! I feel like the biggest fool! I want to just die! I can't believe that he chose my best friend over me. He had a baby with someone I considered my best friend for years! He had sex with someone that was that close to me! I knew it was out of spite. I can't go on with this truth! I don't deserve to be a mother to such an innocent little princess! She will never be able to live the way she deserves if I'm here. She needs to have a chance to be great. I can't give her that. I can't shake this feeling of emptiness. I can't let go of this dark hole I'm trapped in. I can't pull myself out. I don't think I want to. I'm sorry Tricia and Liz for not turning to you all for help. You all have tried. You have been beyond patient with me and your niece. I would never harm a bone in her body so I'm leaving her with you. I love you two with all my heart and I know mom would never be okay with this. I'm glad she is no longer here with us to stop me. She would have been an amazing grandmother. I wish Cedric would show up now to stop me. Tell him I will apologize to David myself. He'll understand. If only he was here. Cedric would be the only one to keep me from ending it all. Unfortunately, I KNOW that's not going to happen so goodbye forever. Love my princess hard. I wish I could have. Sorry. Love, Charlene."

As I finished reading it with sweat falling on to the paper, Tricia walked back in with the baby. "What's her name?" I asked as I wiped my face. "Her name is Joy." Tricia replied as she gave her back to me in exchange for the letter. I didn't take my eyes off her as I fought back the tears from falling on her. I held her so close to my chest. I didn't want to leave her ever. I was torn between the fact that Charlene would leave such a precious gift and why she didn't seek others for help. Tricia went to put the letter away. She told me she was going to call the police and it was up to me to stay or leave. I decided to hang around for the support. Liz didn't care what I did but Tricia was very appreciative of the gesture. I didn't want to go home nor did I want to leave my Joy.

The longer I was there the harder it was to keep my emotions in as we started to talk about how Carlene and I ended up with a child together. I got choked up a few times telling them the story on how and why David was killed by Rico. That's when Liz started to ease up on the tough sister role. They both cried after that. We were all trying to piece together

Charlene's actions and reasonings after that. How we ended up with that letter she wrote? None of us understood the dept of Charlene's process of thinking. One minute she was cool and normal around them then she was this torn and hopeless person that wouldn't listen to anyone about anything. We cleared our faces as the doorbell rang. It was two police officers. I was glad it wasn't Officer Jackson. I didn't have anything in me to give him. I nervously sat on the couch as the officers took about twenty minutes to take statements from Tricia and Liz. They teared up as they told their story of Charlene and the days that led up to the letter. The officers both stared at the letter for a few minutes. After they read it, they both asked who the Cedric guy was. Both sisters pointed at me as I sat there catching the sweat from falling on Joy. Everyone's attention was on me. I was asked about my relationship with Charlene as well as if we had any arguments or fights that may have triggered her. The cops somewhat grilled me about my statement as if I were leaving something out. I promised everyone in the house that I had nothing to do with her leaving the way she did. After reading the letter myself, it hurt to know that I could have done something to help.

They had all the information they needed to put out a missing person report. They started questioning us all about the baby. They said they weren't going to take the baby then because they wanted to give me a chance to go and take care of the responsibility of doing what was right. I promised them I would do whatever it took to make sure I gained full custody of my baby if Charlene didn't show back up. We didn't want to say it, but we were planning for the worst-case scenario. The sisters didn't give me any push back or had other plans for Joy. They encouraged the gesture and felt it was the best thing to do. The officers wanted us to reach out to any and everyone that Charlene could have come in contact with. People she might reach out to in order to hide or run away to.

All I could think about was heading to Rico's house as soon as I had the chance. I figured he knew something. The cops finally left and promised to keep us all up to date on the investigation to find Charlene. "I'm sorry for swinging on you earlier. I didn't know you like that, nor did I know y'all had such a hectic past. I'm not sure how you're dealing with it, but I hope things get better for us all." Liz said after coming back in the house after walking the cops out. "Yeah, I'm sorry you had to go through that. No one should have to lose a friend to something so selfish. I'm sorry we all have to deal with this now as well." Tricia added. I realized that we all were struggling with it from different perspectives but wanted the best outcome. I did feel better after hearing them apologize, although it wasn't in their control what happened between Charlene and me. "Thank y'all for that. Y'all didn't have to. I know this is difficult for you two. I wish Charlene changes her mind and come back. I know we can work this out." I replied. We all shook our heads agreeing with hope painted on our faces.

Another thirty minutes went by and I was sure someone was looking for me since I felt my phone vibrate several times during all the craziness. I asked the girls to give me some time to go home and figure some things out. I told them I would reach out to some people. I needed a few hours then I would return. I didn't mention anything about the baby because I knew it was going to be a matter of time before we needed to decide about me taking her to spend time with her. They were fine with that as they needed to make some calls themselves. I gave baby Joy a kiss on her cheeks then gave her to Tricia.

I left wondering how and when I was going to reveal the news of Charlene's disappearance to Mrs. Anthony and Tammie. I first needed to address it with Rico before the news spread and he denied knowing anything. It was after noon as I glanced at my phone checking the time. I disregarded the missed call notifications. I wasn't in a huge rush as I took my time looking down every alley and the side of every house as I made my way to Rico's house. I had one lady eyeing me funny as if she wanted to ask me what I was looking for as I stared down the side of her house. I tried my best not to look too suspicious. I continued my hunt as I was just a block from Rico's place. I saw him walking towards his house coming the opposite direction. He didn't notice me until I was about twenty yards from his house. He looked spooked! That kept that gut feeling I had about his knowledge of Charlene front and center. He walked on slight past his house as I approached him to cut me off. "Hey man, what are you doing over here? Can I help you?" He whispered as he was within a couple of feet of me. "You know why I'm here. Come clean now so we don't have to make things worse. Please..." I replied. He looked confused as he looked around to see who was paying attention to us. There was no one else around. Just him and I. "Make what worse? You know you're that last person that has any legs to stand on, confronting someone?" He said as he stepped back a little. He knew he was walking on a thin line with his choice of words as the tension began to thicken between us. "Really man? You don't know why I'm over here? Remember, you're smarter than people think? I know it. Very clever. I just need you to be straight up. I know you know something." I said as I stepped closer to him looking him straight in the eyes. "Hey Cedric, whatever your ass think I know. I'm telling you right now, I don't have a clue what you're talking about. I would appreciate it if you just say whatever it is you trying to figure out. I promise I don't want this to turn out to be something more than it should." He replied as he took another step back. I immediate got as close to him as I could without touching. I did it so fast that it caused him to flinch a little! "I'm going to make it whatever the hell I want to make it if you keep acting dumb! Now where's Charlene! I know you know something! Her sisters are worried! We need to find her as soon as possible!" I yelled at him! His face glared up as he started looking around some more trying to understand what I was saying. "Wait what? Is Charlene missing? How do you know she's missing? What are you talking about?" He asked with a nervous look on his face. I was starting to think he was telling the truth. If he was lying, then he was playing the best innocent role of any movie actor I've ever seen. "Cedric! What are you saying man?" He added. "Yes! She is gone! No one knows where she's at. She wrote this letter saying she didn't want to be here anymore. We just talked to the cops about it and her sisters think she is in trouble." I finally replied. He immediate turned that lost look in his face into a hateful expression after he heard that. "Damn it! I can't believe she did it! Damn!" He said as he tried to walk past me. I immediately grabbed his arm! He snatched his arm away from then kept walking.

I wasn't going to let him get away that time. I walked closely behind him. He kept mumbling to himself as we walked swiftly down the sidewalk. "I knew your ass knew something! Why don't you tell me where she's at so we can go get her? Stop with the games. If you know something, just say it!" I kept saying to him as he was making his way towards Charlene's house from the turns he was taking. He ignored me as he continued to talk to himself as we approached her house. I walked up on the side of him before we made it to the steps. "What are you doing? I already told you what's going on! Just tell me where she's at!" I said as I tried to step in front of him, cutting him off from going up the steps. He didn't say a word as he pushed me down on the side of the steps! I couldn't believe it. I sat there for about two seconds then jumped back up!

Before he could reach the door, I pushed him hard into it! He slammed up against the door then rushed me! He tackled me to the ground then hit me on the top of my head as I avoided a direct hit in the face! I was able to twist out of the force he was putting on me as he tried to pin me down. I was able to get up on my feet first then laid a punch on his jaw just as he was looking up at me! The blow caused me to fall back down with him! He was trying to hit me in the side of my stomach as we wrestled on the ground! The loud commotion was heard from inside the house as the sisters came out screaming at us! "What are y'all doing? Cedric! Rico! Stop it!" Tricia yelled! Liz came grabbing and tugging to pull us apart. We both untangled ourselves as neither one of us wanted to accidentally hit Liz.

"You made her do this! You selfish fool! You did this!" Rico yelled at me! "I didn't do shit! I came to fix things!" I replied. "Too late! I tried to stop her! I talked to her so many times about not doing something crazy! She wanted you! For what reason, I still and never will understand!" He said as he dusted himself off then walked back down the steps. "I knew you knew something! Guess it's too late for you warning anyone! You knew she was going to do something so you're just as guilty as me! I would have said something to someone!" I yelled back at him! He suddenly rushed me again! I punched him in the neck as he was in arm's reach before he grabbed me again! The girls then stood between us shouting at us again! We both were out of breath, huffing and wheezing for air.

"Charlene is responsible for her own damn actions! No one is to blame! She made the choice she made because she wanted to. We are not going to do this like that! None of us... Are to be blamed for what she decided to do on her own free will. I hate it but... Please stop this now!" Tricia said to us both. Rico and I looked at each other with a mean mug on our faces until it faded away from realizing the truth in Tricia's words. We both dusted ourselves off and walked down the steps. "I'm sorry we came over here like this. I needed answers and I was sure he was hiding something. Tricia… Yeah… You're right." I said to her. She nodded her head appreciating the responds from me. "I didn't know she was going to go missing or anything. I just thought she was going to move out of town with the baby without telling Cedric. I didn't think she would leave Joy like that. Yet alone harm herself. I'm sorry for not saying anything about our talks to any of y'all. I agree, Tricia. Charlene know what she's doing and how it's going to affect others. I'm sorry for coming over here causing more trouble." Rico said then walked off. I whispered that I was sorry again to the sisters before following up behind Rico.

    "Hey man! Hold up!" I shouted at him as I had to jog a bit to catch him. "I apologize man for real. I just wanted to make things right. I will do whatever to get Charlene to come back. I need your help. Please man." I said to him as we continued to walk down the street. "I hear you. I'm pissed and I let it get the best of me. I have been working on that ever since you know. I don't want to cause any more pain or suffering for anyone. I need to go check one spot I know she could have gone. I need to get my mom's car. You can come if you want to?" He replied. "I appreciate that. Let's go!" I said then we both sped up the pace heading back to his house. He went in the house quick to grab the keys. I waited as my phone notification signals continued to light up and vibrate. I knew Mrs. Anthony was getting worried but I had to make this one stop with Rico before I did or said anything to her. He came back out with two bottled waters then we jumped in the car. We drank the waters as if we had cotton mouth.

    He drove down towards the old skating ring where Melvin was shot. He turned on the street after it then headed down a gravel road where the river started that flowed all the way downtown along the Riverwalk. There was an old factory that stood along the brim of the river opening. It was empty garbage cans, trash and a few dead animals that gave off an awful smell that came rushing into our noses from the windows being down in the car. "Who the hell comes out here? I know this is a joke. You trying to kill me? Don't try no slick shit with me!" I said looking around then planted my eyes on the side of Rico's face. He kept glancing between the road and me, confused. "Man what? Never! I'm not dumb. Nah you're not worth it! Calm down. Charlene and I would come back through here and climb up in this old tower back here. See it's right there!" He replied then pointed off to the right. I looked over at this tall abandoned tower that stood nearly forty feet high. He pulled over then we got out.

The scent wasn't as bad once we started walking and made it to the tower. There was an old rusty metal ladder that laid beside a few worn tables. Turned over wooden chairs with broken legs and arms on them were scattered everywhere. "That ladder may look beaten but its strong. I have to go up in that tower. We had many talks up there. Hold it for me please." Rico said as he tussled with it then placed it on the bottom of the tower. The tower had its own ladder attached to it that wasn't close enough for anyone to reach without standing or climbing on something else to get to it. I helped him with holding the ladder steady as he began to slowly climb up it to reach the other part of the tower's ladder. He went up all the way then vanished in an opened door of the tower.

I stood there looking up for a minute until some stray dogs came along! It was a pack of about four or five dogs! They looked hungry and on the prowl for something. They sniffed around the grounds until one of them spotted me! I was as quiet as I could have been with Rico's name on the tip of my lips ready to call for him. I hesitated to think they would just continue away me as I had nothing to give them. These were some big dogs with huge heads! All their tongues were hanging out their mouths with slob dripping from them. That was enough to alarm me as I started to reline the ladder in case, I had to go up it. The car was in the opposite direction with them standing in my path. As they all started to raise their heads gazing right at me. It was a stare down as if they were waiting to see what I was going to do. My heart was pounding as one of the dogs slowly trotted towards me. "Cedric! She's not here but she left me a letter too!" Rico shouted as he reappeared with a piece of paper in his hand! His voice stalled the dogs long enough as I grabbed on to the ladder! They all started barking loud and viscously at us! Suddenly they all ran towards me as I slipped a few times hurrying up the ladder! I nearly had to jump to the other part of the tower before one of the dogs knocked the old metal ladder down from against the bottom of the tower! I dangled a bit until I lifted myself on up the tower. The dogs barked while surrounding the tower for about five minutes off and on.

That gave us the chance to read over the letter that was addressed to Rico from Charlene. I stepped in the tower to see that it had a blanket, some used food containers and empty soda cans that weren't as old as the dusty boxes and other miscellaneous trash left up there. Rico paced around the tower nervously as if he was crushed about what he read. His hands were shivering as he held on to it tight. "What does it say?" I asked. He didn't say anything. "Give me the letter!" I demanded as he was not budging with sharing the details! He finally handed me the paper. He shook his head then rubbed it a few times as if he was thinking of other places or the reasons Charlene was nowhere to be found. The letter wasn't as long as the one she left for her sisters. Although its words were just as sad with shocking new information!

The letter said: "Rico, if you are reading this then I'm sure you came here hoping to find me. I'm sorry. You tried your best to help! I know I promised you I wouldn't do anything stupid. Unfortunately, this is the end. I can't go on pretending that I'm happy. I know you said if you can change, so can I. You have changed. I'm so proud of you. You were a mess growing up! I can't change what I did and that's why I'm done with this life. Maybe in the next one, things will be better for me, you, Joy, and my family. You asked me if I was sure Cedric was Joy's father. The truth is… She could be yours or his. I had no way of determining who. You know what happened. I know this doesn't help. I didn't want to worry you. I hope you all find out that she's yours! Cedric won't love her like you will! She will need you! Take care… Goodbye now and forever, Charlene."

My heart dropped through the floor of the tower to the ground below! My head was spinning with denial that Charlene had sex with us both like that! It was karma whispering to me. My teeth pressed down hard on each other as I was stunned by what I read! Rico never mentioned there was any possibility Joy could have been his child! I looked around to see that he had mysteriously left out of the tower! I thought he took off on me, but I walked out to see him sitting on the edge of the platform with his feet dangling. The dogs were gone. I didn't know what to say. For a second, I thought he was about to jump and end it all for him. I almost balled the paper up then threw it at him. Being that high in the air on a shaking tower ledge wasn't the brightest idea to start a physical fight. I took a deep breath then sat a few feet beside him. I handed the letter back to him. We both scanned all over the place as traffic and people could be seen up to a mile away. I knew his little secret. I was patient with my reaction to see what he was going to say or ask. I pulled out my phone to see what I missed giving him more time. Mrs. Anthony called several times. She sent me a text message asking me to call as soon as possible. There was one unknow number that had called twice. No voicemails. To my surprise I saw Lauren's name come across the missed calls list as well.

Rachel also sent a text saying, Junior has been saying 'da da' for hours so I needed to come get him. I guess she had a change of heart.

"I didn't want to say anything because she swore that Joy was your child. I wouldn't have held that info back if I knew more. I hate this. Man… We did hook up. When I tried again, her whole attitude wasn't the same. After I was arrested and finally got out, she was sick. She was always sick. I stopped coming around her after she told me she didn't like me anymore. Many months later she had a baby! It was all about Cedric and her being this happily ever after couple one day. I knew she needed help, so I tried hard talking with her. I told you, I was seeing her as much as I could to ease the stress. I didn't know she was hiding that from us all!" Rico finally said. We all got played one way or another. I saw signs of relief thinking that I wasn't the only guy with a child to feed in that crazy endless debacle. I was starting to feel happy about the news that Rico could be the daddy. "I need to get home and spread the word. I hate this for real. I don't know what Charlene is doing right now, but it seems like she doesn't want to include any of us. I hope you're the father as well. Maybe she's right about some things. I'm sorry man." I replied. Rico finally looked over at me with tears in his eyes. "Yeah man. I didn't think it would all come crashing down like this. This is crazy. Why would she leave? Me a dad? I know she kept saying things and how she felt. But… No signs at all pointed to this! Damn… She may be gone for real." He replied as he stood up.

We both had to climb down to the very last inch of the ladder attached to the tower then had to leg go to a hard landing on the ground. The ladder was broken when Rico went down first and tried to sit it up for me. I was nervous about letting go with such a hard landing. Neither one of us twisted or broke anything as we both limped a little back to the car. Rico dropped me off at my house. The ride was quick as he sped down the street making hard turns to my house. I knew he was scared and frustrated because that's how I felt when I found out I would be a father. I told him I would keep him posted if I heard anything. He agreed to do the same. I gave him my number since we never exchanged any information like that before. He drove off once he saved my number in his phone.

I looked around just in case Charlene was sneaking nearby, spying on me or anything. I don't know why I had that feeling that she was nearer than we imagined. I entered the house quietly although it didn't matter. Mrs. Anthony and Tammie were sitting on the couch. They both jumped up and started yelling at me! "Where the hell you been? You don't answer any of our calls nor have any respect to let someone know you were leaving!" Tammie said. "Cedric, I've called you several times! What is going on? I don't like you ignoring my calls. Rachel called asking about you. Some coach from Texas called my number too. Where have you been?" Mrs. Anthony said. "I'm sorry. I was wrong. I can't explain everything now. Charlene, the girl that told all those lies. Well... She is missing." I replied. They both looked confused. "Okay... I'm sorry to hear that. But umm... What does that have to do with you Cedric?" Mrs. Anthony asked. Tammie eyes glared at me with fire. I needed them. I needed to be truthful. I didn't owe them anymore lies. I came clean. "Charlene had a baby. The problem is it may be mines. Or Rico's. We don't know. She wrote these letters saying that she couldn't live anymore. She didn't want to be a horrible mother. So... We don't know... if she... you know. Or if she just ran away for good?" I replied. "Are you serious Cedric? Please no... What happened? Why would she do anything to herself?" Mrs. Anthony immediately asked then placed her hand over her mouth fearing the worse. "You were having unprotected sex with everyone? What kind of games where you playing? Cedric this is not good! Not good at all. Two babies, seriously dude!" Tammie yelled as she faked at me wishing she could punch me! Her fists were bawled up ready to swing at me! "Tammie, no! Don't do that!" Mrs. Anthony said to her. Tammie shook her head slowly at me looking worried then walked away back to the couch breathing heavily with anger. "Cedric... What have you done? Did you all call the police. Where is her family? Where is the baby? Is the baby okay?" Mrs. Anthony started rolling in the questions with concern.

"Yes, we called the police. Her sisters have the baby and she is fine." I replied. "A baby girl? Wow! You better go out there and find a job right now because you're taking care of those babies!" Tammie yelled from the edge of the couch as she sat there listening to everything. "Yeah her name is Joy. She so pretty. I don't know for a fact if she's mines so chill out over there! Right now, we're letting everyone know that Charlene is missing. We need to find her! "I said then glanced over at Tammie. "I know that's the truth. Well if the police are involved that's a start. Maybe we wait to hear from them. In the meantime, you need to call that coach back. He sounded extremely excited to talk to you. He said he has an opportunity for you in Texas to get back on the field to play." Mrs. Anthony said. I scratched my head thinking about it. "You need to do something!" Tammie said then stood up. "Tammie... I'm just as upset as you. Please... He needs our help." Mrs. Anthony said to Tammie. "I'm sorry but Cedric knew what he was doing. He knew better." She replied then tried to walk in the kitchen. "Oh! So, you get a pass because what you did happened so long ago huh? I tried to keep my mouth shut but no! You knew better too! You left me remember! Maybe if you stayed you could've shown me how it was supposed to be done you know! Living flawless! Not making any mistakes! Oh, but you didn't! Because you made some major mistakes that had you running your ass back here! Get off my back! I'm trying to make things right! Yeah, I did some dumb stuff! Sorry I'm not perfect like you!" I yelled before I rushed upstairs to my room! Tammie was frozen in shame. She stood there looking as if I hit her with a brick in her face. Mrs. Anthony didn't know what to say or do. She tried hard to keep us from going to that painful past we all wanted to forget. I didn't care what Tammie felt. I slammed the door behind me once I made it to the room!

I could hear some chatting downstairs as I pressed my ear to the door for a second. I kicked my shoes off then sat at the window. I wanted to call Lauren back, but I wasn't in the right mood to say anything to her. I was sure she wanted to catch up. I didn't want to talk to any coaches about anything baseball. I wasn't in the best position to leave again. I couldn't abandon my child or children. I knew what it was going to mean to have to stay. Tammie was right about that. I needed to get a job or do something for money. The thought of talking to some of the local fools still hanging around the park for something to sell sounded easier than going to work for someone that wasn't going to pay me much. I didn't have any experience in anything. All I knew was baseball. With that out of the picture, things didn't look promising when it came to the different possibilities of employment around town. I was sure Samantha would give me a chance if I ever wanted to work at the store, but the pay wouldn't take care of a child and me. Rachel situation looked more hopeless than mines. Her dad worked but her mom was a stay at home mom. I couldn't imagine how much pressure they were about to have in their house. I was running out of options that brought me back to thinking I should run away too. If Charlene had the nerves to leave everything and everyone, so did I.

I looked at my phone again. I scrolled back through my call log to find that Texas coach's number to call back. I wanted to hear his offer. If this was going to be a tough hill to climb being at home, then I wanted to see if there was another chance to roll out. As I was pressing the button to return his call, a light knock on my door was heard. I instantly hung up the call and laid my phone on the dresser! "Come in..." I said. Tammie cracked the door opened then poked her head in. "Can we talk?" She asked. As much as I wanted to say no, I couldn't. I knew she meant well. I took it to an extremely low place with what I said. "We can..." I replied. She came in then sat on the bed. We both look at each other as if we were thinking the same thing. How did we get there? "I want what's best for you. That's all." She said. "I know. I didn't know what I wanted. Now that I'm facing the consequences of my actions, it's hard when everyone is beating me down even lower. I know where you're coming from. You're right. I knew better. And umm... I do apologize for what I said. That wasn't cool. That wasn't nice. I shouldn't have said any of that. I'm sorry." I replied. She shook her head at me with a slight grin on her face. "What?" I asked. "Boy I was about to knock your whole head off your shoulders! That shit hurt what you said but... You were right as well. I shouldn't have done what I did. After mom and dad, then grandpa... I shouldn't have left you. I'm back now... I'm here for you. Let's be open enough with each other so neither of us go down any roads alone when it comes to making tough decisions. Deal?" She said then stood up with a smile on her face. I took a second to think about it. There was hope with Tammie reassuring me that I wasn't alone. "Deal!" I replied then stood up.

"Well I do have one other thing to confess." She said. I could tell it wasn't good news by the way she changed her tone. Her smile was gone. "You sure you want to say it? You don't seem too excited about sharing. You don't have to." I replied as I stepped over to her. "No, I have to say this. It's more to the reason I lashed out at you." She said as her voice cracked. "Tammie it's okay. We're good. Don't worry about it." I replied as I touched her on the shoulder, staring at her. "No... You need to hear this. Cedric... I was pregnant. I was about three months in before I knew it. From the drugs I was using to a terrible fight with my ex, I had a miscarriage. I didn't know I was pregnant, yet alone knew I had lost the baby. I went to the hospital to get treated from the bruises I had after the fight. I was all alone when I found out. Alone in that hospital debating if I should tell the doctors the truth or just lie like I had been doing. I was completely broken. One, because I lost my child. Two, because of the amount of damage to my body the drugs and injuries had on me. I was told I could never have children. I screwed up bad Cedric! I can't have kids!" She cried out!

I grabbed her as the tears came rolling down her face. We both hugged each other tight! "I'm sorry. I'm sorry. I'm sorry. I'm sorry." She whispered to me. "It's okay. It's okay. We got each other now. We got each other. I'm sorry. We will make it through it all. Together. I'm sorry. I love you. I love you. We got this now." I whispered back to her as we both slowly sat back down next to each other. We looked at one another as if we were both replaying our childhood memories. The feeling of never letting each other down again had us back on our feet hugging once more! We both took a few deep breathes. Finally, we pulled away from one another. Tammie dried her face then said, "With all those kids you have, I don't have to have any now. Thank you! I have a niece and a nephew!" Her smile returned after she said that. "Not so fast. I told y'all. I'm not sure that baby girl is mines. We will have to see." I replied. "Yeah yeah. I hope you understand now. Please forgive me about my view of kids and being careful out there. I don't have that opportunity anymore. I need you to promise me two things." She said as she finished wiping her face. "Anything. What is it?" I asked. "Don't ever put your hands on a woman. Don't run away from any pain you caused. Promise me you will stay during the healing." She said. "I promise. I'm not going anywhere. I remember what dad use to tell me about raising my hand at woman. I will never do that. I am making a better effort than ever to man up for the things I've done. I promise I won't leave without making peace with anyone of any situation that I have caused any troubles with." I replied. We hugged again then she walked out. Again, I was left thinking about how weak I've been. Thinking I was the only one with all the pressure and issues. Tammie had truly been to hell, around the devil's front yard and back which was going to hunt her for the rest of her life. I wanted to live up to the promises I made her and myself. I was getting closer and closer to finding the man I needed to be. I needed to be the best I could ever be going forward.

Chapter 14
WTH

A week went by with no calls, no texts, no leads or anything on or from Charlene. Her sisters were doing everything they could to find her. We all participated in several search walks through the streets from block to block, neighborhood to neighborhood passing out pictures of Charlene and posting them up in high traffic places. The police did thorough searches along the riverbanks from our neighborhood to downtown. They did underwater dives in the river around the old tower area Rico and she hung at. People were getting worried yet had faith that she would return. Her sisters wouldn't let up. They went to other surrounding cities with pictures. I had the duty of being with Joy when they traveled. It wasn't easy emotionally not knowing who her dad was. Rico didn't have it in him, nor did he want to confess anything to his family about potentially being a father. I understood that feeling too well. I didn't complain too much about it because none of us could have predicted that outcome.

Also, at the end of the first week, Rachel and Mrs. Gloria decided to cremate her stepdad. Yes, that's right. My mind was blown when she shared that information with me. She said since he passed, so many details about him were revealed. Mrs. Gloria felt he wasn't worthy of a traditional funeral. It was an easy decision since he didn't have any other family they had to reach out to for any permission. There were many questions I had yet I didn't desire to be too pushy about any of them. They were trying to get him out of their lives for good and quickly. I don't think anyone came by or said much of anything to them after that.

The word around the neighborhood was that he had a heart attack and pretty much died from natural causes. There wasn't a whisper or anything about what happened that day. Rachel nor her mom ever questioned me about what I did and why. It was like I did them a favor or some sort. Each day went by with Rachel and Mrs. Gloria becoming more opened than ever with one another. Spending more time together. They became inseparable. The upside about it, it gave me more time to spend with Junior. The challenge with it all was that Rachel didn't stay long when she would drop Junior off. She was purposely short with me at times. Strangely at other times, she would have twenty to thirty-minute conversations with me. I never knew how she really felt during those times. I was patient with whatever mood she was in. There was a lot going on with her emotionally that she fought hard to hide around me. I wasn't sure if she didn't think I cared enough to comfort her, or she didn't trust me as much as I thought. I offered nothing but compliments and sympathy whenever she was in a talkative mood. She talked in every direction accept directly at me. She struggled with eye contact with me. She would play with Junior while going on and on about the things Junior was doing day to day when he was with her.

Heading into week four of the random conversations with Rachel, I decided to grab her by the hand. Mrs. Anthony was standing on the porch when Rachel and Junior arrived. Instead of me taking Junior from her, Mrs. Anthony reached for him. She picked him up then rushed in the house with excitement. Mrs. Anthony was always ready to see Junior to kiss and squeeze on him every second he was over. Rachel was slow to walk away back to the car giving me a chance to ask her a few questions. "Hey... How are you?" I asked. She hesitated to walk off for a second as if she wasn't sure she wanted to talk that day. "I'm good. Thanks." She barely said as her voice sounded unsure. "No...Really. How are you? I don't want to sound to aggressive but... How are you? Are you good?" I asked again as I pulled her hand in mines. She was tight for a split second then loosen her arm enough to allow me to hold her hand gently. She was uncomfortable yet didn't reject the gesture. It was my rare shot to plea to her my concerns and guilt. "I'm sorry. I know we haven't talked much about anything to do with us nor about what I did. I been feeling so bad about how it happened. You've heard it before. I have been a selfish asshole for way too long. I apologize." I said as she finally looked up at me. She stared at me as if she were trying to see the truth in my eyes. I couldn't recall the last time she gave me that much attention without us doing anything sexual.

Everything was in slow motion as our hands started to sweat. She pulled her hand from mines suddenly! I grabbed it back before she could walk away then leaned down kissing her on her lips. I placed my other hand behind her head as I held her kissing her softly. Her hand fell from mines as I stepped back after the kiss. She looked at me as if she was shocked at what was happening or if she was dreaming. She instantly stepped closer to me pulling me back down for another kiss! It was unbelievable to me too! The nerve of me thinking I could just sweep her off her feet with a forced kiss. Somehow it was working. She didn't say anything after we detached from one another. She didn't smile nor did she look disappointed. She took a few steps back then turned slowly as she walked to the car. My feet felt like a ton of sand were in each one of my shoes keeping me planted on the porch. Just as she was cranking up the car, I gathered enough courage to run down to her!

"I don't know what to do. I do want us to be. Help me love you. I want you for real Rachel. Please tell me how or what

I must do. Anything. Please!" I said as I begged for her to say something. She held the steering wheel with both hands then laid her head on the back of her hands. She was fighting with herself on what to say or do with me. She was rocking back and forth as if one voice was telling her to go, with another voice telling her to stay. "I know I ain't shit! I can change. I don't have a choice. I need your help. I can't do it without you. I want you Rachel! Nothing else matters anymore. Please!" I said then opened her door. I sat down low on the side of her. She still had her head down as I could she her shaking all over. She was trying so hard to figure it out. I placed my hand on her thigh to test the restrictions she had towards me. Nothing. I then reached for her hands. I pulled them both from the wheel as she tried to keep her head glued to them. She glanced up as I was pulling her down towards me showing the tears that had filled her eyes. I kissed her hands repeatedly. "I'm sorry. I know. I know what I've done. Please let me make things right. Let me show you. Please let me give you what you deserve. I know you've been through so much. I don't want you to ever feel alone or helpless. I don't want you to hurt anymore. Please give me a chance to make this right." I pleaded as I started to brush her hair with my hand trying to get her to look at me.

She had goosebumps all over her arms. She was breathing heavily before she took a deep breath. She looked at me finally. She slid her hands from me then wiped her face. I helped with one side as she did the other cheek. I sat upright giving her a second to catch her breath. I was getting adjusted sitting as one side of my butt check was numb. I knew she had a lot to say so I wanted to give her all the time she needed. "Okay Cedric..." She whispered. That was it. I waited for another minute as I was certain she had more to add. She didn't. She shifted the gears to drive then let off the brakes enough to get me up on my feet! She then shut the door. "Okay? That's it? So... That's a yes?" I asked as I was confused. "Yes Cedric. Yes..."

She replied then cruised slowly off down the street. I pulled out my phone then called her! As she was out of sight the phone rung with no answer. I called like four or five times trying to get a clear answer. Mrs. Anthony came out on the porch to let me know Junior had a stinky diaper beyond her ability to change it without barfing. I had to smile without giving off concerning vibes as I walked back to the house. "That little fella know he can lay down some funky loads! Wonder where he got that from?" Mrs. Anthony said as she laughed. "I'm not sure. Maybe his momma. I don't do that much damage. Well... Maybe a little." I replied as we both laughed heading on in the house.

Month two had come quick with nothing about Charlene's whereabouts. Rico and I were doing our best trying to spend time with Joy. It wasn't as pleasant for any of us still not knowing who her real dad was. Charlene's sisters were beyond exhausted financially and mentally. They had spent so much money, time and effort with private investigators, feeding and even paying groups of people every week for search parties. They had traveled further and further away to relative houses in Kentucky, Michigan and Nebraska in hopes Charlene had ran away to a place where she knew someone. All dead ends. No one knew anything about Charlene's disappearance. That was still the belief. She was not dead she was just missing. No one would hint or whisper about it that way except Tammie. Tammie and I talked about two things the most. Me wasting time finding out if Joy was mines and how very possible Charlene may have harmed herself. Tammie would go on and on about how close it was for her to end it all herself. She didn't let me forget that. She stacked up all the reasons why Charlene would do it. Every time it started to make more sense to why Tammie was speaking the truth. I couldn't bring myself to talking with Charlene's sisters about that logic. I made Tammie promise me she would always keep those conversations between her and myself. I didn't think Tricia or Liz could handle that emotionally especially after all they've put in to find her.

It was a Tuesday morning when I received a call from Officer Jackson. It felt like I had just fell asleep since I had Junior staying all night with me. He fussed all night until Mrs. Anthony relieved me around midnight feeling sorry for me. Although I was getting better with getting him to sleep, I guess that night he was struggling due to a stopped-up nose. I was nervous a bit. I was also hopeful thinking he was calling so early with some good news. I debated about answering it and letting him leave a voicemail. I finally answered. "Hello... This is Cedric..." I mumbled pretending to be half sleep. "Morning Cedric. This is Officer Jackson. I know it's early... But umm... I wanted to tell you personally before you heard it from anywhere else." He replied sounding as if he hated he had to call. My heart started pounding as I sat up in the bed. My knees started to shake as my foot wouldn't stop bouncing on the floor. "Okay... what's going on? You find Charlene? Is she okay? She's not dead, is she? Please tell me she's okay!" I said as my voice was choppy and slowly getting louder. "No... no... I hope we find her soon. It's not about Charlene, son." He replied in a calmer voice. "Oh okay... yeah me too... It's crazy that she's still missing. Well... what's going on then?" I replied sounding more at ease.

There was a twenty seconds delay before he hit me with the reason he called. "Well... it's about Ms. Harris. I know that's the last person you care to hear about. Umm... I don't have the full details on how it happened but... Umm... Well... She's dead. She killed herself in her cell." He finally said with his voice sounding somewhat disappointed. I was dazed for sure! I held the phone as I started to see her face. I started to see her office and the things that took place that day. I started to see all those other guys I knew she violated. Anger hit my first followed by grief then I felt dull. "Wow... That's crazy..." I whispered.

That's all I had in me. I didn't know how to respond. "Yeah that is crazy. I hate it! She took the easy way out. That's the ultimate action of selfishness. After all the pain and suffering she caused. I hope she rot in hell!" He replied with his tone changing to anger. He was disgusted with the news. I continued to drift back and forth with the things Tammie had said about Charlene doing something to herself and then news of Ms. Harris doing it. "Thanks for calling. I don't know how I feel. I can't say I'm happy nor sad. I've heard about how people get to a state of complete loneliness or can't live with the consequences of the horrible things they may have done. I just never had it happen so close to me like that. I can't say Charlene would do it. Ms. Harris knew better! It was selfish of her or anyone not to live with the choices they've made. I am! At least I'm trying, I guess. As bad as it's been, I feel for me as well as for Charlene that there is always hope." I replied. "You're absolutely right Cedric! I'm not a bad cop. I've busted my ass for years trying to do better. I had to make tough decisions that were best for me. I promise you that. There were a series of events that I sometimes question that I was involved in with Melvin for years! Which makes me feel the same way about him. That's a whole other story! He had many opportunities to change. He didn't want to put the effort in. He couldn't leave our past in the past. I wish I could share the dark details of how we ended up with those results of him but what's done is done. I've made mistakes just as any other human. Charlene was... I mean... Ms. Harris had those same choices. Many opportunities to change. Accepted what she done then deal with the repercussions. Never should taking yourself out be an option. Never!" He said as I could hear him choking up a little.

Not sure why he mixed up Charlene's name. Sometime strange was felt when he did that. "It's not an option for me at all! Never will I! I understand without a doubt how important it is to think things through. I've mastered the dumb choices lifestyle. I get how my actions have a significant impact on my future. It's understood more than ever now." I said with conviction. "I'm happy to hear that Cedric. Ms. Harris could have faced her penalties, got help for herself while locked up then served others who have the same addiction. That's a sick and sad addition. I hate to say it but that's what it is. I wish more people would own it and seek help! Own your shit! Then give your testimony to those that need that help so they never cross those lines! We all need help! Everyone is suffering or challenged in areas that if, just if others would speak up more about their regrets, it may change lives! It would reduce the pain that others have to live with!" He said sounding beat.

I didn't have anything else to say. I was curious about the history he had with Melvin for a second. I wanted to ask more about it. It wasn't the best time. I left it at that. "I know that's what I'm going to do. I'm going to probably start speaking to some of these younger people about how a moment of pleasure can turn your whole life on its head. I need time to process this though. It hasn't hit me yet about why you called. I honestly don't think it ever will. I've forgiven her so I could have control of how I feel about it. Enough people have prayed for me to be a better person through and through. I'll be fine. I can only speak for me. Although I know things around here will never be the same. I'm here for it which gives me more courage to move on so other can see how I kept fighting for a better life. Despite it all, I will be a better person and a great father. It's in me. I was raised to be responsible. I can't let the people that love me down. Thanks again for calling." I replied with confidence. "You got it Cedric. You got it son. That's it. I wish I could have done a lot of things over. I can't. I'm pushing forward with so much myself. I can't say things will be perfect for you, but I think you'll be fine. Keep that attitude son. You're going to be alright. I'll see you around. Tell those people to say some prayers for me too!" He said as I could tell he was seeing a brighter side of it. "Will do sir. I'll let them know. Talk to you later." I replied. We both hung up.

I sat my phone down then laid back on the bed. I just stared up at the ceiling thinking about my life. I started to make decisions about everything right then and there. I told myself I wanted to know if Joy was my child. I wanted to make Rachel my wife. I wanted to live a life like the one my parents gave me. I wanted to be a provider and a protector for Rachel because that what she deserved. That's what Junior deserved. That's what Joy deserved if she was mines. I wanted to make Mrs. Anthony proud of me again. I wanted Tammie to smile when she saw me. I wanted to be who I knew I could be. Life had done its work on me. I was scared. I was afraid that if I didn't make those decisions then that the opportunity wouldn't come around for me again. Rachel gave me an okay that screamed she needed to be loved. I wanted to be the one to love her like that. I got up then walked in the restroom.

With tears starting to form in my eyes. I was exhausted from failing. I was tired of letting myself down. I was drained. I started to look at myself. I looked myself in the eyes and made several promises. I promised myself that I would love myself no matter how hard things got. I promised myself that I would never ever do anything to harm myself. I promised myself that nothing should ever come between me and providing for my kid or kids. I promised myself that I would listen to those that wanted what's best for me. I promised myself to hear them out. Process it all before I made a move. I promised myself to be straight forward with everyone about how I felt. I promised myself never to hide anything that would cause pain or hurt to anyone emotionally. I made promises that gave me my life's principals that I would never forgive myself if I didn't live accordingly.

I finally got on my knees and prayed. I prayed like I never had because I didn't recall me ever doing so. I prayed hard for all my promises I had made to myself. After I was done, I turned on the shower. I took a long shower standing in the water repeating the things I knew I needed to do until I couldn't think of anything else. All I had on my mind was the things I had control of. I blocked out my wrongs so I could focus on the right things I wanted to do. My first order of business was to find out the truth about Joy.

The next day I decided to call Charlene's sisters to make sure they were okay with me pushing forward with it. I talked to Mrs. Anthony and Tammie about it as well. They both were proud of me for finally stepping up to do what was right. I contacted Rico as well to get him to finally agree to take a DNA test with me. It was hard for him to tell someone else. He said he told his folks which went over smoother than he thought. In a way I was hoping he waited to be sure, but I was glad he was sharing his truths as well. Mrs. Anthony helped with finding the place to do it. She went ahead and paid the fees to get it done for us. It didn't take long to get it scheduled.

Although Rico showed up late after several calls and texts that day after I thought he was bailing out on us. We planned it that way so everyone would be held accountable. Neither Rico or I could lie or deny anything going forward if we were both there at the same time taking the test. Everyone was there. Charlene's sisters with Joy, Mrs. Anthony, Tammie, Rico with his Mom and myself. We filled out paperwork and was briefed by a lady about how wonderful it was that Rico and I were doing the responsible thing. She was very pleasant and caring the way she spoke to us about everything. She thanked us all for doing it as family. She went on about how sad it is that so many kids grow up fatherless just because the dads didn't want to do their part. She even went as far as to tell us that she wished her dad had done the same thing for her. Her mom wasn't an angel which caused her dad to walk away from their family, but he still had the opportunity to be her father regardless of how her mom and his relationship ended.

We finally took the test. My heart was heavy as we waited in the waiting room thinking we were going to get immediate results. The lady came back out to tell us they have what they needed, and it was going to take about two to three weeks for the results. Since none of us had ever done such a test, the only one that looked pleased about waiting was Rico. Everyone else looked sad or gave off a sigh of letdown thinking we were going to have closure that day. We all whispered amongst ourselves about the wait and being okay with knowing that it was at least in motion. They scheduled us to return in two weeks unless something came back sooner. His mom was standoffish at the office during everything and we all had the impression that she didn't want to get too involved with anything until the results came back.

Tricia and Liz offered us all to come back to their house to spend time with Joy. Rico and his mom declined the invite. Of course, Mrs. Anthony and Tammie didn't hesitate to go. No one was too bothered by Rico's mom and his reaction about turning down the invite. She had made comments while we were there about how this should have never happened. She was saying it in many ways but not directly on Charlene's behavior of having sex with two different guys so close together. Everyone tuned her out or talked over her about other things like the weather, news and food. Rico and his mom left out first followed by the rest of us. They didn't say anything to any of us once the wait was on. We trailed the sisters to their house and stayed over for a few hours. Mrs. Anthony ordered pizza for everyone. Mrs. Anthony and Tammie were all over Joy.

We agreed to have Joy over a few days a week alternating between her and Junior.

Every day waiting for the results, it was Junior or Joy over. I found myself changing stinky diapers and my own clothes daily from poop or baby vomit. I thought I had a bullseye on me because it only happened when I was either playing with the two or rocking them to sleep. We didn't say much to Rachel about what was going on. I wanted to wait before I told her how I felt about her and having a future with her. I continued to have small talks with her about any and everything she had on her mind. I texted her randomly giving her most of my attention if I wasn't with the babies. Neither Rico nor I said much of anything to one another during the wait. I reached out to him one time after a few days to make sure he didn't change his mind about seeing Joy. My call was ignored and the voicemail I left was unanswered.

It wasn't hard juggling everything since I didn't have anything else going on. That's when the reality sat in. I needed something to do to provide. I hadn't thought about it too much since Mrs. Anthony had me spoiled with her footing every bill, pamper, wipes, toys or whatever was needed. She didn't complain or confront me about it, not once. She was making it all happen and had been doing it without effort. I was sitting downstairs just watching her enjoy Joy's company with the biggest smile on her face. Tammie was grabbing the keys to the car to go to the store for food for dinner that evening. I was curious to know how she was able to do everything without missing a beat. With calm and peace within her as if she were the happiest person alive. "I can't thank you enough for everything. I want you to know I mean it. I wish I could repay you. I need a job to help soon! I don't want to run you dry." I said to her when Tammie left. She laid Joy over her shoulder as she patted her back to burp her. She looked at me then smile.

"Cedric, baby... I'm doing what any mother or grandmother would do. Loving on my babies! I know you're a man now but you're still just as much my little baby as they are. I'll never stop taking care of y'all. I know it's scary for you but we're going to get through this. I'm not saying you should run out there and find a job right this minute. At some point it should be something you want to do. You must take the role of provider, protector and leader. Money isn't the whole package, but it helps. I'm not worried about any of this. I'm doing what I suppose to do because I want to and love to. I hope and pray you understand what I said. No pressure. One day at a time. You're going to make it happen. It's all going to come together." She said. I nodded my head agreeing.

I could see the picture she was painting. "Yeah I get it. I must step up to do my part. You inspire me. My dad would agree with you without a doubt. You sounded just like him. He would be applauding you right now. Once we get the results, I'm going to make the best efforts to put myself in those roles for my babies too. Thank you! You are my angel! That's what you are. You must be! Tell the truth. God sent you here to watch over me and take care of me, right?" I replied with a big grin on my face. She laughed softly as Joy was heading to dreamland. "Between God and I, he told me you needed someone to be there for you no matter what. I couldn't ignore the shame and loneliness you had within you when David first started to bring you over. I knew there were some things you were dealing with as a young man especially being abandoned in this mad world. How could I ignore God's voice telling me to welcome you not only in our home but in my heart? You didn't turn out too bad." She whispered as laughed again as she laid Joy down in the baby pin. "Thank you." I replied.

Just days later was results day. All parties arrived minutes after one another. Again, Rico and his mom were late.

Not telling Rachel everything, she had dropped Junior off that morning so she could go on a couple of interviews she had applied for. I didn't want her to miss them since it was already planned for me to have him that day weeks prior. Finally, we were all in the family room which was a smaller room from the waiting room. It's were they gave the results for privacy purposes. I'm sitting there with Junior and Joy walking all over everyone's feet. They both were starting to walk with some stumbling here and there! I had to pull Junior up in one arm with Joy in the other after chasing them before I sat back down. Tammie leans down and whispers, "See, you're already getting used to it. You know these are your kids." I looked up at her giving her raised eyebrows and a half smile thinking to myself she must got an inside scoop on the results before we did. She said it with confidence.

By then, the doctor entered with a big smile on her face as soon as she saw me with the babies. "Well hello there, little people! Good morning to you all! We all know why we're here. I won't waste another second as I know how nerve wrecking these things can be. I have the test results here!" She said with excitement as if she has too much fun doing that for a living. Everyone zoomed in on her every move of the manila envelope she had clutched in her hands. I hugged both babies tighter as Mrs. Anthony and Tammie had their hands on both my shoulders. Tricia and Liz stood at attention while Rico laid his head face down on his mom's shoulder waiting to hear the results. "In the case of baby Joy, with a 99.9 percent rating, the DNA results has found that... Rico Gardner... You are... Not the father..." The lady said as she slowly read through it. The entire room gasped. "Yes! I knew it! I knew that wasn't his baby! We can go now!" Rico's mom yelled with relief! Rico looked like he had just caught a bullet with his bare hands. He wore a giant smile on his face then tried to downplay it once we all looked over at him. His mom darted out of the door as Rico followed. He looked back to say, "I'm sorry."

The door closed behind them as the doctor pulled out another piece of paper. "Well that's unfortunate that people cheer not being in a position of blessings. Babies are blessings. I'll never get that part while people feel that way. I apologize for that, but I have your results. Okay... So, in the case of baby Joy. With a 99.9 percent rating, the DNA results has found that... Cedric Mason... You are... Not the father..." She said with a softer tone towards the end. She knew that it was a shock and a concerning one. Everyone looked around confused! Mrs. Anthony was in tears. Tricia and Liz were crying and lost! "Wait... What are you saying? I don't get it?" Tammie asked. "Yeah, so... Neither one of them is her father? Are you serious?" Liz asked. "Something doesn't add up. If she's not mine or his baby? Then who?" I asked trying to be calm. I was torn on the inside. I didn't want to believe what I was hearing. I didn't want to believe that Charlene was with someone else. I didn't want to see her any other way. She wasn't there to explain. Joy and Junior were teasing and giggling with one another. "Yes, I'm afraid to say. These two gentlemen are not the father. I wanted it to be wrong. It's been a while since I've had to resubmit results. I did it in this case. I needed to be sure. When it came back again with the exact same results, my heart melted. I'm so sorry about this. I hope that whoever the father is will reveal himself. I would hate for that precious baby to go fatherless her entire life. It's hard not having your parents in your life. I'm crushed to know that baby Joy doesn't have neither one of them right now. I ask you two aunts to love on her as hard as you can! She needs that. I'm so sorry again." The doctor said as she rubbed Joy's little arm. "Take as much time as y'all need in here. I wish you all luck." She added then left the room.

There was complete silence from all the adults as we all watched Joy and Junior spit and laugh at one another. Sounds of sniffing and heavy breathing followed from everyone as I held the babies in my arms kissing them both on the top of their heads. "I just don't know what to say. I love this little princess now. I don't care what that test says. She's my daughter!" I said as kissed Joy again on her head. It just came out of me without hesitation. Whoever her real dad was wasn't in the picture. I couldn't imagine her without me as her dad. Again, an ongoing thought and feeling that wouldn't leave my heart nor my conscience. "I can't explain how crazy this is. No answers at all. This is hard to process." Tricia said as she wiped her tears away. "I'm with Cedric on this one if you truly feel that way. It sounds crazy I know but I feel something in my spirit that makes me want to be in Joy's life too. I know we don't have the final say so with that. This is a hard one to deal with I know for you two ladies. I'm sorry..." Mrs. Anthony said as she too wiped the tears from her eyes. "Wow... Man this is a tough one. Baby Joy makes my heart smile just like baby Junior. I would love to be her aunt. This is so sad. I'm supporting whatever you all decide." Tammie said. "We all need to think this through. I'm not saying I don't think that's a good idea. Joy does need any and everyone who cares to be there for her no matter what. I will love on her the best I can. We need time to think about this new information. Thank you all so much for being here and your kind words. Thank you, Cedric, for wanting to step up and be in her life even though you don't have to. None of you have to. I appreciate you all." Liz said.

We all nodded our heads as we allowed the two babies to play for another five minutes before one of the aunts picked up Joy. Mrs. Anthony picked up Junior as we all exited the room then out to our cars. I kissed Joy once more then Liz strapped her in her car seat. They promised to keep in touch. I had every right to see Joy as much as I wanted to. They wanted us to give them a couple of days to figure it out. They said they would reach out soon. They pulled off as I could see them both fighting with keeping the tears from falling down their faces. We got Junior in his car seat as well then, the rest of us headed home.

On the ride home Tammie asked, "How serious were you about what you said? You sure that's what you want?" I was teasing Junior while I sat in the back with him thinking about Tammie's question. "Cedric, I'm surprised at your eagerness to make that kind of decision. When you said it, my spirit moved with love and protection. Something was telling me to protect that baby. Something was telling me to agree with whatever you felt. It was strange but I felt your desire to want to be there for that baby. Same way you've been working on getting better with being there for Junior. I'm so proud of you." Mrs. Anthony said as she glanced a few times at me in the rear-view mirror as she drove. I was done with little boy stuff. It was all happening rather I wanted it to or not. I was a dad indeed with more in me. I saw myself raising them as if they were twins. I had the support. I didn't fear anything. "Yeah I meant it. I can see the man I want to be. I see the dad I can be. I see better days are ahead of me. There must be something out there better for me. I've done enough wrong. Up is the only place I can go. You all have been the best support team any fool could have. I think it was a verse or something from the Bible my dad would say. All childish things must come to an end. I believe that." I answered. Tammie turned around at me to make sure it was me who was talking. "Okay grown man. Sounds like a real adult in that back seat. I hear ya little brother. Pops said that a lot. Please believe I get it too. He was always trying to prepare us. I'm so glad you remember so much of what he said to us. Sometimes I wish I would have taken heed to it a long time ago." Tammie replied. Mrs. Anthony just smiled at me in the rear-view mirror with happiness. "I see the changes Cedric. I can see that change. Don't stop. It's a beautiful thing son. A blessing." She said when she placed the car in park after we pulled up to the house. I smiled back. "Thank y'all for all y'all do." I said.

"Oh, there's Rachel! Hope she wasn't waiting too long." Mrs. Anthony said. Rachel was parked across the street waiting. "You going to keep her out in the dark or you're going to make the right decisions with her. She really likes you. Please stop wasting time. Okay." Tammie whispered to me when Mrs. Anthony got out the car. "I promise I'm trying. I'm not wasting anyone's time. I'm trying to make sure I'm good enough, you know." I whispered back quickly before Mrs. Anthony opened the back door on Junior's side. "Yeah yeah." Tammie mumbled at me before we both got out the car. Rachel got out her car then walked over. "I was just stopping by for a little. Junior can stay longer if y'all would like. One of my interviews was shorter than I thought. I got the job right on the spot!" She said with a big smile on her face. "Well congratulations Rachel! So glad to hear that!" Mrs. Anthony replied first. "Thank you!" Rachel replied. "You know we can't get enough of our sweet baby. I'll take him on in then." Mrs. Anthony added. "Look at you! Congratulations lady!" Tammie shouted! "Thanks!" Rachel replied. "I'll get his bag Cedric." Tammie said as she took Junior's diaper bag from me then winked at me. She then walked off following Mrs. Anthony into the house.

Rachel stood there watching them walk in the house as I closed my door. "Wow, that's good news. I see ya. That's nice." I said as she finally turned her attention towards me. "Thank you. Thanks..." She said softly. "What's wrong? You good?" I asked. She was holding something else in. She changed her mood quick when it was just her and I standing out there alone. "Am I going to be the only one working? Am I going to be the only one trying? Am I going to have to wait forever for you to take anything seriously?" She said looking worried. I wasn't offended. She had very fair and reasonable concerns I was ready to answer. "As long as you'll let me, I'll never leave it to you to do any of this alone. I meant what I said. I want you. I want a family I can call my own. You've been nothing but real with me. I'm going to be a man about everything. I was childish back then about too much. I've decided to finish school here at the community college. I want to become a coach at our old high school someday soon. I want to not only help some guys with getting better on the field. I want to help influence them on how to make positive and wiser moves off the field. If you give me this last chance. A chance to show you what I've been dreaming off. I want to show you what I've learned. I want to give you my good. You've seen my bad. My wrong. Please allow me to show you that there's some wonderful things deep within me. The only catch with it is… Can you teach me your language? I want to speak your language. I want to understand what makes you smile and what not to do that'll make you stab me!" I said as I stood there with a passionate fire in my eyes like that of an ancient king adoring his true queen!

My words didn't have much weight to them for her ears, but she was going to know I was speaking from my heart. She stood there looking impressed. She was staring into each one of my eyes one after the other. She looked all over trying to see if it was really Cedric telling her those sweet things she desperately needed to hear. "It sounds so good Cedric. I don't want you to say it if you don't mean it. I need you to show me all of that and more. I can hear the change. There is someone in there that sounds like they want to be a better person. You sound like the guy I thought you was in high school. I love what I'm hearing. I admit it sounds like magic coming from you. I would do almost anything with you and go anywhere with you if you show me, I'm worth it. Please mean it Cedric. Please…" She said as she continued to look at me as if she was searching for the doubt in my eyes. "I've said everything I needed to say. Now with your permission, let me show you. I want you to be mines forever. I love you Rachel." I whispered to her as I stepped up to her. She quickly stepped back as she slowly raised her hands up to cover her ears. I was puzzled for a second. "Please don't ever say that if you don't mean it! Please don't play with my feelings like that Cedric! Please don't do me like this! I don't think I can take it!" She begged me as tears started to fall down her face. "I do mean it! I'm sorry if it's hard to believe. I just wanted you to know how serious I am about you. Rachel... I'm serious. I will show you. I love you." I replied as I slowly stepped back over to her. She moved her hands away from her ears. I leaned down and kissed her. She didn't move away that time. She was trembling as her hands and arms were shaking. I pulled her into my arms. I held her for a few minutes. "Please Cedric. Don't hurt me... I love you too..." she whispered back to me. My mouth fell on top of her head kissing her softly.

Chapter 15

Actions over Words

Later, that evening after Rachel and Junior had left for the night, I included Mrs. Anthony and Tammie in on my plans to finish college at home. I told them about my vision I had about coaching and helping other young guys. They both loved the idea. They couldn't believe I had thought through it so well. I admitted to them that it all came in an instant. It felt right. I was going to be as close as I could be to my family. I needed Rachel to believe that I wanted a life with her beyond coparenting. Tammie was excited and wanted to help with making sure all my grades and credits from Northwest were transferred immediately. Mrs. Anthony wouldn't let me refuse her support of paying for whatever classes I needed to get me going as soon as possible. As much as I fought with the thought, I knew where I could go for some quick, easy money.

I finally called Samantha to patch our friendship up. I needed her help with a gig so I could start making some money. She ignored my calls for about two days. She finally answered with frustration as if I was stalking her! For about an hour I begged and pleaded with her about my behavior and selfishness until she gave up being upset at me. I told her all about what happened with my baby situations, my change of heart, my willingness to do whatever it took to make peace between everyone I wronged. I apologized several times throughout the entire conversation. I told her I needed a favor. I told her about my plans. She took a few minutes thinking about it all. She said she forgive me for my selfish games. She not only agreed to make sure I had a job, she told me they were opening another store. She needed a new manager to run one of the old ones so she could manage the new one. She said they were growing fast! She needed all the help she could get. She mentioned she was prepping Rico for the role, but he didn't want that kind of responsibility. It couldn't have been a better time for us both! She told me I could start manager training within the next week if I was ready for the job. The pay was way more than I thought I was going to get with some other side gigs I was fishing around for.We agreed that I could take some evening classes then she would work around my classes whenever I started back up at the college. I promised her over and over that she wouldn't regret doing that for me. I didn't want to get off the phone realizing how well that call went with Samantha. I couldn't believe what was happening. She literally had to hang up in my face because I couldn't stop saying thank you!

I shared the good news with Mrs. Anthony and Tammie. They were excited for me and had already started getting everything in order for me. Tammie was able to get my transcripts online. With Mrs. Anthony's help, they were able to apply and enroll me in the school at home. They were waiting for some other papers to be mailed to us, while some were being faxed over to the school. I was believing in the idea more and more as it all fell in place.

A couple more days had passed. Although everything was moving faster than expected. It was all going along as planned, but something felt off. I realized I haven't seen or heard anything from Charlene's sisters about Joy! I knew they wanted some time to think things through. I was convinced that they were going to reach back out within a day or two. Something wasn't right. I called the number they gave me but no answers. I called late in the evening thinking they were busy. It was well passed seven days! I got up early calling and texting. Still no answers or call backs. After about three voicemails went unanswered, I decided to go check on them later that evening. I asked Mrs. Anthony and Tammie their thoughts which they too agreed that something was off. They even went as far as to call from their different numbers. Same results, no answers. I asked Tammie to go over to their place with me in case they thought I was trying to strong arm them about their decision. My logic was to go ahead and move forward while the feeling was there. I didn't think trying to adopt Joy when she turned eleven was the best idea. I committed to raising her as my daughter along with Junior. It reminded me of Tammie's and my upbringing. A family with a mom, dad, sister and brother. I was ready mentally so there was no turning back. I just needed the sisters to agree or at least to trust me with their niece.

The sun was making it's escape for the day, a chill from a cold front that was heading our way made us both wear a jacket. It was a more bearable windchill than those Chicago blizzard like winds. Of all the houses on the street, we could barely see the darkness of their house sitting back as if it was a gray cloud hiding it. All the other houses had their lights on from the inside as well as a few flicking on their porch lights as the sun continued to disappear. My heart was starting to sink from my chest as the butterflies in my stomach danced. As we pulled up to the ghost house, I felt a sharp pain shoot through my entire body. "Are they home? You can see straight through the house. Wait a minute. Did they move?" Tammie whispered to me as we sat in the car looking at Charlene's house. I couldn't see it. I couldn't imagine them leaving like that! I couldn't see them not calling or texting letting me know what was going on. "This is the right house, right? I mean I know it is... I'm just... Damn..." I mumbled to myself.

Tammie slowly got out of the car then headed towards the steps of the house. I immediately followed hoping our eyes were misleading us. We both walked slightly past the house checking on both sides to see if anything was on through the side windows or back windows, downstairs and upstairs. We walked up on the porch to see if could see anything through the porch windows. I placed my hands on them carefully peeping in to see an empty house! Nothing was there! Not a damn thing! No furniture, not even a picture on the wall was seen. I turned and headed back to the car feeling sick to my stomach. Tammie peeped through the windows to witness the same thing. I leaned on the passenger side of the car scratching my head in disbelief. I checked my phone making sure I didn't miss a text or call that may have slipped past me from them. I dropped my phone shattering it because my hands were shaking so bad! I had this tingling feeling throughout my entire body. I couldn't control my limbs. I tried to pick up the pieces but only to be frustrated even more because I couldn't get them all up quick enough. I began to throw them into the street with anger!

Tammie ran down to me and grabbed my hands to keep me from causing more of a scene. A couple of neighbors came out on their porches to see what all the commotion was for. Tammie quickly helped me up from the street then escorted me back to the car. She helped me get in, waving at the people as if she was sorry for disturbing their peace. I didn't cry, I was just mad. "I just don't get it. No explanation. Nothing. Why?" I said to myself as Tammie was starting the car up. We drove down the street then Tammie said, "I know you're upset. I would be too. Hell, I am upset! Don't worry. I just hope Joy is okay and they do right by that baby. There's nothing we can do." I sat there thinking hard. All I could see was a blank space. After a few minutes I could see Joy's precious face and hear her giggle. I knew that was it. The way they left like that was a sign of how determined they were about getting away from me.

Maybe they thought I was going to take Joy away from then and never let them see her. I didn't know nor was I going to get any answers anytime soon. I sat there in silence as we rode back home. Once we were back, we both took a couple of minutes before we went in to collect our thoughts. "I'll explain to Mrs. Anthony what happened. I'll do that part. You're going to have to tell her what happened to your phone." Tammie said as she smiled at me. I nodded my head agreeing as I smiled back. "Look on the bright side. You have a job to buy your own phone. You can afford it since you don't have to take care of two babies now. I know how much Joy meant to you. I'm hurt too. Just know, things line up a certain way for our good. Don't beat yourself up for something that was totally out of your control. You have Junior and you're doing a damn good job. I'm so proud of you man!" She said then leaned over and gave me a hug. "How you got jokes and encouraging words all in the same breath? You're right. I appreciate you and those words. It's going to take me a minute to get things rolling. I won't complain. I have so much to do. I just hate how they did that. Damn… I love that little baby. I'll be alright. Junior will keep me busy enough. You know I was so close to telling Rachel about raising Joy. Glad I didn't." I replied shaking my head at it all. "Yeah I was wondering when you were going to include her on that very important information." Tammie replied as we both got out the car. "Well, it is what it is. I can move forward with everything else. Forward and up is the only way I want to go. Anything that's going to lead my back down the wrong road, I can live without it." I added. "Yeah boy you done been through enough. Let's keep it together. This may be your last shot. Don't mess this up. You're lucky. Well, I'll say what Mrs. Anthony says. You're blessed baby." Tammie said jokingly before we walked in the house.

Two weeks later I started working at the store. It was clear that Samantha and I were just friends. I didn't flirt or try to bring up any old feelings I once had for her doing my training. We got along, fine. It was a bit awkward at times being alone with her going over policies and procedures. She would explain things to me while showing me and as we switched seats or moved certain ways, we brushed up close to one another. Neither one of us acknowledged any discomfort or took other measures to avoid it. Everything flowed in a way as if we were close friends instead of potential lovers. I called or texted Rachel on my breaks and lunch time to keep from spending any extra time with Samantha that I didn't have to. I was working on trusting myself being around her more and more. I wanted Rachel to know that I was only doing what I had to do to take care of business. I didn't want anyone getting any ideas or worrying about me not behaving the way I promised I would.

After that first week, it was smooth sailing. I talked to Officer Jackson once more in hopes he knew more about something with Charlene and if he understood why her sisters would leave the way they did. He revealed some disturbing news that only left me even more confused and lost. He told me that an unknown source they couldn't verify with confidence, gave them tips that Charlene was seen with a guy, two young ladies and a baby leaving town in two big moving trucks. They crossed checked everything, but nothing made them suspend their missing person search on Charlene. He didn't believe it. While on the phone with him, he said, "It didn't seem logical or consistent with the sister's behaviors after all the efforts they put in seeking answers to find their sister. If they all worked together to plot and play some twisted fake missing person's lie just to leave town than that's probably the dumbest reason." It was calming to hear him be just as perplexed about it like I was.

At least once a week for the next eight weeks after that, he would call or stop by to say they were still looking and following up on Charlene but with less efforts since the leads started to become few. Even after I had given up thinking about Charlene, it was a little strange Officer Jackson kept me in the loop. It became clear that her case was becoming colder by the day.

Nearly six months with nothing but the disappearance of her and her sisters with Joy is all we had. By then I was in full rotation as the store manager while going to class at night. It was quite the load at the first but with the help of everyone making sure I didn't get burned out. It wasn't as bad as I expected. Rachel helped me study while Mrs. Anthony and Tammie entertained Junior many nights. I had started volunteering at my old high school. When I finally spoke with Coach Thompson about wanting to follow his footsteps with coaching, he was beyond anxious to get me back in the school to help. We sat down and had a heart to heart about me not wanting to continue to play since I still had a for sure chance to make it all the way to the major. He was torn yet understood the 'why' more than forcing something I had no desire to go after anymore. He shared a story that I had never heard from him in all the years I played under him.

We met for lunch the day before I came out for him to introduce me to the team since they were having weekend practices. While eating, he told me how he ended up coaching and missing out on playing in the league himself. "Cedric, there was this girl in college I would do anything for! I would skip practices just to spend more time with her. She would treat me like crap sometimes, but I looked past that because of the way I felt when I was around her. My playing time was shortened to missing a few games. I was starting to be more interested in her than playing or even getting to class to keep my grades up. It was getting closer to the last straw the coaches had given me! I knew how upset my mom would have been if she knew I was failing due to some girl I was chasing around. My mom had worked two jobs trying to take care of my four siblings and me. I was in school being a complete fool for this girl. On the day, my coaches gave me one last chance to make it to practice on time and to meet a study buddy to help with my grades, I had to see her! I went to her apartment that was within miles of our campus. Which was one of the main reasons I was so into her. Having an apartment of your own being so young was a huge no no for some. Especially for the ones that never experienced that kind of freedom, if you know what I mean. It was the worse decision of my life! I approached her door then pushed it opened as it was slightly cracked. I heard some moving, followed by sounds of her sweet voice as if she was in destress. To my surprise, it was her and one of my buddies I use to hang out with nearly every day! He was like a brother to me! They were having sex right there on the couch! They were so into, that they didn't even see me standing there in the doorway. I didn't know what to do. Someone was walking by so I pulled the door close slowly as quiet as I could. I walked back to my dorm room crying. Not because of what I saw, but because I had let my mom down. I was kicked off the team. I couldn't go back home. I didn't say another word to the girl which I still don't think she knew the real reason why. I never spoke a word about it to anyone. I stayed in school and got my grades back up. I told my mom I had a career ending injury that wouldn't allow me to play anymore. I promised her I would graduate and that's what I did. That's why I love coaching high school guys so much! I get the opportunity to steer them in the right direction. That's why it broke my heart to see you come back. I understand your reasons and I respect that. I'm more than honored to have you here helping us out. Now I hope that gives you a better perspective on why I'm the way I am and my goal for every young man that comes to play on this team." He said with a straight face.

That took some thought to trust me with that past life changing testimony that basically shaped the rest of his life since then. I thanked him for sharing and being transparent with me. I knew the role I needed to play which was the same as he was aiming towards. I was helping them with workouts as well as giving them life advice during early morning Saturday practices. That gave me a great feeling of responsibility. An opportunity to work on my leadership as well as my coaching skills. The coaches and players were all excited to have me. The young guys started to show more interest as I became more involved after hearing the stories, I shared about how hard I went in practices which helped my game time play. Coach Thompson cosigned everything I was telling them and showing them. They all were showing up thirty minutes earlier or staying later to do extra sets and drills. There were a few players still on the team that were freshmen when I was leaving which helped me to fit in even more. They were the captains that helped confirm everything I was telling them. It felt right being there with them. It felt good working with them on and off the field. They enjoyed it and started to trust me more since I wasn't too far off from their ages. They shared so many struggles with me that they were having which made it easy for me to tell them my similarities and how I overcame them.

Three years of that and I couldn't believe I was graduating from college! Staying home and trying again with school turned out to be one of the best decisions I could have ever made! It didn't take long for Rico to find his way back around. After his mom came by and apologized for being incentive to the whole thing, Rico knew something wasn't right overall. He said to me on several occasions that no one truly knew what Charlene had done when she was out roaming the streets. He said as much as she came across everyone else as if she had lost her mind, she showed him she had plenty of sense. We didn't dwell too much on any subjects about Charlene or Joy. I didn't hold any grudges with him. Plus Mrs. Anthony was happy to have him back around too. I didn't like the way Tammie and him would hang out sometimes, but I had my hands full to give any pressure. Rachel and I had falling deeply in love with one another. At times I had to think back about all the mess I put her through. I never imagined how stress free it was loving just one girl with all that you are as a man. I was giving her the attention she needed and deserved. She didn't hold back with her feelings and actions proving to me she too wanted something greater than our past. If it wasn't Mrs. Anthony or Tammie saying it, it was Mrs. Gloria saying we looked great together. Every hint they could give was mentioned to me on making my relationship with Rachel very official. Little did they know I was already on top of it.

I was making some decent money which allowed me to spoil Rachel with little gifts here and there. We were doing more as a family, Rachel, Junior and me. We were out growing the normal visits back and forth from my house to her house. We had to sneak just to mess around sometimes. That became old fast and expensive. Having to get hotel rooms just to have some privacy! Out of respect for the mothers, we started planning to move in with one another. Not because of more sex opportunities. Well, we did need more space and to relax under each other while we walked around in our underwear. That was more of my reasoning, but Rachel mentioned several times about coming home from work to lay up with me as we watch Junior play. Junior was getting bigger by the day, eating everything in sight as he had phased out of the terrible two-chapter. He was walking, running and climbing on everything by then. She said there were so many things she had always wanted to do when she settled down with someone. She would go on and on about how she saw herself being a mom and wife. I would always throw in the fact that that was how I was raised so I wasn't against any of it. Particularly the whole wife part. As if I didn't have enough notice on the direction, we needed to go in. We reached that point in our lives that we were ready to do certain things completely on our own. We knew Mrs. Anthony, or Mrs. Gloria wasn't going to be okay with us shacking up. I had a long talk with Pastor Clayton days before my graduation because I had a surprise for Rachel as well as everyone else.

It was early in the morning when I walked down to the church as I agreed to meet Pastor Clayton the prior day. I needed to make sure I was ready and wasn't going to do anything out of guilt. We started the conversation off with congratulating me on my accomplishments. "I must say Cedric, we thought we lost you there for a minute. I can't tell you enough how proud of you everyone is. A lot of us prayed hard for you boy. God doesn't make mistakes. I'm sure you've heard that many times. I just hope that you believe it now. What's on your mind? How can I help you?" Pastor Clayton said as he shook my hand. We both sat down in his office or whatever it was they called it. He had a desk, chairs, a sofa, a few bookcases, and file cabinets. It was about as big as my room with a computer on the desk as well. Looked like a fancy spiritual meeting room to me. I was nervous but I had made it all the way up there to ask for his advice. I couldn't leave without hearing what he had to say. I took a deep breath in then told him how I was feeling and my plans. "I can't thank you enough for those prayers. Lord knows I needed them. I think I've been through enough and it's time for me to take things to new levels when it comes to being a better man, father and hopefully a good husband. I need some advice. Who be..." I was saying before he shouted! "Praise God! Amen! Thank you! Thank you, father!" He jumped up screaming to the top of his lungs as if he was possessed! I was scared as hell as I raised my forearm up towards him thinking he was going to jump on me! It was like something took over him! I remained seated as he settled down then sat back in his chair. "God is good! My oh my... Cedric Mason. God is good son..." He whispered as he pulled a handkerchief from his packet wiping his face and around his mouth.

"Son I am so proud of you. This is truly a blessing! This is amazing to hear it. It is just as sweet to see it happening." He continued as he was calmer. "Yes sir. Thank you. I want to do it the right way. I've found myself in good hands with the love and support of all those around me. I have a son and a lady that loves me. I have been blessed with another chance. Another shot at doing things the way they're supposed to be done. I came to ask for your blessings and guidance. I feel it in my heart to do this. I want to marry Rachel. I want to raise my son the way I was raised. With his mom and dad loving each other together in our own home. I have been blessed with the opportunity to work and make good money. I am graduating with a degree to go teach and coach at my alma mater. I don't have any complaints about my life. I need to know that this is the way. I can't think of any reasons sir, not to do it." I finally replied as I started to choke up thinking on how far I had come. He sat there staring at me as if he didn't recognize me for a second. He nodded his head several times before he said anything. "You hear yourself son... You are right on it. You have realized your trials and tribulations have brought you to this point in life. When I say it is a wonderful thing to realize that at your age. I mean God has worked on you. You are moving in the right direction. I don't have to second that for you to know that. I am grateful that you decided to come to me. I'm honored! Yes. Yes. Yes! Don't look back. Keep moving forward with love, peace, patience and selflessness. You are blessed. You have my blessings as well. We are all here for you. Always have been. Can we pray together?" He said with so much joy in his voice.

He had the biggest smile on his face. I agreed to his prayer request. I found myself smiling as well as I bowed my head. He prayed for my sanity and my self-control. He prayed that I allow love to control my decisions and not my flesh. He prayed for Rachel, Junior and our bond. He prayed for all evil doers or distractions to be cast down by God that try to alter the path that I was walking on. After that we both stood up and hugged. "Does anyone else know about this leap of faith you're about to take?" He asked with curiosity. I shook my head smiling. "No sir. Not at all. I was thinking it would be a big surprise to do it at my graduation dinner. I hope that you'll be there to give me some confidence." I responded. He hugged me once more then said, "Of course I'll be there! Wouldn't miss it! Only person you may want to say something to is Rachel's mom. Mrs. Gloria, I believe... It's out of respect and tradition. She would appreciate that." I thought about it for a second. "Sounds good. Yeah, I will." I replied. He was cheerful about the good news I gave him. "If it helps. I will love for you all to be married here. Wouldn't cost you a penny! I'm sure Mrs. Anthony is going to be so excited when she finds out! I know she's going to want to plan everything. I'll make that part easy for her." He said. "Yes sir. That's one of the reasons why I came to you first. I was hoping you could do it for us. It would mean so much to me. Thank you!" I replied as we shook hands before I left. We both smiled and he told me he would see me at the dinner. He welcomed me to call him or come back if anything changed or if I needed anything else from him.

My next order of business was to go to Mrs. Gloria to ask for her blessings too. I couldn't have it lingering on my mind too long so I called her while I was walking back to the house to see when I could catch her alone to talk. I made it seem as if it wasn't anything of importance, since I didn't want her to alarm Rachel about my desire to talk to her mom privately. She said she would be out and about within the next hour. I asked her to meet me for coffee. I hated coffee but she didn't know that. She couldn't go a day without it! It was easy to get her to meet me.

I made it back home to find everyone moving and grooving to their normal tune. Mrs. Anthony was cleaning, and Tammie was getting ready to go to class. Yes, Tammie wasn't going to let me one ups her. She decided to enroll in some classes to get her degree in computer science. There something about cellphones, computers, software and downloading things that excited her. I was happy for her because I knew she was loving the new life we all had. She was believing in herself just as much as I was. I couldn't wait to see the look on her face when she found out I was proposing to Rachel. I was a little afraid she was going to start dating Rico and force his hand in marriage. It was funny to think that, but I was praying that didn't happen. I called Rachel to make sure she was indeed at work. Rachel worked at the bank. She challenged herself every day there that landed her the branch manager position. And that kept her very busy during the day. I didn't want anyone catching me with Mrs. Gloria. I wasn't sure how well I was going to do, lying about what my purpose was. I asked Mrs. Anthony for the car. She didn't question my reason which was great for me. I didn't think of a comeback as I asked not thinking twice about it when she passed me in the living room before I went upstairs. I didn't drive much back then because everything was in walking distance. After having a child, it made me never want to hardly walk anywhere anymore. There were way too many toys, cups, snacks, pampers to keep up with to be walking with a child. Plus, I had to improve my driving skills before I purchased a car. We were getting around fine in Rachel's mom's car because she didn't go anywhere very much.

After quietly moving through the house without speaking much to anyone, I grabbed the car keys then headed to the coffee shop. I cruised down the street playing out how I wanted to deliver the news to Mrs. Gloria. Halfway there my phone rang. I was started to cringe for a split second when I saw Mrs. Gloria number come across the screen. She was already there waiting on me to get there. I sped up to make sure I didn't put her in a bad mood. She was sweet yet a little impatient at times. Finally made it there. She had Junior with her since she wanted to keep him that day. He jumped up on me when he saw me. I had to wrestle him off, to get him to sit down in the seat at the table we were sitting at. Once she received her coffee order and Junior was chowing down on a blueberry muffin, she asked, "What's going on Cedric? Is there something wrong?" I wondered how bad things were at one point that everyone I ever asked to talk to would always think that something was wrong. I laughed to myself thinking about all those times someone asked me that. "Nothing is wrong. I promise you that. I'm a little nervous so bear with me." I replied.

I glanced over to see Junior murdering the muffin which indicated there was a small window I had before he turned his fun levels to the max from the sugar rush he was about to be on. "Okay. That's fine." She said as she sipped on her coffee never taking her eyes off me. "Alright... I know things started off very rocky for Rachel and myself. I know I've done some things I shouldn't have, and I do appreciate your forgiveness. Thank you for accepting me in your family. Thank you for being a wonderful grandmother as well as an amazing mother to Rachel. I love your daughter. I want to be in her life forever. As long as I'm on this earth, I will love her, protect her and be there for her through whatever." I said as she dropped her coffee on the floor! "Oh my God! Cedric! Are you serious? Are you going to marry my daughter! Oh Cedric!" She yelled in shocked! I had to shift my feet to the side avoiding the coffee volcano! One of the servers there rushed over immediately to clean up the spill! "Yes ma'am. I want to marry Rachel. I love her. You have raised a great woman. I want to make her my wife." I replied as I moved one of the chairs out the way to let the server wipe up the small coffee puddle. "Wow! I'm so sorry for that. Sorry. Whew!" She said to the server. He looked up smiling saying it was okay and he understood. He overheard everything then said congrats on the news. "Yes! Cedric that is the best news I've heard in a long time! Aww… You have come a long way. Thank you for loving her! You two need each other! Yes! I'm so happy right now! Thank you!" She shouted then pulled me in as we both stood up and hugged. She hugged me so tight that I almost suffocated! Junior pushed in between us trying to get involved in the hugging, basically saving my life. She was crying with happiness as I gave her napkins from the table. A tear or two did fall from my eyes as I felt the joy from her. "Thank you for your blessings. I don't have to say it but, please keep this between us. I want it to be a surprise during my graduation dinner." I whispered as I gave her more napkins. The tears were rolling down her face. "Grannie okay? Grannie okay?" Junior soft voice asked as he looked up at her while she wiped her face. I picked him up then said, "Yeah Granny is okay son. She's okay." She smiled at him then leaned in as she kissed him on the cheek. "Yes sir. I won't say a word. I'm so happy for you two. Granny is okay baby. Granny crying happy tears!" She replied to him. Junior smiled as he repeated, "Okay. Okay."

It was all done. The nerves had settled down. I had her blessings and was now ready to ask the big question. I walked them to the car after they made her another coffee. I kissed Junior as we all hugged again before they got in the car. I drove back home. I needed a power nap before I headed to school that evening to get my cap and gown since they had my measurements off. They did a rush delivery on getting me the right sizes that had me going to get it that evening.

Chapter 16

It Was All Worth It

It was graduation day with everyone that has ever had any part of supporting me, loving me or cared about my well-being was in the building cheering for me! It was a magical moment in my life. From the tears of triumph to the endless applauses I received when my name was called to walk across the stage to receive my degree! It felt great! The speaker they had there gave us all something to hang on to. She was a retired veteran who opened her own beauty supply chain as one of the first in her family to ever reach the level of success she had. She spoke on the doubts of those around you, should never penetrate your faith to smear the picture you have set for yourself. She talked about the many challenges she faced not only as a woman but as a black woman. She gave examples on how she overcame those stereotypes and how she kicked opened the doors that were shut in her face by staying true to what she desired. Her voice was heard loud and clear with so much passion that people began to clap after everything she said. She moved the entire room with her story of determination and will power. I was inspired by every word she said. I needed to hear that someone else had been through so much from the many mistakes they made. She was able to forgive herself then on to fighting for everything she knew she deserved. I needed to her it from a woman's perspective to have even more respect for all the women that put their all in making sure I had everything I've ever needed to make it. I wanted to love them all more knowing how difficult it was dealing with some of the things men may never experience due to how women are treated in the work place, homes and other places she had to keep her chin up at. She closed with stating that we all have great gifts that we were born to give to the world. It was something I heard my mom say as well back then.

It was an emotional speech. It was the confirmation I needed. She was given a standing ovation what felt like five minutes. She authored a book that I was able to purchase after the ceremony. Once everyone had all the hugs and pictures with me, we all headed home. Mrs. Anthony was hosting the graduation dinner at our house. It was early evening since the graduation had started around four that day. The weather was gorgeous as I was changing into something more comfortable with the cool breeze blowing through the entire house since Mrs. Anthony wanted all the windows up. Fresh air with the smell of good food traveling in one room to the next. Had me rushing to the kitchen to do a little taste testing! I had to put something on my stomach before everyone else showed up. I was nervous but I wasn't sweating or noticeably moving different. I had the ring tucked deep in my pocket since I threw on some cargo shorts with multiple compartments in them. I wanted to help with serving to make sure I could do some seating arrangements.

The ring I had was from our parents. It was one of the only things that survived the plane crash. It was sent to us right before our granddad had passed. Since Tammie wasn't around, our grandfather wanted me to have it. It was something I never spoke of or told anyone but David. I intended to mention it to Tammie but what better way to show it than to use it the way our parents would have hoped for. I was able to get it resized to fit Rachel's finger after snagging one of the rings she wore during our date nights. As everyone made their way over, I was cornered by Pastor Clayton. He told me he had been praying for me. He told me to relax and let my heart take control. He had my back if I needed him. As soon as he released me from his grasp, Mrs. Gloria stepped over to me as everyone was heading towards to kitchen. She wanted to be sure that I was still feeling the same way about her daughter. I promised her nothing could change my decision. I couldn't wait to marry Rachel. She smiled then jokily said that it's been so hard holding the wonderful news in, to herself. She thanked me again for doing it the right way. She finished up by saying she couldn't have asked for a better son in law. I was all smiles as I waited for everyone to crowd in the kitchen.

Rachel was looking like a full course meal as if she wanted everyone to know she was dating the guy the dinner was for. She was glowing which made me want to hurry up to get her alone to see what she was wearing under that fitted lavender colored dress she had on. Junior was sitting at the table already with a mouth and hand full of Mrs. Anthony sweet cornbread. Pastor Clayton was asked to bless the food once everyone was circled around the table holding hands. Rico and his mom were there, Tammie, a few old school mates, players from the high school baseball team as well as Coach Thomas. Officer Jackson crept in at the last minute since he was off duty that day. He claimed he didn't want to miss Mrs. Anthony's fried chicken she had made for some of the officers during law enforcement appreciate day at the church back to back years.

It was the most people we've ever had over at one time since David's funeral. I didn't realize how big the kitchen was until I was amazed at how many people were standing around bowing their heads before we ate. Pastor Clayton didn't let the moment go to waste without praying for everyone in the room. He made sure everyone was fully aware that God was in the house and that if we wanted to fully receive God's blessings we had to turn away from our sinful ways. I caught him and Officer Jackson having a stare down while everyone else either had their head down or eyes closed. There were some bad vibes or something going on between them that no one was aware of. I lowered my head back down as he closed the prayer by praying for me and my future endeavors. Once we all said Amen, both Rachels's mom and Pastor Clayton looked up at me wondering if it was the time. I waved my hands in a downward motion to them both as if to say not right now. I wanted to wait until everyone had eaten or at least had food on their plates. I wanted everyone to get comfortable. I had to beg the women to let us serve them. I had the high school baseball guys including myself serve everyone. I wanted to teach them about helping others before themselves. I talked to them how acts of kindness went a long way. They weren't stubborn about it. It was a lesson they appreciated. Coach Thomas was happy to see it as well.

Took about fifteen minutes to get everyone something to eat. Everyone was enjoying the food in the living room and kitchen table. Both rooms were filled with laughter and many conversations. I was back and forth in both rooms talking and serving refills to everyone. Mrs. Anthony announced the desserts she had made were ready to be served. Which was the perfect timing for me to make my move! Everyone jumped up after hearing she had banana pudding and peach cobbler. We were all gathered back in the kitchen as I slowly moved closer to the entrance door. I gave Pastor Clayton the thumbs up and winked one eye at Mrs. Gloria to alert them I was about to do it!

Mrs. Gloria walked over to take Junior from Rachel as she was sitting at the table playing with him. Pastor Clayton without hesitation said, "Hey Hey! I think brother Cedric has something he wants to say! Can he have your attention please!" Everyone quieted down within seconds then turned their eyes and ears towards me. Mrs. Anthony, Tammie and Rachel all look around at me then to one another as if to ask with their nonverbals what was happening. Neither of them had a clue as Pastor Clayton had a grin on his face as he gave me a head nod to go ahead and speak. I looked around then took a deep breath as everyone wanted to hear what I had to say. I walked over closer to Rachel as she was seated at the end of the table. I didn't look at her just yet.

I started with how much I appreciated everyone being there and showing me so much support. I thanked everyone for their time and all the efforts that went in helping me reach that milestone in my life. I thanked Mrs. Anthony for her love and deep pockets. I thanked Tammie for everything she's done and coming back into my life. I thanked Pastor Clayton as well for everything he had done for me. I then turned to Rachel. Before I could get one word out, her mom burst out in tears! I continued by saying to Rachel as I looked into her curious eyes, "Rachel, last but never least. Thank you for everything you've done for me. For being an amazing mother to our little guy Junior. I am truly a lucky guy to have you in my life. I want you to know that you mean the world to me. I know I've put you through some troubles I regret. You have brought so much happiness to my life and sunshine to my dark world. I was once at a point in life that I wanted to give up on myself. The strength and courage I've seen in you made me change my mind. I would have felt like a fool to give up seeing what you've been through. You have become my favorite person to be around. You are my best friend. I don't want to ever lose that. I'm ready to make this bond, our friendship more serious. Rachel, can I have you forever? Will you be my wife?" I pulled the small box out of my pocket then opened it up as I got down on one knee. Rachel's eyes lit up like a firework show! "Cedric... Really? Are you serious right now? I mean like... Wait! This is happening right now!" Rachel said with doubt as if I was pranking her. "I'm serious. I'm as serious as I could ever be. Will you marry me?" I replied as I slid in closer to her. She looked around at her mom then at Mrs. Anthony as they were all in tears with excitement waiting for her to respond. "Yes! I will!" She yelled!

Everyone applauded then shouted congratulations to us! I took the ring then slid it on her finger. It was a perfect fit. Rachel stood up then pulled me up to her. We kissed as everyone continued to cheer for us. Mrs. Anthony walked over and hugged Rachel then me. Her whole face was dripping with tears as she couldn't stop them from falling. Tammie was in shocked as she walked over as well hugging Rachel then stepped back looking at me up and down. "I see you little brother. It's about time! Making some real giant leaps in life! I'm so happy for you two! I'm so proud of you!" She said before she hugged me tight. All the players, Coach Thomas and Officer Jackson walked over to shake my hand. Everyone was shocked and happy for us. I don't know who cried the most, Mrs. Anthony, Mrs. Gloria or Rachel. Those ladies were on cloud nine with delight!

We all had desert to end the evening with even fuller stomachs and happiness from the good news of Rachel and I tying the knot. I had the players to help with the cleaning duties. Rico and I helped too as we dumped plates, washed dishes and took out the trash. They were helpful while we gave the ladies some rest in the living room as they couldn't stop talking about the plans for the wedding. Rachel probably talked more that night than any night ever there at the house. I stood in the doorway of the kitchen looking on as I could see her glowing while she went on about being a wife. Coach Thomas and Pastor Clayton talked amongst themselves near the front door. Once the kitchen was squeaky clean, the boys were given extra helpings of desert to take with them for their willingness to help. Everyone headed out congratulating us again. I walked them all out to their cars. Mrs. Anthony thanked the boys for the service they provided with serving and cleaning. She told them that they were always welcomed over. Pastor Clayton and Coach Thomas both joked with me about the responsibilities I was going to have to take care of when your girlfriend becomes your wife. Coach also joked about how she will change a little so enjoy every second of it. Pastor Clayton ensured me that things will be fine if I prayed first about whatever decisions we had to make. He made sure I understood how necessary that was. Rico and his mom left as they both were all smiles for us. The players carpooled and as they were leaving Officer Jackson stood out watching them and told them not to do anything crazy going home. He made them promise him they were going straight home and for them to be careful. They were learning valuable lessons, but they still had work to do. Some of them had been in some trouble a year before that upset quite a few people in the neighborhood. That's another reason why I wanted to work with them. Officer Jackson kept an eye on them.

Once everyone was gone, I made sure Rachel and Junior was okay. They stayed for another hour longer until Rachel's mom started yawning. She said she was mentally tired after having to keep in the secret she was so close to telling. We all laughed as Mrs. Anthony gave Junior kisses as we gathered their things. Mrs. Gloria had sat some banana pudding to the side she refused to forget about. It was the last of it. I was hoping she didn't remember it as I had my mouth set on eating it since I didn't get any. It was selfish of me to plot to do it but I'm glad she recalled she had it in the fridge. I didn't need it. They were all finally in the car as I kissed Junior then my future wife. Rachel's mom thanked me again for being a good son in law and told Rachel and I that she will do whatever it took to help us get through whatever it is that we needed.

I went back into the house as they were pulling off. Tammie and Mrs. Anthony were standing there staring at me with huge smiles on their faces still in shock about what I did. "I just can't believe you did it, Cedric! I mean I do! But I am just amazed at how things have worked out for you. Not just for you but you know… Basically for all of us. I love you so much! I won't bother you about any plans we talked about. Just know I am so excited about this! Everything is going to be great! Not perfect but great!" Mrs. Anthony said. "Yeah I am excited as well. I know I've seen that pretty ring somewhere. I'm just curios on how in the hell you get it?" Tammie said. I thanked Mrs. Anthony for her kinds word then told Tammie about how I received the ring from our granddad. "Well I'm so happy one of us got to use it! Now, if she doesn't act right, I need that ring from her, okay… I'm kidding! I'm kidding!" Tammie said as she started laughing. "I got you. Thank you, ladies for everything. I'm beat. This has been a long week, keeping that in from everyone and now finally doing it. I'm going to call it a night. I love y'all." I said to them both. They both went in the kitchen as they both admitted to not being able to rest their thoughts with the ideas for a wedding taking control of them. I hugged and kissed them both then excused myself upstairs to my room. I waited until Rachel called me to tell me they made it home before I laid down. I was out within minutes as I could hear the chatting from Tammie and Mrs. Anthony downstairs. I rode the soothing breeze still flowing through my room from the cracked window to dreamland.

Just under a full year, all the planning and the mothers not wanting us to stay engaged too long was over! It was a beautiful wedding! The mothers had gone far beyond Rachel's imagination to create a magical and memorable day for us! From the fresh flowers that were placed throughout the entire church and Junior's stroll with the ring in his little tuxedo to the extra-long white limo that awaited for us and the all paid vacation to Hawaii neither Rachel or I expected! It was a dream wedding overall. Nothing was wrong or out of place. It was well thought out and executed to the finest and classiest scale. We were beyond grateful and thankful for everything everyone had done. We did it! We both said yes! We were standing there at the alter after saying our vows. I thought I saw a ghost! I looked over the church as everyone were glued to us before we kissed. I would have bet everything I had to my name that I saw Charlene walk past the doors of the church with a pretty little girl. Pastor Clayton nudge me to make sure I wasn't losing my mind as he noticed the change in my facial expression! "You may kiss your bride!" He repeated as everyone began to clap. I lifted the laced white veil that was covering Rachel's face as her eyes locked in on mines. I leaned down towards her giving her a long soft kiss with the cheering and clapping echoing throughout the church. "I now pronounce you Mr. and Mrs. Cedric Mason! Congratulations to you both! May God forever be in your hearts and in all your decisions!" Pastor Clayton yelled out! I lifted my head as I quickly scanned the doorway area to make sure I didn't see any other person or anything that was off. I lifted Rachel's hand in mines to signal our victory as we began to step down the few steps from the alter! Once we were outside jumping in the limo, I did one last scan to make sure it was indeed my mind playing tricks on me. We had a police escort by Officer Jackson to the reception. They rented out a place downtown that had newly opened. They had a DJ and some of the best food you could imagine. It was by far the happiest day of my life for sure! We had a blast with all the friends and family that attended. We couldn't have asked for anything else or more that would have topped that experience and day!

A few weeks after the honeymoon and we had moved into our new place, things were going great. I didn't have any complaints. My life was everything I needed and wanted. I was starting my full-time teaching and coaching at the high school. Rachel started working as the regional manager for all the busiest banks in Mississippi with a lovely pay raise. Junior was in elementary school being a big boy learning and growing like a little giant. Mrs. Anthony had started selling her desserts that were being bought at all the local grocery stores ran by Samantha and Greg. Rico and Tammie were officially dating which I had to sit him down to go over the ground rules before I gave him my permission. Well he didn't need it because Tammie was going to do whatever she wanted to anyway. Rico and I were best friends by then and I had no issues with what they were doing as we were all adults. Things were the best they had ever been in my life. I was thanking God every day for the lessons and the chance to change my directions. My life had purpose and was as close to a dream come true as you can get!

One day, the craziest thing happened when I was on my way to the school as the sun was shining on a beautiful day. I was at the intersection with the police precinct to my right. As the light was turning green for me to go, my attention was drawn to a squad car pulling in fast in their parking lot! I was starting to cruise through the light when two officers got out of the front seats then opened the back door. To my surprise they pulled Officer Jackson out! He looked dazed while in hand cuffs! Then it was something that Melvin had said to me that I remembered at that very moment. I couldn't help but think about it! "If Officer Jackson has anything to do with catching up with me, and he has me dead to right in his crossfire, he will kill me with no remorse. I promise you Cedric, it won't be for what you think it is." He told me during that conversation I had with him after he pulled up on him. At the time he said as if it wasn't something to worry about, so I never questioned it. As I continued driving on by the precinct, more officers came out to greet them. Officer Jackson slowly raised his head then somehow looked right over at me! He dropped his head once the other officers grabbed him in an aggressive way as if he had never been on the force a day in his life...

THE END...